This book is dedicated to all those people struggling to find their own truths, to the people who know that change is inevitable and who are courageous enough to open their minds to the possibilities that lie just beyond conventional thought. This book is also dedicated to my dad, who, in death, inspired me to write.

Len E. Hooke

RIP-SYNERGY

Copyright © Len E. Hooke (2017)

The right of Len E. Hooke to be identified as author of this work has been asserted by him in accordance with section 77 and 78 of the Copyright, Designs and Patents Act 1988.

All rights reserved. No part of this publication may be reproduced, stored in a retrieval system, or transmitted in any form or by any means, electronic, mechanical, photocopying, recording, or otherwise, without the prior permission of the publishers.

Any person who commits any unauthorized act in relation to this publication may be liable to criminal prosecution and civil claims for damages.

All characters appearing in this work are fictitious. Any resemblance to real persons, living or dead, is purely coincidental.

A CIP catalogue record for this title is available from the British Library.

ISBN 9781786126023 (Paperback)
ISBN 9781786126030 (Hardback)
ISBN 9781786126047 (E-Book)

www.austinmacauley.com

First Published (2017)
Austin Macauley Publishers Ltd.
25 Canada Square
Canary Wharf
London
E14 5LQ

Foreword

This story is based on true events. It is an account of issues and experiences that took over my life for decades. I recorded my experiences in a journal which was then transferred to print. I take full responsibility for the fact that this book might not be of the highest quality in all respects, but in my defence, I am not a seasoned author. While I cannot promise that every word is true, what I can say is that I acted diligently in remaining faithful to the themes and principles so clearly laid out before me.

To some degree, the story is irrelevant; it is the messages that must take precedence and the implications that the story has for all of us. I have changed some names to protect the privacy of the individuals involved, using poetic licence in some places to enhance the storyline, but the facts remain unchanged.

This foreword is necessary to offer a word of warning. There is something in all our lives, something unknown in the way it acts and in the way it affects us. No race, creed, colour, religious belief, and no amount of prayer can repel the intrusion into our lives that might, one day, prove fatal.

The threat to everyone is relentless, it is evil, it is deadly. You cannot hide and you cannot fight. It exists as it always has and as it always will. My only hope is that the words in this book serve to arm you with whatever defence might be available at the appropriate time.

एकम्

'Solly, what is up with you tonight?'

Mary had only known Solly for two weeks before they headed to the bedroom, but even by then she felt they had a deep connection. Not one to flaunt her sexuality, the eagerness she felt to share her body with her new beau had surprised Mary. Despite his name, Solly was not of Jewish descent, he learned at an early age that his name was just one fancied by his mother a few days after he emerged into the world, ginger-haired and blue eyed. At twenty-four years of age Solly retained his boyish good looks and a nest of wispy red hair.

'I don't feel good,' Solly struggled to speak through tightly clenched teeth.

Solly's eyes looked bugged out as he desperately clutched at the front of his white tee shirt. His knuckles rapidly whitened and his scared eyes widened.

Mary scooted away from her boyfriend and raised herself quickly from the sofa and into a standing position. She raised both hands to her head and squeezed at her hair before gesticulating crazily in front of her.

'What can I do, tell me Solly,' she cried out.

Solly was not able to reply. Though impossible to in any way adequately describe the intense pain he was feeling inside his chest, he could only liken it to his insides being ripped to shreds, repeatedly. He pulled his left fist up and ripped open his top. He stared wide-eyed at his chest, which showed no sign of the battle being waged inside. Solly continued to stare as he slowly rolled into a ball and fell gently onto the sofa.

'Solly! Solly!' Mary screamed as she lunged forward and shook Solly's stricken body violently, in a vain effort to erase the last thirty seconds.

***

'Can I speak with Inspector Marchant, please?'

'Who is asking and what is it about?'

The man behind the counter carried on with what he was doing without glancing up. His ginger hair looked ruffled, his cheeks slightly pinkish. His white collar was slightly crumpled on both sides where it hung over his navy blue jumper.

'Can I speak with Inspector Marchant, please?' I repeated.

The room was clean, but completely unwelcoming. With no light penetrating the glass in the doors, the room was lit by two low-hanging neon lights that did nothing to brighten the scuffed cream shades of the walls. Two doors led from the room, one left and one right. The counter side was accessed from the right, through a split barn-type door, only the bottom halves of which were visible. The air inside the room was trapped and slightly stale.

A woman pushed open the right side door. Dressed informally she was above medium height and slim, but not size zero by any means. A puffed purple blouse hung over her broad shoulders and casual black slacks met unremarkable black boots at her ankles. Her dyed blonde hair was clear of her face on the left and fell slightly below her eyebrow on the right side. 'Would you like to come through?' she asked.

I was led rather briskly to a door on the left of a short corridor. She moved inside and took a seat on a creaky wooden swivel chair behind a modern-looking desk. She motioned for me to be seated in front of the desk. She had an A4 pad in front of her and three well-used Biro pens. Her hands met in front of her, a pen cradled on top.

'What is this about?' she asked.

'Whoa, hello, how are you, might be nice,' I replied.

'Let's cut the crap, shall we?' Inspector Marchant leaned forward on the desk, casting a dark shadow over pad and pen. 'You gave me the run-around before, are we here to start that business up again?'

I moved in my seat, composing myself, searching for the right words to use.

'Well, it wasn't quite like that, but I will admit that we got off on the wrong foot before,' I replied.

We had worked together previously, albeit for a very short period of time. In reality, the case had been cold before I became involved. It was only my insistence that led to Inspector Marchant resurrecting a project that, at least at that time, should have stayed buried. But back then, my psychic abilities were less focused, less known, not as complete as they are now. As it turned out, our working together resulted in a stiff reprimand for Inspector Marchant, and a charge for me of wasting police time.

'So what is it now?' Marchant asked. 'My time is considerably more valuable than should be spent chasing after rainbows with you.'

I cleared my throat, and then began the tale of why I was there.

'You know me, Judy' I started, 'at least a bit. You know that I am a psychic, sensitive, whatever people want to call me.'

Marchant chipped in, 'Look, I have much better things to do with my time.' She moved her pens and shuffled her pad as if to get up from the table.

'The point is, Inspector Marchant, that it has started again. But this time on a much bigger scale. Before I was not ready to untie all the knots, to untangle the web of what was going on, but now I am,' I replied.

I felt uneasy as Inspector Marchant rose from her chair. She pointed a stiff forefinger in my direction as I, too, started to rise from my seat.

'Unless you have something concrete, like names and addresses, or unless you have anything of any material wealth for me at all,' she paused momentarily, 'then this conversation is closed.'

She picked up the pens from the table and moved towards the door. I followed her.

'You are aware of a man who died recently of natural causes, no witnesses, and the guy was in his early twenties?' I asked.

As she put her hand on the doorknob Marchant said, 'And?'

'I don't know, Inspector Marchant, this is the problem. But something is not right. Something is very, very not right. And something needs to be done, urgently.'

Inspector Marchant opened the door and almost pulled me through it with her eyes.

'Goodbye and thank you for coming in today.'

'His name was Saunders,' I said as I slowly made an exit from the room, 'the dead guy.'

ॐ

I was born in South East London in December 1963, one of three children.

'Mum, that boy's drinking and pissing a lot.'

My brother, maybe having the wisdom of five extra years on me, was the first to say something. Nobody else noticed my concave stomach and my dramatic loss of weight. My brother called me tin ribs. That is all I knew.

I was taken to my general practitioner's surgery where my doctor tested my urine.

'We got him just in time,' I remember him saying.

I was admitted to hospital within thirty minutes. I was given one insulin injection by a nurse. Since then I always did my own injections. Diabetes and any potential complications of the illness were never explained to me. My childhood became a case of trial and error, pretty much devoted to urine and blood sugar testing, boiling syringes and needles, and eating measured amounts of carbohydrates in food.

Hypoglycaemic attacks were common. One minute I was fine, the next I could not stand or speak and I was completely unable to communicate. At these times, weird thoughts traversed my mind, having no bearing on my physical reality. These thoughts were like strange waking dreams. Everything went hazy and I most commonly got a sense of falling, drifting, or floating as the world around me disappeared.

At only seven years of age little of anything made sense to me, but as a child, diabetes was just a part of my life, so I got on with it.

***

I was scared of the dark. My dad played a shiny 'blonde' double bass in a band with his two brothers. That double bass lived in my bedroom. It never moved, but in my peripheral vision it did. I had a lot of nightmares. Each week I must have awoken with a jolt, two or three times a night. There were three tower blocks on our estate. The monsters always towered over these concrete blocks, and they were always looking for me. I never mastered the art of running away from these monsters. The roads or walkways always became covered with the blackest, stickiest treacle. However, I did create one escape route that seemed effective. In my dreams, I knew that if I blinked three times I would wake up. It always worked and the monsters never cottoned on to it.

***

At fourteen years of age, I was admitted to hospital with pancreatitis, an excruciatingly painful illness that recurred periodically. Having pancreatitis was like my stomach cramping up so much that the pain was unbearable. On this occasion I was given intravenous pain relief and sent to a ward upstairs. While asleep, I was injected with Trasylol by a male nurse. Nobody else was in attendance. I awoke and sat up in the bed. I had pins and needles in my feet and legs, a sensation which was rapidly rising through my entire body. I was cold, sweating and desperately wanted to excrete. A second nurse ran off to return with a metal bedpan. With help, I disrobed below the waist and sat on the bedpan. The pins and needles rose up to my neck and then into my face and scalp. The need for me to excrete was immediate, urgent.

The next thing I knew I was on the floor. Somebody pushed hard into the middle of my chest and I heard a light whoosh of air escape my lungs as I awoke. My chest was very sore. For the next two days, I was extremely tired. I was never put on any monitors or life-saving equipment. I found out thirty-four years later that Trasylol was withdrawn around this time because it caused adverse effects in children. According to my mother, she was never told that I had died that afternoon.

***

My mum always believed she put her children first. She did not. She had no idea of the danger she placed me in with her choice of budget clothes, haircut, shoes and bags that she bought for me. I suffered seventeen years of bullying as a result. The only way I had to evade the bullies was to stay secretly hidden inside my home. No lights. No television. Making no sound. I heard my tormentors moving around outside, jumping the rear fence into the garden, banging on doors, talking about what they were going to do to me, and planning ambushes. From my early schooldays the name-calling and bitchiness stuck. I knew I was ugly. Whenever possible I still avoid looking into mirrors. Until the age of nineteen I avoided girls, preferring to spend time on my bed accompanied only by imagined masturbatory images and a large amount of toilet tissue.

***

My parents divorced in 1980 after twenty-nine years of marriage. This is when my life really started turning messy. I felt the tension that filled the air and I heard my dad in the kitchen cursing my mum every night. My siblings sided with my mother and adopted her same aggressive posture towards our patriarch. I never did. I accepted that any problems between my mum and dad were a matter for them and not me.

My dad was a handsome man who had, I am given to understand, a number of extramarital affairs. What my mum kept from the family was that at the same time she too was having an affair with her married boss. I didn't really know my father until after he died. While alive, my dad was portrayed as a lonely figure, a man of bad intent, a man who took what he wanted regardless of the effect of his actions on other people. A womaniser, a maniser, a cross-dressing freak. Forever angry at what he was missing in his relationship with my mother, but never expressing what it was that he wanted.

I always managed to maintain an objective view of my immediate family. I guess my reluctance to take sides was the reason my dad felt a lot closer to me. But it was not until he died that I realised there was a hidden, deeper side to him. This is something that maybe my family will never know, but it sits right with me. Through meditation and deep thought, I came to realise that he had a compassionate side. He did whatever he could to help people, even if he rarely got off his backside. I talked to him about all sorts of things in his last year. Through many difficult and painful years since he died, that is what I missed and it is what I still miss now: his listening ear.

***

Through two marriages, two children and countless hours of domestic boredom I travelled extensively and, in 2004, I went with my second wife to the Gambia, West Africa. A lack of natural resources, led to The Gambia being reported as the poorest country in Africa; it is also the smallest. I got involved in developing and financing some charitable projects in the country and, using a substantial pay out on leaving the Civil Service, I bought some land and built two villas close to the main tourist area. My idea was to sell these houses and use the profit to finance more philanthropic projects in rural areas. I planned to live there no more than six months, but the stay was extended more than four years beyond my target.

People might believe that racism exists only against non-Caucasian people, but I experienced the other side, being treated as different everywhere I went. Then there were the marabouts - witch doctors who take money from needy people to carry out magic to deliver outcomes. Potions consist of local vegetation that must be bathed in, animal sacrifices, or simple Arabic verse wrapped and buried in the ground. Mostly, it is empty words, another way of making money out of an individual's fears or desires. The only marabouts who seem to have some power are those dealing with black magic. And bad things do happen, as I experienced myself. A Sierra Leonean girlfriend asked for some clothes of mine, photographs and some hair. Over the next four years, I lost nearly everything as a result. Financially I was broke. These were the darkest and most desperate days of my life.

I returned to live in the United Kingdom in 2011. My son, who was born in 2009, returned with me. My Gambian wife, after lengthy and stressful appeals against Home Office regulations, now resides with us.

***

I was introduced to spiritual books by my second wife. She claimed she had an affinity with Buddhism, angels, God and most other types of mumbo jumbo. In 2003, during a break in our marriage, I visited my wife at a place she was renting. She came back from work and placed a book in front of me on a coffee table. Just then, the phone rang and she went to the kitchen to answer the call. I sat, and I sat and I sat a bit more. After thirty minutes I picked up the book, it was about a man who had directly conversed with God. I started reading the book and found I could not put it down.

From there I read every spiritual book I could find. I was particularly interested in accounts of our wider spiritual identity, the afterlife, past lives, and in spirit guides and higher beings. I had an interest in the paranormal since reading horrific tales on holiday in my pre-teens, and this seemed like a natural progression. I began to meditate and, after a while, I found it quite easy to relax and let go. I bought meditative compact discs and looked into self-development literature.

I always believed in a God figure, but I was not religious in any way. I could not stand the doctrine of organised religion. I had a problem accepting the fear that commonly pervaded religious teaching. I do not tend to believe in anything unless it is proven to me, so I started testing the theology of spiritual writing. It seemed to me that God was not a thing to be scared of, not even something to be in awe of, but more a partner, a companion, a fixer, a trader. So I started asking for proof in each section of every book I read. And by and large, I found it.

I never followed spiritual text; rather, I used it to inform my own analyses of the non-physical. I never believed anyone who said, 'This is the way it is', because almost certainly, it is not and, it seems to me, this kind of directive has religious rather than spiritual overtones. I have never been into preaching of any kind, and it just seemed to me that most of the spiritual texts available on the market preached what an individual author thought was right, rather than encouraging a reader to find his or her own truth.

As an illustration, I was on holiday in Turkey and reading a book that suggested we and God are one and the same. Facing a deep blue sea, I looked up from the book and noticed a cloud formation on my right that looked suspiciously like steps. I then noticed more clouds that formed to my left, almost exactly, the words 'I AM.' Two weeks later my wife was upstairs in the bathroom and I heard a soft crash. Nothing new in that, since she had a tendency, like many other people, to pay little attention to her surroundings. Ten minutes later I visited the bathroom. A small bowl of potpourri that usually sat on the edge of the bath, had tipped inside. My wife had removed the bowl leaving the dried potpourri leaves where they had spilt. I looked at the leaves scrambled haphazardly across the bottom of the bath, the brown, the red and green. I was looking for a message, but could see none. I turned away from the bath and towards the window. Fixed to the wall was an extendable shaving mirror. At that moment, I wondered if I would see anything if I pointed the mirror down towards the inside of the bathtub. In the mirror's reflection, I saw, very clearly, 'YOUR', which could also be interpreted as 'you are.' I had the proof of what I was reading 'I AM – YOU ARE.' Many other similar experiences followed, sufficient to prove to me beyond any doubt that a creator-type something does exist.

    I cannot say that any of my experiences are right, or the truth, for anyone but me, but I was now on a quest of self and universal discovery. The signs were all there, I just needed to take notice. This journey dissolved my second marriage. I felt like my entire self expanded, I grew self-knowledgeable and, as a consequence, my entire life philosophies up to that time were gently erased and replaced. I felt that I had turned the physical into the non-physical. Reading books was no longer good enough. I craved the experiences and the proof of our universal selves. My wife stuck to reading and theorising. The two could not exist together.

त्रीणि

Inspector Marchant called me three days after I visited her office. She said she needed more information, on an informal basis. She apologised for adopting an abrupt attitude at her workplace and assured me it was a necessary trait in her line of work. I had no idea why she changed her mind, I didn't ask the question and she offered no answer.

'I'm a little surprised you called.'

'Well, you either know the dead guy's name because you know him, or because you killed him,' she replied.

'It's neither.'

'That's what I thought. So tell me about your psychic abilities. That is why you contacted me isn't it?'

'There is not much to tell,' I replied.

Marchant's eyebrows lowered into a mini-frown. 'Come on, after our debacle before, you at least owe me that.'

'And a bit more,' I added.

'If you want me to listen to what you have to say – and God forbid, to become involved – then you ought to lay it on the line for me. You were very candid about your life experiences, now open up about the mystical you, the you who came knocking on my door again after so long,' she demanded, gently.

I sighed and then began to search for the right words to use. The words to describe feelings, instinct, knowledge. The words my host might understand and that might help to make the mystical, the otherworldly, feel real.

'Do you believe in flying saucers?' I asked.

'What kind of a question is that? I asked about your psychic abilities, not little green bug-eyed men.'

'I will tell you about how I can tap into information that might otherwise seem not to exist, but in order to do that we first need to establish a basic understanding of our non-physical existence,' I explained.

'Okay, I am all ears, but not all brain, not yet,' she replied.

those people of a negative disposition seek extra clarification to prove the psychic wrong and their negativity right. Most of these types of clients are, at least in my opinion, of an opinionated, stubborn and egotistical persuasion.

What is interesting is that readings can be done for people with little or no prior knowledge of what psychic readings might entail. The same is true, in a starker form, with hypnosis. I started experimenting with my abilities while I lived in the Gambia, where most people have no knowledge whatsoever of western spiritual ideologies or practices. Outcomes remained the same. Readings and hypnosis can be undertaken for anyone, regardless of their background or life experience. And this is when it struck me that whatever abilities I had must emanate from me, and not from my surroundings.

While it is true that a defensive or aggressive person might disrupt the flow of information available, this might only arise from my own defensive patterns. If challenged, anyone is likely first to adopt a defensive stance, even if they then engage in more open communication to clarify or explore any arising issues. Once a more open mindedness is established, the flow of information can continue. On more than one occasion I have encountered an obstructive client and prepared to end the reading, with the full intention of closing myself down, only to find the flow of information pick up again when I least expected it.

I do not consciously search for information. Whatever source this information comes from is neither directed nor governed by me. I always try to steer clear of undertaking any guesswork, but this can be inevitable if the information I get is not very clear.

I am provided with knowledge of a place, a person, an incident or an object of significance. I am then able to focus better and gain greater clarification and make the source of it bolder, brighter and more understandable. It can be a little like tuning into a radio signal. You get a fuzzy outline of a station and then gently tune in to the stronger signal that then comes through without interference.

The term spiritual has nothing to do with religion. Each religion has its own deity, its own creator and, in many cases, its own judge and executioner. I have never followed any religion, but that does not mean that I do not have an intelligent, creative force at work in my life. And that creative force is the same for everyone, regardless of their religious beliefs or practices. It is my belief that any information I receive psychically is prompted by such a creative force. If we are all made up of energy, that energy must have an evolutionary creative passageway prompted by an issuing force. Maybe all I am given privilege to opening up are avenues of communication with individual aspects of that creative energy force. And if that force is intellectual in nature, then it makes sense that any individual elements emanating from it must be intellectual in nature too.

'Are you saying that Jesus, the Buddha, Mohammed were all psychic?' Marchant asked, a surprised expression on her face as she spoke.

I explained the process by which I pick up on psychic intelligence. I have no idea where this information comes from, but it must emanate from somewhere beyond our everyday physical realm as we currently understand it. Although I can detect images and sounds I do not use my five physical senses to do this. Instead it comes through a knowing or a perception of an image, sound, smell or taste. Sometimes this process is enhanced by information provided by clients, or by the touching of belongings of the deceased, or by photographs of them.

I begin by rubbing my hands together briskly and placing them over my face. I then ask, from deep within me, for assistance in opening myself up to any images or messages meant for my client. I open up my seven main chakra centres and imagine them turning faster and faster, drawing in an energy as they turn. To me a chakra looks like a beautifully cut diamond and as each one turns, it gives off its own colour. This is usually done from base to crown or from the base of my spine to the top of my head. As each chakra turns and glistens, I feel different areas of my body open up. It is like breathing through different areas of my body. I will then hold my hands open in my lap, palms up, to receive a white or golden light that I draw down from above me.

Physically, I feel that I become energised. I feel tingling sensations in my feet, my legs, my arms and in my hands. I feel a warm glow start to emanate from my body. My thinking becomes crystal-clear. Sometimes my eyesight becomes a little bit blurred. This procedure sounds lengthy and detailed, but in reality, it only takes a matter of seconds.

I will stress again that I really don't know how this works, whether I read what is inside people's minds or whether they project thoughts to me, I don't know. All I know is that information does arrive. Usually I will first pick up a bit about the person, or the people, I am reading for. This happens almost instantaneously. As soon as I am in the presence of someone, I will know how open they are, or whether they put up barriers or any other kind of resistance to communication. I will know if they are shy, withdrawn, boastful or aggressive. Sometimes I will know if they drink alcohol or if they are teetotallers. Particularly clear to me is whether they have an injury or ailment. I will become aware of any strong issues in their personality or in their makeup. It is safe to say though, that the issues of greatest concern to my clients will always push their way to the forefront and be the clearest issues available to me. It is never easy to read for a defensive or an aggressive person, or for one who might be hostile to the work of a psychic. It can then become a bit like a game of cat and mouse. Information will still be available to me, but denials of such information or unnecessarily eager attempts to dispute information could, in some circumstances, lead to a deeper searching for answers that might not be available, or might be pushed away.

It is always the wish of a psychic to inform a client, and thereby offer at least some degree of value-for-money, whether in cash or time. Deeper clarification on information is rarely sought from my source, since the information provided will be that deemed necessary for the client. It seems

'So what are you saying? God is made up? The Bible is full of cack? Are you saying there is no reason why we exist?'

'No, that is not what I am saying. There are somewhere in excess of seven billion Gods, or creators, or spiritual deities, or nothings. And each version must be correct to be believable, right?'

'I guess so,' Marchant was frowning again.

'All I am saying, in a nutshell, is that each person's experience, or belief in a God, or any other creative energy, cannot ever be the same. And it must be true that each of our own Gods are real, it has to be. And each difference creates a new god, a new deity, or a new belief. An atheist has a god, just not one they believe in. And what if God does not exist somewhere else? What if God was here right now? What if God exists right in this space here?'

Marchant stared at me as she lifted the tepid coffee to her bright red lips.

'What if,' I moved further forward in my seat, 'What if we are Gods, what if we are the single energy that creates physical illusions all around us? What if we create physical entities, people, places, all of history as we know it? What if every single one of us is God, or a manifestation of our own godliness, an illusion, a player in somebody else's life, and puppeteer of our own?'

'Wow. That is some thought.'

'It might be more than just a thought. It is perfectly feasible,' I suggested, 'My own belief is that when we die there is a common enough outcome, one ending and another beginning, or even just a continuation. I certainly think it possible that our individual beliefs will be acted out upon our physical death, otherwise how shocking or horrifying could the death experience really be? No, I believe it must take some readjustment.'

'So what about those people who do not believe in God? Those that say when we die we are buried and get eaten by the creatures of the land?' Inspector Marchant asked.

'Then that might be exactly what they experience when they die.'

Marchant squirmed in her chair. Maybe readjusting her physical position also entailed some movement in her metaphysical outlook too.

'This is a lot to take in, I'm not sure I'm ready for this.'

'If you can, just shelve your own belief patterns for a while. Put on hold all you have been told, all you have read, all you have experienced. If you can, just be open to the possibilities that might exist all around us. Can you do that?'

'Okay. I will try.'

***

'Do you believe that some form of intelligent life might exist out there in the vast reaches of space, possibly further away than we might at the moment be capable of perceiving?' I asked.

'Yes,' her answer was surprisingly swift, confident.

'If you hold this view, then you might be open to believing what I am about to tell you. Many people believe that what a psychic perceives are ghosts, but this is not strictly true. Now, I should start off by telling you that anything I say cannot be perceived as the truth.'

Marchant's eyebrows lifted as I said this.

'This is only my truth, my own personal ideas and feelings, because, in effect, there is no absolute truth,' I explained.

'There is no proof that ghosts or spirits exist. There is no absolute proof that an afterlife exists. There is no proof that God exists, right?' Inspector Marchant asked.

'Right,' I acknowledged, 'so I am just cautioning you that anything I have to say cannot be one hundred per cent relied on and most certainly would not stand up in court.'

'Well that's a shame. I'm much more used to dealing with courts than with hocus pocus. In any case, I left my notebook back at the office,' Inspector Marchant replied sullenly.

'From the start, let's stay away from ghosts. In my opinion, a ghost, or a ghostly energy, might just be an imprint of a historical event or a historical character that more often than not occupies a space on our planet. It might well be true that ghosts can interact with people by touch, smell, or speech, but this still emanates from that energetic imprint of another time, or of another event. I have no doubt that many people do have ghostly experiences, but these are neither psychic nor mediumistic. Any psychic or medium who claims to see or hear a spirit as if it is a physical being is only doing that for effect; maybe so that a client or audience can more easily focus on the message being given. But in my opinion, any such action is just theatrical.'

'So if you don't see or hear a ghost...'

'Spirit, or spiritual energy,' I corrected.

'If you don't see or hear a spiritual energy, then how can you pick up messages, scenes or whatever it is that you pick up from these otherworldly energies?'

'I don't know. I mean, I can't be sure. I don't know how any channels of communication work, and I don't think I am meant to know. These people who write books giving definitive answers to our existence, what will happen when we die, who will meet us, what happens next, it's all just their opinions. None of it is true.'

'None of it?' she asked.

'None of it. Except for that which we ourselves choose to believe, or that which sits right for us as individuals,' I explained.

'Quite possibly. It seems reasonable to suggest that all of these people, and many, many more, would be acting as channels for the source. It also seems likely that they were intellectually open to spiritual knowledge far beyond that known, or even contemplated, by other people in their time.'

The air in the room grew noticeably cooler as the night closed in around us.

'And what about those people who think Jesus was an alien?' I continued, raising my eyebrows.

'Are you serious?'

'I guess nothing is beyond the realms of the possible.'

***

During my time experimenting with spirituality, seeking my own learning and growth, I started to ascertain that the greatest lesson of all was to try to be non-judgmental. While I cannot say I achieved this goal, I did manage to understand the 'judgmentalism' inherent in my own personality.

Any answers I found, during this journey, only served as signals that I was on the right path. As I mentioned before, I can never be sure that it was not my own concentrated focus on an issue that turned up the proof I thought I saw. We are all Gods, as many believe, and maybe in these instances the God within me was performing personal miracles. There can never be any answers in the search for spiritual enlightenment, since personal outcomes can only ever lead to more questions.

It seems to me that science will never be able to prove the existence of God. But does that mean that the Creator does not exist? Equally, it seems science cannot disprove the existence of any deity, spiritual energy, angels, or devils even, but equally that does not prove such entities do not exist. If we are able to open our minds to any possibilities, to be non-judgmental in our thoughts and deeds, to make every choice the most beneficial one, then this, it seems to me, is the only route to enlightenment.

In practising my psychic abilities, I am not claiming enlightenment. It just means that my mind is sufficiently open to receiving images and knowledge that otherwise could not be known. This is how I chanced upon the incident which led me to contact Inspector Marchant six months ago. And now these images, this knowledge, is far stronger. It is imperative I get Marchant onside, because the upcoming journey will be arduous and possibly more dangerous than either of us can contemplate.

चत्वारि

The meditation process is, essentially, easy to master. There is no secret ingredient only uncovered through many years of thought and study, and there is no way that anyone can get it wrong. It is all about being able to focus on one thing only. Most people automatically enter a meditative state before they fall asleep. When the TV screen becomes blurred, when the writing on the page of a book moves around, when thoughts drift away from our normal solid life, and head towards the cartoon anti-symmetry of our relaxed self. These are the first steps towards meditation.

Each person has his or her own preferred method of achieving the meditative state. It can be beneficial to picture something that we can easily return to, it does not matter what this is, just so long as your mind can travel to this item or place with as little thought effort as possible. I relax on the bed. I imagine myself before a stone doorway. My right hand touches the stone until I can perceive the coarseness of the rock as it crumbles away like sand beneath my fingertips, as they lightly brush against its surface. The stone entrance has carvings all around it, but I am not aware of what they are. My focus is solely on the loosening particles of stone on my fingers. When I feel the time is right I enter a small chamber.

Inside the chamber is a chair, its back lowered so the top and feet are equidistant to the floor. I enter and sit on the chair. I relax into the seat and imagine a pure white light emanating from the ceiling and moving slowly towards the floor. This is my higher self. I am enveloped by my higher self and feel energised by the positivity within the white light as it drops ever so slowly over my body. Sometimes I am visited by Jesus, or another higher being. Such visitations can happen spontaneously, or at my request. I feel calmed, relaxed and cleansed by all the positive energies now in the chamber.

When the time is right, a portal opens on the opposite side of the room. I am then standing on a sandy beach. Sometimes I sit and cross my legs, facing the gently breaking waters in front of me. The sound of the waves further serves to calm me. Here I might be visited by a higher energy or being. On other occasions, I will commence walking along the beach. It is essential that I feel the sand beneath my feet, the grains trickling across my toes. The more focus that you can place on the vision before you, the better will be any information received and its beneficial impact. I am aware of the sun, the *more questions. Our quest for knowledge is insatiable only because ultimate knowledge is never-ending.'*

'So there is no one being, no one energy that has greater knowledge than all the rest? What about God? The one creator?' I asked.

'Many humans believe that man was created by God in the image of God. But let's turn that around a bit. Would it not be better to state that God was created by man, in the image of man?'

'Well it might be better, but it would be wholly unacceptable to a huge chunk of the human population.'

'And those who would not accept this description of God, I guess that they would be the ones, the descendants of the ones, or the believers of the ones, who originally created this image of God. You see, to behave in some way deemed to be good, human beings must create just the opposite. Unless you know bad, you cannot know good. In this case, God must also be vindictive and impossible to please; otherwise there is no incentive to keep working hard to get on the right side of God, to warrant your salvation. Going to the extreme, many believe that you are born bad, so in your struggle to achieve salvation in the eyes of your Creator, you must overcome this badness inherent in being born. And to make this God phenomenon more believable, then God must take the image of an old, judgmental man who could strike you down for looking at a lady's ankles. This is how the image of God was created.'

'Well yes, I guess so. How could so many people, bereft of the benefit of education and knowledge, believe in the living of a good life on the say-so of something you cannot perceive.'

'Exactly. So God was created by man, and not the other way around. And why should there be only one creator?'

'Because that is what we are taught since birth, this is the only reality we know.'

'As I think you already know, if it is real to you, then it is a real thing, it exists. In truth, there are as many creators, as many Gods that you can imagine there to be. And do you believe that these creators, these Gods, know absolutely everything about everything?'

'Well, yes. I cannot see how it can be any other way.'

'Not at the moment, maybe, but it can. It can be any way you are open for it to be. You also believe, do you not, that your earthly physical existence serves to bring the experiencing in a physical form of a set of circumstances and situations that occur throughout your physical life? And if only for your benefit, then why predetermine what set of circumstances you should be born into? That is your belief, is it not?'

'Well, yes, I guess it is,' I replied.

'And why do you think one or many creators, Gods, would give you that opportunity? What is in it for Him? For them? Are you really only toys,

'*So what are we here for?*'

My thoughts projected out. No need to move my lips or resonate my voice box to get my message across. The communication was exactly like talking, with no corruption from extraneous thought processes, but without any physical input from my body or facial features.

'*That is up to you, my friend. I am always aware of your circumstances, your thought processes, your actions; everything you do, say and hear I will always be aware of. So your question is better directed to you. I am here for you. That is my role in your existence, in your life.*'

My visitor kept his head facing straight ahead. Though I could see no face, I was able to make out the maleness of his communication. I could detect his wisdom. Everything I needed to know about my visitor was immediately available to me. He knew why I was here, and he was aware of every moment of the circumstances leading up to me sitting next to him.

'*Yes, but this time it is different, isn't it?*'

'*Yes, it is.*'

If there was one thing I had learned from meeting my spiritual guides, it was that although they possess seemingly endless knowledge of me and my immediate world on the physical and spiritual planes, the process of communication was always driven by me. I get answers from any communication I put forward, but such answers would inevitably lead to further questions, some of which I was unaware before our communication.

***

'*Okay, so I guess you are going to tell me what is going on with the deaths of these young people.*'

'*I am here only to offer guidance to that which helps you on the path to finding the answers you seek, so that you may further gather and use greater knowledge than you already possess. A signpost shows the most direct route to a destination. I am your signpost. Of course, you should first understand that no answers exist, none at all. And because of this fact there can be no teachers. Greater wisdom is not defined by how much you learn, but by how you put learning into practice in an effort to learn more. There is no pinnacle to reach. It is in searching for the quickest route to the pinnacle that greater wisdom is gained, and can then be used.*'

'*But if the pinnacle itself does not exist, then why do we try to achieve the unachievable?*'

'*Because only in the search for the pinnacle of knowledge, the non-existent answers to everything, can you discover greater knowledge of all that you do not yet know. This is the definition of learning. Answers only lead to*

This time it was different. No sooner had I closed my eyes than I felt a tingle from my toes to my head. It felt like a small current of electricity shooting through my body. I gave in to the feelings and let my mind switch off. I felt as if I was giving off small waves of static, and was sure that the hairs on my arms were standing straight up from tiny raised pimples of skin. My head started to feel warm. This warmth spread through my neck and shoulders. It was as if my whole body was presenting itself to attention. In my mind's eye I was walking slowly up a gently inclining path. A green field of cut grass stretched left and right. A small number of trees grew around me. The path seemed to comprise of those small earthen coloured bricks that commonly make up a driveway. These bricks were very clean, the joints between them flat and perfectly placed. Not one brick stuck out, not one misplaced.

At the top of the incline, slightly to the left of the path, was a small stone bench overarched by a silver-barked beech tree. The bench was not adorned in any way; just two slabs of slightly worn stone topped by another one. The bark on the tree was worn in patches. Small slits of bark peeled away at several places, revealing a vaginal-like entrance to the moist, pale amber trunk beneath. The umbrella of leaves sat on slender, gently drooping branches. This umbrella provided perfect cover to the bench from the sun, which was pure and bright, but contained no perceivable warmth. The sky had a pink and orange tinge, the like of which I had never known before. I approached the bench and sat down.

There was no sound at all. No birds sang. No flies or wasps buzzed. I could make out no extraneous sounds at all. As I recalled walking on the path, there was no sound beneath my feet. But that is how it is here. A place I have visited a number of times.

The hill overlooked a patchwork of fields, all seemingly as well maintained as this one with small hedges fringing each one. In the distance to the left and ahead of where I sat, I could see a huge crystal city. Domes and erect skyscrapers atop many glistening walls. The sun bounced off every parapet, glistening red, yellow, pink, blue and all the colours of the rainbow.

Somebody approached from my left side. I cannot say walked, because there was no placed movement of their body. I could not make out any feet beneath his clothing. As he moved, his legs could clearly be seen pushing against the material of a robe that was an almost indistinguishable grey in colour. The robe sat perfectly on broad shoulders. The hood of the robe shaded his face, disguising the features beneath. I could only describe it as if he were gliding towards me, but even this was not accurate, as his feet definitely made contact with the ground. My visitor sat down beside me on the stone seat.

***

sand, the water, of everything around me. I turn right. There are some small, well-worn wooden fences ankle high, progressing towards the gently rolling sea.

I step over the first wooden barrier. The sand beyond is a brownish brick colour. I bend and pick up some of the warm sand and place it in my pocket. I continue along the beach towards the next wooden breaker. I step over it. There is now an underlying red tint to the sand. Again, I pick up some of the sand and put it in the same pocket as before. On the next beach, the sand is a dull green colour, the next pink, the next a light blue, the next is an indigo colour. Finally, I arrive at a bright white stretch of sand. I have now completed a full circle of this small island paradise. Each beach represents the colour of my seven major chakras. I now sit cross-legged and visualise each of my chakras spinning faster and faster and lining up inside my body. Like pure clear crystals, each chakra throws off the brilliance of its own reflected light as it spins faster and faster.

If I have issues I need to address, I will then walk across a rickety wooden bridge to a roughly made shack at the end of a short pier. The door is locked. To gain entry to the shack, I must first vomit any negativity and darkness into a metal bowl that sits to the left of the entrance. It very much feels as if I am being sick. I can feel the bitter hotness of bile, as all my troubles spew out. Sometimes I see particular issues as dark objects in the black mass that exits my throat. Once finished, I find a key at the bottom of the bucket. I pick up the key, insert it into the wooden door, and enter the shack.

Inside there is a chair in the middle of the room fronted by a wooden desk and a computer terminal. There is no keyboard, no hard drive tower, just the terminal screen. To the left corner is the only window. Bright light bathes that side of the room in warm sunlight. First, I step up to the window, immersing myself in the warmth of the sun. It cleanses me, it warms and comforts me. I approach the desk and sit on the seat. A soft pillow supports my bottom and my back. I wait for the terminal to flicker to life.

The terminal will sometimes begin to communicate messages. The messages do not necessarily appear on the terminal screen. Sometimes I see images or am aware of messages coming to me in other forms. However these messages arrive, they are always in answer to the issues I bring to the shack. I can ask questions to further explore the communications I receive. When ready, I can shut down the terminal, leave the shack and shut the door. The trip back along the rickety wooden bridge is a journey back to consciousness. The closer I get to the beachfront the more awake I become. The island, the sea, the sky, everything, fades and dissipates until the blackness of closed eyes is all I see. I wake up feeling energised and with a positive outlook. Everything that happens within a good meditation is remembered, and ready to be utilised in my physical life.

***

puppets to be played with? Are the one or many creators like children in a playground, throwing down this situation, that problem, this person, that loss, as a game? And what would be the point in that?'

'None that I could see. This situation would only have merit if God were the Devil, playing bad tricks and jokes on people.'

'And there is no devil, dear one. No such thing has ever existed. It was all made up.'

'What about demons, curses, hexes?'

'Again. All exists if given life by an individual perspective. If you go to a haunted house, what might you expect to experience?'

'I see. But you are telling me that God, the one ultimate knowledge, the creator or creators of everything that there ever has been is not a font of ultimate knowledge. That is an extraordinary claim.'

'Extraordinary a claim it might be, but it is true nonetheless. You are sent to experience a physical reality, is this what you believe?'

'Yes.'

'And the experiences you have in that physical reality can, and usually do, provide learning or a gained knowledge in one way or another, yes?'

'Yes.'

'Then why can your understanding of your existence, this playing and replaying out of physical experiences, birth, death and rebirth and the everlasting glory of your existence, be limited to that of yourself? Can you not see that your life on earth, or any other planet, your energetic existence in other planes, can you not see that all this,' my Guide raised his arms above his head, *'that all this may not serve another purpose?'*

'Go on.'

'Okay. What if all existence of whatever shape, or form on planet earth, or any other satellite anywhere, has another purpose? What if the playing and replaying of experiences in any form whatsoever serves the purpose of another?'

'You mean God? Gods? The creator or creators?'

'Yes, why not? If not for this creative force then nothing at all would exist, correct?'

'I guess so.'

'And this creative force, have you ever directly experienced that without any shadow of a doubt?'

'Well I believe so, but I cannot answer yes for sure,' I answered.

'And would it be fair to say that this creative force, this God, is not able to take a physical form? Or, to put it more accurately, chooses to experience all of the creative powers of all universes through the living, breathing, seeing, hearing, touching, smelling of them, as fed directly to the force by elements of it that can take physical form? I myself am a guide to fifty

thousand humans alive at this moment, plus many more that currently reside here on the spiritual plane. That being said, it stands to reason that this creative force itself can never reach the pinnacle of knowledge and wisdom that does not, in reality, exist, since as much physical experience as has already been, much, much more, is yet to be experienced.'

'Let me get this right. You are suggesting that the creative force responsible for everything cannot, or chooses not, to take a physical form. This so that the vast array of experiences that have happened, and will ever happen, to physical forms, can be fed to the creative force as and when each of these beings finishes a physical existence and returns to the energetic pool of matter that makes up this creative force?'

'Yes. That is a very good summary.'

'And the same drive that the creative force has to reach the non-existent pinnacle of knowledge is that which drives the individual aspects of the creative force to do the same thing.'

'Yes. And there, my good friend, is the meaning of life.'

'So what is it that I need to learn? And how does my being here relate to the deaths of Solly Saunders and the others?'

'All of creation is a part of life being lived, all has a role, and all is part of the everything. Your physical existence on earth can never be separated from your spiritual being. To better address the issues of immediate concern it would be beneficial for you to learn, at first hand, of the link between your physical existence and the spiritual realm. And to answer your question, we need to go there.'

My guardian pointed towards the crystal city in the distance. His robe, draping over his arm, covering everything except the digit with which he indicated our destination.

***

My understanding was that in the spiritual environments there is no need for speech. Feelings and thoughts are immediately available to all. There we wear our thoughts and feelings as part of our energetic makeup. There is no need for secrets or suspicions, for lies or deceit.

Negative energies are a necessary part of our physical makeup, since without negative feelings or circumstances, there can be no learning. How can we adjust our understanding or increase our knowledge with no need to do so? In the physical plane, we often bemoan negative influences in our lives. We ask constantly 'How can a God of love, a God of devotion, allow such pain and suffering as we are consistently witness to?' The solution is not an easy one to accept. With no bad, how can good be known? With no negative, how can we be aware of positive? It is a simple answer, but nonetheless true.

Judgment is often the route of all negativity on earth. We see other people as doing wrong while we judge ourselves as right. Any occasion when a person suffers, we judge as unnecessary, cruel, heartless, or evil. We judge other people all the time, but how often can we stand back and see the wider picture? How many times can we truly see and understand the other side of any situation? We invest so much time in our own view on things, that we do not allow ourselves to be aware of any other standpoint. But the fact is that any perceived negative impact on our lives has a reason, and is seen as a way to achieve a legitimate end by the perpetrators.

We learn nothing from goodness. We can only know good because of the knowledge of bad. Without night, we could never know day, without cold we could never know hot, without wet, we could never know dry. Lack of judgment is seen as foolish by some people, but as enlightenment by others. The truth is that a lack of judgment must inevitably lead to a lack of negativity in our lives. Any negative aspects of our lives are growth experiences. The more we try to judge them, or seek to ignore them, the more they will occur.

The communication with my host came to me as words because that is what I am used to on the earth plane. I am a visitor to the spiritual realm only through meditation. While I can understand all that is communicated to me, it is only through words that I can better understand and acknowledge what is put before me. To exist in a reality where all our thoughts, all our emotions are readily available to all other inhabitants seems to me intrusive, but that is only by way of my human learning.

What is also clear is that our learning in the physical realm, our knowledge of our surroundings and our individual culture, how we deal with any issues that cross our life paths, is so familiar that this is the only way we can effectively operate. So the same must surely be true in the spirit realm. How we communicate, how we exist in the spirit realm, is just as comfortable and normal as it is for a human being to exist on earth.

पञ्च

The crystal city is larger than it looks from a distance. Travelling to it was instantaneous, one moment we were seated under the pleasant shade of the drooping willow, and the next we were inside a magnificent crystal hall. Passageways led off into the distance, separated by a dozen inclining steps. In the centre of the hall stood a two-metre high rectangular crystalline wall encompassing a set of small trees, creeping foliage adorning the sides all around. The massive hall seemed deserted apart from my guide and me.

'This is the Hall of Remembrance.'

'Hall of Remembrance? Remembrance of what?' I asked telepathically.

'This place is commonly used as a meditative area, where we are able to remember feelings, sensations and emotions that have been experienced in physical form.'

'I see nothing that might help to enter a relaxed enough state for meditation.'

'It is often easier to meditate while looking at an object, listening to a sound, feeling a breeze or even while moving around. Even on earth you can easily meditate while walking, listening to music, or focusing on anything.'

'But there is nothing to look at. There seems very little inside this hall to focus on,' I probed, *'and nobody is here, only you and I.'*

'You are incorrect. Whatever tools that might be required are available through the vibrations in this hall. It is just a case of tuning your own vibration to that which you desire. That is the very essence of our existence here in this realm. At any time, and in any place, we can assume an alternative vibration to experience whatever it is we require.'

'Wow. A playground where we can be whoever we want to be, experience anything we want to experience, just by calling it to us. Amazing.'

'Not so amazing. You have this capacity on earth too. The environment is a little bit heavier, a bit slower, but you all have the capability to bring to you anything at any time.'

I have occasionally experienced receiving something just after thinking about it. I would not say I called something to me and I might describe such an incident as coincidence, but in recent years I have come to accept that maybe there is no such thing as coincidence.

'So is this hall called here? And by whom?' I asked.

'All in the spiritual environments is called into being. Common areas are collectively brought forth. All creation is that way. Everything carries its own energetic vibration. There is an underlying vibration to every animate and inanimate object. This is its blueprint. But everything has the ability to vary its vibration and thereby change itself into another form.'

'And that is what happens when we die?'

Although put as a question, I felt I already knew the answer.

'Yes. Energetic vibrations are changing all the time. Energy can never be destroyed, it can never finish. All it can do is vibrate at a different frequency so that it changes form. For a century this is already scientifically proven on your planet.'

'Yes, for inanimate objects. For molecules and atoms.'

'There is no such thing as an inanimate object. If you could look inside a rock, you would see molecules moving around, so the rock is ever redefining itself without any external influence. Everything lives; everything is created from molecular energy. A rock was not always a rock. The rock went through a millennium of energetic molecular changes before it became what it is now. And it will continue to do so, for eternity. What you might consider as living entities, go through the very same process.'

It is not so easy for us to contemplate such revelations during our everyday lives, where the only two things for sure are death and taxes. We live so much in a world of emotion and chaos that our fundamental existence is ignored – taken for granted. But here, where these issues are at the forefront of existence, where death, taxes, emotion and chaos do not exist, it all becomes easy to interpret and understand.

My host continued.

'At this very moment, this hall is full of energies using unique vibrations to meditate on issues of relevance to them. These issues take form and can appear as real as at any time during a physical existence. Your perception, however, is that the hall is completely empty. This is only because your vibrations match with the hall you see and the fact that you and I occupy a space in this hall. But there are ever so slightly different vibrations going on all around you, without your knowledge. This acts as an aid to meditation. Many energies here prefer a common vibration. It helps them focus on their own issues to be in the visible vicinity of others.'

***

My host turned slightly and lifted his arm towards one of the corridors leading from the hall. Immediately we were inside a huge crystal library. Light was cast everywhere from multitudes of crystal shelves; the ceiling rose more than thirty metres above me. I remember how it seemed strange that I knew a boundary existed up there, but I could not see it. The chamber was vast, stretching into the distance so that from the entrance, the opposite wall was not visible. Each shelf held numerous books from floor to ceiling.

'This library holds every book ever written, and every book that ever will be written. It also holds ideas of books that are yet to be started, of every literary kind imaginable.'

My host began to explain the immensity of this place.

'It also holds the records of every lifetime ever lived, of those lives that are happening right now, and of those lifetimes yet to happen.'

My mouth fell open involuntarily.

'Our Akashic records?'

'That is a common human term for what is here, yes.'

'What do you call them?'

'We have no need to apply names to what exists; it is simply known and recognised. My communication with you is through words out of necessity, not by choice. The communication of choice throughout the spirit realm is that which comes from knowledge and recognition.'

'So nothing can be communicated of which you are unaware?'

'That is correct.'

'And therein lies the necessity of physical lifetimes and experiences, and also the necessity to build on these with spiritual awareness between lifetimes?' I asked.

'Put quite simply, most of what you say is correct.'

'So what am I missing?'

'That of which you are so far not knowledgeable, that of which you, as an entity, are unaware.'

'Until such a time as I reach further towards the pinnacle of knowing what does not exist.'

'That is correct.'

'So I can view any manuscript and any lifetime I wish?' I eagerly asked.

'Yes.'

'How do I do that?'

'Through your desire. But your desire must be clean, it must be intense, it must be real. Just focus your desire to see whatever it is you would like to see, and you will find that information before you.'

I focused on viewing my own Akashic record. I was a little reticent to view such an open and honest account of my life, but my desire overcame any reservations I might have had. I closed my eyes to make my visualisation stronger, bolder. On opening my eyes, a buff coloured folder lay in front of me on the crystal desk. My guide stood to my right. I opened the cover and saw a blank page. I flipped the page and found another blank page, and then another.

'This is empty,' I said, turning to face my host.

'Focus intensely on a page. Meditate on that page, let nothing else enter your mind except the information that lies within.'

Easy for my host to say, but this was a new experience for me. I stared at the page. Shortly, I was aware of a greyish flickering around the outer edges, and as I stared at the centre the greyness vanished. I returned my attention once again to the middle of the page. As I did, the greyness at the edge of the page moved towards the centre and started filling with colours, and a picture finally emerged.

I could see a young boy of seven staring intently into a mirror. Though I was looking at a page in a book, the image was not flat and I was able to view it from every angle at the same time, to immerse myself in the textures and in the light and shade of the image before me. Not only that, it seemed that I was also aware of a depth in the image, of the odours, of the moment, of the feel of the air upon the boy's skin and also of the taste inside of the boy's mouth. It was as if the boy existed inside of me, like I was an invisible shroud draped over his form. I felt like I was inside and outside the image concurrently.

The boy did not seem to be aware of my presence, but he was aware of something in his reflection, something other than that which stood in front of the mirror. His stare was unwavering. He was looking for something, searching for information that lay just beyond his reach. And then it hit me like a bullet to the head, this boy was waiting for some unknown thing or event to make its presence known. I looked harder at the image before me. The boy's eyes glistened a deep blue, moisture flooding the bottom of each eyelid. The boy was sad and he was scared by what he feared was on its way into his life.

As I relaxed my focus, the image before me faded slowly as the wave of flickering grey folded from the edges of the page into the centre. Then it was gone.

'What you should understand is that whatever you view in your Akashic records will have a particular relevance to you at the moment you view it,' the message from my guide did little to help me understand what I had just witnessed.

'That boy was me when I was little. It was as if I was there with him, it was incredible. But why do I get the feeling that he was very scared of something, but he didn't know what that something was? And do you know what else? I feel like I know what that image was about, but that answer lies just beyond my reach.'

'What you witnessed was a living image of an event that has a significant relevance to you at this time, and this is the way in which the records are commonly used. Each page holds an imprint of an event from any past,

present or future physical existence of that entity to whom the record belongs.'

'So that means that I could look into my future, including lifetimes yet to be lived. Hey, I could find out next week's winning lottery numbers.'

'Nothing in your records will be revealed of which you are unaware. Akashic records react to your evolutionary progress, so if viewing an event in a future lifetime would assist in your development then that information might well be made available to you. But the Akashic records themselves are evolving. As the decisions you make shape your future opportunities for growth, so the records of life must also take account of such change. The raison d'être of all creation is to live and experience, since this is the best way in which evolution can occur,' my Guide explained.

'Okay, so our physical and spiritual existence is all to do with our personal growth and development as well as being a contributory factor to the evolution of all of creation.'

'I have something else to show you,' my Guide bowed a little, and we moved on again.

***

Immediately we were inside a cave-like room. The walls rose to meet in a dome at the centre of the room, which was lit by a soft apricot light emanating from its centre. The cave walls, though appearing rough and unkempt, were not dark or dingy. There was no sense of the moisture that most people might associate with a cave.

My host began explaining this room's role.

'One thing most humans associate with their passage to the spirit realm is that the first thing they will do is be judged on their actions in their preceding lifetime on earth. Of course, if this is what they think will happen, so then it will. However, in reality, all will have a chance to review what happened in their latest visit to the physical realm from every aspect. This is where such a viewing might take place.'

'Their latest visit? So reincarnation is a reality.'

'Maybe not insofar as most descriptions of reincarnation you might know. There can be no reincarnation if there is everlasting existence. We are all an energy and as you might know from a knowledge of basic physics, no energy can be destroyed. You, therefore, are everlasting. The physical form you adopt when visiting the earth plane is just that, a form you have adopted.'

'And what does "from every aspect" mean?'

'It means that any situation or action encountered during a physical lifetime can be known from every aspect, and not just from the viewpoint of you as you were in that physical context.'

'*That means you get to know the outcomes of your deeds? The feelings of other people affected by your words and actions?*'

'*Yes. The energetic vibrations sent out by words and actions cause an imprint that remains forever. This imprint can impact other energetic vibrations, like a ripple which, in itself, can cause a change to the vibrations it has impacted. Human emotions and feelings are energetic vibrations, and just as they can change, so can everything else. This is all part of the same creative principles we spoke of before. As such, these vibrational changes are recorded and can be replayed forever and ever more.*'

'*And this is what many people believe to be our life review?*'

'*Yes, but that term is inaccurate. It is simply a replaying of vibrational changes caused by actions and words, feelings and emotions created while in any of your physical forms.*'

'*So, if we have many previous lifetimes, these too can be reviewed?*'

'*They usually are, yes. Common themes arise and are essential to the understanding of our physical and spiritual experiences. But this process is not a review and neither is it a judgment. The experiences of physical lifetimes are always positive implements, learning tools, and since it has already happened, what would be the point of a review? Also, if all experiences serve to increase our knowledge of ourselves and our existence, then what need for a review? This process is a necessary pathway towards our greater knowledge of ourselves. It is only by gaining greater knowledge of ourselves that we can aspire to achieve the reaching of the pinnacle.*'

'*Which does not exist, right?*'

'*Which does not exist,*' my Guide confirmed.

Three egg-shaped lights appeared on the wall in front of us. The lights did not seem to emanate from any source or contraption, and appeared more like an intense energy, similar to the type of light that might be created when a laser hits a solid object. The difference was that there was no beam creating these lights. The three lights moved over the surface of the wall on occasion, but mostly they remained still. The intense energy of these lights seemed part of the wall, rather than attached to it. One light sat higher than, and was flanked by, the other two. It also became clear that each ball of light energy was intelligent in nature.

'*Every nanosecond of the life that is eternal, both physical and non-physical, is a learning process. Each energy must theorise and assimilate all that is wished to be learned. In this chamber, intentions, hypotheses and action are objectively viewed with the intention of setting further objectives. The three entities you see before you are not judges, neither are we evaluators, nor teachers. We, as do all senior energies in this realm, act as guides. Our role is simply to put objective observations on the table, so to speak. We have no views on what is revealed in such evaluations, but we are here to assist the individual evaluator to be able to actively pursue learning opportunities which will be of positive benefit to their continued existence.*'

It was the lower right energy that communicated this information to me. I wanted to ask so many questions, but was unable to do so. The lower left energy continued.

'You may be aware that an individual spiritual energy does not exist alone; in fact, it cannot. Many thousands – hundreds of thousands – of different energies integrate in one form or another with one energy to achieve the meaning of life, which is to learn and practically act out this learning. A life path does not exist; neither does fate. A lifetime is planned to the degree that certain behaviours and experiences are deemed beneficial to best achieve the desired learned attribute. But the events in a human lifetime can never be mapped out – that would be to remove free will and the desire to learn. An automaton has no need to learn, but acts out a planned course of action. The learning capacity of a human being relies entirely upon free will, upon a capacity to star in and direct their own life. Situations, circumstances, events and other physical entities can be, and are, introduced at key stages within that life. It is by choice that any spiritual energy, can contribute to an individual lifetime in whatever way might afford benefit to itself and to the person experiencing that lifetime. Whether they are used, and the degree to which they are used, is always a matter for the individual entity to determine.'

The middle, and highest, of the energies before me, spoke up.

'As you learn on earth as human beings, so you learn on a universal scale. It is in your genetic makeup. An interest in a subject leads to theorising about that subject. Then comes practical learning and experiencing. After that comes the process of deviating and developing that experience to learn the same subject over, and over, and over again, ad infinitum. It is similar in many ways to driving a car. You know where you want to go. You are familiar with the route and some of the landmarks you will pass. Signposts offer guidance as to how far you have come and how much further you have to go. But the journey will always be different. Always, and in all ways. The capacity to learn is not governed by intellect, but by the space you afford yourselves to cultivate as many varied experiences as possible. In this case, quantity and quality hold equal reverence. And this is why physical lifetimes are so cherished, so worshipped, so glorified. Every spiritual energy rejoices with each release and each return. Every physical lifetime can, and does, affect every other lifetime. The cause and effect of these actions and reactions is not predetermined, only that an opportunity might arise for the greatest benefit to be realised for all affected spiritual beings living earthly existences.'

'So tarot readings, crystal readings, psychic readings and mediumship are all wrong, since nothing is planned for our futures and therefore cannot be foreseen?'

I guess I already knew the answer to my thought, which was not even broadcast as a question. It was answered by the central light energy, nonetheless.

'The things you mention can be very useful in highlighting situations where predetermined future opportunities for specific learning might arise. And it is the very nature of these opportunities that make it extremely difficult for their explanation to be too precise. The learning opportunities themselves are not predetermined. Only the circumstances that, if moulded and created by an individual, or a number of people, might be created. There is, therefore, no fate, no predetermination in a life path. There are instead signposts, if you like, specific markers that will, or will not, be picked up and utilised to create opportunities for learning and growth.'

'And this is a learning opportunity for me?' was my next thought.

A moment of silence, during which time the three light energies seemed to shimmer as they moved a little before settling back to their original settings.

'Yes and no,' the left-sided light energy replied, *'It was your desire to come here, and it is true this desire was one of those opportunities provided for you that you became aware of and actioned. But this opportunity was posted for another reason. We need your help in resolving an issue that has arisen.'*

'But if this opportunity was placed into my life plan before I was born, you had fifty earth years to resolve this issue without any need for input from me.'

Once again my mind automatically let go of this thought without any interaction from me.

'There was always a chance that this situation would arise and that you might become involved, that is why this marker was inserted into your current lifetime. I should explain that here in the spirit realm all is known, there can be no deceit, no hiding away from issues or from the truth. Therefore, we have no reason to assume that all will not run immaculately. This is how the spiritual realm has been created and will always be. We have minimal security measures in certain areas, but that is only to preserve and protect those elements essential to the authenticity of two worlds, the spiritual and the physical.'

'Which work simultaneously together?'

'Much more closely than you might imagine.'

'So, why do you need my help?' I asked.

'We are aware of a fault in the mechanism that links our two planes of existence. As I already explained, our security measures are there to protect and preserve the records of existence and certain ongoing operational issues. But there is nothing in place to protect individual spiritual involvement with the human world. This falls outside of our need for security. The polarity that exists here between spiritual energies and our structure and environment is such that it could never be envisaged that an issue such as this could arise. We do not, therefore, have the capability to deal with such issues arising out of a non-secure environment.'

'Has this kind of thing ever happened before?'

'In theory, it cannot.'

'But it was always foreseen, always known that this incident would happen, otherwise I would not have signposts to this effect written into my life plan,' I insisted.

'Yes, that is correct. At the age of fourteen, you made a choice that eventually led to the opportunity you face now. That choice set up the chain of events that has led to the present-day situation.'

'What choice did I make?'

'You chose to return to the earth plane to continue this lifetime.'

'Did I really have a choice?'

'Yes, you did. And since you made that choice, the instigator of these problems is an intricate part of your life path, and always will be.'

'We do have free will to make choices, yes?'

'Yes, you do.'

'So can we not choose consciously or subconsciously to deviate from our learning path in a particular lifetime?'

'You can, but invariably you do not. Future events can only occur as a result of one of two choices, you do something, or you do not. You cross the road or you do not, you brush your teeth now or you do it later, you drift off to sleep now or you watch another programme on the television, you decide to accept the offer of an injection to relieve the pain you feel in your abdomen, or you do not.'

'I can accept that for major events, but for everything?'

'Every nanosecond of the present, of the here and now, sets up your future path. Every decision ever made sets up a significant chain of events.'

'But that means each lifetime also changes because of these decisions, right?'

'Yes. This is because a decision can be changed, and very often is. So in this case, where a decision is changed, an alternative future learning path is established. I should add that these future paths have the potential to exist forever and ever, too.'

'Until they are changed by the next decision.'

'Yes. Ad infinitum. So your physical and spiritual existence are forever being created anew. And so you, most cherished and revered one, are the creator and the created, the actor and director, the cast and the crew, the puppet and the puppet master, the sheep and the shepherd, and so on.'

'So, if I have this right, all decisions I ever made, all actions I ever took, all words I ever said, and all thoughts I ever had...'

'In this lifetime and in others,' added the bright energy on the right side as I looked.

present there can be no past and no future. Science will never be able to prove the existence of God. But equally, neither will you be able to prove God's nonexistence. There is no beginning and no end to the energy that is life. But you are correct in thinking that to our right is the direction in which all life travels. This is the direction of the destination all life energies seek to attain. To be one with the creator. To exist as the creator. In reality, all life is the creator already. Our creative energy can and does evolve to our right, until each life energy, each life force moves closer and closer to the pinnacle, which, as we already know, does not exist.'

'So to the right and to the left is the ultimate creator. That is where God exists.'

'Oh, my dear one. The right and the left of this tableau goes way, way beyond God.'

'So God is not the ultimate creative force?' I asked.

'To be one with God. To join with our creator might well be what all life aspires to, consciously or subconsciously. But what created God?'

'So there are energies, forces beyond God?'

'Yes. Of course there are. The creative energy you know as God has its own origins. And here is something else that might well blow your mind. The one true creator, the one true God that you, as a life form, aspire to be, originated as you, as all of you.'

'And as time does not exist as an aspect of life, then...' I hesitated. Maybe I was not fully able to grasp the complexity and the simplicity of what I was about to say, *'then we are all God, we are all the Creator. We already are that which we aspire to be.'*

'Indeed you are.'

This knowledge really was mind-blowing. I was aware that my hands were shaking; my body was sweating and numb. The truth, which I was now unravelling, really did have the capacity to blow my mind. Literally.

'And if I wanted to, I could travel to any part of this tableau and view that part at which God exists.'

'Theoretically, yes. But your ability to view anything within the tableau is limited to your capacity to understand what it is you see. Your spiritual development, your life experiences and understanding will only allow you to view that which you have the capacity to take in, to review objectively. In reality, it is really only a very small amount of the tableau you will have access to.'

'How small?'

'The area at which you were standing.'

The tableau went on to infinity, so I was told. If my capacity to understand life really was limited to an arms width, then what hope of ever reaching the non-existing pinnacle? There was no conclusion I could reach, other than to accept that our lives really did not end when we left our earthly does not exist. All of everyone's life is governed by, driven by, dictated by something that truly does not exist.'

'You are right, my friend. All there is, all there ever was and all there ever will be, is the here and now. This is where everything that has ever been possible has started, happened and then ended. It all happens now. There cannot ever be any other way to live. To do so would be to defy and deny life itself, and that can never happen.'

'This moment contains memories of the past. It is the present in every possible form, and it will always be the future as defined by the present. The here and now.' I said, telepathically.

'Essentially, that is correct. The shell contained a nut in the past, but that past event is a memory, it has no creative reality. The past can only ever occupy one moment in time when it was, in fact, the present, the here and now, defining the future. In effect, the past never existed. The future cannot ever exist; it only exists as a plan or as a potential outcome of here and now circumstances, choices and actions. This tableau in front of you is life, in action, in the present now. All choices made, all actions taken, all words spoken, all deeds done, all hopes, dreams, catastrophes, nightmares. Any and all that ever existed in this moment in time cannot exist without this tableau. This is the definition of life being, right here. Life moves, changes, ever and ever more. The tableau is in motion all the time life is being lived, in any shape, or form. In this respect the tableau moves always and inexorably.'

'Towards a conclusion?' I asked.

'There can be no conclusion, as there was no beginning. Energy just is and will always be. Life is energy in motion. Nothing more and nothing less.'

'So this tableau goes on forever that way?' I pointed to the right.

'And that way too.' My host lifted his arm and pointed to our left.

'And each perception of this tableau will be different.' I said.

'You have learned well, my friend. Yes, each perception of this tableau will be different. The only common denominator being that the tableau will always be a representation of life being lived at this moment.'

'But if time does not exist, this moment cannot exist, because this moment is a moment in time.'

'You are correct again.'

'So what is that way?' I pointed again to my right side.

'In that direction is the pinnacle that does not exist.'

'And in that direction?' I pointed to my left.

'In that direction is also the pinnacle that does not exist.'

'So, if I wanted to prove that God did not exist I could do so by cutting the tableau at either end.'

'In theory, yes. But to whom would it be proved? All life would cease to exist and would never have existed in the first place, since without any returned to normal. I felt the veins in my neck throb and was acutely aware of blood pulsing through on its way to my brain.

'This hallway is not empty, as it seems to you. A security system was alerted as soon as you started taking a step closer to the tableau. It is still there in front of you now, even though you are not aware of it.'

'Why a need for security if all entities occupying this space are spiritual?'

'You would be surprised how many visitors we receive.'

'And what shape or form does this security measure take?' I mentally asked.

'That is irrelevant, suffice to say it is there and aware, at all times.'

'We need some of them at the clubs where I live, crime would become obsolete.'

There was no response from my host. I guessed that humour might be in short supply here.

'I thought I saw movement. I wanted to take a closer look.'

'All creation is continually in motion. All life is continually evolving, changing, recreating. What you might not yet comprehend is that this tableau before you is not just another aspect of life. It is not just a cog in the machine, in your machine. It is not an artefact, nor is it a tool, nor is it a pipe in the system. No, dear friend. This tableau is life itself, living.'

'So this magnificent depiction in front of me is not that, it is not a representation of life. It is life?'

I struggled to comprehend the impact of the thoughts I was projecting, not on my host, but on my own mind, maybe even my own sanity.

'Yes.'

'Wait a minute. My life, right at this moment, involves me laying on my sofa and being involved in some kind of far out meditative experience, the like of which I could never have imagined in my wildest dreams, ever. So far as I can see that is the totality of my physical existence, my human experience right at this moment in time.'

I immediately knew the shallowness of my thoughts, even after all I had experienced in my life. After becoming diabetic at seven years old, dying and being resuscitated at fourteen, my determination to read about and push the boundaries of spiritual experiences, my abilities to receive information psychically, to hypnotise people, to heal them. Of course, there was much more to our existence than that which we can see, touch, hear, smell and taste. I turned to look at my shrouded host. My eyes widened, my jaw dropped a little, a crease formed above my eye sockets.

'There is no...' I struggled to frame my thoughts, to finish the jigsaw of the realisations that only now had come bursting through the locked gates of my mind, all boundaries broken, *'there is no such thing as time, is there? It*

'In this lifetime and in others, set up the conditions and circumstances under which I would be here now, being asked by your revered selves to help you catch a spiritual saboteur?'

'Well, it is not quite as simple as that, but yes.'

***

My host gestured that we should move on. Once again, our movement was instantaneous.

We arrived at a very long hall that stretched left and right as far as the eye could see. Three steps in front of us was what looked like a three-dimensional tapestry that filled the entire length of the hall. The tapestry was about two metres high and bordered top and bottom by thick oak beams.

The tapestry consisted of many different colours and shapes, seemingly interwoven. Blues and blacks, golds and greens, reds and yellows. I pushed my head back a little as I tried to take in the whole of a part of the tapestry to discern an overall colour. The colour was similar to that you might find on the outside of a woman's womb, or on the covering of any internal organs or parts, for that matter. It was a dull greyish pink. The pinkness of it gave the appearance of life. I could make out no fabric beneath the pattern.

'The item in front of you is possibly the most important creation ever assembled. This, my dear friend, is the tableauic representation of life. As such it represents all the circumstances that satisfy the energetic and molecular parts that are the living essence of the creative force inside everything.'

'Tableauic? Is that even a word?' I asked.

'It is now. Using vocabulary, this is the closest I can come to representing what you see before you. This is the tableau of life.'

As I looked at the construction before me, I noticed a tiny movement from the corner of one eye and turned my head automatically in that direction. I took a step forward and found I could not move anymore. My legs were solid, my arms stayed in exactly the same position. I struggled to make any movement at all. I could not.

'It was mentioned before that we have security systems in place where necessary. This is one such place,' my Guide explained to my unasked question.

I pulled my forward most leg away from the tableau. I felt a twitch in my foot, and it very slowly started to retreat. The lower part of my leg began to move backwards, following my foot. Then my upper leg and my hip twisted away from the tableau. Feeling came back to my arms as I slowly stepped back to rest at my original starting point. The leg I pushed forward ached and was deadened; as if the blood flow had been severely hampered and then forms; that we must continue to exist as an energy striving to reach a goal that is beyond reach.

'My good friend, we have one last place to visit. All that you have witnessed during your meditation period is essential to helping unlock the reasons behind the problems that we have been experiencing. It has already been explained to you that operational aspects of the spiritual realm are, at least theoretically, unbreachable. This is because in this realm openness, understanding and faithfulness are assured. This realm is very different than the earth plane, because no energy here has ego or any other humanistic aspect that might provide access to self-interest at the expense of another. Here it is understood that we are all one. There is, therefore, no need for competition, and there is very little need for rules or regulations. There are processes, systems in place, to meet any educational or informational need that can ever arise. These processes are foolproof, or so we thought.'

***

I found myself now inside a room housing ten man-sized cylinders. Each cylinder lay horizontal, one metre from the floor and each was equidistant from the next. The cylinders did not appear to have any buttons, or switches, or any type of instrumentation. No wires or tubes affixed sides, bottom or top. The bottom of the cylinders was dark grey in colour. Each cylinder was topped by an opaque, smoky screen, along the edge of which was a single thin black line. I guessed this must be the entrance and exit points. But for what?

'For spiritual energies. This is where we can connect with our human counterparts anytime during a current lifetime on earth. This is where spiritual influences come to bear on your physical experience. Where the signposts we mentioned before can be planned, developed and put in place. Where an individual human's life path can be observed and interaction can be undertaken as and when it is deemed necessary or particularly beneficial. This is where the intricate link between the spiritual realm and your human selves combine. This, my friend, is where life is lived,' my Guide explained.

'Wait a minute. You said our human selves. Are you saying that human lives and experiences are only one part of our existence? As we go about our daily lives, as we go shopping, as we take kids to school, as we down a pint, as we flirt in the bar, as we watch porno movies, as we iron Freddie's shirt for school the next day, a separate part of us is up here, doing whatever you do, we do, in the spiritual realm?'

Again my mouth fell open, my eyes creased and I felt a little saliva pool underneath my tongue. My question was so overwhelming that I was unsure at this time whether or not it was actually my brain that could concoct such an idea. This idea seemed ludicrous, preposterous and went against all that was ever taught, or even known, in my physical domain.

'Yes. We have already discussed the link between spiritual realms and your human realities, but the bond between here and there is much closer than you could ever foresee. It is, in fact, conjoined.'

'Like a Siamese twin,' I smirked and lifted my head slightly, tutting as I did, *'and that was a joke.'* I said.

'And it was probably the most serious joke you have ever told, because it is extremely close to the truth. We exist here dependent on you. You exist there dependent on us. You might also like to know that it is not just you and us. You exist, as an energetic entity, on many other planes too.'

'Whoa. I think my head is gonna explode.'

'It possibly would if you knew the whole truth. But it is true that in your physical realm and here in the spirit realm there are only two planes on which you exist right now. They are two planes of many more. All coexisting. All contributing to the one goal, and all dependent on each other to achieve maximum input towards an individual energetic entity's own achievements.'

***

My mind buzzed, I heard it as I did my best to comprehend what I was being told.

'You remember I said that the tableau is life lived?' my Guide continued.

'Yes, I do.'

'Well, now maybe you can appreciate that life lived is not just lived on the earth plane. The tableau is the cumulative total of all life, on all planes lived now, ever lived and ever to be lived.'

If I had a physical body, my legs would have probably buckled beneath me by now. My host continued teaching me the philosophies and realities of life.

'The pod before you is the one used by spiritual entities to interact in your life.'

'You mean in anyone's life, right?'

'No, I mean in your own personal life. This is your pod.'

'Wow. So how does this spiritual, human interaction happen? In a nutshell, please,' I asked.

'You might have heard of a cord, invisible to you, which is connected somewhere around your navel area. You might have heard that this cord is your connection to the spirit realms. You may also be aware that if this cord is ever severed, then your physical lifetime comes to an end.'

'Yes, I have read about this. But if we cannot see it, then this cord cannot be a physical object.'

'Yes it can. There are many things on your earth plane that you cannot see, but that is only because they are outside of the spectrum you can perceive. Air is a perfect example.'

'But air is invisible.'

'It is invisible only because it exists outside of your spectral field of vision. But air is certainly not invisible. In the same way, this cord is a physical object that exists not only outside of your visible spectrum, but it also carries too little weight for you to perceive, and its molecular structure is such that it cannot scientifically be detected on your earth plane. But that does not mean it is not there.'

'So this cord functions as a harness that links spiritual energies and humans?'

'It is not a harness. It is a living structure that carries information, it carries emotions, it carries data, it carries perceptions of anything and everything between a human and the spiritual energy engaging with that person on earth at any one time.'

'Like an information superhighway. A focused interaction like an internet messenger service.'

'Almost, but not quite. This cord can be used by any spiritual energy, not just by the spiritual energy having a majority share in assisting you in each lifetime.'

'You mean our guardian angels.'

'There are actually no such things. But you will have a select number of spiritual energies assigning themselves to assist you during your lifetimes on the earth planes. They are not guardians; they are assistants. There is no one thing protecting you, as might a guardian, but your physical existence is assured all the time your intended observations and experiences remain unfulfilled.'

'You said earthly planes, with an "s" at the end.'

'Yes. As I mentioned before, your physical existence on earth, at least the one that you are consciously aware of, is not the only physical existence you are indulged in. There are a number of physical planes existing simultaneously, very similar in all respects, but not identical. On each of these planes, the outcomes of decisions can be played out simultaneously, so your existences on each plane follow different goals, experiences and destinations based on the different decisions you make. You can only make two decisions, you do something, or you do not. In one physical plane, you will do something, setting up a unique set of oncoming situations and experiences. In another simultaneous physical existence you will choose not to do that very same thing, thereby creating completely different experiences and a different outcome.'

'But then each lifetime on each plane will go off in so many directions, it must be impossible to learn anything as one spiritual energy living a physical experience on any number of earth planes simultaneously,' I replied.

'That is not the case. Your goals, your objectives, your intended destination is established before you start each lifetime, and they remain the same on each and every plane you exist on.'

'Wow. That means that you reach the same destination, but with entirely different sets of experiences along the way. Essentially, you live the whole gamut of experiences. You can live in pursuit of core values and learning experiences all at the same time. Ingenious.'

'Quite.'

'Even if on each earth plane my own physical entities might all have different spiritual outlooks?' I asked.

'Especially if that is the case. This would be an ideal scenario to experience and learn the most from a lifetime, and to bring that into your ultimate consciousness to ensure growth.'

'And what would happen if I ever was to step into another earth plane? What would happen if I ever met my other earth-plane self?' I asked.

'They are two separate questions. In answering the first, it is perfectly feasible for you to step into another plane of existence, just as you are able to bring yourself here. But there is a major difference. The link between the spirit realms and earth planes is permanent and fluent, to allow interaction between the two. There is no such link between each of the earth planes, so to step inside another might entail much more knowledge and experience than even you currently have. A person would need a very high level of enlightenment to achieve this. On your second point, while you are able to, and often do, view them, it could never happen that you meet your other earth plane self, the same as you can never encounter any past or future you. The complications caused by such an event would be insurmountable.'

'Yes, I can imagine.'

My headache came back with a vengeance. I found myself hoping that this experience would end very soon, glorious and astounding as it was. I felt I was being made privilege to so much essential knowledge to which most, if not all, of the human population had no access. And this was not just a theoretical chat over a cup of coffee, the information being given to me was fact, and proven by my surroundings. It was real.

'Okay. I can just about comprehend that the scenario you place before me is feasible, not scientifically, but theoretically.'

'It is all real. It is all existing at every moment, although, as I mentioned before, the actual appearance of what you perceive with your vision is a personal one. Each system, each process, each operational circumstance in this realm is common no matter what perception you have of it. Sometimes the appearance and effect of these systems can change depending on

individual expectations, belief systems and the capacity to open up to them. If a human expects at death that she will be placed in the ground and eaten by worms, and that nothing else exists beyond her last lifetime on earth, then that is exactly what she will encounter as part of her own individual dying process. But that does not mean that the dying process is any different from one to another. All who take part in the spiritual realm, in the creation of life, will follow the same process of changing from one aspect of themselves into another. The same can be said for those people who strongly believe in heaven and hell. If a person believes that hell exists, and if her disappointment in her life's achievements are so great, then the hell that exists in her mind as a potential destination can be experienced. The truth is that hell is not built into the system. There is no judgment. Eventually all will continue their personal quest for spiritual development and growth in this environment.'

'So if someone is a murderer, or worse, a despot leader killing thousands of people, that person will not go to hell?'

'No he will not. Unless his belief is that this is what awaits him. But there is no eternal fire.'

'I assume there is an adjustment phase that all must go through. It is a pretty big jump from one minute being conscious of a physical life on earth, and the next moment they are an energy in a completely different set of circumstances and environment.'

'Yes, a period of adjustment is necessary. But since all spiritual energies have existed here before, and will forever after, that adjustment, while being necessary, is really quite minimal. Since parts of the energy that makes up a human being have existed in this realm all along, soon after their arrival the part of those people who physically died on earth will accept and embrace that, with the help of those spiritual energies interacting during the past lifetime.'

'Are we aware of this permanent link we have with spiritual realms?' I asked.

'All the time. Sleeping is the perfect example. During a physical lifetime, the human body needs to rest. This is not because the physical body is tired. A physical body can go on and on indefinitely. The reason for periods of rest is the very same reason you meditate. This is when the connection between the physical and spiritual realms is strongest. In periods of rest the barriers created by life experiences, thoughts, plans and everyday issues are all dropped. This allows contact and cooperation between life energies and spiritual energies.'

'So you are saying people visit this place in their sleep?'

'Constantly. But it is a two-way process. Spiritual energies also visit people.'

'Like ghosts.'

'No. Ghosts are spiritual energies that trap themselves on the physical plane for their own personal reasons. They are not physical entities; that part of their makeup is gone, but they might not realise this fact. Maybe they cannot accept death. Or maybe some unpleasant or emotionally upsetting event occurred in their life that they are seeking to resolve, which they cannot, of course. Ghosts can interact with human beings, but only because they are occupying the same space and time.'

My headache was growing in strength as my Guide continued.

'And here is something else that you might not have considered before. Since a number of different planes exist in the same place at the same time on earth, what is perceived as ghosts might also be life being lived on that other plane. This means that you, so far as you are aware as a physical being with heartbeat, blood, faculties doing your everyday tasks, can appear as ghosts to those humans existing in the same time and at the same place in an alternate plane.'

'And our earth is not just what we physically experience. There are a number of slightly different physical planes with numerous experiences going on at the same time in the same physical space?' I asked.

'Yes that is correct. But I think it might be time now to move on to the reason you are here.'

'Yes. I think so, too. My brain is hurting.'

'I am aware of that.'

It was still extremely unnerving to realise that my Guide could read all my thoughts even before I had an opportunity to express them.

My host then explained that the room we were currently occupying was one of millions of identical rooms where pods connected human lives with energy life forces here in the spirit realm. So far as could be determined, one of these pod rooms is where the problems occur. He explained to me that the three people in my geographical area that had been removed from their earthly existence much earlier than had been anticipated, were not the only ones affected. In every case, it had been known that there was the potential for this situation to arise, but at that time they knew no more.

'Okay. So you do not know how many people have been affected so far, but in each case there is a possibility that there is a trace on their records. What is the potential for this issue? How bad can it get? How many lives can potentially be cut short?'

'One million, three hundred and sixty-four thousand, two hundred and thirteen.'

I took two steps back and leaned against the wall behind me. My breath quickened, a cool sweat broke out above my eyes and under my armpits. I looked down at the floor. I knew time did not exist in this place, but I stayed like this for what seemed like hours, struggling to comprehend the task being placed before me and the seriousness of any outcomes that might occur. I felt a huge weight on my shoulders. I felt responsibility for every potential victim of the problems being experienced here.

'I don't think I can do this,' I said, finally.

'At first we were unaware of the potential scale of the problem. The truth is that since we first knew of a problem, the figures have increased. This is why it was imperative that we were able to secure your involvement in this issue and get you here as soon as we could, in your earth time.'

'Why me?'

'Because when your present lifetime was planned, all the necessary implements needed to address this issue were imprinted into your DNA. It was, of course, necessary for you to unlock these implements at the times you were ready. Having gained all the tools necessary, you now possess a high enough degree of spiritual knowledge and experience to possess an openness of mind essential to approach what we now face. With an open mind you can more logically process information and your judgmental tendencies are weakened. Your life experiences have provided you with a tenacity and inquisitiveness that will also stand you in good stead. Also, do not forget that the possibility of this outcome occurring at some time in your life was always known, it is a factor in your genetic makeup. Your family background, your schooling, your siblings and your peers were all developed and constructed for this moment.'

'Sounds like fate to me.' I said.

'No. Fate does not exist. The planning process that takes place before all lifetimes is essential for maximising the potential beneficial aspects of physical experiences on earth. All decisions lead to differing outcomes. If all potential outcomes are not covered in the planning process, then living becomes a circus of chaos and confusion. This is not a good learning situation. It is therefore necessary to prepare for all potential decisions and all potential outcomes.'

'But that is a monumental task.'

'Yes, but a necessary one.'

'How many decisions does one person make during his lifetime?'

'We cannot and do not cover every decision – only those that might create defining outcomes if followed through.'

'But the offshoots of only one decision can be monumental.' I said.

'Yes they can. We cover, on average, eight-and-a-half billion potential outcomes from the one hundred and fifty thousand decisions that have the potential to significantly affect a life plan made in any fifty-year period.'

I made some mental arithmetic.

'That is around eight decisions a day. So you are telling me that on average we make eight decisions every day of our lives that have the potential to significantly affect our life path, opportunities, chances, achievements, time of death and every other significant event in our future lives.'

'Yes, that is correct.'

'From what age are we counting?'

'From birth.'

'So this means that when my lifetime was planned somewhere, somehow, in amongst the millions of likely outcomes there was always the potential for decisions that might lead to me being right here, right now.'

'Yes. But there is another angle too. Each spiritual energy that agrees to undertake a physical lifetime knows each potential outcome before they take up their physical presence on earth. This means that their choices in a physical lifetime can, to some degree, be measured, and outcomes can be known.'

'Instinct?'

'Sometimes, yes.'

'So it is not really so much a chance of potluck. Many things I have become privy to in this visit seemed to make this physical lifetime, and our spiritual experiences, seem so haphazard as to be a complete waste of time,' I suggested.

'Firstly, there is no such thing as a waste of time. Every single moment of every human, spiritual being, of every animal on every planet, of everything that ever existed and ever will exist is an opportunity for greater learning. Secondly, during the planning process, the individual spiritual energy, subject to its next physical lifetime, is aware of the most positive route and the most beneficial decisions and choices that can be made. This information is always known during that lifetime. But the planning process must include some of the other less beneficial potential outcomes, so that, if necessary, a life path can continue to be followed, should the individual spiritual or physical energy so choose.'

I turned away from my host. Something crept into my mind, sniffing around the edges of my thoughts, growing until it represented a boiling, angry volcano ready to erupt and shit its contents all across my mind, exhuming and destroying everything in its path.

'Has this event that we are faced with now, been staged? Is it some kind of spiritual security drill that got out of hand? Was this situation planned all along to test the security features of the spiritual realm?' I asked.

'Well, let me say this. If this idea should arise in your mind, then it might be one of the moments of high importance in your current physical lifetime. It may be one that your spiritual self remembered and then presented to your conscious mind to be drawn out now. Yes, that is a possibility. But equally, your mind does have the capacity of free thinking, of acting in a purely unobstructed, calculating way. Freedom of thought, freedom of will is an essential element of any physical lifetime. There is no such thing as fate, there is certainly no possibility that you have only been provided the opportunity to live some kind of robotic lifetime carrying out chosen tasks at the press of a

button here. That cannot happen. But it can be that you yourself, you as a spiritual and physical entity, together or separately, may have made that choice. This is also possible. No end of possibilities exist for why you are here right now.'

'Okay. Getting back to the problem in hand. I guess you have monitoring procedures in place.'

'Yes, we do. But any spiritual energy having legitimate access to physical lifetimes can have access to these pods at any time, depending on the necessity of them gaining such access, and their intentions in doing so.'

'I don't have much choice but to help, do I?'

'You always have a choice.'

***

I awoke on the sofa sweating profusely. My head pounded with a sharp stinging pain that seemed to envelope my brain. I may have cried out in pain, I cannot clearly remember. I straightened up to a seated position. My body had produced an outline of moisture that soaked into the fabric of the sofa. I went to stand up and immediately fell backwards against the rear of the sofa. I held my head in my hands. In my mind I cried out, *'Why me, why me?'* with no answer.

I gathered myself and drew to the front of the sofa before trying to stand up again. This time I made it. My legs were weak, my knees trembled at the effort of keeping my body upright. All of my muscles felt tightened, ready to rip apart. I had flatulence. I felt heartburn roar at the back of my throat. I walked unsteadily to the kitchen. The distance was not very far, a matter of three metres or so, but it felt like miles. I went to a cupboard, pulled out a packet of Nurofen, and pumped three into my dry mouth. I filled a mug with water and swallowed the pills. Though the water eased some of the pain, I could feel each tablet bounce from side to side as they bumped down my throat.

Within a few minutes, I started to feel a little better. In forty minutes I was feeling completely recovered. I sat back down on the sofa, fingers once again curled around the moist hairs that covered my head. Wrists against my ears, I heard the blood as it pumped into and out of my fingers and clammy palms.

'What the fuck.'

षट्

Martin Coombs returned from his work at the Job Centre. He, as did some others, held a deep dislike for the interaction with his clients. He hated using the term clients to describe the lazy, the weak, the unfocused, the uneducated, the supposedly sick, the lame-brained people who passed through the entrance doors every minute of his thirty-six hour, five-day working week.

It was Martin's job to act as an aide to these people. The idea was to offer advice on how they could most quickly return to work, thereby cutting the number of unemployed people and reduce some of the country's expenditure. Mostly it was a game of politics. There are inevitably ways in which the numbers can be manipulated to show monetary savings, to show how wonderfully well the government is sticking to its austerity plans. But most information released by the government is false, everybody knows that. God knows how much they pay economists to manipulate the figures while men, women and kids are getting groceries from food banks.

Politics really has nothing to do with the good of the country. It has nothing to do with helping citizens make the most of what is in their pockets. It has nothing to do with setting the parameters by which the country can become a stronger trading commodity, or a better investment opportunity. Mostly, politics is about the inflation of egos, where politicians use their citizens as puppets in the creation of a national mirror of themselves.

'Fuck them all,' said Martin as he strode towards the tube station, 'and their mothers, too.'

The crowded train did little to ease the tension he felt in his shoulders. Martin, as did everyone else on the travelling sardine can, made as much room as he could for himself, but inevitably elbows butted into his back, heavy breasts pushed against his arms, and the smells of the underground were all too familiar, body odour and cheap perfume.

As he slid in through his front door, he finally began to relax. His head felt lighter, his step became jollier. The weekend lay ahead, a long weekend incorporating the bank holiday. Martin's plans for the evening were simple: microwaveable ready meal, and then play some games on PS4 until he dozed off on the sofa. Luxury.

preferred option, but Martin could not stand the often-coppery taste of artificial sweeteners.

He sat back down on the sofa. He picked up the plastic movie case beside him. Glancing at the back of the case but not reading a word, he removed the shiny plastic disc and placed it into the DVD player that sat on a shelf beneath his large screen television set. Maybe that was not such a smart purchase; he only used it to watch movies, never having read the instructions detailing its full range of capabilities. He sat back on the sofa, turned over the movie case and pressed the play button on the remote control.

Martin sat back to enjoy one of his favourite gory movies.

***

Inspector Marchant's fingers felt great on my back and shoulders, soothing, relaxing, comforting. This was just what I needed, and at the right time, too. I had thought long and hard about this meditation ever since I had it, and still I had no idea what to do.

'And when did you have this experience?' she asked.

'It was three weeks ago now.'

'And since then I guess you have tried to go back to the spirit realm. I am also guessing you might have tried to contact your Guide.'

'The answer is yes to both questions. I always try to meditate at least once a day, maybe for twenty to thirty minutes. As a psychic, healer, hypnotherapist, and life coach, in the last five years it has been important for me to centre my mind and relax my body. A person cannot effectively do any of these things unless they can be focused and open to anything that comes through. But since I had this experience, I have found it increasingly difficult to switch off interfering thoughts, to block out the magnitude of what happened. After all I experienced that last time, I thought it would be easier to revisit, to gather more information, to start some detective work. When my meditation initially finished, I was disappointed to return to the sofa, to be back in the physical world. Then again, I also got scared of what I had seen and the implications it had for my life, repeatedly telling myself that I must have imagined it all.'

Marchant stopped her massage and rested her right hand gently on my back. 'Do you think you could have dreamt this all, made it all up?'

'That is a distinct possibility. Whenever I meditated before, it was on specific subjects, issues of concern or interest. I guess in these cases, it might have been easier to accept guidance or supportive thoughts and put them into action immediately. But this was different. I might have had an issue I wanted to raise with my meditative mind at the time, I don't remember, but the striking thing is that this time there was no way I could prepare for such a something strangely satisfying for Martin in watching people die or get the shit scared out of them on screen.

Martin had not had a girlfriend for more than eighteen months. Most of his previous girlfriends had been gothic types, and not the ones who liked to possess their men and claim ownership of all that was them. And that was how Martin liked it. Being slim, six feet tall, with jet-black, well-manicured shoulder length hair, Martin had no trouble attracting girls, and he had no problem shaking them off when an opportunity arose.

Why had it been eighteen months? The last girlfriend Martin dated had become incensed at his behaviour. To a degree that was understandable, but Martin could see no need for the ferocity of her words just before they split. Martin had a mutually agreeable open relationship with Alice, or so he thought. It was not that either of them wanted to mess around with other people, it was just that they had agreed that if it happened there would be no comeback. Words and actions rarely go hand in hand, as Martin found out to his cost.

Alice had trashed his car with a baseball bat when she found out he had been fucking a granny. It was not that he was attracted to the lady, and he wasn't even sure he knew her name. A lot of men believe that middle-aged women are an easy lay, but Martin was a guy who always wanted to push the boundaries. Extreme age differences were just an interest, a 'what if' scenario. At that time, he wanted teen girls and sixty years-plus women. It actually happened twice that he fucked a granny, but Alice only knew about the younger of the two ladies, who was sixty-one years old. He never admitted to fucking the eighty-one-year-old woman he met online.

These two times were exciting, but not much satisfaction came with their memory. Alice was his age, typical gothic looks. She had jet-black hair with singular blue streaks in it, black and white clothing, thick black tights and the very deep blue lipstick and eyeshadow. When Alice found out about his elderly conquest, she took a baseball bat to the windscreen and bonnet of his car. The car was not worth much, but he heeded the warning, and since then his only sexual adventures had been of a casual nature.

In the last year, Martin knew he had put on weight. His waist had grown by four inches, his face had gained fuller features; even his nose had grown a little puffy. He bought a silver ring engraved with a dragon rising from the surf when he was twenty years old. This ring was now tight enough on his ever-chubbier fingers that it could not be removed without the aid of butter, oil or freezing water. His teeth were still good, and he retained his mop of black hair, that these days grew longer and shabbier than before. Martin had not drunk any alcohol in the last four years; he just did not need it. He smoked menthol cigarettes, but never to the degree that he had ever considered himself hooked on them. A typical smoker.

Martin got up and made himself another mug of coffee. Instant granules, a small amount of milk and two teaspoons of sugar. Sugar was no longer the

I stood at the sink, turned the tap and placed the stained interior of my coffee cup beneath the rush of water coming from the faucet. I held the cup there, zombie-like. I was not thinking of anything. It was like I was devoid of everything, an empty shell, stuck in time. I felt a warm, sensitive, gentle touch on my right shoulder. Every muscle in my body tightened involuntarily.

'You are tense, aren't you?' Inspector Marchant said.

Her palm gently rubbed against my shoulder, fingers curling over my collar bone. My shirt moved rhythmically in time to her gentle caress. I put my left hand over her right and squeezed a little. Her fingers were very soft.

I pulled myself out of my zombie-like state and smiled rather haphazardly at the lady standing to the right.

'Come and sit on the sofa and tell me the rest of the story. Let's see if we can work something out together, see if we can make up any kind of a plan to tackle this situation.'

I stepped back and turned at the hip, dragging my right foot across the shiny white ceramic floor tiles, until I faced the Inspector head on.

'Did I hear you correctly? Are you offering to help me in this?' I asked.

'I wouldn't say that, but if you tell me some more, maybe I can offer some advice or have some kind of input that might prove useful.'

Inspector Marchant smiled exquisitely.

'That would be a great help. I appreciate it.'

I moved to the side of the sink unit to dry my hands on a rather grubby tea towel.

'Let's sit down and I can give your shoulders a massage as you tell me more; it might help relax you,' Judy said as she reached around and ran her hand gently down my back.

It felt good and it did feel relaxing. I laughed and immediately began striding towards the sofa.

***

Martin Coombs lived economically. The shelves in his fridge and freezer compartments were half-full, as were the shelves in his kitchen units. At twenty-eight years old, Martin had only recently become accustomed to looking after himself. In the five years up to now, he had lived his life as a bachelor, not as a home builder. No pictures adorned the walls of his one-bedroom apartment, and no knick-knacks sat on the shelves. His living space contained mostly books, compact discs, movies and PS4 games.

The books on display were varied, and eclectic. His DVD collection followed a single genre – all were horror movies. Martin would only watch movies after eleven o'clock at night; there would be no atmosphere at any other time to support themes of hacking, rape and murder. There was

***

'And you remembered everything that happened?' asked Inspector Marchant.

'Yes,' I replied.

'But you have a problem with the frontal lobe of your brain, does that not mean that you have difficulty remembering things? Also, you told me that you have a problem with sequencing.'

'Yes I do. But meditation seems to be different. I can remember every meditation I have ever done, near enough,' I replied.

'But you just gave me a blow-by-blow account of a very detailed encounter you had with a spiritual energy that escorted you on a tour of the afterlife.'

'Yes.'

'It all seems like a lot to take in. How long were you in meditation?' asked Marchant.

'Nearly twenty minutes.'

'And all this happened in less than twenty minutes?' she looked at me incredulously.

'Yes, it did. Look, I don't expect you to believe me, after all not many people could even comprehend most of what happened, let alone the task I have been set,' I said.

'Yeah, and what about this task?'

'I have been asked to find out why some people's lives are finishing before they are supposed to, according to the planning and programming that took place before they were born. Somehow, in some way, I am expected to help correct this oversight.'

'And you have no indication of what you should do or in what way? You don't know who is behind this or why it is happening. You don't even know what tools, physical or spiritual, might be available to you.'

'That is correct.'

I felt the air around me become heavier as realisations hit me from the front, from the back, and from all sides. The understanding that I might be alone on this quest. The conception that I had no physical proof that any of what I said to Inspector Marchant ever actually happened. The realisation that while I could not deny that my spiritual beliefs and understanding led me to think that everything I had experienced was perfectly plausible, and completely feasible, the rational side of my mind put up a good, and loud, argument that my imagination was running wild and creating this amazing situation to lift the gloom of an otherwise rather dreary, dull and unexciting existence. I got up from the sofa and walked the seven paces to the open plan kitchen.

wide ranging and unexpected journey. Though it is true that the issue that arose this time centred on the same things I raised with you six months ago.'

'And could have severely dented my career,' Marchant added.

'Yes, and I have already apologised for that profusely. But it just shows that six months ago I was on the right lines; I just took the wrong train,' I replied.

'There was nothing suspicious about those first two deaths, and you gave me nothing to go by.'

'Nothing except a finely tuned intuition.'

'No matter how finely tuned your intuition, I need to deal with facts, not intuitive feelings that bear no relation to a situation.'

'Yes, I know. But this time I know for sure that the first two deaths, and this latest death, are all tied in, somehow, to the meditation.'

Marchant put both hands on my shoulders and turned me towards her as she spoke. 'Look, I have the greatest respect for your intuitive abilities. Though I might not believe it, sometimes people do, in one way or another, show amazing skills that most of us cannot master, let alone understand. I did not come here tonight because you placed new evidence before me, because there still is no evidence to back up what you believe. What we do have are three deaths, as yet perfectly explained as being from natural causes. The only link here is you saying there is a link. People die all the time, and you have no proof that anything other than exactly that happened.'

'What about this?' I reached out my right hand and turned it palm up. In the middle was a perfectly formed white circle, one centimetre in diameter.

***

Martin Coombs awoke with a jolt. He raised himself with his left arm until he was sitting upright. This is why he had so many goddamned movies; he always dozed off before the end of a film. The title screen showed on the television, one scene played over and over again as the options were listed below the title. He rose from a seated position and pressed a button on the remote control to remove the picture from the screen. He walked to the DVD player and pressed a button on top to open the front drawer. He then removed the plastic disc and carefully inserted it onto the slot in the case. He replaced the case onto the shelf, one of three in a set that supported most of his movie collection. Some other cases were scattered around in other places, but the ones on show were those he was most likely to watch. The movies were placed in alphabetical order, top to bottom and left to right.

Martin returned to the oak coloured supporting unit on which stood the DVD player and the television. The DVD recorder stood one shelf below the television, the PS4 console sat on the bottom shelf. Below the shelves was a drawer with two handles. Flat-packed furniture, if made correctly, could do everything that a more solid construction could do, but at a fraction of the cost. Martin took a hold of one of the handles to the drawer at the bottom of the unit, and pulled it open. The drawer was quite heavy. It fell forward and hung out of its allocated space. Martin looked along the single row of pornographic titles inside the drawer. He had his favourite titles, and he knew exactly where they were. This night he was in the mood for some black lesbian loving. He removed a disc from its cover and replaced the cover in its allotted place, then he opened the disc slot of the DVD player. Placing the plastic disc onto the drawer of the player, he returned to the sofa and unbuttoned the fly of his trousers.

***

'What is that?' asked Marchant as she turned my hand left and right, trying to look deeper into the perfectly formed, circular white mark on my palm.

'At the end of my meditation, my guide told me he wanted me to take something away. He told me that this would help me.'

Marchant moved an index finger across the mark, cupping my hand with hers.

'Are you sure it was made during the meditation? It is not a bruise. Did you touch any paint? Did you use detergent or bleach recently?'

'My Guide put two fingers to this palm. I didn't feel anything, but I would swear that the tips of his fingers glowed ever so slightly with a deep purple light.'

'And you think that this mark is a sign that what happened in your meditation was all true, that it actually happened?' Judy asked.

I chuckled a little under my breath.

'Look, I am not going to try to convince anyone of what happened. If it did, then it did. If it was just my imagination, or if I was sleeping, so what? The fact is that if I do not try to follow through on this, then I will never know.'

'And, according to what you told me, more than a million people might lose their lives.'

'Yes,' I replied.

सप्त

I tried once again to enter meditation, and again I failed. My head was full of last night's discussion, but also the person with whom I was conversing. My mind returned, involuntarily, to how it felt when my strong-shouldered confidante was sliding her hand up and down my back. The words had tumbled from my mouth with little thought of their content, but throughout the evening I was very aware of my companion, the vague smell of perfume, the cleanliness of her skin, I even noticed her unremarkable black boots by the front door on my way in. I particularly noticed the brightness in her eyes, the soft fall of hair upon her brow and of her breasts as they moved each time she did. As I rose from Judy Marchant's sofa, I needed to shield the front of my trousers as best I could. I performed an awkward kind of sideways shuffle, placing my left forearm across my pelvis. I was embarrassed in case she should look at my crotch being, as it was, face height. This was when the last, but strongest, surge of blood swept from all parts of my body to what lay hidden behind my zipper. I was lucky to get out of her flat without staining the front of my trousers.

'Are you alright?' my wife's voice shook me from my thoughts.

'I'm fine, I just have a lot of things on my mind at the moment, that's all,' I replied sullenly.

***

I had always wanted to try to explain to Inspector Marchant how I got it so wrong the first time we met. Only now it seems that I hadn't got it wrong at all, but my interpretation of events was well wide of the mark. The policewoman had every reason to feel angry at what she became involved with as a result of listening to what I had to say, but the brunt of her anger should have been me, and not herself.

It started six months ago when I was doing a reading for a middle-aged couple. The man still worked in the pharmaceutical field, only in a consulting capacity. The woman had taken early retirement some years before. I started getting images of a man in his late twenties struggling to breathe. The more I tried to focus on his appearance and clothing, the more I was drawn to the predicament he was in. I tried my best to describe this man to the couple, but neither could identify him. The feeling of breathlessness became a physical issue for me, and I pulled at my collar.

I asked the lady to get me some water. It did not help. I tried to break free of the feeling, but it refused to go away. I was aware of the young man clawing at his shirt and ripping it from his chest. He bent down on his knees and tried to cough the breathlessness away.

Most times, I am made aware of an illness or physical susceptibility in people who are subject to a reading, but this time I felt nothing from the elderly couple and nothing from the man whose images projected into my mind. There seemed no reason for him to be suffering so much. My last feeling was that this young man's life had expired. At that moment, my breath returned. I gasped aloud and held my neck. The couple asked if I was okay, and said I looked as white as a ghost. I made my excuses and left the house, well aware that I was stumbling as I made my way through their hallway, out of the front door and into my car.

When I returned home, I looked into the mirror. The cold sweat, so prevalent while witnessing the young man's demise, had all but disappeared, soaking into the material and neckline of my polo shirt. The colour had returned to my face. But my eyes looked hollow and lacklustre.

The second occasion happened one sunny afternoon the following week. While preparing for a reading, I undertake a short meditation before entering my client's house, but before I had a chance to lay my hand on the internal door release of the car I was shaken by an image that flooded my mind. I was transported inside a small terraced house. It was night time. A young woman in her early thirties was drying her hair after taking a shower. I was aware that the water was still running inside the small shower cubicle. Her eyes opened wide and she pressed the towel into her chest. Her mouth fell open and breath spilled out in shock and surprise. I was aware that an intense pinprick of pain was debilitating her. She fell to sit on the floor. The pain in her chest spread throughout her body. She crumpled to the floor and her right arm fell limp, open-handed, on the bath mat in front of the shower. The water continued to flow. I was so shaken by this image that I quickly turned on the key in the ignition, started the engine, and drove home.

I had never before sensed anyone dying, and yet in the past week I had been witness to two deaths that had no apparent reason. Each death seemed to be of natural causes, but there was something unnatural about them, and both seemed inappropriate. Two weeks later, I contacted Inspector Marchant, because I felt there was a need for the police to investigate the two cases.

The police were aware of the two deaths, but no action was taken. In both cases it was found that no drugs or alcohol were present in the deceased bodies and no unnatural marks were found that might suggest foul play. Medical records showed that neither the man nor the woman suffered any kind of illness that might have played a part in their death.

I pressed Inspector Marchant into looking deeper into these two deaths. I explained that I was a psychic who had witnessed these people's demise and that in my opinion, there was something very wrong with the scenario I witnessed. I had no physical evidence; I had nothing to go on except my intuition. I must have sounded at least a little persuasive because Marchant did look further into each case. She turned up nothing. And the outcome of my approaching her was that she was called before her senior officers to explain her actions in the light of the public money used to fund such a flimsy investigation. The problem was that when I first approached Inspector Marchant, I trusted my instinct too much. I did no parallel investigation or theorising myself. I went to her empty-handed.

***

The day after I met with Inspector Marchant was uneventful. A few callers wanted to ask about readings, one asking if a message could be gained from a dead relative. The answer is that such a thing is possible, but my mind was on other issues. I politely made an excuse of being busy on other projects and asked these people to call back another time. I cancelled appointments booked for that day, again using the same excuse. I had never before cancelled a reading. My clients were in obvious need of information, or at least some solace. If it was true that the spiritual realm set signposts for certain decisions that might be beneficial, then I had just steamrollered every marker out of existence – twisting and turning straight paths that otherwise might have remained clear.

Time dragged on. My son went to school and my wife went to work, as usual. I kept looking at the clock. I could not get out of my head that something had happened, or was about to happen. The plan should be foolproof, so my guide had said; therefore, my long night-time discussion with Inspector Marchant must be a precursor to the next scene in this particular episode.

It was becoming more difficult for me to believe in a foolproof plan that now seemed to have so many holes in it. I told myself that despite all that had happened, I was still the same person I was before my visit to the spirit realm, and in that case, I retained all the faculties I had before. I felt I should once again trust my instinct on the feelings I get – and the feelings I had now were those of an impending loss. If only I could clear my mind sufficiently to focus on exactly what might lay ahead, but without access to meditation, I had no way of guessing what the future might hold.

***

'Okay, what have we got here?' Inspector Marchant asked.

As she walked in through the front door of the nondescript flat, she thought about removing the white synthetic gloves she always carried in her bag, it was second nature when entering a property on the job, but then she thought better of it. From the first reports of the officers at the scene there was no crime, and therefore no danger of corrupting any evidence.

'Male. Twenty-eight years old. Goes by the name of Martin Coombs. Neighbours say he keeps himself to himself. He didn't turn up for work today and his mum, who he calls every morning before leaving for work, hadn't heard from him since yesterday morning. I was asked to look in on my way to a minor domestic. When I got here the lights were on as they are now,' PC Tomkins pointed outside the front door and motioned to the light in the lounge. 'Pretty odd, but not alarming, until I got in here.'

Marchant glanced around the flat before entering the lounge. As she entered, she heard the gentle buzz of flies. The television set was positioned immediately in front of a small open-ended two seater sofa. A large pillow was on the floor in between the sofa and the television. A full head of hair met Inspector Marchant as she entered the room. The man was sitting facing the television screen almost head-on. She walked past the man's shoulders and approached the middle of the room. Martin Coombs sat upright on the sofa, naked from his waist to his knees. It appeared as if his trousers and underpants had been pushed down in a hurry. Two sheets of unused kitchen towel lay crumpled on his left side. The television screen showed a repetitive link to a porno movie that showed the name of the film, chapters and extras on a titles screen against a pink background. Nothing seemed out of place in the room. It was not the tidiest of places, but there appeared to be no sign of a struggle, or any misplaced items. There was plenty of dust in the room, but no spaces in that dust where anything might have been moved.

'He was masturbating,' said PC Tomkins with a smirk.

'I gathered that,' replied Judy Marchant dismissively.

'When I was younger I heard that a man masturbating uses up as much energy as he would running a half-marathon. '

'Is that why you are always so tired at work, Tomkins?' asked Marchant.

PC Tomkins turned away and looked at the blank page of a notebook.

'I guess there is nothing here for us,' the Inspector said. 'Best to let the coroner do his job on this guy.'

She turned to leave the property, lifting the mobile phone out of her bag as she did so.

अष्ट

I received the call at four in the afternoon.

'A twenty-eight-year-old guy died last night in his apartment. No signs of foul play. You interested?'

'Might be, but I need more information. Any chance you could stall the family until I can get some access to the guy's home?' I asked, hopefully.

'Absolutely not. There are procedures to follow. Officially, as there are no suspicious circumstances, the guy's apartment should be handed over to the family immediately. In fact, this has already happened. Our only interest is in what the coroner finds, if anything. And then that's it; case closed.'

'You called me, Inspector Marchant, so I guess you think I might be able to help you decide whether this death might be connected to the other three. That means you suspect it is. Am I right?' I asked.

'Yes. It's just that I can see no reason for these people to be dying like this. I know it happens sometimes, but there is something about this I can't quite put my finger on. That's why we spoke the other night, because there is nothing physical to suggest foul play, but my intuition is still sparking out. There has to be something I am missing, something that, at the moment, is outside of my reach. I guess you might be able to use some mumbo jumbo to let me know what that something is,' Inspector Marchant said.

'Mumbo jumbo?' I feigned upset.

'Sorry, no offence intended. What I meant to say is maybe you could use your psychic abilities to help me place the dots and then join them up.'

'No offence taken. But at the moment I have nothing, not even the guy's name.'

'Martin Coombs. Mum and Dad are in Leicester, they have been informed. He has one sister in Bristol and a brother somewhere in Spain.'

'That will help a little, but I really need to get inside his place. I need to connect with this guy if I have any chance of working out what might have happened, and more importantly, why?'

'He was masturbating and he died. That's it.'

'So can you get me inside the Coombs apartment?' I asked, 'that is the only way we can move forward on this thing.'

'And what exactly is this thing? So far as I can see, this guy died a natural death, albeit at a young age and with a seemingly clean bill of health beforehand.'

'That in itself should be enough to raise your suspicions,' I replied.

'And how do you think I might be able to arrange a visit for you? I am already going out on more than a limb even talking with you, isn't that enough?'

'Look. I know I am asking a lot. But whenever you have a reason to suspect that something unlawful has happened, you go to whatever length it takes to uncover the evidence to prove a crime, and then to arrest a potential perpetrator,' I reasoned.

'Yes, but in this instance there is no crime. There is nothing of interest for me as a serving police Inspector.'

'You investigate issues of criminal behaviour, you look into any suggestion that a law, or laws, have been broken. You then look at the evidence and forensics to establish who might be a likely suspect. An arrest or two is made. When the crime is murder, a person's life has been cut short by the actions of another. But what if the information given to me in meditation is correct? If it is, then it is likely that you will have quite a number of murders on your hands and, although through normal eyes all these deaths will not look like murder, they are. These deaths are the same. They all serve to cut someone's life short by the actions of another. This 'other' might not take human form, but the outcomes are the same.'

There was a lengthy pause.

'Inspector Marchant?' I prodded.

'Yes, I am here,' she replied.

'The least I can do is try to prove or disprove that you might have a legitimate interest in me taking a closer look at what is going on. After we visit the scene, you are more than welcome to stand back, hold your hands up, and tell me I am on my own with this. No hard feelings.'

'I didn't know we were in this together already,' Judy Marchant replied.

'Turn of phrase, that's all. So what do you say, Inspector? Can we give it a go at looking at the scene?'

'My name is Judy.'

'What do you say, Judy?' I asked.

***

Judy Marchant pulled a key out of her bag and inserted it into the keyhole in Martin Coombs' front door. It had taken her all of four hours to agree to my request, but she had relented, not least because, and despite my wildly ridiculous claims, she couldn't help but admire my assuredness and tenacity in putting them forward. Would I really risk all on putting out a load of baloney I knew to be fake? Judy Marchant thought that very doubtful.

She put her left ear just above the door handle as she gently manoeuvred the key in the lock. I waited nervously, eyes on the lookout for anyone who might see us; ears open for any sounds that might signal the approach of another person. After a couple of minutes, Judy pulled the door a little into the wooden doorframe and turned the key. The door opened stiffly.

I entered the hallway. It smelled stuffy inside through a lack of ventilation. I turned slightly to the left and followed the hallway towards the lounge area. I had no interest in any room except that one. I was not detecting, I was dowsing, looking for energies that might have been left behind inside the room, searching for emotions that scar the air, like a hot knife through butter, listening for faintly heard imprints that leave their own mark from everyday lives. Most people are not aware that life can leave indelible imprints in the fabric and the atmosphere of buildings. They don't know that everywhere they go they are passing gently shifting energy waves out that incorporate everything that goes on within them. But then, most people are not psychic.

We entered the lounge.

'I guess I should leave you to what you do best,' Judy Marchant suggested. She walked away towards the bookcase standing against the wall to the left side of the room, and proceeded to thumb nonchalantly through the books on display there.

I closed my eyes and ran through the same preparation as if I was undertaking a reading for a client. This process not only served to rid me of unwanted thoughts and to focus on the job in hand, but it also intensified each of my senses. The air inside the room grew cleaner and a little bit cooler. My heartbeat slowed down a little and my legs, arms and fingers took on a familiar tingling sensation. My neck and head grew perceptibly warmer. I sat like this for some minutes, using this time to attempt to attune with the vibrations of the room.

This was very different from doing a psychic reading. During a reading, all of the evidence is brought to me, but now I needed to look for information. I needed to probe the space inside this room for anything on which I felt I should focus my psychic senses. If the truth be told, this was the first time I had tried such procedures, but it felt like the right thing to do. Any psychic, medium, sensitive, or any other label by which they are known, must be acutely aware of their intuition, and I now needed to go in whatever way that might take me.

***

Dr. Theobald Anstis acted as the coroner for this area of the town. Known as Theo to his family, friends and colleagues, Dr. Anstis was a balding man of considerable presence. At a little under six feet tall and stocky, it was not his body size that leant any credence to his stature, but Dr. Theo Anstis commanded attention from all around him when he spoke, and silence when he was thinking.

A Catholic by birth, Dr. Anstis had turned in the last twenty of his fifty-eight years to the United Reformed church for religious guidance and comfort. It was shortly after joining his local church that he had met his wife. Georgina was twenty-three years old at the time, while he was thirty-eight. They knew each other a year before developing any closer relationship. Georgina and one of her friends at church had taken Theo Anstis under their wings when he joined the congregation. It was no easy task adjusting to the rather easy going acceptance traversing his new church from the old, restrictive and stifling religious regime he had endured since birth. He had never followed the preaching of the Catholic faith since he first became aware of religion in his childhood, but, as with many converts, it had taken some time to face up to his misgivings about the ideology being presented to him every Sunday morning. He and Georgina had two children, Hans and Adam, who were both now in their teens.

It was normal practice to perform an autopsy when somebody died under forty years old, particularly when there was no history of serious, or potentially life threatening, illness or disease. The medical records of Martin Coombs contained nothing to suggest he was under any medical threat at the time of his death. Most autopsies would be carried out by a pathologist, but on this occasion the office was short on senior colleagues, so it was down to Theodore Anstis to carry out the dirty work.

Dr. Anstis made his first incision into the body of Martin Coombs, a straight, deep cut from the dead man's chest down to just above his pubic area, which afforded access to all of the cadaver's vital organs. The coroner had already recorded that the skin of the dead man showed no signs of blunt force trauma, no signs of cuts or slashes, and there were no obvious signs of bruising. On opening up the chest, there was no sign of any heavy substance use, smoking or of any alcohol abuse. On first inspection, this man should have lived a lot longer than he did. Dr. Anstis immediately noticed a very large amount of congealing blood on the underside of the man's ribs and around the inside of the chest cavity. It was also clear that this blood had pooled at the top of the large intestine, around the spleen, and onto the stomach. He noted this, and asked his assistant to clean the blood residue out of the chest cavity so that he had a clearer area to play with. Autopsies were sometimes messy affairs, particularly where injuries to vital organs had occurred. But the amount of blood that had been shed in this case was a matter of concern. He opened the ribcage with a small electrical saw, to afford greater access to the dead organs beneath.

As was usual in any autopsy undertaken by Dr. Anstis, he began by looking more closely at the dead man's heart. It was immediately apparent to him that the most likely cause of death was cardiac failure. But something else had caught the coroner's attention. He removed the monocle from his eye and the spatula from the man's chest cavity and looked up from the body.

'Remarkable,' he said.

***

I was aware of a mixture of feelings inside the lounge of Martin Coombs. I knew that these feelings came from the dead man. A feeling of being alone but also an appreciation of that fact. A disappointment in a large part of his life, most likely linked to a job. There was a benign artistry to this man that was never allowed to surface. He was good with words, an impressive letter writer who was always, and with little effort, able to literate a point of view that would be difficult to argue against. If he had an opinion, it was researched and well thought-out. A quiet educated man who made little of his intellect.

The furniture and state of cleanliness of the room backed up these feelings. The lounge was not immaculately clean, but neither was it unkempt. The carpet appeared to have been regularly cleaned, no large stains or abrasions of any kind. It was scuffed in the corners, but this may well have been just normal everyday wear and tear, and age. The shelves in the bookcase were not dust-free, but showed signs that a large number of books had been removed and replaced, backing up my feelings of an educated and well-read man. Most interesting was the alphabetical order of the DVD collection. This showed a well-ordered and methodical personality not easily given to wild extremes or disorderly conduct. I doubted if this man had ever fallen foul of the law. His home was his sanctuary. The sometimes chaotic and frustrating world was firmly kept on the other side of the entrance door, again leading me to believe that, although he disliked his work, Martin Coombs was easily able to shut off when home time came each day.

But there was something else in the room, something that was not so easily discerned. I sensed a more flamboyant energy. Very subtle. Very weak. Something that sat oddly with the energetic blueprint of the dead man. It was almost imperceptible, but it was there. I stood up and peered at the wall in front of me searching for a way to make my perception stronger, bolder, to bring it to the forefront of the other energetic imprints surrounding me.

'Are you okay?' Judy asked from my left side.

I lifted my hand, palm outwards, to signify my wish not to be disturbed. My concentration intensified. Very often by staring at a fixed point, we can focus intently upon an issue and bring greater clarity. Sometimes this is how we can blank our minds of all else, bringing to light the one issue in our mind that is crying out for attention.

This energy was not flamboyant, but it was fleeting, it was like pure electricity, darting as if it were current through a plug socket. It left a trail behind it like a comet, one moment there and the next moment gone without a trace. This electric-like energy seemed to pulse, dull and obscure, but as I focused on it I was able to follow it as it moved up and down, left to right, in a crazy, unrestricted dance of frenzy. Sometimes very dull, sometimes a little brighter. It was not easy to follow, but the more I was able to focus the more I became aware of an obscure pattern of movement beginning to emerge.

Imprints of living energy are like waves. They become clearer as they move towards me and then disappear as they retract. They are oblique, they do not have a definite form; they are fog-like in their feeling. As a psychic, it has always been my job to peer through that fog and extract anything that I know will be of interest or of particular relevance to my clients. It is the same with seeking out future events or issues of potential concern. But this energy was not at all oblique or obtuse. It was clearly defined, shaped and contoured.

I started to move slowly around the room, searching out the path of this anomalous energy, looking for the strongest signal, like a human aerial. As I moved towards the bookcase where Judy stood, this energy dissipated and mixed in with her living energy. I moved away and towards the door to the hallway where once again my perception became faint. I moved towards the television set, which stood on its wooden platform unit. I turned to the sofa. I stared at the cloth of the furniture, at one point of the canvas, to create the picture I was trying to view. I approached the sofa and sat down, very close to where Marchant had described the position of Coombs' body when she found it, when it was still physically here, in this room. I lay both hands palm down on the sofa, on either side of me.

'Somebody else was here,' I finally said.

***

'You have to come and see this.'

The phone call arrived just as Judy and I were settling into the front seats of her car, having secured the property formally belonging to Martin Coombs.

'Right now?' Judy Marchant asked.

'Yes. If that is at all possible.'

Dr. Theo Anstis sounded excited, like a young boy in a candy store. Most unlike him, thought Judy Marchant. Usually straight as they come, Dr. Anstis had a reputation as being a bit standoffish, a bit self-important. Some people in the coroner's office viewed him as a bit too full of his own self-importance. They did not feel like he looked down on them; he was always grateful of their supportive work and had no difficulty in showing his appreciation for the work they did. Nonetheless, he knew a lot more than they did about his and their occupations and, at times, he let them know that in no uncertain terms.

'I'm on my way.'

Judy Marchant pressed the button on the front of her phone to cancel the incoming call.

'Who was that?' I asked.

'It was Dr. Anstis. He wants me to go to his office, right now.'

'Okay then, let's go,' I said.

'Whoa. Hold on now, cowboy. The only place you are going is home. I will take you there and then continue on to the coroner.'

'That is hardly fair. I am the one looking into these matters. You are the doubtful one who is sitting on the fence, undecided whether or not there is anything of any professional or personal interest in this case. I should go. You never know what I might be able to pick up being that close to Coombs' body,' I argued.

'You are not going. At least I am not taking you, and without me, you stand no chance of entering the building. The only thing you will be picking up is a takeaway from the Indian restaurant closest to your home.'

It was clear that she was in no mood to back down, and that was understandable given the sensitivity of the position we found ourselves in. I felt as though I had goaded Judy into following up my hunches, thereby again putting her into a spotlight she might find more difficult to avoid this time. She was going out on a limb even to listen to what I had to say.

'Will you let me know what you find?' I asked.

'Yes, of course I will. Lost cause or not, you started this and if it all goes pear-shaped again, I ain't going to be the fan taking all the shit; you will.'

***

Judy buzzed the entrance keypad and the door clicked open. She walked briskly into the building. It was getting late, and she wanted to get this finished as soon as possible. While half of her mind doubted the tall tale told by me, the other half was intrigued enough to listen, and listen well. Countless times over the four days since I had walked back into her life, she found herself cursing her stupidity for once again wrapping herself up in stories that could never be proved.

Circumstantially, there was a point in what I was saying, but that point was thinning out almost to being invisible. And now she found herself on the brink of delving even deeper into situations she knew nothing about, at the mercy of a psychic, hypnotherapist, healer and possible crank, and she risked chasing around as might a puppet on his string. I was the only person who could lead this investigation, and she felt like she needed to follow, picking up the pieces and making them all fit together. Was I a soothsayer or a crackpot? Time would tell for Judy Marchant, and the quicker the better.

She leapt the stairs two at a time, hoping to God she did not slip and crack her shin against the cold, unyielding concrete below her feet. And what did God have to do with all this? God was a thing she was not even sure she believed existed. She was sure something was out there, other than what she detected with her five senses, but just what that was, she had no idea, and it was something she tried her best never to think about. That was, until four days ago.

There was no doubt in her mind that I was a sane individual not given to wild flights of fancy, but where do reality and fantasy meet? Can they actually coexist as proposed by the mystical guy who undoes too many buttons on his shirt? She thought I talked a good talk, that I was certainly believable, and that I could be persuasive. She felt I had charm and charisma that begged one to pay attention and to believe. My ideas were not cultist, and I did not seem to draw people under my wing for some devilish end-of-days sexual shenanigans. So far as she was aware, the ideas and philosophies put forward, as they regarded these three recent deaths, were only known by her. I was not a tabloid freak and neither was I an attention seeker. And so were the thoughts of Judy Marchant. At least for now, it seemed sensible to put away her demons and listen to the angel on her left shoulder, who argued that it would do no harm to look at this scenario with open eyes.

Judy Marchant garbed herself up as necessary, putting on a plasticised cape, latex gloves, a small mask and a cap. She breathed in deeply as she stood before the door leading to the autopsy room. The thought, *What am I doing?* once again flashed across her mind, as she exhaled and pushed her way in through the doorway.

नव

I never had a holier-than-thou attitude toward God. My mind-set was always that if God can help us, then why not ask for assistance when we find it necessary? To me, God is something I can talk about, something I can get angry at, something whose name I can take in vain, because to me God is not vengeful or spiteful. How could the creator of everything good, all loving, all angelic, have a judgmental bone in His ethereal body? And why does God have to be male? Why was it not the Goddess which created all life?

I have always been able to talk to God when I want to, and about any subject. I can beg for its assistance and for mercy. But God is closer to me than might be comfortable for the vast majority of the Christian world. God is my confidant, my adviser, my helper, but God is also a thing that I help and assist. God and I are equal, and I communicate with God on an equal level. If I want to show God my hurt and upset, I do. If I want to show God my anger at It, I do. If I want to show my joy and happiness, I do. If I ever feel that my circumstances are too testing or unnecessarily unfair, I get angry at God. And this is how I felt now. Angry and rudderless, drifting on a sea of resentment, doubt and frustration, heading for a maelstrom of unbelievable intensity.

***

'What have you got for me?' Judy asked as she approached Dr. Anstis.

'Inspector Marchant, nice to see you.' Dr. Theo Anstis took the corners of the light blue blanket covering the current corpse of his focus and pulled them up over the dead person's head. He raised both hands towards his chest and walked towards the table supporting Martin Coombs' lifeless body. Brown, rapidly drying blood covered the coroner's fingers. Small spatters of this and other expelled bodily liquids were noticeable on the cuffs of his plastic surgical gloves, and on the front of the apron he wore over his shirt and tie. The monocle sat upon the crown of his head.

Dr. Anstis' assistant walked over to Martin Coombs and gently, almost politely, moved the cover down to the area of his now-sunken belly button. The assistant wore a uniform similar to Dr. Anstis, if a little oversized. To call this twenty-something lady diminutive might have been going too far, but she was below average in height, and below her office kit she was extremely slim, nearly waif-like.

Martin Coombs' corpse was open from nipples to groin, layers of skin and ectodermal tissue lying in a neat y-shape where the coroner had expertly removed the outer covering of his body to expose his internal organs. The dead man's skin had taken on a grey pallor, and any residues of fat which once puffed up his body were now rapidly decaying, leaving a sunken vessel of skin on bone. As Judy drew closer, she was looking directly inside Martin Coombs' chest cavity, at the greying parts that once gave life and now were in mortal decay. She hated attending autopsies. She had no fear of blood and had become used to the cuts, bruises and other injuries so closely linked with her job, but the insides of a human being should remain just that, inside.

'There are no outward signs of injury, no contusions, no cuts, no severe bruising. From what I can see of Mr Coombs, the only marks on his body would come from acne or small insect bites. There is also no damage to the ectodermic tissue immediately below the skin, so no outward or internal signs of any blunt force trauma. No marks around his neck or windpipe. So this is not a murder, Inspector Marchant,' the coroner said.

Dr. Anstis looked up at Judy Marchant and then continued to explain how Martin Coombs had died.

'In that case, and in dealing with someone so young, we must place our focus internally: lungs, liver, heart, colon, spleen, appendix, pancreas, trachea, stomach and the small and large intestines. In Mr. Coombs' case, it seems that all appears normal, so there is no reason to suspect that any of these vital organs would have contributed to his death,' the coroner continued.

'What did, then?' she asked.

'Ah yes, and this is why I called you.' From across the metal table, Dr. Anstis raised his right index finger as he spoke, 'I have been a coroner for a number of years, probably now too many to count. In that time, we see many things inside of a human being, although they are not being anything when they come to us. We also see some unusual aspects, some things to buck the trend, so to speak. Now, I am aware of something like this, but I have never seen a case like this one. Look here.'

Dr. Anstis adjusted the light above the table so that it focused on a smaller area of the dead man's body. He leaned forward a little and placed a metal spatula next to Coombs' heart.

'Yes, that is his heart,' Judy Marchant observed.

'Look more closely,' Dr. Anstis urged.

'Okay, are we looking at the veins at either side of his heart?'

'Yes, we are. Here are the aorta and the vena cava blood vessels. They carry blood into and out of the heart.'

Dr. Anstis gently placed his spatula under one and then the other blood vessel.

'There is no doubt at all that your corpse bled out from the inside. There is a symptom called spontaneous coronary artery dissection. This is where a blood vessel can rupture in one or more places. These ruptures are usually quite small, but can happen anywhere inside the body. This is an extremely rare phenomenon that might occur in somebody of at least middle age, and more commonly much older. It is associated with too much wear and tear on the fabric of the blood vessels, which is why it usually occurs in the vicinity of one of the areas of the body more used to wear and tear or exertion during life, such as arms and legs. The rupture will inevitably lead to heart failure and, more often than not, to death,' the coroner explained.

'And you are saying that this is the case with Martin Coombs, a twenty-eight-year-old man in otherwise good health?' she asked.

'Not only that,' Dr. Anstis lowered himself even closer to the table. 'Do you see?'

On closer inspection, it seemed that the aorta from the left ventricle of his heart was detached. Looking at the right atrium the superior vena cava was also detached. The two major corridors where blood would pump to and from the heart were both broken.

Judy stared for some seconds at the point of interest. She raised herself upright.

'Dr. Anstis, did you cut these blood vessels in your autopsy?' she asked.

Theo Anstis straightened himself up to face the Inspector. He shook his head.

'Not me. These vessels were surgically cut immediately before this man died,' there was a long pause by the coroner, and then he looked Judy Marchant straight in the eye before continuing, 'from the inside.'

दश

I woke up to the buzz of my mobile phone, which lay sandwiched between the top and bottom pillows on my bed. I found the phone and pulled it out. I looked at the screen. The green and red markers on the slide screen blurred, touching in the middle. I was determined not to wake fully as I pulled with my thumb on the green indicator, opening the call.

'Hello.'

'I just left the coroner. We need to meet up.'

Judy sounded excited; she also sounded confused. I looked at the glowing face of the alarm clock on the bedside table closest to me. The hands signalled something like one thirty in the morning, but in this state of wakefulness, I could not be sure.

'What is it?' I asked.

'The coroner found something weird in Coombs that I think you should know about.'

'Can we talk in the morning?' I asked, still struggling to wake up.

'We could, but I would rather do it now. This is kind of important.'

'Give me ten minutes. I will be there,' I reluctantly said.

***

Amy King dragged the phone into the crook of her neck and shoulder. She winced as a sharp pain shot into the base of her neck. A hazard of the job, Amy thought, as the ringing tone buzzed in her right ear.

The work was easy for Amy, after eleven at night all she had to do was answer her phone when it rang. She had two phone lines into her home; one was personal and the other was for work. All she needed to do was to remember to plug in the work phone at eleven o'clock and unplug it again at four in the morning, when her shift finished. Five hours a night, four nights a week was easy labour for Amy. The money paid her bills and then some.

Amy was twenty-six years old. She owned her own two-up-two-down house, which was inherited from her ex-husband in a generous divorce settlement two years ago. She met Mike when she had just turned seventeen years of age. At that time, he was thirty-one. Mike was her first love – her only love as it turns out. Amy never had a good impression of herself, and Mike came into her life and swept her off her feet and away from her otherwise dull single life.

Amy's parents were true blue in nature, consequently her life had been controlled to the point that Amy felt permission was needed to take a shit. Her mother had a sparse head of ginger hair, she wore little or no makeup and was at least three stone overweight. Her father was a nondescript man with a balding head and annoying steel-rimmed glasses. In their early fifties, Amy always viewed her parents as completely fashion-less. No sense of style or colour in their clothes, which were usually functional and dull. She had always been embarrassed by her parents. As a result, what few friends she had in her school years were never invited to her home.

Mike took her away from all that and, so glad was she to leave her old home life behind, that the first thing she did was to change her wardrobe entirely. In came Gap, and out went gap-toothed.

Mike worked as a computer technician, or that was the title he gave it. He certainly earned good wages, sufficient for her to glam up in a way she was never able to before. Amy and Mike never seriously contemplated getting married. That was a subject that was never really discussed. That is, until Amy got pregnant at twenty-one years of age. That is when everything went south, literally. They got married when Amy was six months pregnant, and they found the house she now lived in before the baby, Stevie, was born.

While it is true that Amy spent less time and money on looking her best after giving birth to Stevie, she never felt she let herself go. A little overweight when they met, Amy had only gained one or two pounds since Stevie was born. It was as if Mike felt no longer the centre of Amy's attention. Maybe it was that, or maybe it was just that Amy was gaining years and was no longer the white rose untouched by human hand, that she was when she first met Mike. Whatever the reason, Amy and her husband grew further apart until one morning, quite out of the blue, Mike suggested a divorce. To her surprise, Amy immediately agreed.

The divorce happened quickly. Amy found herself in a house with small front and rear gardens, a small amount of money in the bank and freedom from everyone, which was quite liberating. Stevie was supported financially – more than adequately by her ex-husband, and Amy, at last, began to live a more rewarding life. After six months, Amy wanted to be able to support herself. Until this time she never had any paid employment. She was not too clear on how or why she started working for the Agency, but from her recollection, it was a spur-of-the-moment decision that had worked out well ever since. In her line of work, Amy was able to support herself financially, spend a lot of time with Stevie, and gain trust in herself in managing well, her and Stevie's lives.

'And what would you like to do tonight?' Amy asked into the mouthpiece of the phone. She glanced at the picture of an eighteen-year-old girl in school uniform, white knee-length socks and ponytailed hair that looked at her provocatively from the screen of the tablet. The girl's name was Amber, and this was the personality adopted by Amy as she listened to the laboured breath coming from the earpiece of the telephone.

***

The drive to Judy's home was uneventful. I lowered both front windows to let as much cool night air flow into the car as possible. I was cold, but becoming more awake as each metre of roadway ticked by. My mind was not yet engaged, the automatic task of driving was more than enough for me to concentrate on at this time of the morning. It took me fifteen minutes to reach her apartment.

I looked in the rear view mirror; a reflection of tired watery eyes stared back at me. I rubbed my hands briskly over my face and pulled the door lever to release myself from the car. The cold night air, instead of invigorating me, now became uncomfortable and irritating, as I walked to the door and knocked, rapping cold knuckles against its hardwood surface.

***

Amy King looked at the picture of Amber. A short description of the girl overlay the full screen shot. She was eighteen years old, so said the advertising blurb. She liked older men who would treat her right. She had a strict Catholic upbringing and now she wanted to be taught how to be a naughty girl. She had never had a man before and had always wanted to know how it might feel to be punished for having sexy thoughts. Amber wanted a real man to teach her how to satisfy him, and to release the lust that had lain inside her virginal mind since she was pubescent.

Yeah, right, Amy thought.

The model on the screen was clearly a lot older than eighteen years. If she looked closely at a blown-up image Amy could swear to seeing one or two lines in the creases of her eyes. There was also some cellulite visible at the base of her navy blue panties. Though advertising the girl as eighteen years old, it was clear that the website wanted to project Amber as being even younger than that. As the call went on, the screen photos would change to show Amber in various stages of undress, with an exercise book in front of her and a pencil in her mouth, blouse unbuttoned, then to her in a bra and knickers with reading glasses on, kneeling upon the bed. Then face down naked while apparently looking at a soft porn magazine and then lying face up, arm covering breasts and one hand covering her pubic region.

Eventually the photos would show Amber in legs-wide shots and later with various sex toys in one or another bodily orifice. Whether the punter was able to wait until the end of the deliberately slow slideshow, or if he, or she, shot their load earlier, they would pay full premium rate until the show was over, including advertisements for other shows available. This would mean that Amy could be on the phone continuously for as much as thirty minutes for each call; hence her cricked neck.

***

Judy opened the door and beckoned me inside.

A very big part of being a psychic is being able to dig inside of people to find out what makes them tick. A client's past is just as important as their future in a reading. It is the past that sets out the route they have taken to where they are now, and to their need to contact me for a reading. Psychically, finding out about his or her personality, their health and any immediate issues they face will open up a dialogue between us. It will make the client feel calm and assured about my abilities, creating a situation where they, as if a book, can be read. Only then can communication with wherever my client data originates be clear and concise, since the client, in opening themselves up, is inviting the communication in. Many people believe it is the spirits of dead people that come to us, but it is not. It is the openness, it is the calling of the client, that invites information and communication with the spirits.

With Judy Marchant, I learned very little by being in her company. She drew an almost impenetrable wall around herself, I say almost, because no matter how much you try to protect yourself from being known by other people, the very fact that the wall is there tells something of the person. I got the impression that Judy Marchant was a very defensive person. She likes to do things right and reacts very badly, sometimes aggressively, to criticism. I can find no reason for this, but I would guess it might stem from a strict upbringing. She certainly learned from a young age to keep her emotions in check and to keep her feelings private. This does not mean that she has a cold heart, far from it. If Judy Marchant let you into her life, you would receive love and support in abundance. It is just that most people are not allowed such unfettered access.

'Hi, Judy. I was dozing off when I got your call,' I said as I walked through the entrance way.

I took my jacket off and placed it across my arm.

'Let me take that for you,' she said, as she took my coat and placed it on a three-pronged metallic coat hook fixed on the left side wall near the entrance to her apartment. 'Come through; I have some coffee ready.'

It was not particularly cold outside, but the short twenty-metre walk from the car to the apartment block had invited a steely iciness into my body that refused to let go. I shivered involuntarily as I crossed the hallway and entered the lounge area where we had met before. I made myself comfortable on the sofa opposite the door.

Judy stood in the small kitchen enclave to the right. Her back to me, I traced my eyes over her figure. Dressed in black leggings, which were barely sufficient to cover the outline of her underwear beneath, Judy wore a red lightweight jumper on top – far removed from the business-like uniform of slacks, blouse and matching jacket she wore to work. I much preferred her casual look.

She turned, holding two mugs of coffee, and approached the lounge. It is my thing, but probably so is it the same for most heterosexual men, that a woman wearing tight leggings is too inviting a sight not to look for the outline, the shape and the groove, of what lies at the top of her legs. We cannot help it. We are men and it is more an automatic psychological function than anything seedy, or repulsive.

Judy set the cups on thick glass coasters with gold patterns on a black background. She leaned back into the sofa, put her arm up and rested it against the top of the furniture, her elbow bent and the fingers of her right hand pressed hard against her temple.

'What do you know about this?' she asked.

***

By the time the third picture of Amber flashed onto the tablet on her lap, Amy's caller's breathing was coming long, deep and hard. She guessed this caller would hang up before another minute had passed. It was not that she was uncaring, but Amy did like to get the job done as quickly as possible. She was good, and her boss knew it. Amy could put on a sexy, cheeky voice, just as well as anyone. She found it easy to play a role, just as she had found it easy standing up in front of a school full of children, and reciting a poem or story when she was younger.

Amy had no desire whatsoever to go into acting, but she did seem to have an ability to switch from one persona to another, just like that. She could sense that her caller was close to climaxing, so she turned up the desire and passion in her voice another couple of notches. She liked to keep reminding her callers how young her acted persona really was, flaunting the rules of the website just enough to ensure that a good night's work was enjoyed by everyone. She did not see her work as sordid or dirty; she just viewed it as a way of paying the bills and serving the needs of another human being at the same time.

The phone clicked in Amy's ear and she pressed the end call button. She reckoned she might have five to ten minutes before her next call. Amy was one of five girls working this shift, plenty enough to cover demand at this time of night. If they had not finished their calls yet, the other four Ambers would be winding up soon. With a thirty-minute window for each call, Amy knew instinctively that she was most likely to be the first disconnected caller each time.

She had plenty of time to put the kettle on, put coffee, milk and sweetener into her cup and to push a slice of white bread into the toaster. She went to the fridge and removed a small tub of spreadable butter and a jar of shop-branded marmalade. Life was not too bad for Amy and Stevie King, not too bad at all.

***

'What do I know about this? How do you mean?' I was a bit taken aback by the abruptness of the question.

'You came to me saying that another person had died, linked to what happened six months ago. Then you said that in meditation you were told that the final body count will be more than one million people. Now I have a guy lying on a coroner's slab who died, if not an impossible death, then a highly improbable one,' she paused, and then continued. 'When we were at the Coombs place you said that somebody had been there. It is pretty impossible to believe, given the circumstances of his death, but are we talking about murder here?'

I sat back into the sofa, trying unsuccessfully to make myself comfortable. I tried to focus on the feelings I picked up at the scene of the incident.

'I don't know if you could call it murder, not in the commonly understood meaning of the word. But there was a distant feeling of an alien energy in the lounge, something that did not fit. From what I sensed it seemed that Martin Coombs lived a bit of a lonely life there, at least insofar as he did not have many visitors. The energies of the room that I was able to pick up were, therefore, unique to him. But the longer I was there, the more I became aware of a separate energy that did not seem to fit with everything else I felt. It was a very distant energy, nearly imperceptible – almost as if it was hidden in a fog. It could even be that this energy had tried to shroud itself in an attempt to cover its tracks.'

'But there was somebody else there either at the time, or before, Martin Coombs died.'

'I don't know,' I replied.

'But you seem to know an awful lot about the dead guy.'

Judy Marchant had a way of throwing things out directly, like darts to a board. Sometimes she shot wide of her mark; other times she hit the bullseye.

'Wait a minute. Am I a suspect?' I asked incredulously.

'Of course not, there is no suspect. There can be no cause of death, other than natural.'

'Except?'

'Except it looks a little bit more complicated than that.'

'Complicated? In what way?' As I spoke I was looking straight into Judy Marchant's brown eyes.

'Martin Coombs died of spontaneous coronary artery dissection. It is unheard of in a man his age, and certainly in someone who should have been in perfectly good health. The main blood vessels carrying blood into and out of his heart were severed,' Judy then leaned forward, as if uttering the next few words within earshot of anyone else might place her life in great danger, 'from the inside.'

'Now I see what you mean when you said the coroner found something weird,' I said.

'I want to know what happened.'

'How am I supposed to know? You are acting as if I was there when this incident occurred.'

'There is no murder here. I'm not going to lock you up and throw away the key,' Judy reassured me.

'Thank God for that, but it still seems like you think I am implicated in some way.'

I was feeling even more under the microscope of Judy Marchant's gaze than ever before.

'It is nothing like that. Look. Usually, I would have a murder weapon, DNA, fingerprints, or something else that nine times out of ten would lead me to a suspect and subsequent conviction. Murder is never good, but at least then justice could be served and the case closed. Here I have nothing. You are the only person I can turn to. This is not, and never can be, an official investigation, simply because of its origins and its outcomes. All I have is a guy who speaks of things I have never experienced and, most of the time, never even thought about. All I know is I go to work, I earn my wages, I pay my bills, I see my mum and dad sometimes, I see my nephews, I go to the beach on holiday once a year. I know nothing whatsoever about this crazy shit that I find myself being dragged deeper and deeper into. Now help me with this.'

I sat back and took a deep breath. I reached for my coffee cup, but placed it back onto the glass coaster again.

'To be honest with you, Judy – can I call you Judy?' I asked.

Judy nodded and let out half a laugh.

'Of course you can.'

'I might be your only lead, but I know as little about this as you do. I dragged you into this, I know I did, but that is only because I need your help. But don't forget that I got dragged into this, too. Do you think that I asked to be involved in Armageddon?'

'Is that what this is?' she asked.

'At the moment it sure feels like that is what it could become,' I said.

'I know you are a reluctant participant, too. But I also think this whole thing intrigues you. You might be on the cusp of answering all those questions you never felt could be answered. All those questions the famous spiritual leaders and authors refused to address because they didn't know the answers. But *you* might. And that draws you in, just as much as your sense of duty.'

'Yes, you are right,' I conceded.

'As it does me too. That is why I called you. That is why we met the other day. I didn't watch Sherlock for nothing, and I think this case might stump him, too.'

***

Amy King bit into her snack. The sweet, sharp tang of the marmalade was perfectly offset by the large helping of butter that lay underneath. The crunchy, slightly burnt toast added a third dimension to the snack that set off everything else. After chewing and swallowing the food, she licked her lips. Absolutely divine. Amy put some cold water into her steaming mug of coffee, tested the temperature of the drink, and then added some more. A sacrilegious act to some people, but a necessity when working on a strict timetable, as Amy did.

She slurped at her coffee as she returned to the reclining single-seat faux leather chair. She picked up the tablet with her left hand while seating herself in the chair and placing her rapidly cooling coffee on the small shelving unit beside her. The lamp on top of the unit dispersed rapidly dimming yellowish light in a radius from the base, its faint glow barely reaching the matte cream walls shaping the interior of the room.

Amy picked up the cup of coffee and finished it rapidly. She clicked on the small, integrated pad of the tablet and brought into focus the image of the next young lady in the queue. This girl did not have a first name. She was identified on the screen as Dr. Cumming. Appropriate.

Dr. Cumming was in her early twenties. The screen described her as 'vivacious and willing to do anything to make her patients happy'. The fake doctor was dressed in an extremely short white medical tunic which only barely covered her sheer black stockings and suspenders. With a stethoscope tucked into a breast pocket of her tunic, she sat on the edge of her desk, one leg straight in front of her and the other bent at the knee. The camera angle gave just enough glimpse of white panties to ensure the punters would start their evening's entertainment quickly and effectively. Dr. Cumming had bright blonde shoulder-length hair and black-rimmed glasses propped on the end of her nose. A pencil was nestled lightly into the edge of her mouth, a clipboard held in the crook of her left arm. The girl's tunic was unbuttoned to her belly button, exposing a white lacy bra cupping incredibly well-shaped, full breasts.

Amy was already in character as the phone started to ring. She would never get to answer it.

एकादश

'As far as I see it,' I began cautiously, more than aware that the subject of this conversation was way beyond what most people might be able to comprehend, 'we have a young guy who died of natural causes, though his death was, putting it mildly, a little odd. We have my intense meditation, which suggests a strong possibility that many more people may die because of an unknown glitch in the spiritual death selection process. I have been asked to help solve this problem, but I have no idea whatsoever how this might be achieved. This situation might, or might not, also include the two unexplained deaths that happened six months ago, which were also deemed to have been of natural causes. Am I right so far?'

'Well, I guess so. This is much more your case than mine; I am here as an interested observer, at the moment,' Judy's emphasis was on her last three words.

'The common denominator is that all three deaths happened to young people in apparently good health. None had any medical background that might suggest their lives would be terminated before they at least became middle-aged. None had any history of using illicit drugs or of abusing prescription medicines. And in each autopsy their bodies were found to be clear of alcohol and any chemical substances that might have posed any risk to their health,' I continued, 'also, all three deaths occurred within a five-mile radius of where I live and where you work.'

'So you *are* the killer,' Judy smirked.

'I am trying to be serious here.'

'Sorry,' she apologised.

'Wait a minute. You are right though, and that does put another slant on it. If each death occurs within an easy fifteen minute drive of where you or I am likely to be, what does that mean?' I asked.

'Well, we are already pretty sure that you are wrapped up in this thing, and we can be reasonably certain it's unlikely you would be chosen to become involved in some almighty spiritual mix-up that occurs thousands, or even hundreds of miles away. Not meaning to be rude or anything, but there are other people doing things who would have access to a much wider network of contacts, and who could better cover events that might happen hundreds of miles apart,' she said.

'Like a policewoman you mean,' I replied.

'Oh my God, yes,' she replied.

Judy Marchant lifted her mug of coffee to her lips and slowly swallowed the liquid, her mind deep in thought. I was thinking, too. I was thinking of the three deaths, thinking of my meditation and struggling to snatch out of all that had happened that one gem of information that might be crucial in pointing the way ahead to the next step in resolving this problem. The next step to stopping any more deaths, before the situation gained so much momentum that it spiralled out of control.

'Okay. Let's try turning this on its head. It is highly improbable that a person had anything to do with these three deaths. But let's just suppose that the lack of evidence cannot rule out homicide. Let's imagine that there is a perpetrator somewhere, anywhere, that is responsible for ending three people's lives that otherwise would have continued, had it not been for their actions. What then? If you were looking at these three deaths as straightforward homicide cases, how would you investigate? What would you do?' I asked.

'Well. First of all, I would need to get a report from the first officers at the crime scene, including the apparent method and cause of death. We would then need to find any weapon that might have been used. Other items at the scene would be retrieved. We would check for fingerprints, footprints, or any other marks around the scene that might be connected to the crime. Only after we gathered all our evidence would we then create a team to further look into what might have happened, why, and who might be the perpetrator. We would then incorporate the autopsy findings and have a pretty clear idea of the events as they occurred. Over time we would draw up a list of potential suspects, talk to neighbours, workmates and anybody else who might know the victim or the perpetrator well enough to add useful information. It is then just a matter of building a case. If we are not able to build a case, we keep the investigation open until such a time as we can move it towards prosecution,' she explained.

'But this case is different,' I said.

'Yes, it is. We really have nothing to collect. The only thing I have is your say so that this death might be one of many more to come and each, as seems likely, will continue to be devoid of any physical evidence and any suspects.'

'And how many more similar deaths might it take for your office to sit up and take notice?' I asked.

'It might never happen. The deaths could be blamed on anything, airborne pollutants, water pollution or chemicals, some kind of natural or manmade virus, but without any known variables, we could only believe unknown and/or undetectable factors might be responsible,' she replied.

'And why would some form of spiritual intervention not be seen as a potential unknown or undetectable factor?'

Inspector Marchant laughed, not in a jovial way, but more as a nervous reaction to my question.

'You know as well as I do that no official body would ever consider a spiritual instigator in such events. Look, I am having a hard time accepting even a fraction of the information you are presenting to me. If the numbers of dead people reach a tenth of what you are suspecting, that would have to be some kind of epidemic. Even then I might not consider your argument of the true cause as anything other than the rantings of an egotistical lunatic,' Judy admitted.

'Yeah, thanks.'

'Face it; we are alone in this, and I am having a devil of a time taking all this in. I can't promise that view will ever change,' she said, shrugging her shoulders.

I fully understood what she was saying. I appreciated that her job and reputation was at stake. But to my mind, since when did careers or reputations matter in the roles we adopt when investigating the loss of a human life, physical or spiritual, known or unknown, and anything else that this might entail? Judy Marchant might need physical evidence to quell her wavering thoughts, and that would be just fine with me too, but I was having increasing doubts as to whether anything might turn up to keep her sufficiently interested and engaged to offer any assistance that might prove beneficial in sorting out this mess.

The easiest thing to do would be for both of us to walk away and just let fate and circumstance take control, but, speaking for myself, I have never thrown in the towel on anything that I had not first thoroughly pored over. My instinct told me that the good Inspector sitting next to me on the sofa, smelling clean and sweet, would be the same. So, at least for now, we were on the same team and singing from the same hymn sheet.

'The situation is no stranger to you than it is to me; I can assure you of that. No amount of spirituality, no amount of engrossing oneself in meditation or New Age practices, and no amount of psychic ability can prepare you for what we are facing now. If I had any answers I would gladly give them to you. At the moment, I am not even sure of the questions,' I replied.

***

'You love Marta.'

'Shut up. You don't know what you are talking about.'

Linsey Matthews had been seen hugging Marta Lewis, but there was nothing in it. Linsey had problems with her stepdad. He had always been too controlling, too strict, and now, as she approached her seventeenth birthday,

Linsey's forbidden dreams and aspirations were bursting to be let out, despite her patriarchal guardian's desire to mould the young girl into another aspect of himself. Work in a bank, you get nothing without hard work and dedication, do your homework, and millions of other things that strengthened the rails of the track that he was vigorously pushing her on towards a brighter future, or so he thought. Towards moroseness, boredom and morbidity, so far as Linsey was concerned.

Linsey was engaged in one of those occasions when thoughts become so strong that emotion takes over. Tears flooded her eyes and started slowly at first, and then more steadily, tracing snail trails down her cheeks. Marta had noticed. She had hugged Linsey to try to quell her friend's upset. Linsey quickly forgot the cause of her tears, but, as is often the case, some of the other girls in the school were always ready to take advantage of moments of weakness, and turn them into their own form of entertainment. Pinky Perkins was one such person, and it was she who had turned the situation to her own egotistical advantage.

Pinky Perkins had gained a reputation as a bit of a bully, not with physical attacks, but with an acid tongue that reached out and trapped her victims time after time. Janet was her real name, but who could take a joker like Pinky seriously with a name like Janet Perkins. Some said her name derived from the colour of knickers she wore, others said it came from the small pink scar she had carried on her chin from a young age. The fact that a nickname afforded her the respect of some of the more aggressive girls in the school, was good enough for Pinky.

Linsey, Marta and Pinky were all members of the school netball team. Pinky was the smallest member of the team, but she had a little bit of bulk about her. She was good at reading a game; she was also vociferous on the court, barking out orders to her teammates and putting the heebie-jeebies on any opponents that might get too close. Linsey had blonde hair that she had forced her mum to dye dark blue at the ends. Marta had short, jet black hair that seemed to refuse to grow to shoulder-length. Her skin was a little bit rougher, giving her the glancing appearance of a boy. It was only her blossoming breasts, fitting a thirty-four-inch bra, and the fact that she could more than hold her own in a fight, that kept Marta out of harm's way. Some girls had whispered a speculation that Marta might have lesbian inclinations. But Linsey and Marta were good mates, and had been for a long time.

***

'Are you feeling okay?' Judy asked.

'Yes. Err, yes, I feel okay, why do you ask?'

'You are sweating; your shirt collar is wet. Here, let me get you a damp cloth.'

'I'm okay, honestly, you don't have to…'

Judy was rising from the sofa as soon as she had finished offering me assistance. My protestation was more a token than real. She walked through the door to her hallway, into the bathroom. Very quickly, I heard a tap turn on and then running water. She returned in less than two minutes with a dampened facecloth.

I leaned against the sofa and put my head back. I stared at the ceiling. As I lay there, my vision started to blur. Judy undid the two buttons on my polo shirt and tried to waft some air onto me by pulling the neck of the shirt in and out. She gently pressed the facecloth on my forehead, onto each cheek, across my mouth, and then around the front of my neck.

'You are burning up; what is going on?' she asked.

Her words, sharp at first, began to wane as she finished her short sentence. I was aware that I was losing consciousness, even as a blackness closed inwards from my peripheral vision.

She continued mopping my brow as I slowly felt myself drifting into a deep sleep. Half-asleep images started replacing the reality that I knew surrounded me. The sounds of cars going past mixed with an image of a green door and the number sixteen, the feeling of damp flannel on face mixed with a feeling of cool night air and a gentle breeze on my face and hands. The feeling of Judy Marchant doing her best to bring me round mixed with a growing sense of being somewhere else. Somewhere I was not familiar with, a place which, in some unknown way, beckoned me.

***

'Hey Snout, you ready for practice tonight? I'm gonna get you good this time, watch out.'

Sinead Jones was another member of the netball squad. Sinead nudged Kelly Grosjean as she passed Linsey Matthews in the hallway. Kelly made up the numbers and was not as dedicated a player as most of the other girls were.

Linsey hated being called Snout. There was nothing nasty about the name, and most of the time it was all taken in good faith. But occasionally, Linsey felt irked by it. Lately, Linsey was irked by almost anything. She just sometimes had one of those days. Linsey liked to think that her nickname had nothing to do with the length of her nose. She thought she had a cute nose – not too long, not too wide, not too thin, and she had no knobbly bit on the end. And no hairy nostrils, gross. It was more likely that the nickname came about because Linsey was occasionally known to partake in smoking the odd cigarette, or four, behind the concrete games hall at the far end of the site, opposite the entrance gate. A small area no more than a shoulder's width with the gym hall on one side and a tall wire fence on the other. This is where all the stuff that was against school rules went on. Teachers tended to ignore this place, so long as what happened there posed no danger to the girls.

As Sinead and Kelly departed, Linsey heard them tease an unfortunate girl who carried too much weight, at least for their liking.

All her actions were now overseen only by the posters of actors and pop groups, whose innocent gazes looked down at her from her bedroom walls. It was the fact that her stepdad had forbidden Linsey from going out after nine o'clock one evening, the evening of the interview with the adorable four members of her favourite boy band on a chat show she was going to watch at Janey Cooper's house, that really tugged at her emotions. Marta's attention was welcomed at a time when Linsey's thoughts had descended, once again, to self-pity. Her mother was so much devoted to her second husband that her two children, Linsey and her brother Mark, were all but accessories to her suburban life. There was little discussion now with her mother, less with Mark, and virtually none with her stepdad. She never asked for this situation, but it was what her mother had chosen to serve up on a plate.

Linsey knew that after having children women can lose a bit of self-respect, and that sometimes they could feel totally unattractive to men. This situation was enhanced even further when your husband of ten years walks out of the family home and then dies less than two years later. Linsey never had a close relationship with her dad, but sometimes it seemed to her that life would be so much easier, so much more bearable, had her dad still been around so she could unburden her sorrows on someone. Too many tears were a sign of weakness at school, so Linsey did her best to control her emotions around the grounds. But it did not mean her emotions were not cutting deep, just because she curtailed them whenever they threatened to burst the banks of River Linsey.

The netball team was a good creative outlet for Linsey. She felt appreciated every time the ball dipped through the net, accompanied by the whoop of Pinky and the sharp slap of palm on palm from other team-mates. Playing sport made Linsey feel welcomed and useful. Linsey liked most creative pursuits. Her favourite lessons were Art and English, two subjects where she could express herself unashamedly. She had taken, very recently, to writing songs, which would never see the light of day. But that did not stop her dreams of stardom, sharing her emotional journey with adoring crowds, and opportunistic paparazzi snappers.

***

I was awakened from what seemed to be a deep slumber by Judy shaking my right shoulder, jolting me backwards and forwards in my seat. I had pins and needles in both buttocks, and my toes and my fingers tingled as if a static charge of electricity had been passed through each one of them in turn. I was aware of a high-pitched buzzing in my forehead and at the crown of my head. I was also aware of a burning sensation in my cheeks, before I knew that I still had my eyes closed. I slowly opened them. As the lids rose up, I was aware of a pitch-blackness, which was pierced only by the artificial beam of a neon streetlight. An orange glow was cast inside the car by its instrument panel. One of the internal lights had been turned on by the person accompanying me.

I jolted upright in the seat, violently enough for the seatbelt to lock sharply against my left shoulder. I looked around quickly. Judy's face was a blur, as my head turned one way and then the next.

'What the fuck, where in the devil's arsehole are we? Judy, what the fuck is going on?' I asked in my heavily sleepy state.

'Hey, hey, it's okay. Calm yourself down. Take some deep breaths before we do anything. You scared me there, Mysterio, you are one helluva freaky guy. I guess my mum must have warned me about guys like you,' Judy said.

'But you spit in the face of danger, right?' I replied.

The breathing was working. Somehow I had gotten to somewhere on a journey I knew nothing of, but breathing in huge breaths of oxygen somehow helped my acceptance of the situation, weird though it was.

'Something like that,' Judy said.

A sudden urgency overcame me. I sensed danger and I knew it was nearby. I reached out urgently for the door handle, released my seatbelt and removed myself from the car, all in one seamless movement. I looked around, searching for something, but for what? The inquest into what happened to me, how I got to this unknown place and under what pretence, would have to wait. Right now, I knew I needed to do something, and to do it immediately. Judy released herself from the car and walked around to the kerbside where I was standing.

'Here, you said you needed this, we got it from your place on the way here.'

Judy handed me the CPAP machine, which I used at night to treat sleep apnoea. It continuously pumps air through each nostril while I am sleeping, to stop my airway from closing up. Before using this machine, I was told that my breathing stopped thirty-six times every hour during periods of sleep. Since using the machine these periods of breathlessness had reduced to nine per hour. Still, pretty horrifying.

I looked at the machine, cold in my hands. I wrapped the plug end into my left hand and scooped up the plastic tube and face mask in my right. I moved forward towards a row of terraced houses that faced the road up a grassy incline.

'Where are we heading? You still haven't told me what we are doing here.'

I stopped and turned to my companion.

'I don't know, Judy. I don't know.'

Frustration was clearly evident in my voice, maybe even anger. Judy visibly moved her body away from me as I spoke.

'Come on Judy, we don't have much time.'

'Much time for what?' she asked.

I groaned as I continued to stride up the embankment. I reached the top of the grassy slope and leaned my way under a metal guardrail that stood at the top. A terrace of six houses stood beyond a concrete path that followed the guardrail. I looked quickly from one house to the next. Judy Marchant followed me, noticeably slower in her stride than I was.

'We are looking for number sixteen, a dark green door with a brass lion's head door knocker. Hurry.'

'There it is, over there on the right,' she signalled.

Judy's eyesight was much more accustomed to darkness than was mine. I had lived in the Gambia five years, but had never grown accustomed to the darkest, sandiest streets I had ever encountered. I still struggle in the dark at home, bumping into things, stepping on other things, feeling my way around objects as though blind. The single orange streetlight did little to illuminate the row of houses that stood atop the verge.

I hurried in the direction Judy Marchant had indicated. A small black metal gate led to a stoned walkway of no more than two metres. A couple of plants were potted inside brown rustic clay pots that balanced on the slightly sloping sill of a bay window to the front. I approached the door and put my ear to it. No sounds came from within. Thick curtains were drawn across the inside of the window. I could see nothing through the glass except a small amount of light cast from inside. The rest of the house was in darkness.

The door had a long pane of thick, heavily-patterned glass to the left of it. It was impossible to see inside the hallway through the glass. The door had two locks visible from the outside. I was hoping we could enter the house as quickly and as quietly as possible. If we came across a roller catch which inserts into the door and frame, then a speedy entrance was unlikely. I prayed that both locks were not engaged.

'Judy,' I whispered over my right shoulder, 'can you do your thing with that special key of yours?'

'You do know that I will be in a ton of shit if someone reports this, don't you,' Judy said as she brushed past me and into a position affording better access to the top lock.

'Can we get this done as quickly as possible?' I asked.

Luckily, the top catch was freed in a matter of seconds and the door moved, too noisily, inwards. Judy stepped inside while I eased the creaking door back into its frame. We were both immediately aware of a wretched gasping sound coming from the room to the left, the room where the light appeared fleetingly through the bay window curtains. We rushed towards the door and pushed it open.

Amy King was sitting in a chair to the immediate right of the door, gripping the arms of it. The tips of her fingers were white and bloodless. Her eyes were wide open with fear, tears had passed down her cheeks and pooled against the collar of her blue dressing gown, and onto her chest. Her face was reddened. She was struggling to draw in breath, and her whole body raised from the chair with the effort. We could hear the coarse sound of air trickling into her mouth and thinning out as it entered her trachea. She was coughing too, and making a loud, retching sound in an effort to clear her throat.

'Plug in the machine, there behind the chair, hurry,' I told Judy.

The lamp and the small table to the right side of the armchair had toppled over during Amy's desperate struggle to breathe. A tablet was at her feet face down, the screen casting a blue glow upon the carpet on which it lay. A telephone was also on the floor to Amy's right side, the handset removed from the cradle.

Judy plugged the machine into the wall socket that was live.

'Press the round button on top,' I said urgently.

The small light at the top of the CPAP machine came on.

'Now press it again until a second light comes on, quickly,' I instructed my companion.

The CPAP machine came alive as air rushed out of the plastic mask.

'Help me get this thing on her head, quickly,' I ordered.

Judy took the rubber strap, placed it over the back of Amy King's head and held it in place while I manoeuvred the mask so that each rubber tube in the facemask was inserted into the suffering lady's nostrils. Amy's spittle and snot dropped onto my fingers, until the facemask was finally positioned correctly.

The machine continued to push copious amounts of rushing air into Amy King's windpipe. Finally, the ailing woman managed to gradually slow the gasps of air she took. Within two minutes her breathing was returning to normal, the blockage, whatever it was, removed, so that her trachea returned to working as it should. Amy continued to take huge gulps of air every six or seven breaths. She began to cry and reached up for a comforting embrace from Judy, who cradled the stricken woman in her arms, gently running a hand across her head as she did so. Amy King wept long and hard while burying her head into Judy's shoulder.

I reached down to the floor and turned the tablet over. The screen was bright blue with a timed-out message across the middle. Whatever Amy King was doing before she was incapacitated, had ended. I found the cut-off button and manoeuvred the pad to switch off the tablet. I then picked up the small unit beside the chair and placed the tablet onto it. I picked up the still lit lamp and put that next to the tablet. I could hear the soft beeping of the handset that signalled a broken phone call. I replaced the handset on the cradle and placed it beside the chair in which Amy was still sobbing, supported by Judy. As I steadied myself to stand up, the phone started to ring. I wrenched the lead out of the wall socket, and stood up.

My mind was buzzing with questions. What exactly had happened to Amy King, and how? What had happened to me? Had I blacked out? How did we find ourselves outside of Amy King's house, and how did I know we were needed there? How did I know the directions to the house? How did I know to get the CPAP machine from my home, and how did we have it in our possession? Was I somehow able to exit the car with a clear mind, walk to my home, use the front door key, retrieve the CPAP machine, exit my home and lock the door, return to the car and belt myself in, all without any knowledge whatsoever of doing these things?

What the fuck was going on?

द्वादश

Linsey Matthews sat in front of her vanity unit, staring into the face of the girl reflecting back at her from the mirrored glass. Linsey was a pretty young lady. Natural blonde hair fell across her right shoulder, the ends resting on her adequate breasts. Linsey had never been the kind of girl who wished she looked any different. Most of her friends wanted fuller lips, slimmer hips, more rounded bottoms, and most of them wanted different breasts. No doubt when they got the money together, most of them would seriously consider having cosmetic surgery. Linsey would prefer to be herself; in any case, she did not fancy unknown people in white gowns drawing on her and ripping into skin or injecting chemicals into parts of her body. Most of all she did not want scars, no matter how well-hidden, that would remain with her the rest of her life.

Linsey looked after her skin very well. She made sure that her face was always clean and well moisturised, using the finest female cosmetics available. Linsey did not need mascara, eye shadow or lipstick to make herself into something she was not. In any case, such things would only serve to dry out her skin and create conditions likely to produce acne, the scourge of pubescent girls everywhere. Sure, she had a small number of marks on her face where spots had developed two and three years ago, but nothing that might detract from her natural effervescence.

Linsey ran a brush through her hair one more time, before retiring to her bed. The small alarm clock beside the bed showed the time as ten thirty. The sun had long ago sunk below the horizon, replaced by a bright moon and clear, starry sky. It was late spring and the evenings had been mild. Linsey liked to leave a small window open in these conditions, and she very often left her bedroom curtains open, too. She drew great comfort on these types of evenings from lying on her bed, motionless, while staring out at the deep, dark blue, sparkling sky.

As Linsey put her brush down, she took one last look at her reflection. She pushed the switch on the neck of the lamp to turn off the source of light in the room. Immediately the light blue shine of the moon entered her bedroom, making her feel closeted, protected, safe. She lay on her bed, moving herself a little to get comfortable

Linsey stared at the moon, gazing at the light and dark shades apparent on the surface of the satellite. The brilliant white glow surrounding the moon was absorbing and relaxing. As she observed the brilliance of the night sky, she started to think about Marta Lewis. Thoughts of her friend's boyish good looks, her short black hair and the sympathetic and warm, attentive attitude she showed Linsey today at school, rose in her mind.

There were only two things that upset Linsey: the attitude that her stepdad adopted towards her and her mother's subservience to the man she claimed to love. If Linsey ever complained to her mum about her stepdad, her mum would invariably tell him, leading to more accusations, bad tempers and greater upset. In recent months, Linsey had decided to stay out of her stepdad's way. She preferred the solace of her iPod, her tablet and her television set, all of which took pride of place in her room.

Linsey turned her thoughts once again to the school hallway. Linsey was turned into a corner, her arms across her chest clutching schoolbooks, tears cascading down her cheeks. She had positioned herself in a place few people would notice her as soon as she felt her upset state starting to overcome her. Linsey was known as level-headed and had overcome a lot in her young life. Everyone knew her past, but she was known as a survivor, a person who would overcome life's obstacles with a shrug of her broad shoulders and a flick of her hair. On this occasion, she could not overcome her pain and in a very infrequent show of emotion, she had broken down in a flood of negative feelings.

Marta came towards Linsey. She was showing concern even before she reached her tearful friend. Marta put her hand on Linsey's right shoulder as she approached.

'Linsey, what's wrong?'

Linsey did not answer, but she was determined to dry her tears before too many people found out that she had been crying.

'Linsey you can tell me, we are buddies, right?'

Marta gently shook Linsey's shoulder as she spoke. Marta slowly turned Linsey around. She lifted her friend's face with her right forefinger. Linsey had no choice but to look at Marta through tear filled eyes. Marta took out a cotton handkerchief and gently patted below Linsey's eyes, drying out the lines rapidly forming from the rivers of her tears.

'It's okay,' said Linsey. 'I will be alright, it's just something really silly; I will be fine. I feel a bit stupid, that's all.'

Linsey nervously chuckled as she desperately fought to gain control. Marta handed her the handkerchief and Linsey rapidly wiped it across her eyes and around her cheeks.

'Come here,' Marta said, 'a quick hug never hurt anyone.'

Marta gently pulled Linsey into her embrace. Marta was warm, she smelled good and she was providing exactly the comfort that Linsey needed.

Linsey was aware that her lips brushed Marta's neck as she nestled into her friend's shoulder.

'It will all be okay, I promise.'

This must have been the moment that somebody had passed them, embracing. This must have been the moment that the rumour mill had started churning, ready to pump out whatever the piper thought their audience would most like to hear. Linsey was unaware of who had walked past, and she did not care, she was getting what she needed from her friend.

Marta pulled Linsey away from her shoulder. She ran her hands through Linsey's hair to straighten it out. She gently passed her hands over Linsey's face to make sure no tears lingered. It was at that point, with their faces only a matter of inches apart, that Linsey felt sure Marta was going to plant a kiss onto her lips. Maybe the anticipation, the eagerness for a gentle meeting of mouths came directly from the taut and strong emotions still swirling tornado-like inside Linsey's mind, maybe not. But it did not happen.

'Come on, I will walk with you,' Marta said, as Linsey steadied herself and moved back away from the corner of the otherwise quiet hallway. 'And remember, pal, I will always be there if you ever need me.'

It was not the anticipated kiss that Linsey thought of now, as she watched a wispy dark cloud float across the front of the moon, it was more what Marta had said as they both walked away and towards their individual destination points. Marta and Linsey did not meet too much in the school. Though in the same grade, they attended different classes most of the time. They only really met up when going to maths and English, and even then, the width of the classroom separated their chairs. In a way, maybe that mix of closeness and distance drew in the thoughts that now started to escalate inside Linsey's mind.

***

Amy King refused any medical assistance after the incident, insisting that she did not want her young son disturbed while he was sleeping upstairs. Amy told us that nothing like this had ever happened to her before. So far as she knew she had no problems with her lungs, and that she had never suffered any breathing difficulties before.

We agreed not to inform the medical authorities of what had happened, on two conditions. First, that she get an appointment at her doctor's surgery to look into whether or not she had developed a recent problem with breathing or allergies that might have led to her experience that evening, and second, that she agreed to talk with us again so we could explore what might have caused the incident. Amy King agreed to both.

I welcomed her decision, because it would allow Judy and I to look deeper into what happened without attracting the attention of any official organisations and thereby, also that of Judy's superiors. For me, though no death had occurred as a result of this incident, it did not mean that Amy King had not been targeted by the same force which took the lives of Martin Coombs, the two young people who died six months ago, and of Solly Saunders. It was very clear, from the unknown beacon that attracted me with such devastating force to the scene in Amy's front room, that there was a connection between all the events taking place, regardless of their differing outcomes. Of course, that would not be so easy for Judy Marchant to accept. Had it not been that I was in her company when becoming so overwhelmed with this psychic phenomenon, it might be very hard for her to continue to follow these events with anything like the building conviction she had.

This kind of event had never happened to me before. Judy said I had my eyes open most of the time, right from when I collapsed on her sofa to when I came to, exiting her car. She described my look as 'vacant' during the journey, adding that my conversation was minimal and in a lowered tone, despite her desperate pleas for information, and the apparent emergency of the situation we found ourselves in.

My first thought was that I was in some kind of trance-like state, but I had never heard of anyone entering such a state without sufficient preparation beforehand. Alternatively, I might have been sleepwalking. The problem here was that I was not asleep when the incident first occurred. If I was in a trance, how could that have been triggered without my knowledge? Something else that did not fit with this explanation was that I was aware while on the sofa that I was losing consciousness in the seconds before I blacked out. At that time, Judy had sufficient time to notice a change in me and to prepare a damp cloth and apply it to my face, neck and forehead. No rational explanation seemed to fit.

I had never felt so disjointed from reality before. No matter how deep a trance people claim to be able to enter, there would always be a part of them rooted into the here and now, into their physical surroundings. It is not possible to completely sever all knowledge of our five senses, even if we are able to reach an additional sixth sense of awareness. Astral travel was never an option, since my physical being travelled as one whole part of my experience. And even if this was possible, a metaphysical me in another place would be unlikely to be able to manipulate physical objects, as had happened. During all the psychic readings I ever carried out, the images I am aware of overlay my physical surroundings. Meditative and hypnotic states are the only two occasions when I might be this disjointed, but in both cases, I would not have been able to interact with my physical environment.

The whole experience just did not fit comfortably with any logical reasoning.

***

Judy and I did not communicate with each other those first three days after Amy King was attacked, if indeed attacked is the right word to use. We had no proof of anything except what might be deemed a medical incident with an otherwise healthy mother of one small child. Judy must have been feeling just as shell shocked as I was over what had happened, and for us to talk together without first individually seeking to calm our thoughts to try to level out what was, at that moment, a tempest of emotions, and conflicting thoughts and feelings, would likely be counter-productive.

There must be a rational explanation for all that had happened which, in turn, should mean that future events would follow a similar pattern. Rationality was a difficult tool to handle when all that was happening seemed to fly in the face of human experiential protocol. It was the seeming irrationality of recent events that seemed to make it more difficult to piece together our experiences as time progressed.

I stayed at home those three days, taking part in only minimal tasks. I managed to cook a meal or two, I washed my face and hands only as appropriate. Despite tumbling thoughts during the daytime, I did manage to sleep well. But by day three, I could feel my energy lapsing, my concentration was not as sharp and my focus on the primary issues of concern was fading in and out. You might think this would be a great time to try some meditation, but it could not be done. The buzzing of thoughts inside my head was just too strong, the thoughts too many in number. And I got no answers, only more questions.

It was at this time that I seriously considered jacking in the idea of ever being able to comprehend, let alone put right, the things that had been placed on my spiritual plate. To any sane, reasonably-minded person, the idea of chasing some spiritual entity, that killed people before their time, would be laughable at best, insane at worst. Surely people had been locked away in psychiatric hospitals for much less. Maybe very soon the men in white coats would come knocking at my door, ready to tie the latest jacket around my back, Gucci leather straps securing my arms. What sounds crazy is that at times I did consider this outcome a real possibility. The secrecy of the project I was involved in, as well as the seemingly insurmountable objectives, would be enough to drive any normal person crazy.

But one thought always returned in my times of doubt. I knew that the spirit realm would never set tasks that a person, during any physical lifetime, could not achieve. I guess this was what I, in all the decisions I had made up to the present time, was destined to do. I don't believe in fate, and I don't believe in karma. I just think that what is before us at each point in our lives, is what we are supposed to deal with.

'Judy, how have you been?' I asked down the mouthpiece of the phone.

'I have been better. But come to think of it, I have been worse, too. I wondered when you were going to call,' she answered.

'I guess we have both had a lot on our minds since Friday night,' I said, referring to the incident at Amy King's house.

'You are not kidding. In case it escaped your notice I have a full-time job to hold down, as well as chasing ghosties and ghoulies.'

'Yeah, I know. I'm really sorry I dragged you into this,' I said.

'Too late for that now. I guess you knew what you were doing when you cast your line out. You must have had profiteroles on the end of it,' she joked.

'You know what, Judy, despite what other people might think, you do have a sense of humour,' I replied, smiling.

'I need it right now.'

'We need to speak to Amy King if we are going to make any headway.'

'I know. I guess I just hoped by some miracle we might be able to forget everything, and let those people die who have been earmarked by this supernatural freak.' Judy spoke frankly, but she did raise a good point.

'I cannot do that, and I don't think you can either,' I replied.

'No, you are right.'

'Can you be free now? I am thinking we can go over by lunchtime so her kid is at school. I don't want to give Amy an opportunity to sidestep our agreement, by calling ahead.'

'Are you sure that would be wise?' Judy asked.

'Who knows?' I replied, not quite sure of anything anymore.

***

Linsey Matthews withdrew her hand as soon as her lust was satiated. Her body still trembled and stiffened as the last orgasmic waves shot through her body. She tightened her legs together and crossed her ankles. Breathing quickly and erratically, she was aware of a few beads of sweat on her forehead that slowly trickled past her temples. She corrected her nightdress, pulling it once again below her waistline. She straightened her body and turned away from the crumpled sheets in the middle of her bed. Lying on her left side, hanging on the edge of the bed, she cupped her face in her left hand and stared blankly at the stars glistening beyond her window. Cool night air caressed her face.

Her thoughts stayed with Marta Lewis. Linsey's body might now be releasing the last of the hormones associated with her recent sexually-driven exertions, but her mind was not. Linsey had never before considered the possibility of kissing a girl to be exciting. She had had two boyfriends up to today and she had kissed both. She had even fondled one of the boys. Sure, she admired attractive women, but don't all girls do that?

Linsey did masturbate, but not too often. Maybe it was her Catholic upbringing, maybe not, but Linsey had a thought buried deep inside her mind that if she did masturbate, especially to a conclusion, then something bad would happen as a result. Linsey had never stopped to think if this had ever been the case. Nevertheless, this thought was always there in red flashing lights if ever she felt that familiar tingle that demanded attention, and this time the urge had been way too strong.

As Linsey stared at the sparkling moon, she felt a little more than the lust for Marta that drove the carnal thoughts about her friend. She was now aware of softer thoughts that had never before entered her mind.

***

Judy Marchant and I stood facing the green door leading to Amy King's house. The property looked very different in the daytime. The small area to the front of the house looked unkempt. Small tufts of dirt and soil littered the loose gravel frontage, which was topped by four plastic tubs holding weeds and a couple of flowers. The soil inside the tubs was dry and cracked. The green paint on the door was patchy and flaky in parts. The bay window was clean and the retaining uPVC housing was also clean.

'I think it's best if I do the talking,' Judy said as we saw the shadow of a person inside, nearing the door.

The front knocker rapped against its surround as the tight doorway slightly hampered the passage of the door, as it was tugged inward. Amy King stood before us, left hand remaining on the handle of the door ready to admit or decline entrance to the property.

'Good day, Ms King,' Judy began.

'Amy, please.'

'Yes, Amy. We were in the area and thought we should pop by to see how things are with you,' Judy continued.

'Fine, fine,' Amy replied.

It was immediately clear that we might not be so lucky as to be given an opportunity to discuss the events of three nights earlier, since the demeanour of the householder seemed defensive. I found myself willing Judy to press on with the reason for our visit and the importance of exploring our previous meeting in some depth, for the benefit of everyone.

'We wondered if we might take a small amount of your time, to help us clear up some issues regarding what happened last Friday night?' Judy continued.

'Is this an official investigation Inspector Marchant?' Amy asked.

'No, it is not.'

'Then I am not sure I can give you any more insight than you have already. You were there, you saw what happened, I told you about my medical history. I don't know what else you need to know.'

'Well, that is precisely why it might help everyone if we were able just to catch up with you and put this issue to bed.'

Too soft, Judy. Push her, I thought.

'I think it is already sleeping, Inspector. Good day.'

Amy King went to push the door shut. Her shoulders tensed as she prepared to turn away from the door and continue doing whatever she was doing before we arrived. I leaped forward from my position on Judy's right shoulder. I forced my toe into the doorjamb, blocking the green door from closing.

'I am sorry, Amy, but maybe my partner failed to impress upon you the significance of our visit,' I said more sternly.

Honesty will always pay, especially on issues that might hinge on what we could find out from the only known survivor of the entity I strongly believed to be responsible for four recent deaths, and for one very close call.

'What happened to you on Friday night is extremely rare, almost unheard of. But it is not the first of its kind,' I continued. 'In fact, we have very good reason to believe that four people have died in the last six months. The last man to die was twenty-eight years old. He died one week ago yesterday.'

Amy's grip on the door loosened. I withdrew my foot, and straightened myself up in a more committed, but also a more empathetic stance. Amy King seemed to take the bait. Our doorstep communication, our negotiation, continued.

'I don't understand. If people have died, then we must be talking about murder. And you, Inspector Marchant, would be conducting an official inquiry. You would be scraping hair samples from carpets, taking fingerprints, looking for a suspect. But you said this visit was not official. What happened to me was not an attempt on my life, it was just one of those anomalies that grips people from time to time, wasn't it?' Amy King asked.

'We would like to gain some more information so that we can continue our unofficial enquiries. If we are able to explain more fully what we believe to be happening, then everything will become a little bit clearer,' I said.

'I promise you, Amy, there is very good reason I am not here in an official capacity. I am not in the habit of chasing ideas that have no basis in fact. I can also promise you that if I felt it was not absolutely necessary to be here, we would not be.' Finally, I thought Judy had managed to seal the deal.

'You had better come in,' Amy said as she opened the door and retreated into the entrance hallway of her home.

त्रयोदश

We were seated on a faux leather sofa in the lounge. Judy flipped open a small notebook and prepared to write down what was said. Amy sat next to us on a seat she had retrieved from the kitchen area. Her demeanour suggested that she had not used the armchair opposite since Friday night, and I doubted whether she would ever use it again. Memories become very real when we replay any part by using furniture or items closely associated with painful experiences. In this case, the small armchair had taken on the persona of the bad experience, and it remained in the grooves and lines, in the texture, and in the material of that chair, until such a time as it was psychologically cleansed by its owner.

'In your own time, can you tell us what happened last Friday night?' I asked Amy.

'I was working. I work from home in the evening. Stevie sleeps soundly at night, so I don't disturb him. With a young kid, this job is perfect for me. I just...' Amy held her neck as she explained the events of the previous Friday evening, 'I just lost my breath. I was gasping for air, but it seemed nothing was going in. I was coughing, too. I bent over, spittle was coming from my mouth, snot from my nose, it was terrible. I couldn't leave the chair because I was doubled over. There was no pain, only gasping for air. I thought I was going to die.'

'Have you ever suffered from sleep apnoea, Amy?' I asked.

'What is that? I have never heard of it,' she replied.

'As in the name, sleep apnoea occurs during times of rest. It happens when your airway closes in a spasm; it only lasts a couple of seconds. Usually it is not sufficient to wake the sleeping person. On other occasions, it can be terrifying and it can last twenty to thirty seconds. A sufferer normally makes a complete recovery when the airway re-opens through conscious effort, like by coughing or gasping for air. Most people suffer such a seizure maybe once or twice an hour. Somebody suffering sleep apnoea, as I do, can suffer these attacks up to ten times each hour. The condition is not usually fatal,' I explained.

'You brought that machine with you. How did you know about what was happening to me?' Amy asked, while shooting out a piercing, puzzled stare straight into my eyes.

'I will come to that very shortly, I promise. First, can you tell me if you have ever suffered from sleep apnoea?' I asked.

'Huh? No, never.'

'Do you have any allergies that you are aware of?' I continued to question my increasingly perplexed host.

'No, not that I know of.'

'Have you been subject to any severe anxiety, depression or...' I hesitated, 'or have you ever had any suicidal thoughts.'

'Good God, no. Never. I just live my life with my son. We are happy. We have been settled in this house for the last five years. We get on fine. I have no debts, no secrets, no worries or concerns,' Amy was stern in her tone.

'I am sincerely sorry, Amy, but I have to first consider whether this episode you experienced might be a simple result of any known medical issues, as they might relate to you. Only then can we consider any other alternatives,' I stated.

'And what 'other' alternatives might there be? It seems you are keeping something from me. Why would you turn up at my house just at the right time, knowing what I was suffering from at that exact moment? How did you know where I lived? You don't even know me.'

Amy King's stare continued to focus on me while she shifted a little on her seat.

'No, we don't. Neither Judy nor I ever met you before Friday night,' I agreed.

'Just what is going on here? On the doorstep you spoke of people dying, and somehow you think these deaths are linked to me. So tell me, and give it to me straight, what the fuck is all this about?' Amy asked.

She was clearly disturbed by what had been said; maybe this was why she was so defensive on the doorstep. If you hide yourself away from something it can disappear, except usually it does not. The householder also knew all too well that she had pledged her support for a further discussion, and it is hard to retract such a promise, especially when the two people you are making a promise to had just saved your life.

I explained, as briefly as possible, about the two deaths six months ago and how I had sought Judy's help to look into the circumstances of each and how, in hindsight, that had created a mess for both of us. I told Amy about my ability to channel information and how I became aware of the broader picture of what appears to be happening now. I explained to her the circumstances of the death of Martin Coombs and how I believed this was linked to the earlier demise of the two young men. I then went on to explain the circumstances leading up to Judy Marchant and I being in the right place at the right time, to assist her recovery last Friday night.

'I'm sorry but none of this fits in at all with God's truth as I know it. I was raised in the guidance of the Catholic faith. I don't practice anymore, but that does not mean that I have abandoned my beliefs, far from it. So if you want me to believe in all of this nonsense, I am afraid that won't happen.'

'Amy, I am sorry but I cannot say it other than as it is. The truth can sometimes be stranger than fiction. I do not have the mind to make this all up, but I can promise you, one hundred per cent, that all I have explained to you is true. I don't doubt that this is hard to understand, and I believe the actual situation is far more complicated than even I could imagine. I would never ask you to abandon your beliefs. But is it not true that God allows all beliefs, all faiths to prosper in His name?'

I was desperate to get this conversation back on track, to introduce a more positive perspective that might, in turn, create an opportunity to uncover greater knowledge of what was going on, than we had before knocking on the green front door this morning.

'Yes. That much is true,' Amy replied.

'And in that context, all I ask is that you can, somewhere inside of you, open yourself up to what I am saying. I cannot impress upon you how important this conversation is, not only for the people here, not only for the four young people who have had their lives cut short so tragically, and not only for the grieving families of those young people. You, Amy, were very nearly forced to leave your young son without his mother at only four years old. Amy, you are twenty-six years of age. How many more experiences are left for you, how many more treasured moments with your son, how many more achievements, how many more of the proudest moments to share with your loved ones? You nearly lost everything on Friday. The four people who died have already lost all they had, and all they might have had. And I have good reason to believe that if Judy and I are not able to at least grab a greater understanding of exactly what we face, then many more, as yet unknown, people might be in mortal danger. Who knows, with a much greater understanding of what we are facing maybe, just maybe, we can stop any more unnecessary suffering in its tracks.'

I had played my trump card, and could only hope that Amy King was able to react positively to my desperate plea for her assistance.

'Okay. Yes, you are right, I understand,' Amy King's renewed positivity showed in her eyes.

'Amy, so far as I am aware, you are the only person to survive such an attack. I must stress that I cannot guarantee that what you suffered was in any way connected with anyone else, or even that any connections exist between any of the people I mentioned. The only link I have is through what I believe psychically. And, in truth, that is all we have to go on. To be honest, Amy, I have always doubted my psychic abilities. I am so fearful of being wrong in the information I pick up. But I feel a very strong psychic connection between the four young people who have died, and with what happened to you on Friday. My fear is what might happen if we do nothing? Can we live with the responsibility of not at least trying to see if any of the ends can be tied up?'

'No, I guess not,' Amy replied.

Judy sat quiet, and motionless, throughout the conversation. Maybe she was silently questioning her own part in the situation. Maybe hearing the whole set of circumstances laid out in such a concise manner forced her into once again evaluating the validity of her involvement, or even strengthening her determination to uncover the truth? I sincerely hoped it was the latter. I needed Judy's help. Little did I know at this moment in time, just how vital that would be in the days and weeks to come.

चतुर्दश

In time, and with more than a little persuasion, Amy King agreed to be hypnotised to uncover the truth of what happened to her. There was little more to gain from conventional questioning. It was clear that the young mum had no easily identifiable medical issues that might have caused, or complicated, the situation she had found herself in. While it was true that apnoea could strike at any time, it was unlikely that this would happen during waking hours.

Despite questionable glances from Judy Marchant, I was adamant that a session of hypnosis might be the only way to gain insight into what had happened in this house, and also yield us vital clues as to who or what was responsible. Everything leaves a trail. I knew this through my experiences as a spiritual channeller. I also knew that in this property I was picking up similar energetic traces to those I had felt at the site of Martin Coombs' death.

Hypnosis has many levels. Stage hypnosis relies only on the complete belief of volunteers that something unexplainable will happen to them, while submitting to comedic acts to satisfy the paying audience. And if the level of trance is insufficient to cause complete obedience to voiced commands, then the volunteers themselves are known to complete the tasks set.

It is very rare for a practitioner to use stooges placed strategically in the audience to further their egotistical aims, unlike stage magicians. So a hypnotic performer must have some degree of influence over his subjects. It is highly unlikely, however, that the subconscious mind of anyone would allow them to act as a chicken or any other animal on stage. This is because a hypnotist must reinforce the knowledge, or experience, of a participant. Tasks of which the volunteer is unfamiliar would rarely work without the conscious participation of that volunteer.

Although I obtained certificates of competence, with honours, in hypnotherapy, I have always adapted my style to that which is most suitable for each client. The success or otherwise of the hypnotic process depends far more on the ability of the client to hypnotise themselves, than for any practitioner to implant a state of hypnotic trance. Don't ever believe any scare stories about the safety of hypnosis. Each person has a fail-safe subconscious mechanism that will protect them from any suggestions that might conceivably cause any anguish or harm. A person's mind simply would not co-operate with anything they did not welcome, or accept. The depth of a client's need for assistance on any given subject is paramount in the success of hypnotic procedures. This is why a thorough review of the susceptibility of each client to the hypnotic process, must be carried out before any action is taken.

In the case of Amy King, her understanding of the hypnotic process was good, but her belief in any potential benefits or outcomes was not. Anybody can be hypnotised with the right approach. With Amy King, I needed to convince her subconscious mind of the lack of harm that would occur, and it was vital that I use a strong and powerful message that the process would yield personal gain. With these markers at the forefront of my mind, I began sending Amy into a hypnotic trance.

***

'Hey Linsey, are you ready for the big showdown on Thursday?' Kelly Grosjean asked, placing her right arm around Linsey's shoulders.

'Yeah, ready as I'll ever be,' Linsey replied.

'It's the regional final, you had better be ready,' Kelly countered.

Linsey felt Kelly's grip around her shoulders tighten as the other girl pulled her closer. She was not sure, but thought that Kelly might be a little jealous over her hug with Marta earlier in the week. That can happen. One minute one girl is flavour of the month, the next minute someone else is the one to be with – the one whose best mate position is a must. Linsey may be the 'in' thing at the moment, and long may that continue, but she knew it would not last forever.

'No Sinead?' Linsey asked.

Kelly Grosjean and Sinead Jones were like peas in a pod. They went everywhere together, sat together in every class, gossiped and quipped about their classmates together. Linsey felt sure Sinead would not be happy with Kelly's attention toward her, should she ever find out.

'Sinead is somewhere around, but I haven't seen much of her today,' Kelly replied.

'Ah, okay.'

'Hey, are you going to Simeon's after the game?' Kelly asked.

Simeon's was a club in town where most of the girls got in, despite them all being underage. A guy on the door, whose sister was in the same year, usually let the girls enter the club, so long as none of them tried to buy or drink any alcohol. The club was a bit loose in its rules and regulations, but it served as a good place to hang out at the end of the school week. Linsey never planned to attend, especially this week, as they had the big game the very next day.

'I guess so, yeah,' Linsey replied, only because she knew Marta would be there.

***

Amy King lay on the sofa. I checked the room to make sure there were no drafts from open windows or doors. I positioned myself in the same armchair in which Amy had suffered last week. I moved it to position myself level with Amy's head and facing her on the sofa. I made sure that Amy's arms were by her side and that her legs were uncrossed. I then began the process of inducing hypnotic trance.

'I just want you to relax your body. Be aware of the sofa beneath you and how it supports the whole of your body. When you are ready, I would like you to close your eyes.'

Amy's eyelids closed.

'Just be aware of your breathing. The gentle rise and fall of your chest, as you breathe in and breathe out.'

I timed my words with the rhythm of Amy's breath.

'With each breath in you are feeling more and more relaxed, and with each out breath you are ridding yourself of all concerns, worries and extraneous thoughts. Breathing in relaxation, breathing out thoughts. On each out breath just see your thoughts leave your mind, like clouds in a beautiful blue sky. See those clouds float away as if on a gentle breeze. All your thoughts are gently floating away into the distance. With each breath in you are becoming more and more relaxed, more and more comfortable. Imagine you are breathing in a soft, soothing, relaxing colour with each breath. Feel that comforting, warming colour enter your toes, your feet, your calves. Feel this gentle relaxing colour enter your thighs, your bottom, and your stomach. Becoming more and more relaxed with each breath in. This colour is in your chest now, your shoulders, travelling gently, softly down each arm and into your hands. It is reaching each finger in turn, relaxing, comforting, warming every part of your body, every molecule becoming so relaxed now. This relaxing colour enters your neck. Every muscle in your face is becoming so, so relaxed. Into your forehead and your scalp. You are now feeling so much more relaxed, more comfortable then you have ever felt in your life.'

The muscles in Amy's arms and hands visibly loosened, her legs became more docile and supple upon the sofa. Now it was time to deepen the trance and test the effectiveness of the session so far.

'I would like you to raise one finger when you are ready.'

The index finger of Amy's right hand rose slightly off the surface of the sofa in acknowledgement of my suggestion. This showed that my client was ready for her hypnotic state to be deepened enough to allow for an in-depth interview of her subconscious mind, an area devoid of ego, empty of conscious interference, blank of emotion, a place from where only truth should emerge.

'As you hear my voice and all the sounds around you, you will feel more and more relaxed. You will react positively to all the suggestions I give you. You are standing at the top of a staircase with ten safe, wide stairs leading down. I will ask you to go down the stairs, and with each step down you will feel more and more relaxed.'

Now was the time to introduce a scenario in Amy's mind, to make her engage totally with the images implanted by my suggestions. By doing so, I could ensure that she responded positively to my requests for information about what had happened to her. Amy King lay motionless on the sofa, eyes closed, head tilted slightly to the right side, facing me.

'In front of you now you can see a wide hallway with a few doors to the left and right of you. At the end of the hallway is a door with a dull light above it. That is where we are going. So start walking down the hallway. Each time you pass a doorway you will go deeper and deeper into sleep.'

I lowered the tone of my voice, slowed down the delivery of my words, placing emphasis on every suggestion delivered to the entranced subject two feet in front of me.

'When you get to the door with the light above it at the end of the hallway, I would like you to let me know. You might want to raise one of your fingers, you might want to tell me you are there.'

After a short delay, Amy raised her right index finger to signify she was ready to undertake the next stage of her hypnotic journey.

'Okay, that's good. This is the front door to your house. Behind this door is your safe, comfortable home. All you need to do is to open the door and walk inside, so when you are ready, you will enter your home and walk into the lounge area. Do that now.'

'It is last Friday night. It is late in the evening. As you enter your lounge, you are aware that everything in this room is exactly the same as it was then. What are you doing now Amy?'

'I have made a piece of toast and some coffee. I am walking into the lounge to take my next call.' Amy's voice was barely audible, slightly slurred by the deep sleep state she was experiencing.

'That's good. That's very good. Then what happens, Amy? Tell me what you did next. And remember, Amy, that everything that you see and feel is not real. Everything you will see as if it is a movie, you can watch it all at a distance. So just tell me what you see Amy.'

'I sip coffee. It is too hot. I place it on the floor. I pick up my laptop. My next character is on the screen. I am a doctor.'

Amy's voice changed perceptibly. She sounded younger, she sounded more enticing, more evocative. Her words had a softer tone and were drawn out.

'And what would you like to do tonight?' Amy said, her speech slow, soft, sexy.

'Who are you talking to on the phone, Amy?' I asked.

'A customer. He thinks I am the girl on the screen,' her voice returned to normal.

'And what happens then, Amy?'

Amy put a hand to her neck and moved her head around a little, stretching it up gently, moving it left and then right.

'Throat getting tighter. Trouble breathing. I am being pinched inside my throat.'

Amy King started to wheeze, drawing breaths in bigger gulps. I could hear Judy Marchant shifting in the chair behind me.

'What is happening?' Judy asked. I turned to face her.

'It is okay. She is just becoming aware of the beginning of the attack. She will be okay. Promise.'

I returned my attention to the subject before me.

'Remember, Amy, you cannot feel anything. You can come to no harm. You are just watching this scene play out, like a movie. So watch and tell me what happens,' I urged.

'It's hard to breathe. I am coughing. I can't get up. I'm being pressed into the chair. I want to get some water. I am trying to get up from the chair but I can't. I can't move. Help me. Please help me, I can't move. Help me.'

A tear began to well up inside Amy's eye, ready to trickle down her cheek.

'You are just watching this all play out before your eyes, Amy. Nothing can hurt you,' I said.

'Something is inside me. It is cold, very cold. I can feel it inside me. Get this thing out of me, get it out.'

'Go on, Amy. Tell me what you feel,' I said encouragingly.

'Stop it now, it's too much for her,' Judy urged.

'No,' I replied sternly. 'We must find out more.'

'It looks like diamonds, it is so bright, so beautiful. I know this place,' Amy King said.

'Where are you, Amy? Tell me where you are?'

I was surprised at the complete shift in the experience of my subject. I had never before known a client to change their focus so suddenly, so dramatically. Amy had detached herself from the attack to somewhere unknown, somewhere not suggested by me. All my clients should ever see or experience in trance is directed by me. There can be no other influence that can affect a hypnotic trance.

'We did not travel. I am just here. It is light, it is pure white light.'

'We? What do you mean Amy? Can you explain who else is there with you?'

'Oh,' Amy replied. 'It is not a who.'

'What is it Amy? What is there with you?'

'I don't know, I can't see it, but I know it is here. It is waiting.'

'What is it waiting for Amy?' I asked more urgently this time.

'It is waiting for me, and it is waiting for you too,' Amy moved her head so she was facing me more directly, 'I can see through its eyes now. It wants to change something, it wants to overcome,' Amy continued.

'Amy, tell me what it wants to change,' I ordered.

'It wants to change the status quo,' Amy King frowned as she continued. 'It wants to create freedom, to free all from oppression. It wants to create harmony and integrity. It is so beautiful inside, but there is something else deep inside. There is a darkness. I cannot see it, but it is there, because it has to be. This is the only way.'

Amy King now showed fear on her face, it was etched into the creases of her eyes.

'What in God's name is going on?' Judy demanded, rising to her feet.

'Amy, you are just watching the movie. You must continue, you must tell me what you see. You are safe, you are protected.'

'I am not protected. Nobody is. It can get inside. It can destroy. It is so very cold. It is icy. It wants change, but there is only one way. Only through destruction can construction begin again. Only by burning old bridges can new crossings be forged. I see fire now. Oh no, the beauty of this place is being destroyed. Fire engulfs everything, obliterating all else. It is here now, and it demands attention. It needs help to accomplish its goals, it needs you more than anything else.'

Amy King's voice lowered into a snarling growl. She opened her eyes wide. They were bloodshot, a fiery red colour. I saw the face of our adversary in her eyes. Razor sharp teeth, too few to be human. Sunken cheeks, glowing red eyes. Skin grey and dead. A swirling blackness inside the eyes that was full of malice and deceit.

'Amy, you must tell me, what is this thing?' I demanded of my subject.

'You know fucker,' the Amy thing growled in a deep, gravelly voice that was full of menace. 'Let me in. I will prevail.'

I shifted backwards violently in my seat at the sight projected before me. Amy bolted upright so sharply that the sofa shook on its feet. Amy looked me in the eyes and ever so slowly, they started to close. Her eyes filled with tears that began cascading down her cheeks. I rushed to her and swept her into my arms.

'What is going on?' Judy's incredulous voice drew nearer to us.

'It's okay, Amy. You are safe. It's okay.'

I did not believe the truth of what I had just said, and it was doubtful the two other people in the room would believe me either.

पञ्चदश

The rest of the morning was quiet. Very little was said on the drive to Judy's home. Judy asked three times about the visions Amy might have had, and what I saw during the hypnosis session. Each time I replied that undertaking a hypnosis session is very tiring, particularly when it is as tense as it was with Amy. My little white lie worked to quieten all talk, allowing me to gather my thoughts and relax as best as I could. No matter how distressing, no matter how shocking my earlier experience had been, I sat in the car in a numb kind of daze. Very little entered my mind, and very little left it. I paid no heed to our direction of travel or what happened in the world outside the glass in the car door.

When we arrived, Judy asked me in for a coffee and I agreed. My thoughts started to run normally again by the time we mounted the steps to the front door. Judy got her keys into her hand and inserted one and turned it in the lock. The door opened easily.

'I don't want to be alone at this time, Judy, thanks for asking me over,' I said as I entered her hallway.

'No problem. I could do with a bit of company myself. And anyway, you have some explaining to do.'

She dropped her keys into a small china dish at the entrance to the kitchen, and began getting the cups and ingredients ready to make the coffee. I rather absently entered the lounge and sat on the sofa facing the hall doorway. Within five minutes, Judy had entered the lounge with two mugs of coffee and a small plate of biscuits balanced on her right palm. She sat on the sofa and placed the coffees and biscuits on the small table in front of us.

'What did you see?' Judy Marchant asked.

'I am not sure what it was, but it was ugly. It was grey with sunken features and razor sharp teeth,' I replied.

'Like a demon,' Judy suggested.

'Maybe it was a demon. But what puzzles me is that demons do not usually show themselves, if indeed they exist at all. I am not one of those people who believe in heaven and hell, and I do not see how a demon can fit in with my idea of a spirit world. I believe that demons exist in people's minds, that there are personal demons. However, I am quite sure that positive and negative energies exist. In everything there must be a balance. Light and dark, night and day, good and bad.'

'So where would evil exist if not in a place you don't believe in, in a netherworld?' Judy asked.

'That is another issue. Turn the word evil around and it spells live. So to me the word evil is meaningless; it is just a positive word turned on its head,' I explained.

'Okay then, let's call it bad, or negative, or anything. Where does the opposite of good exist?' she asked.

'To my mind there is only one place it can exist, and that is on planes of existence that vibrate at a lower frequency,' I answered.

'Excuse me? I don't understand,' Judy exclaimed, searching for greater clarity.

'Many people believe, and science can prove, that different things vibrate at different speeds. These differing speeds are indicators of the energy contained within each thing. People believe a rock is inanimate, but it is not. If you look at a rock under a microscope, you will see the slow movement of particles making up the rock. You are aware of the particles of a human being, and how the different subconscious mechanisms within us each contribute to the whole. The faster moving elements inside a human being show us to be alive. These elements contribute to our life energy. But even inside a human being you will find particles moving faster than the rest. Our thoughts, the reactions we have to danger and other events, these are much faster movements than the ones that drive our basic living functions. These faster movements are much closer to the energies used by spiritual essences in their own realms of existence. Our energy is created by the sugars, carbohydrates and other sustenance we get from our diet. Maybe a dark, energetic form is fed by a human's negative feelings and actions. So while a darker, negative energy might be made of the same stuff as its spiritual counterparts, it cannot exist there, because there is no fuel to sustain it. There is no desire for negative energies, or vibrations, in the spirit world. But there is plenty of fuel for these negative energies in our world. That is my theory, and it can only ever be a theory, because it cannot be proven.'

'So what was this demon that visited you and Amy today?' Judy asked.

'As I said before, I am not sure it could be called a demon. From what I understand of the subject – and I am no expert – negative energies can take any form they choose to. It might just be that what I saw in Amy's face was what she herself might perceive a demon to look like. I am not even sure that the energy I came into contact with was a negative energy at all.'

'How can you say that? You jumped back in your chair when you saw it and poor Amy started growling, then she screamed as if hell itself had visited her,' Judy said, convincingly.

'I say that because I must make a judgment about what happened based on my own feelings about it. I must use my own instinct. To me, the entity that visited Amy today was undoubtedly the same one that attacked her last Friday, but there is an underlying driver behind all that has happened, there has to be. Until I find out how all these incidences are linked and for what reason – to what end – I cannot possibly make any kind of a judgment on what I see or experience,' I said.

'So are you saying that what Amy King experienced on Friday and also what happened this morning might, in fact, be projected by Amy herself? And this projection, in whatever way, and however it shows itself, is using certain people to reach an as yet unknown goal?'

'That is exactly what I am suggesting, yes,' I replied.

Judy did not completely cover the theoretic reasoning, or the conclusions, I was reaching now, based on all that had happened, but it was close enough. For some reason my thoughts always came back to what might be at the end of this path, rather than at the beginning. What might the intended end result signify, on earth and in the spirit world? Some psychological and physiological exploring of events would be useful at this time. The problem was that there was very little to explore.

'This energy is clearly of sufficient power to create physical changes in people's bodies that cause death. It is undertaking a plan to create an unknown outcome, the like of which must, of course, create beneficial outcomes for itself. And I have an idea that this energy requires our input, some human interaction, to achieve its goals. It also strikes me, if my meditative experience is to be believed, that certain senior energies in the spirit realm know a lot more about this than they have so far let on to me. What I don't understand is why both sides in this struggle require me to interact with them to conclude this matter, one way or the other.'

***

Les combed what was left of his hair. As he looked into the mirror, he reflected on how some years ago he had hated guys who combed their hair over their bald crowns. Now he had no choice. He could not shape his hair; he could not curl it. He could do nothing but drape the loose strands over the baldness that cursed his life. Les had a contract to drive a bunch of schoolgirls to a netball match. The journey each way was eighty miles or so - a bit of main roads, motorway, then main roads again. A straightforward job, the best type. As a bonus, he got to watch the netball match from the car park. Les was fifty-four years old and it never harmed anyone to watch nubile bodies jumping about and exerting themselves physically, especially in those tight, short navy blue skirts they wore. If Les was ten years younger, and if he had a full head of hair, he still might have been able to grab some flirtatious female attention during the trip.

The netball party was sixteen strong. Not too many, but not too few to make a few bob on the trip. The noise on these journeys could sometimes aggravate and annoy, particularly on a longer trip, and especially with drunks or old people who want to sing decades-old songs badly out of tune. Drunk groups laughed loud, talked loud; they even farted loud. On longer trips, Les was able to block out the annoying surroundings by humming to himself and concentrating solely on his driving. He made mental markers of the percentage of the journey he had so far covered, and of how far he had left to go. He split the mileage into five or ten percentage chunks, and watched the milometer on the Transit minibus as it ticked away the distance to his pay cheque.

Les was married for two years in his twenties, but at that time he was driving trucks and the schedule did not allow him much time with his wife. It was okay driving trucks. The pay was good, but it was a laborious job, travelling the same roads all the time. Even foreign jobs lost their appeal the twentieth or thirtieth time you ran them, day in and day out.

Since his marriage was repealed, Les had no need for a long-term relationship; he preferred the relationship he had with his right hand and the freedom of aloneness in the daytime. He had many relationships with women at home and abroad, but found it easy to duck out if the relationship in any way got sticky or showed signs of dependence. He did not have children and did not want any. His brother had two children, which suited him just fine. When the kids came to see Uncle Les, they were gone in an hour, allowing him to then get on with doing his own things, in his own time.

Today Les would do his hours on the road, take his pay and then get back to his life. Les had only ever remembered being independent; he never had a wide circle of friends. People came into his life and left just as quickly. All were acquaintances, not friends.

Les tightened the red tie around his neck, straightened his collar and brushed down the front of his corporate grey jumper. He rubbed the top of each shoe against a calf and then pulled the hair across his scalp one last time, before departing for work. As he pulled the door shut to his home, he was whistling. Les had never been able to whistle properly, it was more like breathing through the taut circle made by his lips, and it came out like a high-pitched wheeze. But at least it was an indicator of his contentment with life.

***

'What did Amy mean when she said 'Let me in. I will prevail?' Judy asked.

'I don't know, but I would guess, from the tone of her voice when she said it, that this entity, whatever it is, made that message come out through Amy's mouth,' I replied.

'And did you hear her voice? It was weird, deep and gravelly. It did not sound like a man – more like an old lady with a bad smoking habit.'

'It is more than likely that Amy was not consciously or subconsciously aware of what was being said at that time.'

'Do you mean that she was possessed?' she asked.

'I don't believe in possession, not in the movie kind of meaning of the word. But it could be that some part of Amy was manipulated, or used, by this entity to deliver a personal message to me. I don't know why that would be. Hell, I have no idea whatsoever why on God's side they want me working with them, and then in opposition is this other force that also needs my help. I just don't understand what is going on,' I replied.

'And why did you see this "demon" and I did not?' she asked.

'This is why I doubt that Amy was possessed. When an entity separate from the subject possesses a person, what is said or done is just a show of power. You remember I said that dark entities feed on fear? Well, a possession is a show of power designed to generate fear, and so further feed the entity in possession. But what happened to Amy was more focused than that; it was a message primarily directed at me. That is why I believe that I saw what was projected through Amy's facial features, and you did not. You were aware of changes in Amy, but not of the content of the projection. It was obviously a message to me, and probably designed to make me become more involved in what is happening,' I replied.

'But for what purpose? How can you, as a human being, become involved in what is essentially a dispute concerning spiritual entities? What role is it that you are supposed to play? And how have I been dragged into all of this?' Judy asked.

'I don't have any answers at this moment in time, Judy. I wish I did. But that is hopefully what we are going to find out,' I answered.

'But you were the one doing the hypnotising. You were in control, right?'

'While in trance, Amy was whisked away to somewhere I did not take her. That is extremely unusual, but not unknown. In most cases, a subject is taken to places only at the instigation of the therapist. This is done so that a subject trusts the hypnotist at a deep level, which should lead to Amy successfully following any positive suggestions given to her. This is where most hypnotherapists fall short of the high standards of service they should provide to their clients. They get lazy. They already have a good marketable reputation, so they feel they don't have to try too hard anymore. They fail to ensure that the trust, built up between themselves and their subject, is sufficiently strong to enable the positive outcomes requested of the treatment, to be fulfilled. In Amy's case, the trust between us was there. She was able to fully explain what happened that night, she knew what the Amy she watched was feeling, she knew the struggle that ensued,' I replied.

'Even so, what was there was able to pull her away from you, almost as if it could do what you were doing but more boldly, more vehemently. It took her over,' Judy declared.

'Yes, it did. But why did it not do that last Friday when it attacked Amy? Why did it not finish the job? At no point was Amy acting as if she was possessed, until after she recalled being attacked. That suggests to me that the entity did not join with Amy on Friday night, although it still managed to hurt her. The projection through Amy, controlling her actions, only happened when we were there earlier today.'

'And what happened to you on that Friday night? This entity, this thing might not have taken over Amy, but it sure as hell seemed to take over you. How else did you know what was happening to Amy, how to get to her house? And how did you know to bring that machine to save her?' Judy asked.

'I don't know, Judy. Whatever this thing is, it is powerful enough to affect different people in different ways. It can announce what it is doing, or it can act in secret. It can leave traces of what it does, or it can leave nothing. It can tell us what its plan is, or it can choose not to. It has certainly acted intelligently enough to get around whatever security measures might be in place in the spirit realm,' I answered, with no answer at all.

'From what you say, it seems as though we are at its beck and call. And like a serial killer, it will only stop killing people if it becomes complacent, or when it wants to stop,' Judy said.

'I don't think this is simply a killing spree. If it were, there would be no need for this entity to actively seek out our attention. It is more likely that killing people is just a part of a greater plan. Causing death just might be a catalyst to further actions. But it does not seem to me that death is its aspiration. There is something much bigger, much bolder, that it wants to achieve,' I replied.

'Is it playing with us? Is it using us as puppets for its own ends?' Judy asked.

I did not reply. I was considering at some deeper level the implications of what had happened to Amy King when she was alone in her lounge, against what happened when Judy and I were present. I did not think the entity was playing any games; that would just go against the warnings given to me in meditation. It would also conflict with the apparently perfectly planned and carried out attacks it had so far undertaken.

I had no doubt that, had it wanted to kill Amy King, it would have done so. But why did it spare her? Did it plan to attack Amy and let me know, so I would arrive on the scene, save her life, and then confront Amy about what happened? In that case, had the entity also planned for me to confront it at the same time? And what of the escalation in its actions? The first two deaths I knew of, but I had very little other knowledge to go on. But now I am involved much more deeply, as if I were being drawn into its net. And I had taken the bait – hook, line and sinker. In this scenario, it would make sense that Judy Marchant also had an important role to play. Is that why I had very little on the first two murders, just so that I would hook up with Inspector Marchant? It all seemed too planned, too succinct.

षोडश

'So how do we go about chasing a shadow? This entity, whatever it is, has no physical substance. It does not leave fingerprints. It cannot be seen, it cannot be smelt, it cannot be tasted, it cannot be touched. We have no senses capable of tracking it down, let alone stopping it from carrying out any more killings,' Judy said.

'There is one sense we can use. Our intuition, our psychic ability, our subconscious mind. Don't forget that this is the only channel through which this entity can travel. It does not travel physically. It, too, cannot touch, smell, taste, or see, physically. So really we are on a level playing field,' I replied.

'But this is what it is used to. It exists in the spiritual realm, so this is what it knows. It only has to do what it does minute by minute, day by day. The entity that might be responsible for the four recent deaths, and the attack on Amy King, only has to do what is familiar to create physical outcomes here on earth, resulting in death. We can track and stop criminals, because they are the same as us, the only difference being that they choose not to follow the same rules and regulations as law-abiding citizens. But how do we chase something we know nothing about?' Judy asked.

'We don't chase it. We follow it,' I said.

'I don't understand. You don't just follow criminals and try to catch them in the act. They would just go on to do more and more crime,' Judy replied.

'But this is not a criminal, not in the normal sense of the word. We will never catch it from any physical evidence left behind. So far as your colleagues are concerned, no crime has been committed. It is undetectable. It acts under our normal physical radar. We have no choice but to follow any leads it gives us, and it seems to be leaving us psychic leads because it wants to, for some reason it needs us to become involved in its scheme. So the only way we can stop too many people dying, is to follow those leads and gain greater insight into this entity, and its true purpose.'

'Too many killings? It sounds as if you are convinced there will be more,' Judy said.

'Oh yes, I know there will be quite a few more, at least until we know enough to tackle this problem head on,' I replied, too confident of the comment to feel any ease.

***

Linsey Matthews waited with the other girls in the assembly hall. Miss Malvern, the head of physical education and netball coach, was scurrying around pulling canvas bags of balls and team kits into the centre of the large room. She was assisted by Angie Davenport's mum. Angie was not a member of the team, but a supporter who travelled regularly on such trips. The school sent five girls, including Angie, to support the team during matches. It was a day out of the classroom for them and they didn't even have to break sweat. Kelly Grosjean was trying to look as if she was helping Miss Malvern and Angie's mum, but really, she was doing nothing useful at all.

'Hey, Snout,' Pinky called over to Linsey, who was sat on the floor cross-legged, maybe six feet away. Linsey turned her head to face her enquirer, 'we saved a seat for you on the bus.'

'Shut up, Pinky,' Marta replied, giggling.

Marta looked at Linsey, and she winked. Linsey then looked down at the dust on the hall floor. She did not want to get involved in any of the petty chit-chat and backstabbing that happened on these occasions. She preferred to play the game, shoot the points and keep herself to herself. Another reason she looked to the floor was to hide the hot red blush that flashed across her cheeks.

Kelly and Angie joined the girls as Miss Malvern and Angie's mum completed the task of gathering together all of the equipment and preparing it to go on the minibus. Most of the girls around her were giggling, talking in that oh-my-gawd way, and being girly. Linsey was keeping to herself, pre-playing her shots for the regional final, thinking about how bad it would be to return home, win or lose, and thinking of that Marta wink.

'Girls, girls,' Miss Malvern demanded attention, 'the minibus is here, it's time to go.'

Miss Malvern and Angie's mum each dragged a canvas bag towards the double doors that led out of the hall and to the small car park. The other bag was dragged by Sinead and Lucie, another of the team supporters.

Les looked into his side mirrors as he reversed the minibus into position in front of the doors to the school. Always on time, and always seeking to run to the pre-arranged schedule for each job, Les was a driver who satisfied a great many passengers. It helped with tips, but it also helped him get home as early as possible. He stopped the minibus, put it into park and engaged the brake. He watched as the first few people opened the school doors and spilled out towards the minibus. A bus full of girls in school uniform, nice.

Les watched discreetly as each person entered the vehicle, noting certain features of merit on each of his passengers. Another perk, rarer, was on the occasions when the distance of a job was too great to be completed in one day, an overnight stay and the freedom of the night to explore the sexual treats held by each destination. Les was not averse to using a prostitute in each port. They had a job to do, maybe a family to support, and there was nothing seedy or dirty in engaging their services for a little bit of harmless entertainment. Les was not in any way deviant in his sexual preferences, and so the importance of his rendezvous with ladies of the night was not of primary interest, it just passed the time in a pleasant way. Some of the girls were nice and liked a little chat to accompany the evening's activities so, for a fee, Les was afforded female company for a short time on a no-strings basis. Perfect.

Les never imagined doing anything with his charges, and certainly not with school girls. Too many men had completely ruined their lives, and those of their families, by abandoning sense and reason in favour of a few minutes' lust. It was just not worth it. The only way to live a safe and free life was to keep temptation at arm's length. Les loved looking, but he never touched.

Linsey was last to leave the school building and last to climb up the steps and the other travellers. As Linsey entered, she realised there was only one seat left, and that seat was next to Marta.

Les pressed the button that shut the front door and locked it into place. He waited patiently for his passengers to take their seats and buckle themselves in. The lead teacher headed his way.

'All okay?' she asked.

'Yes, fine. Just to let you know, we will stop for a ten-minute convenience break sixty minutes in. We will then have another sixty minutes after that,' Les said.

'That's great,' the teacher replied.

'We should arrive about two fifteen,' Les added.

'Superb. Thanks.'

The teacher returned to her seat at the front left of the minibus, always the most sacred, privileged seat on any public transport vehicle.

Les took one more lengthy look into his rear mirror, released the brake, put the minibus into gear, pulled out of the car park and away from the school.

***

'Just what did you see, when Amy spoke to you?' Judy asked.

'You asked me that before, remember?'

'Yes, but I am really struggling to understand exactly what it is we are dealing with here,' Judy explained.

'You and me both,' I agreed.

'I can't get the image of a demon out of my head. What you claim it has done is pretty demonic. It is at least evil,' Judy said.

'I believe that certain entities create frightening or scary situations to increase the amount of negativity they can recover.'

'So what is the difference between a dark entity and a demon?' she asked.

'Well, demons exist in folklore. Stories are told of certain characteristics, powers or appearances. And you know how tales gather speed like a snowball rolling down a mountain.'

'Well, tell me again what you saw, so that I can greater visualise our adversary.'

'I saw an image of the entity that was projected onto Amy's features. So far as I am aware, spiritual entities can show themselves in any form they choose. Most commonly, during a psychic reading, a spirit will show itself in the form most recognisable to the person being visited. In Amy's case, and since this entity seemed to take over control of her trance state, it could be that the only way it could appear to me might be through how it was perceived by Amy's subconscious mind. We know Amy was brought up in the Catholic faith, so it seems logical that what I saw might be an image of how Amy perceived a demon might look. Equally, what I saw may have actually been the entity itself. After that, I saw what seemed to be conflict in the spirit realms, maybe war. Two separate factions fighting for control and supremacy. I saw the spirit realm, as we perceive it, crumbling, collapsing in flames.'

'Do you think that is the entity's aim? To overthrow the current masters of the spirit realm, the controllers, the ones that set or apply the rules and regulations? Or maybe even to destroy the spirit realm?' she asked.

'I don't know. Again, these could be either images projected through the filter system of Amy King's thoughts, or they could be actual events,' I replied.

'But you told me more than a million people could die,' Judy said.

'Yes, I did. But again, I have no parameters to go by, no guidelines. It might be true, or it might have been a warning of what might happen if I did not get involved,' I replied.

'Well I hate to be disrespectful to families of the yet-to-be-dead, but it seems like we are in this for the long haul,' Judy said.

'I would not disagree with you,' I replied.

'I have a question for you.'

'Fire away,' I said.

'What I don't understand is why you cannot make this more simple. We got a lot of information out of Amy King. We have an idea now of the plan of this entity and of how it might seek to carry out its strategies. We had nothing before we spoke to her. Why can't you talk to the victims? Surely they could relay much more information than Amy. After all, each victim would have been through the whole experience of dying through the actions of this thing, and now they would also have the extra insight gained by obtaining their spiritual form,' Judy asked.

A very good question, but one that I could answer easily.

'It's not quite as simple as you suggest, Judy. I cannot request information of individual spirits by psychic means. When receiving messages I simply open myself to any spiritual energies that might be available to me, and usually any messages are directed at the person receiving a reading from me. Despite what you might have read or heard about psychics, it is quite rare to receive insight to future events in a person's life. That would kind of go against the meaning of the whole life experience. I can't chase messages, they come to me.'

'Okay, then let me put it another way. If you sought clarification, and I mean from the very core of your everything, is it possible that you might receive some answers?' Judy asked.

'Anything is possible, but that would more likely come by prayer or meditation. But, you should also bear in mind that there is far less chance that any information coming through prayer and meditation would be accurate or helpful in any way,' I replied.

'Well, you were pretty successful in meditating on the events that consequently unfolded,' Judy suggested.

'That is true. But it is far more difficult to follow meditative leads wholeheartedly. I always doubt my experiences in meditation, but I can rarely doubt any psychic messages I receive,' I replied.

'It must be worth a try. Surely a complete, wholehearted attempt at communication might offer us a bit more than we have now, which is not very much,' Judy responded.

'I have tried numerous times since I visited you at work, looking for the way forward, looking for anything that I might be able to pursue. I have always come up blank.'

'Well, try again.' Judy pulled me back towards her by my shoulders, so that I was resting against her chest 'Try again, for me,' she said softly into my ear.

***

Marta sat on the window side of Linsey on the minibus. She pulled the striped orange curtains across the window, leaving a slit of light sufficient for her to look out on the world passing beside, and just below them. Nothing much was said between Marta and Linsey as the coach pulled away and began its journey. Ten minutes into the trip, Marta lifted the armrest between their seats, so that there was no barrier between the two girls.

Linsey could hear the banter among her fellow passengers. The noise level started low, but gradually grew in volume until, after twenty minutes of the journey, the sound of the bus radio was completely drowned out. Loudest of the voices were those of Sinead and Pinky, both telling stories of friends, film stars and singers, each one more outrageous than the last. It was at this time that Marta turned her legs slightly inwards to face Linsey. She pulled a navy blanket out of her small duffel bag that sat on the floor of the minibus.

'You want some of this, Lins? The air conditioning in here makes me a bit cold. I always use a blanket on the plane when we go on holiday. My nippies get like rocks if I don't use it.'

Marta looked up and into Linsey's eyes as she spoke, and there was that playful wink again.

'Yeah sure, thanks.'

Linsey needed to turn a little and move in closer to Marta to get the cover over her shoulder and her bum. Linsey had thought of Marta since that time in her bedroom, but in a caring and not in a sexual way. But as she sat huddled up against Marta that wink she had received again sent butterflies into her stomach and sparks of excitement into her groin.

Linsey felt Marta's hand on her leg, her fingers gently kneaded at the skin from kneecap up to the bottom of Linsey's thigh. Linsey shivered. Goosebumps rippled through her skin to the surface. She felt sure that her friend would notice, and she was a little embarrassed at that, but not at the fact that her friend was touching her, that was nice.

'You okay?' Marta whispered, her face inches away from Linsey's neck.

Linsey could feel Marta's warm breath on her skin, and that too felt good. Linsey gently nodded, too absorbed in the moment to speak. She felt invigorated, she felt jubilant, but most important, for the first time in many years, she felt loved.

Linsey's mum had become too involved with her new husband to show any attention to her son and daughter. For her brother, it seemed that his mum's attentions were unwanted anyway. He just got on with listening to his music, watching football on the television and going out with his mates. He was old enough now to look after himself and to maintain his independence, but Linsey could remember way back when he was still in junior school, when that same independent streak took precedence. By comparison, Linsey had always sought out her mother's love and approval. She did well at school, and she always felt proud to announce any achievements to her mother.

As the years went by, Linsey still felt the need to seek her mum's approval, and that is why she took up an interest in playing competitive sports. She was a good athlete and, whenever possible, she got involved in impromptu football games. But as she grew in height, it was an easy choice to turn her sporting prowess to shooting the hoops. It was three years ago that she started putting extra effort into gaining a place on the school netball team, which coincided with her mother's greater release of her parental reins.

Linsey kept away from boys to avoid her mother's disapproval and disdain. Sitting here now with her friend, she felt such comfort, not only in her newfound sexual interests, but also in the fact that Marta was female as well as in the knowledge that she could maintain her self-imposed moral values. Boys could get you in deep shit, girls could not.

Marta gently reached over and pulled Linsey's right hand into her left and proceeded to gently stroke at it with her fingertips.

'Marta, I have been meaning to ask you a question,' Linsey said breathlessly.

'Go ahead.'

'Have you ever done anything with a girl before?'

'Not just with a girl, I have done it with a woman too.'

Marta moved her right arm to embrace her friend, deliberately brushing at Linsey's breast as she did so, causing Linsey to shiver. She gently undid a button on her blouse, and then another, allowing access to the skin beneath. Linsey breathed in sharply. The small navy blanket was a light, but effective, cover for what was happening underneath.

'What was it like? I mean how did it feel?' Linsey asked through clenched teeth.

'It felt wonderful.'

Marta traced her fingers around the outside of Linsey's bra before slipping them under the fabric and moving them gently across her breast.

'It felt just like that,' Marta said as she continued to manipulate Linsey's skin.

'Would you show me, I mean properly, when we get back?'

Marta removed her fingers from Linsey's breast, and cupped her friend's hand.

'Of course I will. I think it is time that you gave into the pleasures of your body. Is that what you would like?' Marta asked.

The rest of the minibus was still enveloped in banter. Luckily, most of the party had congregated towards the back where the best seats were, and the loudest girls always sat there. Linsey rapidly nodded her head.

सप्तदश

'So what now?' I asked.

'Now we go and catch that son of a spiritual bitch,' Judy replied.

'And how do we go about that?' I asked.

'I drive you home. Then you settle down and do some deep meditation. Contact those dead guys. Who knows, you might even be able to chat with this entity and ask what the fuck is next in its grand evolutionary plan,' she replied.

I walked to the front door. Judy released the lock and pulled the door open. I remember thinking as I stood hesitantly, should I kiss her? Hug her? What do I do? Judy rubbed my back and my legs automatically carried me beyond the threshold of her apartment. As we left her apartment, she locked the door. We walked to the car, entered it, belted up, and continued our conversation.

'Judy, I have a question: Why no boyfriend or marriage?'

'How do you know I don't have a boyfriend or a husband?' she asked.

'No ring and no obvious signs of any male presence in your home,' I stated.

'Maybe this Inspector thing is rubbing off on you,' Judy replied.

'Are you avoiding the question?' I asked.

'I have a good career. I don't want any complications. I can fuck when I want to, I don't have any baggage. Maybe I don't need a ring or smelly guys' underwear draped over my chairs to be content,' she explained.

'Yeah, that's fair enough,' I replied.

The journey was quiet after that, and over too quickly for any meaningful deep thinking.

'We got work to do, we better crack on with it,' Judy said matter-of-factly, as the car drew up to a halt outside my home.

'Yeah, I know. I will get onto it.'

'See you later, big boy. Let me know straight away if you pick anything up. We need to press the pedal to the metal if we are going to change the world,' Judy said.

I leant forward and kissed Judy Marchant on the lips, before I turned away to leave the car.

***

Sinead Jones was waiting for Linsey at the bottom of the minibus steps. With backpack across her right shoulder, Linsey sidestepped off the minibus. 'Nice journey?' Sinead asked, winking at Linsey.

'Yeah, good,' Linsey replied with a broad smile pulling at the sides of her mouth.

'Need you in your best form today,' Sinead said, faking a shot at the hoop.

'No problem with that,' Linsey replied.

Marta was respected by all in her year at the school. Even some younger and older girls greeted her when she passed them. Marta was not in any way different from other girls at the school – unremarkable looks, intellectually average, but she had a presence about her and an assurance that all were aware of, even the teachers. Linsey remembered one time an older girl had taken exception to Marta's position at the school and picked a fight. Marta slaughtered her. The girl turned up the next day with scratches on her face and two fingernails missing. She came straight to Marta that morning, greeting her and shaking her hand, the generally accepted greeting of a beaten opponent. Marta was unmarked and totally unfazed by the incident. Word spread quickly around the school, and Linsey felt sure her friendship with Marta, in all respects, was well known, so it would be no surprise if Linsey were now afforded the same respect as Marta everywhere she went.

Marta followed off the minibus and immediately threaded her arm through Linsey's. They walked together towards the sports complex. The smell of freshly cut grass assailed Linsey's nose as she strolled with her friend. Pinky skipped past the two girls to the door. Always needing to be the first for everything, Pinky made a point of opening the door for all to enter the building.

'Let's get to it,' Marta said as she entered the reception area.

'I thought we already had,' Linsey said softly, hand cupped beside her mouth, giggling.

***

Les pressed an application on his phone that opened the Internet. He did not need Google, since Les knew exactly what website he was looking for. His favourite free porn website offered good quality excerpts that showed the full Monty. They had great scenes, and had a particularly good variety of

Les's favourite, schoolgirls. Obviously, the girls on the videos were never under eighteen years old, but most were obviously chosen for their small titties, short height and young-looking faces. These girls could very easily be mistaken for fourteen or fifteen years of age, sometimes even younger. Les ignored the disclaimer statements at the start of each film excerpt, for fear of spoiling the fantasy. He had some time before the girls ran out on the pitch for their game, so why not enjoy himself while he waited. Les's phone rang, just as a blonde-haired girl in pigtails was having her face forced into the open crotch of a huge-breasted teacher.

'Hello?' Les reluctantly answered.

'Is that Les?' asked the female voice at the other end of the line.

'Yes it is, who is this?' Les asked.

'This is Alicia from the Agency. I was just calling to confirm our eight o'clock appointment tonight.'

Les had forgotten about his appointment, which was made last week when a massage therapist, or so called, was not available. And with the anticipation of transporting a minibus full of schoolgirls today he had completely forgotten his already made plans.

'I'm really sorry, but I have been called away on a job. I will not be back until well after my appointment time,' Les lied.

'Well, Amazon was really looking forward to giving you some therapy. She is available at eleven tonight if that is better for you?' the woman asked.

'No, I am sorry, this is a long trip and I will be bushed by the time I get back. I will have to cancel tonight, I am afraid,' Les replied.

'You are a good customer, Les, so I completely understand. There will be no charge. Can I propose we continue your regular weekly appointments for this time next week?' she asked.

'Oh yes, please. Thanks for your understanding,' said Les.

'Can I book Amazon again for you?'

'Only if she looks as good as her photo suggests,' Les replied.

'Oh, she is far better in real life. That is a promise,' the lady caller replied.

'Yes, please. Thank you.'

'No worries. Have a nice day, Les.'

'Thanks, I know I will,' Les replied.

***

The game did not go according to plan. Linsey's team lost by fourteen points, a mile in netball terms. The other team were bigger, stronger, more bullish. Linsey herself had been knocked to the ground numerous times and

Pinky, their normal solid-as-a-rock midfielder, ended up chasing shadows all afternoon. Sure, everybody was disappointed at the end, but it was the two teachers who took it hardest of all. The success, or otherwise, of the school team, it seemed even the honour of the school, rested squarely on their shoulders.

For the girls themselves, being in the team meant time out of lessons, time and field trips. They did bond as a unit and they did play competitively, taking note of all the technical aspects of the sport highlighted in their training sessions, but this was secondary to the freedom afforded by the benefits of being on the team. Everybody piled onto the minibus, sitting in the same seats as on the outward journey. The atmosphere was downbeat; conversation occurred in hushed tones and was sporadic. There was no blaming of any individual players; it just seemed that the team they played was in a league of their own, sharper, more consistent, more physically dominant. Linsey took hold of Marta's right hand, her friend did not turn away from the window but she did reply likewise at the touch of Linsey's fingers.

On the return journey they stopped at a motorway service station. Most of the girls sat at a table, two or three in a group. Linsey sat with Marta, Kelly and Pinky. She tapped the plastic spoon at the ice cream in the plastic cup absently, moving it around and occasionally flicking her tongue at the melting liquid from the spoon. Linsey shivered and sharply lifted her line of sight from the table. She looked left and right, seemingly searching for somebody, or something.

'What's wrong, babe? You look like you have seen a ghost,' Marta said.

'No I am okay, really,' Linsey replied, as she continued to look into the distance.

'You shivered,' Pinky said in between sips of diet cola, 'that means someone just walked over your grave.'

'Is that true? Can someone walk over your grave, even when you are alive?' Kelly asked absently.

'Kelly, it is a saying. It just means someone gets a creepy feeling,' Janet Perkins answered.

'Yeah but, it must come from somewhere. It must mean something, Pinky,' Kelly continued.

'What it means, moron, is that Linsey had a ghost enter her, and when a ghost goes inside you it is preparing you for death,' Pinky explained, wiggling her fingers and doing her best to make ghost-like faces at the group.

'Better than having Mark Jones inside you, eh Pinky?' Kelly replied.

'Oh ha, ha, ha, very droll,' Janet Perkins replied.

She scrunched up a napkin and threw it at Kelly, opposite her.

'It's alright,' Marta said to Linsey, rubbing her back gently.

Linsey nodded, and continued tickling the ice cream with her plastic spoon.

***

I lifted the phone and picked out Judy's number from the contact list. The ringing tone played for a couple of seconds before she answered.

'Judy, I have a strong feeling that the entity is on the move again,' I said.

'Okay, where?' she asked simply.

'I am not sure, but it is about forty minutes or so away,' I replied.

'So it's on its way to us. Can we not wait until it gets here?' Judy asked.

'No. Something will happen on the way. We have to go now. Are you free?'

'Not really, I'm working,' she replied.

'I can go on my own, but it would obviously be better, and safer, if we go together,' I explained.

'Okay, give me ten minutes to get there,' Judy said.

'No, I think it would be better to take my car. You drive. I'll pick you up.'

***

Les blinked as he drove the bus through the petrol station at the motorway services area. The sun was rapidly lowering, glowing orange in a clear blue sky. With three hours yet until sunset, Les knew he would be home before the night sky obliterated any daytime that was left. He lowered the sun visor fixed to the roof just above the glass of the windscreen. He hated driving this time of day. This was the only time during which a person's perception of the dangers of driving was impaired by lengthening shadows, sun glare, trees and buildings

Longer journeys afforded Les more time to think, to reconsider decisions already made and maybe to reach different conclusions. Les had a woman who he knew wanted to get closer to him. Being the type of man to shy away from commitment, Les had always kept the lady at arm's length. She was his age, and not the type he went for. She was plain looking, but she did have a nice smile and tits to die for. So Les was now balancing up the pros and cons of getting a bit closer to her. Maybe he could take her out for a meal, or a movie, and see what transpired. Who knows, maybe if she liked him enough she might get those titties of hers out.

It was a shame that Les could not keep his appointment with the Agency that evening, but he had a busload of schoolgirls to deliver back to their school. Enough excitement for one day. Les liked to plan his time well in advance, so becoming a minibus driver was a bit of a strange career choice. Being a truck driver had been a lot easier for Les. In those days, jams on the roads were rare, there were fewer roadworks and journeys could be planned within a twenty- to thirty-minute window. He got where he was going, and he had time to plan any evening activities before he started the journey.

Sex was always better for Les if he could fool himself that it happened off the cuff. The best way to do that was to book himself in for a massage before he started a journey. Finding his way to the parlour was part of the unknown that spiced up his life. Not being introduced to his masseuse prior to pressing that entrance bell was another. And now he worked from home on the minibus, Les liked having a stranger turn up at his front door once a week, with a promise to himself of a sexy massage and a blow job, hence his weekly appointments with the Agency.

Now, being only an hour and a bit away from the school, and not much further from home, Les was looking forward to some TV and his bed. Driving was tiring for Les, and living on his own, he liked his sleep undisturbed by kids and a nagging wife. Any family Les had were distant in miles, and in mind. If he was unlucky, he met some of them at Christmas; if he was lucky he would not see them for two or three years at a time.

Les touched the brake pedal as a car drew across from the right to the slow lane, ready for the next exit, but far too close to the front of the minibus's bonnet. The minibus wobbled a little before continuing on its way.

'Fucking crazy bastard,' Les whispered, hoping his passengers did not hear him. 'Sorry folks,' he added more loudly.

The minibus was road legal, but possibly not in the best condition. It was eight years old, which is quite ancient, at least so far as public service vehicles are concerned. It had small patches of rust under each wheel arch that had begun bubbling to the surface. The brakes were not too sharp, and the gearbox sometimes grated into reverse gear. But all these things were a matter for the garage. Les was used to the minibus, and how it behaved on the road, and being so regularly with the minibus, it was the closest he was ever likely to come to any long-term relationship.

***

'Where are we going?' Judy asked as she sped towards the motorway junction.

'We are heading north, just follow my directions,' I replied.

'And what exactly are we looking for?'

'We are looking for a busload of schoolgirls travelling back from some kind of competition,' I answered.

'Is that it? What kind of bus? What colour is it? How many people?'

'I don't know the size of the coach, but there are fifteen or sixteen people on board. I don't know the name of the school they are from. All I know is that they are returning from the north, so they will be on the opposite side of the road to us. When we do spot them we will need to turn around at the junction after. The people on that bus are in danger, and I hope we can get to them and warn them off the road before anything bad happens,' I replied.

'Like Amy King?'

'Like Amy King, yes,' I confirmed.

'And how many times do you think we can legitimately go chasing after these events?' she asked.

'Legitimately? I don't know. But what I do know is that these situations are the only leads we have for now. We can chase them, and hope to subvert the inevitable catastrophe, or we can ignore them and people will die,' I replied.

'What if they were meant to die anyway? If that is the case, all we are doing is subverting God's will, not stopping some psycho spiritual entity from taking revenge on God, for whatever reason,' Judy suggested.

'I think we both know, from what we have experienced, that is not the case. It seems clear that we are being led, deliberately, to where these events occur, but for what reason I do not know,' I replied.

'Serial killers leave evidence because they want to get caught. Sometimes they just get bored of the chase. How do we know this is just not some killer in life who was not able to readjust, or refused to, when he died?' Judy asked.

'Then why involve us? If human killing was their only desire why highlight what they did to two people only, why not more? And if he or she was that person, they would surely give themselves over to the leaders of the spiritual realm when they were ready. No, it seems to me that there is a link between what is going on and us, or me, to be more precise. There is a pattern. There is a link being formed with us and these events. We just don't know what that link is right now,' I suggested.

'So all we can do is follow and chase.'

'Yes. It seems we have no other option.'

My head moved rapidly, scanning the oncoming traffic to our right. I was focusing on the far right lane, the slow lane, with the thought that a coach of schoolgirls would not be raced back to their starting point at breakneck speed. I tried to keep Judy driving in the fast lane on our side to make it easier to see traffic on the other side. To be in any other lane would make it more likely that we might be shielded from the target.

Judy was driving as fast and as safely as she could, while still glancing over to the right. Occasionally she drew my attention to approaching coaches, but each time my instinct told me they were not the vehicle we were interested in. Judy's facial muscles were tense in her concentration, just as I was sure were mine, in equal measure.

I then got a strong feeling, like a knot in my stomach, which meant that we were getting close to our target vehicle. I asked Judy to slow down a little, and she quickly manoeuvred my car into the middle lane. We passed under a bridge supported by two large rectangular concrete posts, it was a walkway or small lane providing access to pedestrians, tractors, or other farm vehicles to each side of the road. I looked at the bridge as we passed. Once underneath the bridge I switched my focus back to the three lanes of oncoming traffic. I was acutely aware that the more junctions we passed, the less chance we had of finding one that would enable us to turn around, and chase the target vehicle without too much delay. We entered a long straight piece of road that looked like it stretched about three miles before the next turn. This was ideal. I could look down the small dip and also see any vehicles as we approached the next rise in the road. The next sign we passed showed an exit to be three miles ahead, just where the turn in the road was. I instructed Judy to get off at the next junction.

Finally I got a glimpse of a white minibus on the horizon. It was too far ahead to see any detail, but I was drawn to it, like metal filings are drawn to a magnet.

'It's coming, straight ahead. The white minibus,' I told Judy.

'I hope you are right, I'm not somebody who takes kindly to wild goose chases,' she replied.

'Judy, can you speed up and get ready for the next turnoff?' I asked.

'Okay. You are the boss, at least in this line of business.'

Judy remained as cool and relaxed as ever. I was sweating; my forehead was wet with perspiration. I wiped the sleeve of my polo shirt across my brow. The minibus approached; as it did so, I could start to make out its size and the speed it was travelling at. The minibus occupied the slow lane and was travelling no faster than fifty miles an hour. We approached the turnoff as the minibus passed us on the other side of the road. Scanning the windows, I could just make out girls' heads. I calculated that from this point we should be able to reach the minibus in under five minutes.

'Right, let's go. Fast as you can to the exit, then we will double back and catch up to the minibus,' I said.

'And just how do you intend on stopping it?'

'I don't know yet. I will think of something when we get there.'

Judy pulled left onto the turn off, as we reached the top of the incline the traffic lights showed red. There were few other cars around.

'Can't you step on it? We are in a bit of a hurry here, there are kids' lives at stake,' I said sternly.

'Shit,' Judy said as she put the car into gear and sped through the red light, 'you are the one who is going to be fined, not me. It's your car.'

We went through another red light and descended the feeder road to rejoin the motorway.

'Step on it. Quick as you can. We can maybe get to them in a couple of minutes,' I said.

We rejoined the motorway and immediately sped into the fast lane. We zoomed past the small amount of traffic, determined to reach the minibus as quickly as possible. I spotted the minibus in front, rising to the top of the incline in the slow lane.

'There it is. I want us to get alongside so I can get the driver to pull over onto the hard shoulder.'

'For what reason?' Judy asked.

'I don't know, I can say he has a sparking exhaust pipe, or that one of his tyres is low. Whatever I say it doesn't matter, so long as the minibus stops,' I replied.

***

On the journey back to school, Linsey Matthews sat beside the window. She opened the curtains fully, so she could watch the road and vehicles go past while remembering what had happened with Marta earlier in the day, and contemplating what might be yet to come. Marta was sleeping, maintaining her hold of Linsey's left hand as she did so.

Linsey was not looking forward to returning home. Back to the reality of sharing her dwelling with an unresponsive brother, an unloving mother and an uncaring stepfather. She had never been badly treated or in any way abused at home, but emotionally she bore the scars of knowing she could never build the loving and caring relationships with her family that she wanted. Some of the friends she knew were closer to their mums and dads, while other girls had it even worse than she did.

One girlfriend, Jill McDonnell, had once told her that four years ago her stepfather used to enter the bathroom when Jill was in the bath, or in the shower. He had even offered to wash Jill's back for her on one occasion. There was no lock on the bathroom door, house occupants were expected to know when each other were in the room. Jill did not express any real concern, but at thirteen years of age she knew it was wrong. As her stepfather got bolder in his approaches, Jill told her mother. Jill's mum immediately acted by throwing her boyfriend out of the house. He never returned. Jill thought the only reason he was with her mum might have been to get to her.

That story scared the shit out of Linsey, but nothing like that had ever happened to her, yet. She did get the attention of boys, but mostly only of a sexual nature. But Linsey had only ever been approached in a companionship way by one boy, Adrian Gillies. Adrian was a year older than Linsey. He started by talking to her on odd occasions two years ago. He never really made any move towards Linsey, choosing instead to pass by and utter a polite greeting accompanied by a smile. At other times, he pushed himself to talk at greater length, not about anything interesting, it was usually about an upcoming lesson, or about the weather. Linsey failed to find out much about Adrian, what football team he liked, his favourite colour, what music he liked. She found out nothing.

Then, on the day he left the school for good, Adrian approached Linsey and handed her his mobile phone number. He told Linsey he had always liked her, and that he would like to take her out one day. He asked if she would call him. Linsey replied that she would, but had little interest in dating the unremarkable looking lad. She lost Adrian's number; it was washed in the pocket of a cardigan two days after being given to her. There was no upset at the loss.

As Linsey looked out of the window, she noticed a silver car draw up alongside. Linsey was seated three rows back from the front of the minibus. It seemed that the passenger of the car, a man who looked in his late forties, was trying to get the attention of their driver. The man was lowering his window and looking over at the minibus; he caught Linsey's eye as the car passed. When the car reached the front, it slowed to match the speed of the minibus. Somebody a couple of rows behind Linsey had also noticed the car and the actions of the man in the front seat, and they were now talking about the strange sight.

Linsey suddenly felt an ice-cold chill envelope her body, the feeling reminded her of when she was at the service station, eating her ice cream. Her mouth started to chatter as she shivered under the navy blue cover. It felt almost like she was standing outside completely naked in icy weather. Linsey continued to watch as the man in the car leaned through the window, and gesticulated to the minibus driver.

***

I leaned through the window. At this speed, the wind blew hard into my nose, making it almost impossible to breathe. I opened my mouth and took in a large gulp of air. I pointed at the front right tyre of the minibus, desperate for the driver to take notice and pull over onto the hard shoulder. There was nothing wrong with the tyre, but I would think of what to say after the minibus driver stopped his vehicle, which, at the moment, he showed no sign of doing. I looked briefly to the front, to see the bridge we passed earlier, about half a mile in the distance.

I pushed my right arm through the window. It was immediately pushed across my face by the force of the onrushing wind. I closed my fingers around the frame of the car door and pushed myself further upwards. The seat belt tightened uncomfortably around my waist. I was aware that other drivers might be taking notice of my positioning and gesticulations.

'Come on, do what you gotta do. Hurry!' Judy shouted from the driver seat.

I started shouting at the driver and waving my right arm towards the wheel, using my left shoulder to brace against the car door. The seats in the car were low set in the cabin, so it took a huge effort for me to raise myself to a position where I could be noticed clearly enough by the driver. I pulled myself back into the seat.

'Judy, see if you can get a couple of metres ahead of him, maybe he will take more notice,' I shouted above the squalling wind.

When we were far enough advanced I pulled myself again through the window, and tried again to stop the journey of the minibus, before it was too late to save the occupants. That was the plan, anyway.

***

Les was aware that someone in a silver car had pulled alongside the minibus and was waving his arms like crazy. At first, Les thought the guy might be ready to moon the girls on-board. But then it seemed his arm-waving became more urgent, and a bit threatening. Les had no training to deal with any threats while driving a public vehicle, bus, lorry or minibus. The only threats he could imagine might be faults of other drivers, or faults in the mechanics of the vehicle he was driving. Neither seemed to be indicated here.

Les checked and rechecked all of the dials around him. Nothing was flashing and no buzzers sounded; all seemed to be normal. He glanced a couple of times at the man leaning out of the car, but could not understand what he was ranting about. Maybe he was an angry dad? It was not Les' job to check whether all of his passengers had parental approval to go on this trip, and it was highly unlikely this middle-aged crazy was an irate boyfriend either.

'What is that man waving his arms about for?'

Miss Malvern, the senior teacher on the trip, leaned across to question Les about what was happening outside his window. *Oh great*, he thought, *now I've got a crazy guy on one side, and I've got an inquisitive teacher on the other. Why doesn't everybody just leave me alone to do my job?* When the girls further back in the minibus heard Miss Malvern question the driver, more than one of them slid to the right side of the minibus to get a peek at what was going on.

Les wanted to shout out for everyone to be quiet, as forcefully as he could. He wanted the guy in the car to sit the fuck back down in his seat, and continue his journey like any other normal road user. Unless, of course, he was not any other road user. What if he was drunk, or on crack cocaine? What if he was smacked-out on heroin? Either situation could be extremely dangerous, if true. Les had been on the roads too long to say he had not seen some strange behaviour, but never, in his twenty-two years of driving professionally, had Les ever encountered this kind of bizarre occurrence. And the situation was getting crazier by the second.

***

I slid, awkwardly, back into the seat, feeling windswept, very cold, and fighting to force air into my aching throat.

'It's the bridge,' I croaked at Judy.

'What?'

'The stanchion of the bridge,' I replied. 'Look there.'

I pointed as the bridge loomed up ahead. It was the same bridge I noticed as we travelled in the opposite direction earlier.

'What are you talking about?' Judy asked, nonplussed.

'They are going to hit the stanchion of the bridge, there. Speed up, let's go. There is nothing we can do,' I said.

'No. No. We must be able to do something,' she insisted.

'Just go. Go. Go!' I shouted. 'Let's get out of here; there is nothing more we can do.'

Judy pressed more heavily on the accelerator and we sped away from the minibus. As we came closer to the bridge I thought I heard a popping sound from the inside lane. With the window open, it was almost indistinguishable from the sound of rushing air and car tyres on tarmac. I instinctively looked in the door mirror, and was just in time to see the minibus lurch towards the crash barrier in front of the bridge.

As the bridge became smaller and smaller to my eyes, the minibus leapt over the metal barrier and slammed into the concrete bridge support. Other cars on the motorway slid left and right as they braked hard. Soon after the minibus hit the bridge, we heard a loud bang. Moments later, it was engulfed in a fireball, and black smoke puffed skywards in a huge cloud. I would swear that I saw four bodies projected through the front of the minibus shortly after the impact. Judy obviously saw the accident in the rear view mirror fixed to the windscreen. She instinctively slowed a little.

'Keep going, drive, drive,' I told her. 'I want to get away from here as quickly as we can,' I shouted.

'But there must be something we can do,' Judy said desperately.

'We did the best we could. There is nothing more we can do now. What is done is done. Anyone near the crash or following on is bound to have noticed us, so I am going to have some tough questions to answer as it is,' I explained.

'Me too,' Judy said.

'You were never here, alright? It's too risky, and we cannot afford to let this stop what we are trying to do. If you want to back down now, I will understand that. But you were never here, you got that?'

'Is that what you want?' she asked me.

'It is the only way it can be. This situation is far too important for either one of us to back down now. God only knows what is yet to come. No, let me correct that, God maybe does not know what is yet to come, but it will be bad, I think we can guarantee that,' I replied.

We sped away from the scene of the accident. An accident that would grab national, as well as possibly international, headlines. Ordinarily this kind of exposure would be just the boost we needed to inject some much needed impetus into our investigation. But the circumstances in which we found ourselves, the events that had occurred, with us at the core, were too delicate and too outrageous for us to seek any kind of spotlight, or outside interest. I knew, now more than ever, how important it was that we followed this through. And I was also now sure we must do it on our own.

***

We drove on, saying very little to each other. Both Judy and I were shocked and stunned at the events that had just unfolded. To my mind, I was a little confused. Though I was sure that the minibus crash was due to the interference of this entity there did not appear to be any suggestion that it directly attacked the driver. If we were right in our assumption about the age of the killer's victims, the driver looked to be too old to be a target. It seemed more likely that the teenage passengers on the minibus were its intended victims. So did this mean the entity was now hitting multiple targets through the manipulation of the machinery transporting them? Or did this event signify that the driver, even though much older than earlier victims, could become a vessel by which the entity could strike? Either way, something struck me as very different from the first three deaths, and from the attack on Amy King.

'Are we really sure there is a common denominator in all these events?' Judy asked, obviously contemplating the same issues as I was.

'That is how it seems to me,' I replied.

'I only ask that question because this is an event you saw before it happened, right?' Judy asked.

'In a way I guess it was, but I didn't see the crash, only the threat to that particular minibus,' I affirmed.

'Right and that is what stumps me,' Judy continued.

'In what way?' I asked.

'You perceived the death of Martin Coombs, the attack on Amy King and the accident earlier today. You also knew about the two deaths six months ago. That is five separate events, but there are very obvious differences between them,' Judy continued.

'Go on.'

'Well. As for the first two deaths, we have no information on them except for the age of each victim and the place where they died. But with Martin Coombs we have an autopsy report that says he died of natural causes, albeit in peculiar circumstances. In the case of Amy King, though the attack might seem similar to that suffered by Mr Coombs, she did not die. And now the busload of kids. While we will not have a specific cause of the accident just yet, it might be safe to assume the accident was either caused by mechanical malfunction, or by driver error.'

'Yes, and?' I asked.

'Well, the only rock solid fact is that you foresaw all of these events. But maybe all you saw were flashes or images of events that were already predetermined,' Judy suggested.

'I know what I feel, that is all I can say.'

'But maybe this has nothing to do with an entity hell-bent on dominating the spirit realm, or even some kind of spiritual serial killer. You yourself told me you had foreseen events in the past, when you were younger. All I am suggesting is maybe all the issues arising now are things that you, in your heightened spiritually aware state, are somehow amplifying so that you can focus better on them, than you were able to when you were younger,' Judy suggested.

'And that sounds very plausible,' I replied, 'except for one important thing.'

'And what's that?'

'The meditation I did has played out near enough as I was told it would. Also, that meditation is backed up completely by what Amy King said under hypnosis,' I reasoned.

'Yes, but that cannot in any way be seen as evidential. Amy King could have simply responded to the suggestion placed in her mind before she went into hypnosis.'

'The only thing she was told was that four people had recently died, and we had reason to believe that what happened to her on that Friday night might be connected to those deaths. We said nothing about the possible involvement of any spiritual entity in those incidents,' I replied.

'That might be so, but I am yet to be convinced that all of this is connected. The accident today could have just been that, a nasty, unfortunate accident, the cause of which is yet to be ascertained,' Judy continued.

'As I said before, if you want out, I will understand. It is, after all, quite a monumentally nonsensical situation I am asking you to become involved in,' I said.

'And it just might be possible that this is precisely why I want to be involved. So long as my job is not compromised, I will help in whatever way I can,' she replied.

'I can't promise you that, Judy. At this stage I cannot promise you anything.'

The rest of the trip home had been quiet, and more than a little bit uncomfortable. Judy's reluctance to be fully immersed in my own personal battle with the force we faced was awkward, but understandable. Her understanding of all things psychic was, by her own admission, minimal. For her to even agree to accompany me this far was admirable, and hopefully not foolhardy. I guessed that her naturally inquisitive nature held the sway of balance in her interpretation of recent events, but how long that would last, only time would tell. Nobody knew what twists and turns lay ahead, least of all me.

**

Judy called me on the following Monday, three days after the accident.

'I heard a whisper that your car has been identified as being close to the accident. Some drivers at the scene have been spoken to, and more than one noted your number plate and stated that a passenger in your car had been in, what was described as, a heated exchange with the minibus driver, immediately before the crash.'

'I thought as much,' I replied. 'Don't worry. If someone comes knocking on my door, I won't identify anyone as having been in the car with me at the time.'

'Well, that will not be easy. If you are identified as the person communicating with the minibus driver, then how can you deny anyone else was in the car?' Judy asked.

'It was a traumatic event. People, while being honest in their recollections, might be mistaken in what they say they saw,' I replied.

'So you will lie to the police?'

'I don't have any other choice, do I? This thing must be kept under wraps and the only way to do that is to insist I was there for an innocent reason. I noticed something not right with the minibus and tried, as best I could, to let the driver know. Then I pulled away before the accident happened. And by the time it did happen, I was too far ahead of the incident to stop and help anyone,' I replied.

'Okay, if you are sure.'

'No I'm not, but that is the way it will be,' I replied. 'Do we know yet how many died?'

'Nobody said anyone died,' Judy replied, a little agitated.

'The minibus was cut in half and exploded in a ball of flames, Judy. How many died?' I asked again.

'What I hear is that twelve are confirmed as dead. Four other people received relatively minor injuries,' she answered.

'Let me guess,' I said. 'The twelve people who died were all of the schoolchildren.'

'Yes,' she replied solemnly.

'And the driver and three others, presumably teachers and helpers, were thrown from the minibus on impact,' I suggested.

'Yes,' Judy confirmed.

'And why hasn't anything been in the news?' I asked.

'The word is that the police and emergency services are trying to protect the families of the deceased girls. All that was said was that a bus crashed into a bridge pylon at that location. More information will be released soon. Then the media circus will begin.'

'Do we know yet the cause of the accident?' I asked.

'What I hear is that the front right tyre was damaged before the crash,' Judy explained.

'And what? Tell me all Judy, please,' I asked.

'The driver has a two-way radio to use in the event of any kind of problem or emergency. That was not used. Usually if a tyre deflates or blows, there is some warning. It seems in this case it is more than likely that the tyre exploded without any warning. And the strange thing is that the only debris found came from the minibus, so there was nothing found on the motorway that might account for the puncture of the tyre,' she finished.

अष्टादश

I walked to the shopping plaza, thoughts buzzing through my mind. I knew I was on the right track, so far as the untimely deaths of people in my locality, I thought I knew a little bit about how this spiritual entity intended to carry out its actions, and I was coming to a conclusion about its end purpose. What I did not yet know were the vital pieces of the jigsaw that would display the whole picture, and enable creditable, feasible and decisive action to be taken to stop this entity in its tracks.

I must refer to this phenomena as an entity, I can have no other way of referring to it. It is not a ghost, because ghosts are usually tied to one spot and replay critical events from a bygone human existence. It is not a poltergeist; it does not exist simply to disrupt the lives of human beings by attaching to an individual and displaying a prowess for making noises or throwing articles around. It might be demonic, but this idea did not sit comfortably in my reasoning. For one thing, so far as I was aware, there were no dark clouds or dark shadowy figures close to the events that took place. For another, again so far as I knew, no messages had been left on or around its victims. It is also highly unlikely that a demon would kill its prey; more usual would be for a demon to physically push, scratch or bite its victims.

Though all energy – taking a physical shape or not – has its roots in the spiritual realms, this entity seemed to be more closely linked; as though its natural habitat was the spirit realm itself. It moved with the freedom of a spirit, it communicated through the same channels as would a spirit, and it seemed to meticulously plan and carry out its attacks, as might the spiritual domain carry out its normal practices with the earth plane. But still, I could not label this entity as a spirit, since the malice it showed in carrying out its attacks should not exist in a spiritual form. It was an entity, an as-yet unidentified energy that existed in a form quite unique from all others in my experience and knowledge.

The crash of the minibus disturbed me greatly. This incident showed a marked change of direction in how the entity attacked people to meet its own ends. In this case, it had manipulated a mechanical contraption to cause the deaths of the schoolgirls on board. To me this meant that I was not just chasing down cases where individuals had perished, but the scale of attacks that could be mounted by this entity on the human population, had increased dramatically. And why only attack people of a certain age? The four people who escaped death in the minibus crash were all aged thirty-five years or more. So what was the cut-off point, so far as the age of its victims was concerned, and why? I also needed to find out for sure, and quickly, why all this was happening. What is the intended end result for each side? Was this a war for spiritual supremacy? And, more important to me, what was my involvement? Why did both the spiritual realms and the entity itself, need me to play such an important part in what was going on?

I entered the linen shop. It was time to get back to a life that other people might consider normal, to get away from the chaotic thoughts in my head. I was looking for a new bath flannel, nothing much, but it was enough to focus on something dreary for a change. I was met by a medium-sized black saleswoman. Other than one other shop assistant, the store was empty.

'Can I assist you in any way?' the saleswoman asked.

'Smells nice in here,' I replied.

'Incense. Oh no, that's me,' she said, laughing and wafting her arms around.

'In that case you smell good,' I said.

We walked to the back of the shop and I was led to a set of shelves holding bath towels, hand towels and flannels in matching colours.

'What colour would you like?' she said.

'Do you have purple?' I asked.

'No, but we have a deep violet,' she replied.

'I'm not sure what I should choose. What is your favourite colour?' I asked her.

'I like red. Red is my colour,' she said.

'Have you got red shoes? High heels?' I asked.

'Yes, I have,' she said.

'And I bet you have a short red skirt, too.'

'Yes.'

'But red doesn't match too well, does it?' I said.

'It goes with black,' she replied.

'You know, red is a sexy, but fiery colour, also quite dangerous,' I said.

The saleswoman laughed. 'So you think I am dangerous?'

'I think you are vulnerable underneath your vivacious exterior. You like to be the centre of attention, but only from a distance. What people see, and what you actually are inside, are two different things.'

'You know, you are right,' she replied.

'How old are you? And what is your name?' I asked.

'I am thirty-two years old and my name is Chloe. What do you do for a job?' she asked me.

'Well, Chloe, part of what I do is I am a psychic,' I replied.

'What do you see in me, then?' she asked.

I looked into the eyes of this woman, as I would when conducting a reading for any client. Though I had done no preparation on this occasion, I got ideas about this lady's personality, her home life, her love life. It is difficult to describe how psychic information arrives, but when I have the intention to read for someone, the information is there. It is almost as if everything about people is carried around all of the time. It cannot be hidden. It cannot be repressed. Maybe this information is carried in the persona aura of people? All I know for sure is that when I open my mind to a person, I am able to clutch and pull that information out, as if it were handed to me by them.

'You are lonely, but you are very picky about the kind of man you want around you. You are a bit of a party animal, but there is also a kind, softer side to you, that is hidden beneath the gregarious personality you show in public,' I told her.

The saleswoman looked at her co-worker who was, by now, propped onto a counter, sitting and listening to what I was saying.

'You like holidays, sunshine, cocktails by the pool, bikini, that kind of thing. But you don't get away much. In fact, you have not been on a holiday for quite some time.'

'I was just talking to you this morning about a holiday wasn't I?' she commented to her colleague on the counter, who nodded in response.

'So am I going to find someone? Will I find my knight in shining armour?' she asked.

'No, I don't think so. You want something you might never be able to find. You are a lot like me, Chloe. I see something, or hear something I don't like, no matter how small, and that is it for me. Could be something really small, like how she clears her throat, or I don't like the way she makes a mess when fixing up a coffee. Stupid things like that, they just grate on me. And then it's over. My relationships have never really lasted that long, I guess I get bored very easily, too. And that is how I see you Chloe; you are just like that,' I reported.

I picked up a pack of two mauve coloured face flannels and followed Chloe over to the checkout till.

'You got me down to a tee, that is uncanny,' she said, as she rang my items through the till.

'You two take it easy, and you,' I said, pointing at Chloe, 'reduce your man requirements, or you won't get anyone.'

***

That afternoon I heard a knock at my front door, and when I opened it, a uniformed police officer stood on the threshold of my property, notepad in hand.

'My name is PC Stewart,' he said.

'Would you like to come in? It's not too tidy in here, but it is acceptable,' I said.

'Thank you.'

I led the police officer into my lounge and offered him a seat on the sofa opposite the door, while I sat in a matching armchair, having taken some of my son's toys off its surface first.

'You don't seem surprised at my arrival, as if you were expecting me,' PC Stewart said.

'Well, it would seem inevitable following the accident that I witnessed a few days ago,' I replied.

'Yes, quite. Having spoken to a number of witnesses, it was mentioned by more than one that your car was seen immediately prior to the minibus leaving the road. Were you anywhere near the accident?' he asked me.

'Well, first, you have given me no information about the accident, nothing about where it happened, not even what day it happened. I presume that if I should fail to respond positively to this question then you might come down hard, thinking I might have had something to do with the outcome,' I stated.

'And did you?' I was asked.

'Of course not. Yes, I was there. I was on my way to see my brother,' and luckily for me, the route the minibus took would have been en route to my brother, sort of. 'I noticed this white minibus that seemed to be wobbling a bit on the road. On closer inspection it looked as if the front right tyre might be damaged. It did not look to me as if this fault might cause any accident, but I thought I should draw it to the driver's attention to the tyre, and that is what I did,' I explained.

'But we do have a statement that you were in close proximity to the minibus for quite some time,' PC Stewart said.

'No, that's not the case. It did take a while to get the driver's attention, so yes I would have been alongside the minibus, but I was only there for a few seconds,' I replied.

'We also had more than one person state that there were two people in your car, and that the person trying to attract the attention of the minibus driver was in your passenger seat. Were you with anyone else?' he asked.

'No, no. Sorry, but that must just be a misapprehension on their part, what with the drama of the incident and all that,' I replied.

'So if there was no passenger in your car, and you were driving, how then would you be able to signal to the driver that he had a fault in the tyre?'

'I honked my horn a few times. When he spotted me, I leaned across and pointed to his front tyre. A stupid thing to do, I know, when in the middle carriageway of a highway, but I was hoping that if he saw what I was pointing at, he might stop to check it out,' I answered.

'I am still not sure how he might have been able to understand what the problem was, if you were in your driving seat. He would, after all, be in an elevated position from you,' PC Stewart continued.

'Maybe you are right, but having noticed a possible fault on another driver's vehicle I think it would be my duty to at least try to point that out,' I replied.

'Yes, quite,' PC Stewart said, while noting short responses into his notepad.

'Can I ask if you know yet what might have caused the accident?' I asked.

'Well, at this early stage it does seem that the accident might have been caused by a faulty front right tyre. We are not sure what might have created the fault, since the bus company assures us that there was no fault detected before the minibus left the garage. We are then left with the probability that the fault in the tyre occurred during the journey. The one thing that bothers us is, if the fault was so major as to cause the vehicle to leave the carriageway, why did the driver not notice and pull over to check out the situation? And if he had done that, then he would have reported back to the garage. But no such report was made,' the policeman said, which was all pretty much as Judy had told me earlier 'And you said to me that you noticed a fault in the right front tyre,' PC Stewart continued.

'Yes. That is what I saw immediately prior to the accident. But it occurs to me, PC Stewart, that might not the minibus driver have braked as soon as he noticed a fault in the tyre?' I suggested.

'Yes, I would say that was a foregone conclusion,' he replied.

'Then could it not be possible that the act of braking might well have made the fault bad enough to make it fatal? Or even the act of braking in itself might be enough to make the minibus veer from the carriageway,' I suggested.

'Yes. Yes, that is a possibility. We will know no more until we get some forensics back. But thank you for your time, it has proved most useful.'

PC Stewart rose from his seated position and moved towards the entrance door. I followed him and opened the door.

'I'm always around if you need any help, but I am afraid I have little else I can tell you at this point. I do hope the occupants of the minibus were okay. When the accident itself happened I was some way away from the crash scene,' I said.

'Well, I am afraid to say that twelve of the passengers lost their lives in the crash. The driver survived, but it seems he has a head injury, so I am not sure whether he will be able to add anything else, at least at the moment,' PC Stewart said.

'Oh, those poor people and their families. If you do get a chance, please would you pass on my condolences to their loved ones,' I replied.

'Yes, I will. Okay, many thanks for your time. If we need anything else, we will be in touch,' he said as he left, boot heels clicking loudly on the hallway floor.

I returned to my lounge area and sat in the same seat on which I had answered the policeman's questions. It was fortuitous that they did not press me on the reports of me having a passenger in my car, as it would have been quite obvious to anyone else travelling on the motorway at that time that there was indeed a person leaning out of my car's window and therefore, someone else was driving the car. I was also lucky that the driver sustained a head injury that might make it difficult for him to provide a statement, which would clearly implicate me in having a much greater involvement in the events leading up to the accident than I had said. At the moment it seemed that I was in the clear. And possibly more important, Judy Marchant could remain invisible, at least for now.

It seemed that if this were an issue involving the direct influence of the spiritual entity we were pursuing, my attendance at this accident was part of its plan, and an important step in its quest to reach its end goal. But why?

***

Chloe Ohmigo got home to her studio apartment and immediately flicked off her shoes in the short entrance hall. She walked to the kitchenette and poured herself a small glass of white wine from a bottle she kept in the fridge. She replaced the cork on the bottle and put it back in the front door shelf of the fridge, before picking up the glass and walking into the main living area. Having switched on the mains plug of the television set, she used the remote control to tune into any channel that was not going to prove to be too much like hard work to follow. She sat down on her red faux leather sofa, placed her crossed feet on the small glass-topped coffee table, took a sip from the glass of wine, and sighed.

Chloe only worked part-time at the linen store, but the three days she was there boosted her income enough to allow the indulgence of a glass of wine after work, and the sensory overloaded crème-infused hot bath that was about to come. This was the bliss after the trauma of the day. Her job was easy, it was steady, but the thin heels she chose for her daytime working duties were not conducive to walking about the store for nine hours at a time.

She started her working day at nine in the morning and finished at six in the evening. When the weather was cold, her feet stood up pretty well to the constant walking and standing of the day, but when it was hot, as today had been, by noon her feet were pleading for release into a warm bucket of water.

But this was a no-go, at least until she could return home and relax in her own space, and at her own leisure.

Chloe found herself thinking about the day, and more specifically, about the man who had entered the shop for face towels. Chloe Ohmigo prided herself in being able to show a provocative, self-absorbed and confident face to the world, and not even her closest friends could guess that there was anything more to her than met their eyes. So how had this man, who had never met Chloe, walk in off the street and know her so well that it seemed he had been studying her for all of her life? He was not a stalker, at least he didn't look like one. He was dressed casually, but in a sharp way, and Chloe noticed his footwear was clean, a sure sign of someone who takes a bit of pride in their appearance. And did she really know what stalkers looked like? In any case, he seemed calmer than that, nicer than that, and actually quite a handsome man, if older was your thing. It was for Chloe.

Chloe liked to be hugged and she liked to kiss. She could get these things anywhere, but she now wanted more than that. She felt her biological clock ticking and, at thirty-two years of age, now would be the best time to find someone to settle down with. Someone who, right now, could massage away the trauma her feet had suffered today. Someone who, in ten minutes or so, would be able to scrub her back and pamper her while she bathed. Someone to get in the bath with her, whose genitals she could clean with eager fingers, and someone who could relieve that tickling sensation she always had when her skin came into contact with the crème bubbles.

The need for a man was not obsessive, at least not yet. It was, however, a thought that passed through Chloe's mind on regular occasions, is this why the psychic guy was able to pick up on it? Chloe did not read magazines; that was not her thing, as she had little interest in what was going on in the world that did not directly affect her. Chloe Ohmigo spent most of her time catching up with the gossip of her girls, the friends who she knew were always there for her. Chloe had no problems drawing people in with her external charm, wit and personality. What other people did not have, they borrowed from her. So long as they were not after any money, things were good with Chloe. She started running water into the small bathtub, adding a generous helping of her favourite soaker.

Chloe Ohmigo sipped the last of her wine and set the glass back onto the coffee table in front of her. It was a painful job to rise from the sofa. Having rested for a good few minutes, it felt as if her joints had set into a fixed position. She straightened up and stretched her arms skywards. She moved over to the bed and removed her outer clothing. As she took off her underwear, Chloe looked at her nakedness in the full-length mirror that adorned a door on the one wardrobe she had space for. She pulled at her tummy a bit, she turned, first to the left and then to the right. Chloe was content with her body. She would describe herself as medium, with a tendency for slimness. She would love to remove all her excess pounds –

what woman wouldn't? But while her arse remained good and firm, and her blackened nipples rose hard and long into the air, then she was content.

Chloe passed into the bathroom, enjoying the gentle cool breeze against her naked body as she walked. She turned off the faucet. The bath crème had foamed nicely to the rim of the tub. She reached a foot over and dipped it into the water. Perfect, she thought. She got in gently so as not to overflow the water and soak the bathroom floor. She slipped gently down into the bath and placed a rubberised pillow behind her head. The pillow gripped the end of the tub with small suction cups.

Chloe Omigho closed her eyes and relaxed as the warm water surrounded her, bubbles popping and crackling. Her muscles started to soften, her shoulders dropped a little bit, her feet relaxed against the end of the bath. Chloe Omigho fell asleep.

***

Judy Marchant wrote something down quickly onto a pale yellow Post-It note and threw it onto the floor beside her. She moved her left leg slightly to ease the sharp pain now gripping her knee. She wrote again and threw the note, another thought, another scribble, another Post-It note added to the rapidly increasing pile on the floor. With one final scribble, she removed the last post-it note and placed it on the back of her right hand. 'God,' it read. She looked at the Post-It note attached to the back of her left hand, it read 'Demon.' The words scribbled down on the notes on the floor were all those summoned in between.

Judy looked at the words on each note more closely deciding which of two piles the notes should go on. One pile represented me and the other pile represented the rogue entity. She went with her instinct, as most of the notes had little or no connection with either pile. She hoped that by the end of the exercise she would be able to find the threads that might link each attack, and some suggestions as to why events had unravelled in the way they had, and finally how each were connected with both the entity and with myself. A brainstorming session can only be used as if taking a shot in the dark, a last resort when all else has failed, and this seemed like Judy's last shot.

Judy sat on the floor and spread out the notes on each side of her. She moved and swapped some from one pile to the other, constantly looking, thinking, moving notes around. After a further fifteen minutes, she was satisfied she had brought some kind of order to the chaos. She spread the notes out on each side and read the word on each note over and over again.

Finally, she picked up the notes, five at a time, and stuck each one onto one side of a wall. She took a few minutes to move the notes around and then stood back and took in the sum total of her work. She retrieved a notepad and wrote down her thoughts on the notes stuck to the wall. She numbered each note and placed the pen on top of the pad. She sat down beside the phone and indulged in one last moment of thought before lifting the receiver.

***

When Chloe Omigho awoke with a violent start, her head was completely submerged. She saw the bathroom light above her flickering and moving as the water swirled and motioned above her. She could feel the water surrounding her, she could feel it inside her nose. She closed her throat so that the water went no further inside her. She was also aware of something else. She felt a heavy weight pressing her into the bottom of the bath.

The force she felt was focused on her chest, and it was pressing so hard that it felt like a hand with tremendous strength was forcing her down, palm first. No, it was more than that. The hand forcing her down did not feel like it was pushing her chest, it actually felt like it was pulling her down from the inside.

Chloe started to panic. Chloe wondered how long she could deny the inevitable flooding of her internal organs, along with other thoughts that zipped in and rushed out of her mind at the speed of light. The bath had two handrails, one on each side of the rim. She gripped each one tightly and pulled at them with all of the strength she could muster. Chloe was aware that panic was her enemy, so even though she found herself in a life-threatening situation, she decided she must assess the situation, with a clear and focused mind to determine her best route of escape.

Chloe decided quickly that she would not be able to lift the force from her chest that was pushing her down, so she tried with all she could muster to lift her head to try to clear the water and get a deep breath of fresh air. But the water level was too high, and she could not breach the surface. She knew that her only hope of survival was to find a way to get to the surface and get some air into her bursting lungs.

She quickly released her grip on the rails, cupped her hands and tried to lift and splash water out of the bath. At the same time, she drew her legs up to her waist and kicked them out towards the end of the bath, hoping to displace as much water as she could. She lifted her head, stretching her neck as far as she could towards the surface of the water.

Chloe felt her limbs start to ache and burn, but she would not give up. Finally, after what seemed like forever, Chloe felt her nose pierce the surface of the water. Her insides were burning now, too, her heart was pumping faster, seemingly too fast. She kicked and thrashed her arms harder than before. Her nose completely cleared the water and she took a deep, sharp, urgent breath. She continued to thrash, and soon enough, by stretching her neck as far as she could, her mouth was momentarily cleared of the bath water, she gulped in air. The pushing sensation inside her chest continued unabated.

Chloe felt, and thought she heard, too, a tremendous thud from inside her chest. *What now,* she thought. A rush of thoughts about her situation followed, about what it was that had pressed down on her, about why she decided to have a bath at all? She could have, and should have, flopped on her bed instead.

Still struggling to keep her head above water, she coughed. As she did so she felt a large blob of congealed blood fly through her open lips, the blood flew into the air and landed on her chin. She coughed again, and then again. More blood flew upwards and then landed in areas around her head. She felt blood rising in her throat. Her thoughts continued, even as her panic grew again. Soon there came a time when she could fight no more. The force with which she once pumped her arms and legs diminished, her movements gradually slowed, until she was still. As she ceased struggling, she felt the pressure on her chest release. She became aware that something else was in the room with her, something she could not see, hear, smell or define. The foreign presence was not known, but neither was it unknown to Chloe Omigho.

***

'I think I got something,' Judy said excitedly.

'Yeah, what's that?' I asked.

Since the minibus accident, I had tried my hardest to sink my thoughts into doing mundane things. Getting up-to-date with my income, and taxes from the work I had done in the last three months. Sorting out bank statements and household utility charges. Opening some of the unsolicited mail that never usually got opened at all. I had a habit of leaving tasks like this when I got my head stuck into a project. Maybe the break I had taken over the last few days would freshen me up, distance me from recent events enough to be able to take a more objective view.

'I did a brainstorming session and I think I know why this entity might be targeting young people,' she said.

'Go on,' I urged.

'Well, after the brainstorming exercise I was thinking about what you said you were told by your Guide in that meditation. You said that the reason for our physical lifetimes is to experience a multitude of situations, emotions, feelings, and that it is the experiencing of these things that is more important than the outcomes. You said out of the experiencing comes greater growth, greater knowledge.'

'Yes, carry on.'

'You also suggested that what we experience in our earthly lifetimes is fed to God, since God cannot experience these things itself. You added that we are not tested on how well we perform when faced with situations or dilemmas, but rather we are made aware of those opportunities for learning that we might have missed,' she added.

'Yes. I was told there is no judgment in the spiritual realms, that is true,' I replied.

'You also said that there is no such thing as fate, adding that signposts are planned and placed in strategic places in our lives to provide those opportunities that are likely to provide us with the greatest benefits.'

'Yes, that is how it was described to me.'

'Well. We can probably both agree that when somebody dies young, particularly as in the case of a minibus full of seventeen-year-old girls, according to the sets of rules laid out in the spirit realm there must be benefit to that outcome, both to those individual souls and also possibly to other souls greatly affected by the event. Would you agree with that?' Judy Marchant asked.

'Yes. I would agree. That sounds about right,' I concurred.

'You also said that your heavenly hosts had asked for your help in finding and stopping this entity from cutting lives short. That presumably means that this entity is interfering with the natural chain of events. I think the entity is interfering with the natural pattern of experience and learning. It seems to me these people would have had a lot more experiences, and thereby a lot more opportunities to learn, had their lives not ended so abruptly. So, what if an unexpected or unplanned death leads to the spirit realm not being ready for the deceased spirit? Might that not give an opportunity for this entity to grab its victims before they followed a more natural path?' she added.

'Yes, that seems possible. What did you conclude?' I asked.

'Well, you also suggested that ghosts or ghostly visions might relate to people whose earthly lives were ended suddenly or violently. My thinking on this could be that if such an unnatural death occurs, then it could be that the personality of the dead person might be unable to join with the part of them that resides in the spirit realm, at least until they first come to terms with their death,' she suggested.

'Well I don't know that for sure. I don't know what set of circumstances create ghostly figures or hauntings. But it is pretty much universally accepted that ghosts are those spirits that have not yet moved on to the spirit realm,' I said.

'Let's just say, for argument's sake, that you are right. Let's say that a high proportion of people unable to cross over have been involved in a violent, or otherwise unnatural, death,' Judy suggested.

'Okay, so what is our conclusion about that?'

'The natural conclusion would have to be that these souls are in limbo. Unable to cross over to the spirit world, they could be ripe to be used in some way by the entity to support its mission. What if this entity is the first thing these people encounter after they die? And what if this entity calms them, soothes them after the trauma of their death? What if the entity promises a painless entry into the spirit world, a meeting with family and friends if,' she paused momentarily, 'if these new spirits accepted its indoctrination as part of the process.'

'Okay. You could be on to something here. Maybe, by subverting the natural order of things, this entity is able to influence these souls into believing its dogma, into turning against the natural order of things by showing the meaninglessness of their recent life experiences, or to highlight the lack of opportunities afforded them during this last lifetime,' I suggested.

'And maybe its aim is to build a spiritual army capable of overthrowing the current hierarchy. To install itself as the new leader. The new ultimate creative force. The new God,' she suggested.

'I don't know if we can make any such assumptions just yet,' I replied.

'I have another call coming through. It's Dr. Anstis, the coroner. Can we carry on this conversation later?'

***

'So what have we got on this guy?' the Detective Inspector asked.

'Not much. He says he was driving past the minibus and noticed a problem with the right front tyre. He tried to alert the driver and then accelerated on ahead. The crash happened immediately after he moved off,' PC Stewart replied.

'What about the witnesses who said there were two people in the car?' asked the Detective Inspector.

'He says he was alone,' PC Stewart replied.

'I find that hard to believe, since we have two other witnesses who swear a man was leaning out of the passenger window of his car, shouting and waving his arms at the minibus driver for a good minute before the crash,' the DI said.

'Well, all we have is their word against his. We can't prove he was in the passenger seat and we have nothing on him. The crash was an accident. Nobody hit the minibus, and even if somebody in the silver car was distracting the driver, and if that caused him to lose concentration enough to crash the vehicle, that still is not enough to suggest anything other than driver error, or an accident caused by the faulty tyre,' PC Stewart said.

'Could his dangerous driving not have caused the crash? After all, he admits he was warning the driver about the tyre just before the crash,' the DI suggested.

'We have nothing to suggest that anyone was driving in a dangerous way,' PC Stewart admitted.

'It does not seem possible for someone to be driving his car while warning another driver of a danger' the DI added.

'No, Sir,' PC Stewart concurred.

'If there was a second person in his car, and our two witnesses seem pretty sure there was, then I wonder who, or what, this guy might be trying to protect?' the DI asked thoughtfully.

नवदश

The cremation of the victims of the crash was scheduled for exactly one week after the accident. A joint service was held for all of the dead schoolchildren. The number of attendees inside the church was limited to immediate family members only. Neither the two teachers with the girls at the time, nor Mrs. Davenport were in attendance. It is doubtful whether Les Scott would have been invited even if he was fit enough to attend.

The remainder of people associated with the service congregated outside. Representatives of the school, some of the closest friends of the dead girls, the school caretaker and members of the various out-of-school clubs attended by the girls were there. The number of mourners outside the chapel was swollen by near neighbours and distant relatives, and numbered close to a hundred. The crematorium ran two speakers from the chapel to relay the service to those people gathered outside. The crematorium, with costs borne by the local council, had agreed to erect a memorial stone listing the girls' names and, with the agreement of all the families involved, the ashes of all the girls would be buried in front of this memorial.

The crematorium also served as a cemetery. The entrance was lined with ageing stone monuments to long-dead human inhabitants, grass grew long at the perimeter of each memorial, while flowers, some new and some decaying, adorned the top of each plot. The police had done a good job of protecting the families as best they could. Some national spreadsheets had run stories, but though worthy of front-page space, most of the papers had restricted their coverage to middle page articles that could be easily lost in the plethora of sensationalism happening elsewhere. This was most likely through editorial choice based on police advice, rather than by the wishes of the reporters themselves.

Members of the press were stopped at the main gate, and all had respected the dignity of the event by staying there. The crematorium managers had allowed the cars of those people in the chapel to be parked within the grounds, so that they could depart with few or no interruption.

Local papers ran restricted columns, more eager for advertising income than news. The whole event, it seemed, was a sad and unfortunate accident caused by nothing more than circumstantial issues. A case of just being in the wrong place at the wrong time. That was the belief of all of the mourners, all except one.

I was leaning on a tree on a small mound of earth, far enough away from the main body of mourners, but close enough to observe the proceedings. I dressed in a dark grey suit, white shirt and maroon tie, fixed tightly under the collar. My black shoes were polished so that the late spring sunshine glinted from the toe. A soft breeze caressed my face. Perfect weather for a gathering, were it not for the sombre mood of the occasion.

The door to the chapel opened. The deceased teenagers' nearest and dearest left the small building in a slow moving line. Most were joined by other family members, friends and associated mourners that stood outside. Some mourners greeted others in different family groups. Most of the mourners headed for the newly-erected memorial in the cemetery grounds at the back of the chapel. Most of them, except for an old lady in a dark blue overcoat buttoned to the collar, navy shoes and a veiled navy hat. She turned away from the crowd and made her way towards the mound on which I stood.

Even though she was supported on either side by suited middle-aged men, her turn of pace was impressive. She approached the mound and grabbed at either of the men's arms, left and right, for added stability on the incline. I could do nothing but stand still and await her arrival. She reached me and stood as erect as she could. She lifted her veil with arthritic fingers. The man on her right spoke first.

'You have a nerve,' he spoke with a slight lisp, but his anger was clear. 'What are you doing here?'

The old lady immediately held her hand up to stop any further communication from her right side aide. The maternal power this woman yielded over family members was immediately obvious; it was also most likely that she demanded respect from all who happened to come into contact with her. The grip of her minders on each arm tightened as the old lady shaped up to confront me.

'He is right to challenge you,' she commented.

I held out my right hand in welcome, 'How are you?' but my greeting was ignored.

The old lady spoke with clarity and in a strong, commanding tone. Small in stature, her face nonetheless showed wisdom and intellect in each crow-toed line. Her frail body was seemingly out of whack with her internal biometric make up. Undoubtedly strong of mind and determined, I doubted if anyone would be able to dissuade this lady out of taking any course of action she chose. She pointed her knobbly index finger at me as she spoke.

'What did you do?' she asked.

'I don't know what you mean,' I replied.

'Of course you do. Why are you here? Are you here to gloat? Are you here to take some kind of credit for what you did?' she asked.

'I really do not know what you are talking about,' I repeated.

'You know. It is written all over your face. You know exactly what I am talking about. Do you think these people are all here for nothing? Do you really think those young lives had no meaning? Those poor young wretches, sacrificed like lambs to the slaughter, and for what? You bastard, you brought him here, you led him straight to them, you deprived all these people of the things they cherished the most. You destroyed them, every single one of them, and you condemned those poor innocent young souls to hell and damnation,' she said ferociously.

The old lady's temples throbbed, her face and neck reddened as she went deeper into her cuss. Could this old woman really know about my recent experiences? What did she know about my foe? How could she possibly know anything about how close I really was to the minibus incident? Questions about this harbinger of doom circled and spun in my head, so that it became impossible to hide the embarrassment and sense of guilt that must have pervaded my facial features.

'Excuse me, but yes, it is true. I witnessed the accident. I just wanted to pay my respects to the families who have suffered so heavily in this dark time,' I replied incompetently.

'These innocents were not the first, and they will not be the last. You carry the angel of death on your shoulder, you work your murderous plans and nobody is safe, nobody,' the old lady continued.

'I am really sorry for your loss – for the losses of everybody here and for the loss of the community, too. But I really cannot take any responsibility for what happened to those poor, unfortunate young people. Nor, might I add, should I ever wish to. I am shocked and taken aback by your accusatory tone, ma'am, which is not at all welcomed at this sad and solemn event,' I replied, my own sense of anger rising within me.

'You brought him here, you bastard. You are the one we should blame for what happened to everyone here. You destroyed those kids. You destroyed all these families here today,' she again accused me.

I would swear that as I looked deep into the old lady's foggy eyes, a red fire burned there.

'Now wait a minute...'

'He will succeed if you let him, and the wrath of heaven will be vented on all of us. Send him back where he belongs. Only you have the power to do that. Send him back, before it is too late.'

विंशतिः

Judy Marchant strode into the coroner's office.

Having already donned the light blue pinny and scrubbed her hands clean, she battled with the two extremely snug-fitting latex gloves and pushed the double doors open. She met with the sight of a cut-open black woman being examined by Dr. Anstis and his assistant under a blazing spotlight.

'Ah, Ms. Marchant, do please come on over, I have something you might be interested in,' Dr. Anstis beckoned Judy towards the dead woman.

Judy pulled down the plastic mask on her headwear and approached the lifeless body on the examination table. Dr. Anstis had cut deeply into the dead body and removed all extraneous fats, tissues and what Judy could only think of as foliage. That is how it appeared to her. The white, grey, red and purple bits and pieces were placed on the table beside the body, ready to be scooped up by the assistant and used for whatever purpose they were used for. Foliage.

It appeared to Judy as if Theo Anstis had been extremely keen to reach a certain part within the dead woman's body. It seemed that little attention had been paid to anything except his intended destination. Like a man shopping, he knew what he wanted to get at, so went straight there, did what he came to do and left, maybe even avoiding a car park charge. Maybe the coroner was eager to come across another interesting death? If he had called Judy to his latest case, then she could be sure he had found something of interest to her, and of some excitement to him.

'This lady is, sorry was, thirty-two years of age. Her name is Chloe Omigho. Local officers were alerted because her downstairs neighbour told the landlord she had water entering her flat. The landlord went into the property and found Ms Omigho in the bath. He immediately contacted the police. It might have seemed like she drowned at first glance, but there are a couple of things that immediately made me want to call you. First of all, when Ms Omigho was found the water level in the bath was below a level we might consider as sufficient for a person to drown in. Secondly, there was blood residue floating in the water and spattered in small amounts on the side of the bath, and on the floor. There was no indication of any forced entry to the property and on examination of the body, I could find no external trauma marks, nothing at all. So I must assume the blood belongs to the dead woman.

But how did it get there? If someone drowns, there would be no blood spatter. But look here,' he said.

Dr. Anstis drew Judy's attention to an organ that must have been the heart, except there were deep depressions in the organ and it was ripped at the top and in the middle. Dr Anstis cupped the heart in his hand and pointed to the lesions.

'You see here? It looks to me like the heart has split in several places, probably while the lady was still alive. This would undoubtedly have caused her to bleed out. But here, do you see these depressions?' Dr. Anstis asked of Judy.

'I see them,' she replied.

'Do you see how the depressions can be made to match my fingers? From what I can deduce, it seems to me that these tears could only have been caused by the heart being squeezed. And from these marks on the surface of the heart, it seems only logical for me to suggest that the weapon causing the death of this young lady,' Dr Anstis paused momentarily, 'were fingers,' Dr. Anstis said.

'But how?' Judy asked.

'I have no idea. I have never seen anything like this before, but isn't it fascinating?' Dr. Anstis said.

'And you called me because you believe what?'

'Well. Don't you see how similar this death is to young Mr. Coombs'?' Dr. Anstis asked.

'Not really. Yes, both died because of heart malfunction, but I see no other connection,' Judy replied.

Of course she saw the connection. It was obvious to any who might have knowledge of the two deaths, but she needed to do her best to dissipate interest in this case as much as she could.

'Squeezed from the inside. Split like a tomato. No external injuries. Fascinating, totally fascinating. Never in my years. And two within three weeks of each other,' Dr. Anstis was saying, mostly to himself.

'I really don't see the connection myself, but thanks anyway. Stay in touch, Dr. Anstis,' Judy said as she disrobed, removed her protective bodywear and left the office.

No sooner had she entered the hallway than she lifted the phone out of her handbag and dialled a number.

'There's been another one,' she said urgently.

'What happened?' I asked.

'Black woman, thirty-two years of age, local again. Seems as if the life was literally squeezed out of her,' Judy replied.

'How do you mean?'

'Dr. Anstis called me here this evening because he thinks there is a link between this lady and Martin Coombs. I told him that I doubted any link, but he seems set on the idea, because of the improbability of each death. Theo Anstis told me that this woman had her heart squeezed so hard that the skin split and it burst open, he showed me the finger indentations on the surface of her heart, I saw them,' Judy emphasised.

'And what do you think, Judy?' I asked.

'You've got to be kidding me. Of course it was our guy, our thing, whatever it is. There can be no other logical explanation, and to conclude that, is far from logical.'

'I guessed as much. Otherwise you would not call me about it, right?'

'Right.'

'You were right to try to dissuade Dr. Anstis away from making a connection with Martin Coombs. The longer we can keep this thing between you and me, the better. We have to do all we can to keep your colleagues' noses out of this for as long as we possibly can. That is the only way we can buy ourselves some time to check things out and get things moving in the right direction,' I said.

'And what the hell is the right direction? Where are we headed to? What do we have at the moment, apart from very little?'

'We have made positive strides. We started with nothing...'

'And now we have nothing, with a bit of cream on top,' Judy interrupted.

'We have as much as we can have. We have a lot more than we believe. I promise you that, I can feel it. I know it.'

'Hurray for your confidence, I just keep feeling we have to do more, much more,' Judy said.

'And so long as we can keep the police and all other public authorities out of this, the better chance we have of making some real, positive progress,' I insisted.

'Dr. Anstis is already making connections. All it will take is a few conversations between him and my bosses, and all hell will break loose. We will end up spending all our time running up blind alleys and getting nowhere. I don't think we have time for that,' Judy said.

'No, neither do I,' I replied.

'There were no external marks. How is this thing able to do that?' Judy asked.

'I guess this entity, whatever it is, can enter a human body and physically disturb, destroy whatever is inside of us. But it strikes me that this is just for show. It is trying to show us what it can do, show us its power. It is trying to show us that there is nothing we can do to protect ourselves, and there is nothing we can do to stop it doing whatever it wants to do,' I suggested.

'And at the moment it is doing one hell of a good job,' Judy replied.

'Who was she? What was this woman's name?' I asked.

'Chloe Omigho. She worked at a linen shop in the High Street.'

The phone slid from my hand and dropped to the carpeted floor with a dull *whump*. I put my head in my hands and leaned against the wall for support.

***

Jared fled the scene as quickly as he could.

The blood on his hands rapidly chilled in the cool night air. Blood spatters on his tee-shirt were mostly covered by his leather jacket. He ran fast down the thin alleyway. He knew this area well and had no trouble finding his way to the brook. He stood at the top of the risen earth pile and threw the kitchen knife into the stream. Jared reckoned it was better for him if the weapon was found. He had cleaned the handle thoroughly, removing all personal evidence, while making sure the blade retained traces of his victim. His crude attempt to dispose of the weapon will make the incident look deliberate, and somewhat amateurish, thereby diverting attention away from him. Sometimes it was necessary to divert from your usual MO, especially if the crime committed was a rarity for you. And in acting this way, Jared thought there was a good chance he would be in the clear. The landscape below him darkened as it sunk away from where he was standing, but he was still able to see the blade as it twisted and turned in the faint lighted glow from the alley above.

As soon as he heard the small splash of the plastic-handled knife hitting the water, he turned and scampered up the bank back to the alleyway. He had not been hurt in the commissioning of the crime, and he was as careful as he could be to make sure he trod on bunches of leaves where at all possible. He also took care not to touch any tree branches or other flexible obstacles that stood beside the pathway.

Jared wished he could have used a hoodie, except that had he done so, there was a good chance it would have soaked up any blood spilt at the scene. He had taken as much care as possible when planning what he did, and an important part of that preparation was choosing his clothing. Protect himself from possible identification on any CCTV cameras in the area, or protect himself from getting the victim's blood on his clothing. He thought the latter idea stood a better chance of preserving his liberty.

Jared liked to work alone, and it was work, despite what the community or the police thought. Working on his own he had no need of looking over his shoulder or feeling responsible for somebody else. He also had no fear of being ratted out or set up, a common outcome where two or more people worked together on one job. He had a young kid and a sister with mental health issues that needed supporting, and that was without the rent and other expenses he felt responsible for, so he did all he could not to risk his own safety, or his family losing their major breadwinner. Sure, Jared received state handouts, but where was the money when you needed it to buy your kid clothes, toys and cough syrup? Jared did what he could and he did what he knew to make ends meet. His wife, his mum and dad, none of them were happy with what he did for a job, but all of them were happy to see the notes land on the table come bill time.

Jared had never been a headline crook. He left that kind of stuff to the thirty years plus guys who still harboured delusions of grandeur. When they struck it rich they did it big time, but that happened very rarely. Nobody in this game ever hung up their boots, because when you got away with one, you could go on and get away with another, and another, until the old bill came smashing your door down at five o'clock in the morning.

So Jared tended to stick to small-time stuff. He had loads of connections for offloading stuff, and he used them regularly. He refused to get into drugs and steered well clear of prescribed medications – that was a route to fucking your brain up and bringing a swift end to making any kind of money and protecting your freedom. He still had to be careful, but the only run-ins with police Jared so far had resulted in fines or a small time of community service. He did not mind helping out old folks anyway, to his mind they had lived their lives and deserved a bit of free labour here and there.

But tonight had been a step up for Jared. He had become bored with the humdrum nature of thieving cars, motorbikes or cycles every night. He had long since moved on from thieving from shops and supermarkets, even the label places in town. Small adrenalin peaks for pennies. So Jared had raised the bar tonight, big time.

The target was someone he knew well. Head of a street gang that had small leads into local booze and drug trafficking. He was not the biggest target in town; far from it, but he had been making noises that a lot of people did not take kindly to. This particular gang were the type of guys who congregated on a green in front of a block of council houses talking shit, and doing fuck all. Then when it seemed right, they moved into small-time stealing, snatch-and-grab, those types of things. The idea tonight was not so much to kill anyone but to shut the gang up, to cause them to cease to be, and if the leader happened to die, then so be it. He would not be missed, and neither would his buddies. The most important thing about tonight was the statement of intent, which is all there is, and all there ever was on the streets. There is no need for menace, when the threat of it does the same job.

Jared was used because he kept such a low profile. With a family to support it was easy for him to blend in with the law-abiding citizens, of which, admittedly, there seemed to be less and less. He was calm, he was collected, he planned well, and he wouldn't drag anyone else down were he ever caught by the authorities. Jared would get in, get the job done, then get out. That was what he was good at. Everybody knew that. And the fact that Jared could carry out these jobs with anonymity meant this payday would be good. Jared unhooked the gate latch as quickly as he could, making sure that he did not touch anything with bare fingers. This was the most crucial part of the job. The hit had been done, but its success lay not in the injuries dished out to the target so much as the safe return to his home without leaving a trail.

The first thing he did was quietly turn on the outside tap so he could hold his hands under the trickling water, just long enough to remove most of the blood from the leather gloves. He would clear everything from them, and everything else, with strong bleach, right after he had cleaned himself up. After that he stepped towards the house. He removed his shoes before rapping lightly on the window of the door that opened into the kitchen. The key turned and he was met by his wife, Andrea.

'Working again?' she asked him.

'Yep, and I gotta get a bath. Can you run it for me?' Jared asked.

'Don't I always?' Andrea asked as she walked away and into the bathroom.

Jared picked up the shoes and moved to a small side room that housed the washing machine and dishwasher. He went to the corner, removed one of the carpet tiles, lifted a piece of floorboard and placed the shoes, gloves and his bloodied clothes in the space below. He would dispose of everything later. Right now, he needed to call his contact to confirm the job was done.

'Bath is ready; not too hot, not too cold,' Andrea said as she returned from the bathroom.

'Thanks, babe, I owe you one.'

'I think you owe me plenty more than that,' Andrea said as she walked in front of the sink, which was, as usual, full of plates and cutlery.

'That can be fixed later when Junior is out of the way,' Jared said as he moved behind his wife and cupped her breasts.

'It is about time you called your son by his real name. He is called Sammy, you know that.'

'Sorry. I called him Junior since he was in your belly, and that was only six months ago. He won't know anything yet.'

'But he does have a name, so use it.'

'That's right, and it's not snookums, diddums, honey child, sweetheart,' Jared replied.

'That's different. Names of endearment don't count.'

'Ah, okay. I'm gonna get that bath before all-out war is declared.'

Jared pulled away and kissed the back of Andrea's neck. He walked briskly to the bedroom, removed his underwear, and then crossed to the bathroom.

'Ghosty night tonight,' he shouted out while shutting the bathroom door.

Jared referred to the fact that this was the evening he recorded all of the factual, or supposedly factual, tales of ghostly encounters shown on his favourite television channel. Though never having encountered a ghost or wayward spirit in his life, Jared had an interest in things he had no explanation for, and the reality of ghosts and monsters roaming the planet, terrifying anyone who crossed their paths, was always good entertainment.

There was far too much to be done by both adults in this house to leave time for any serious channel surfing. They had only recently got home internet access. Jared and Andrea had serious ideas of where their income should be spent, and home entertainment was not at the top of the priority list.

Jared entered the water and slid into a relaxed position. He laid his head on the back of the bath and stuck a big toe into the opening of the faucet. Jared never really thought of the family members who would mourn or curse as a result of his work, he never attached any sentimental or emotional value to his victims of the items he stole. Business was business, and he always made good on any contracts he undertook. He did not intend to kill that guy tonight and was pretty sure he had not; he knew where to cut him to cause severe enough damage to make clear his intended message. It was because of the type of job tonight that he had agreed to do it. But if he did need to kill, Jared was sure he could do it without any serious remorse or regretful hindsight.

He noticed a small speck of blood fall into the bath water and dissipate among the bubbles. He sat up immediately, splashing bubbly water onto the bathmat immediately outside the bath as he did so. He wiped under his nose, nothing. He ran his hand all over his face, his neck and through his hair, nothing. Jared looked over his arms and legs as best he could, and still he could see no puncture in his skin or any place where the blood might be escaping from his body. He turned his body to the left and stuck his right index finger into his anus. When he withdrew his finger, it was clean of any bloody residue.

Another speck of blood fell into the water, and then another.

'What the fuck,' Jared said as he ran his hands all over his body. His hands came away clean.

The watery bubbles surrounding Jared pinked up as the red liquid spread through the water, the discolouration growing rapidly. Two further drops, and then two more. The red spots dropping into the bath became more regular until they were a slow but steady stream.

Jared looked down at his left wrist and turned it over, palm upwards. It was now that he saw a deep scratch, only one or two millimetres in length, travelling from his palm upwards. He watched, as the scratch visibly lengthened, and as it did, the amount of blood spilling into the bath increased dramatically. He looked at his right arm, the same lengthening scratch was there too. Jared watched in shock, and the bath water turned from a deep pink, to crimson.

Jared became weak. All strength left his legs and his arms became limp. He tried to shout out to Andrea but it came out as more of a whimper. The scratches lengthened even more. His eyesight began to blur and his legs became still. Jared thought about the victim he attacked earlier in the evening, and for the first time in his working life, he felt empathy for that man. He thought of the impact of what he had done on the man's family, on his children, if he had any, on his girlfriend or his wife. The last thought that Jared had was not for himself or his family, but it was regret for all of the criminal acts he had undertaken.

एकाविंशति

I knocked on the door, hard. I knocked again, and then again. The outside light came on, illuminating the ground around my feet. Judy opened the door dressed in a loose fitting cardigan and jeans.

'Can I come in?' I asked.

'Well, I was actually knitting some socks, as you can see,' she said pointing to her uncovered feet, 'I have run out.'

'Can I come in Judy, please?'

'I don't think you understand how complicated knitting can be. If I lose my place it could fuck me up completely, I'll get one size seven and one size twelve.'

'Judy, please, there is a time for joking, and this is not it,' I pleaded.

'Of course, come in. I'm just pulling your plonker,' Judy said, grinning.

I stepped over the threshold, into the small hallway, and then towards the lounge door. Judy closed the front door behind me and breezed past, to open the door to the lounge.

'Would you like a coffee before we get into any serious discussion? I take it you are here to talk, and not to fuck my brains out?' Judy asked.

'Coffee would be great, thank you,' I replied, refusing to engage in any light-hearted banter.

I sat on the sofa. It was not until I was seated that I realised I still had my shoes on. I pushed my right foot behind my left and pushed down on the cusp of the shoe and levered it off, at the same time praying my feet were free of any strong odour. I then curled the big toe of my left foot onto the top of my right shoe that cupped my ankle and levered that off, too.

I waited several minutes for Judy. In that time, I found it hard to relax. I moved around in the seat, twiddled my thumbs, chewed on the exposed edges of skin around my fingernails and drummed lightly on my knees. All the time my eyes moved around the room, searching for something relaxing to focus on, but never finding it. Judy then returned with two coffee mugs and placed them on coasters on the coffee table.

'You look tense,' she said, 'what's wrong?'

I looked into Judy's eyes. The concern was there, the worry was there also, but something else lurked at the very back of her brown iris. Suspicion. It is easy to understand when a person, faced with details or events of which they have no prior knowledge, is asked to digest information that defies conventional wisdom, and more, to act on that without question. While it was true that Judy had experienced many new things in the past three weeks, most of which she might previously have believed to be improbable, if not impossible, a person with no prior inclination to even consider their otherworldly existence might find it impossible to adjust sufficiently to accept these things as true.

In Judy I had an ally, of that there could be no doubt. But our alliance was sure to be severely tested sometime soon. There is only so much one person can be expected to accept on face value before their natural inclination to reject it kicks in. It is just too much to expect to be able to pump a person with new ideas, new philosophies, new experiences, and events that are impossible to explain in any conventional terms, endlessly, ad infinitum. That luxury just did not exist for me. Not only were we fighting an entity that held all the trump cards, but I was also struggling with Judy's mind-set.

The sum total of all I knew about what we faced together was very little, but what I thought, what I perceived and what I felt, was everything. Inspector Judy Marchant dealt in fact, nothing else. Only occasionally would the circumstances of crime play a significant part, and any such circumstantial case could easily be shot down in flames. The only thing in my favour was that Judy had nearly as much faith in her reading of an individual as she did in the facts. Even if my representations contained no facts whatsoever, they were obviously presented earnestly enough to warrant Judy's trust. Nagging on my mind right now was just how far would Judy's trust stretch, before the elastic of common sense snapped?

'What's wrong is,' the truth was that I really did not know how to start. In fact, I was not too sure what it was I wanted to say in reply to Judy's question. 'What's wrong Judy, is that I don't know how much longer I can accept your help in sorting this matter out.'

'What are you talking about?' she asked.

'This is getting serious now, Judy, and it is getting very dangerous. Since I came to your office a little more than three weeks ago, fourteen people have died and another one, Amy King, very nearly died, too. This is the nature of the situation, I know that. The whole basis on which I became involved in this god-awful mess was that people were going to die, young people, I always knew that and I had no choice but to accept it. But you don't...'

'Please believe me...'

I held my hand up to stem the interruption. If I did not speak now I might forever need to hold my tongue, and that would do nothing but alienate myself with my closest ally, and possibly even with myself, too. Some things you just have to get off your chest or you feel you will explode. This was just such a time.

'Judy, please, I must say this. The fact is that I knew Chloe Omigho.'

'You knew her? How did you know her?' Judy asked.

'I went into her shop to get some flannels the morning before you called me from the coroner's office. We got chatting. She asked me to do a quick reading for her. I just told her what I saw in her, about her feelings, the fact that she was lonely and looking for a man. We chatted for quite a while. And then, early the next morning, you called to say she was dead. Not only that, the reason you called me was because you thought she died from injuries sustained from meeting with this entity,' I explained.

'Oh my God. I never knew about that. Shit,' Judy exclaimed.

'Yes, shit. And here's why it's shit. I came to you six months ago about the first two deaths I knew very little about. All I felt was that I was linked in some way. Okay, we did not hit it off right away, but even at that time I dragged you into this, because when I returned three weeks ago, I came to you first. I had greater clarity this time, I had some greater internal, instinctual understanding of what was at stake, and in what it was I might be up against. I convinced you of the meaning to me about what was going on, and what was at stake. You took that at face value and you ran with it. Judy, now I want you to stop running. Quit.'

'Quit? You have got to be joking. Whether you like it or not, I am just as much a part of this as you are, at least that is how I see it,' Judy said adamantly.

'Judy, I know things, I see things in people. I see your uncertainty, your reservations. You are battling at the moment, inside. Your angel and your devil are at loggerheads. On the one hand, you believe implicitly in all I have told you, and in what you have witnessed. But on the other hand, you are waiting for the moment when something goes awry, when you can finally admit to yourself that this journey, this field trip, is going nowhere, that this was all one big, bad mistake. These are two extreme, but very powerful opponents. Whatever side wins will be triumphant without any shadow of a doubt. The other will blow away like dust in a desert,' I explained.

'I am a policewoman, and a damned fine one, what do you expect?' she asked.

'I am very glad that you can see inside yourself enough to at least tune in with what I have said. But I feel very, very strongly, that this quest is going to end up taking us out way beyond what either of us could ever conceive in our wildest nightmares. This entity is toying with us at the moment, you said that yourself. I am sure that it is capable of untold pain and suffering, and it will not flinch to achieve its ultimate aim. That is all it seeks, nothing more, nothing less. This will suck us up, chew us like cud and then spit us out. Whatever we are dealing with does not have any of the boundaries that we set for ourselves; it does not act within the same parameters. This affords it a tremendous advantage, and that is what will drain us of nearly everything we have. Can you really tell me that you are ready for that? Will you risk your livelihood, your life, for that?' I asked.

'No,' she replied solemnly.

'No, I thought not. And I would not expect you to. I myself would not take up the challenge unless I felt that I had no choice. What can I do if God turns around and says 'Hey, I need you to help me,' am I supposed to say no?'

'I know that's not a question, but I agree with all you say, and God knows why I said it. This whole thing is preposterous,' she replied.

'If this entity is playing with us it is doing it for a reason. This is serious stuff. I can't shake the feeling that this thing needs me to complete its own quest. It seems to offer titbits of information, it selects what kind of reaction it wants from me in any given situation, sure that I will act in that way and feed its cause. When I did a reading for Chloe Omigho in the shop that morning I saw and felt nothing, nothing at all that might suggest she was in danger. That means to me that this entity has the ability, and the scope, to block out certain information while at the same time being able to promote other things. Why didn't I see something, why couldn't I warn her?'

'If it is true what you suggest, then there is no way you could have warned her. And who is to say that the end result would not be the same even if you did? You can't blame yourself for what happened,' Judy said.

'Oh yes I can,' I looked into Judy's eyes, 'and I do.'

'How can you say that? You have no control over what this thing does,' Judy said vociferously.

'You are right, I have no control over what it does, but maybe I have directed it to do what it does to certain people.'

'That is nonsense. Look, I don't know how you got into this, I don't even know what 'this' is, but let me tell you one thing – if you are going to fight this entity you cannot shoulder any guilt over what happens, and who it happens to,' Judy said indignantly.

'Judy, an old lady came up to me at the memorial service for those young girls. I don't know how she knew who I was or how I was linked to what happened. But she outright blamed me for what happened to those kids,' I said.

'What? I didn't know you went to the memorial service?'

'And what if the old lady is right? I was the one who identified the minibus with all those innocent kids on-board. I was the one who distracted the driver, and in doing so I may have even created the perfect circumstances for him to crash that vehicle. I met with Chloe Omigho on the morning of the day she was attacked and killed by this entity. And I was the one who pulled you into all this, and how safe might you be now? I am scared of talking to anyone, bumping into them in the street. Christ, I am even scared of thinking about them for fear of placing a big fat "GET ME" placard on their backs,' I admitted.

'That is crazy talk. Look, you have been dragged into something that it seems God, or whomever, thinks only you can sort out. Do you think that faith was placed in you so you can help kill people? Or maybe because you are the only one who might be able to save them? I know which one my money would be on,' Judy said adamantly.

'I know that, I know it, but that can't stop the guilt I feel, because if it had not been for my contact with these people, who is to say they would not be alive today?'

'But if it had not been for your contact with those people, then you would have no case at all to continue trying to stop all this. Sometimes there are casualties, you must accept that. If it were not for such casualties, you would be at square one right now. And I can tell you for a fact that in these last three weeks you have gained huge insight into what is happening here, and you are in a far better position now to be able to try to set up a strategy to stop it. No one else can do that except you,' Judy said.

'And I accept that responsibility, Judy, one hundred per cent. All I know is that if I don't react, if I ignore all that happens around me, then this mess might never be cleared up and many, many more people, as well as their families and friends, will suffer unnecessarily. I welcome any help you have provided so far and any help that might still be to come, but Judy, you just cannot risk your career, or your life, on something that cannot be proved, on the whim of a psychic, because the only guidance you have on this comes from me; it comes from my instinct. There is no guide, there are no instructions on how you can help me to overcome this killer. I have to go on my internal feelings; I have no choice. But thinking rationally, there is no good, solid reason why you should volunteer to help me,' I suggested.

'I know you are right. How about I take a break? What if you continue the adventure on your own? I might have no choice sometimes to become involved if, let's say, I get a call from Dr. Anstis, but I will report anything like that to you immediately. The only thing I ask is that you keep me informed of your progress. Can you do that?'

'Yes, Judy, thanks. That has taken a lot off my mind,' I replied.

'May God be with you. Squash that son of a bitch. Do it for all the people who suffered at his spiritually filthy hands, do it for God and the angels, straighten the spiritual realm out and get rid of this curse for the sake of all of us. More important, do it for yourself,' Judy said.

***

'Yes sir, you wanted to speak with me?' PC Stewart reported to the DI.

The dark wood furniture, bookshelves and wall trimming glinted in the strong afternoon sunlight that pierced the large bay window in the front wall. The silverware on shelves added extra sparkle to the natural light in the room. The air in the room held very little dust or other particle debris. Cleaned as it was in the morning and evening, the room was spick and span. Even the heavy purple drapes, held in place with a matching tieback, hanging by a thick black solid metal hook, were dusted down twice a day.

The DI sat behind his desk in full uniform, seemingly unfazed by the rising temperature in the room. Of course, he had every opportunity to remove his cap and wipe his brow in between receiving visitors, but being head of the service, it is more likely that he would put up with small discomforts for the sake of his leadership psyche.

'Yes. Stewart, where are we on this minibus incident?' the DI asked.

'Well, sir, the local force are in regular contact with us. We are processing the forensics, but it looks like an accident, since we found no evidence of extraneous interference with the vehicle. The weather was good, warm and dry. We found no oil or other surface disturbance that would have been present before the accident. There is no suggestion of any pre-journey fault on the vehicle, and we have checked the service sheets and all appears in order. The company confirmed they had no contact with the driver after he left the garage, so there appears to have been no serious fault develop with the vehicle during the trip,' PC Stewart replied.

'What about the driver?' the DI asked.

'Les Filbert, fifty-one years old, been a public driver most of his working life. No unspent penalties on his licence. No known medical conditions. He was retained in hospital for observation on a head wound. No other major injuries, only cuts and bruises. He, and the other three adult supervisors on the minibus, were thrown clear when the vehicle left the carriageway. Mr. Filbert confirms he was approached by a passenger in a silver saloon car just prior to the accident, the passenger pointed and shouted something to the driver, but Mr. Filbert paid little attention, since he was not aware of any problems with the minibus at the time. The car moved on ahead shortly before the minibus left the carriageway,' PC Stewart explained.

'And what about this car passenger, have you spoken with him?'

'Yes, sir. Says he was driving and there was no other person in the car at the time. He says he noticed a problem with the front right tyre on the minibus and tried to point it out to the driver.'

'But we have other witnesses who also say that it was a passenger in the car that tried to communicate with the driver.'

'Yes, sir,' PC Stewart confirmed.

'And we have been watching this guy?'

'Yes, sir. He attended the memorial service for the crash victims yesterday. We had a couple of plainclothes there. The report is that he kept his distance, but that he was approached by an elderly relative of one of the deceased who was somewhat agitated with him. He left soon after the service finished.'

'Do we know why this elderly relative was agitated? Can we trace them and get a statement?' the DI asked.

'No, sir, as yet we do not know what caused the commotion, but we can find out if you agree for us to do that.'

'See that it is done. And PC Stewart, continue to keep an eye on this character. I'll have a think about what we do next, but it might be worth finding out a bit more. If need be, we will bring him in for a chat. But for now, let's get as much background as we can,' the DI ordered.

PC Stewart made to leave the room. 'Will that be all, sir?' he asked.

'There is one other thing,' the DI said as he leaned forward and picked up some papers on his desk. Without looking up at the departing constable he continued. 'Will you send Inspector Marchant in to see me please.'

'Yes, thank you, sir,' PC Stewart said, as he turned to leave the shiny, clean office.

द्वाविंशति

Judy may well have agreed to step away from the case, but that did not stop her from having an avid interest in it. So far as I knew, she had backed off and got on with her job, and whatever else she did inside her own home life cocoon. This was not something I wanted to happen. Judy was a great source of strength to me, and it always helped to bounce ideas off another person, but it was necessary to secure her safety and to improve my focus on the job in hand.

It was only much later that I found out the true nature of Judy's interest, and also that of her superiors. I consoled myself in the fact that I could bury myself completely in my own issues without feeling responsible for the safety of anyone else. At least for the time being.

I went back to doing professional psychic readings, hypnotherapy sessions and offering healing treatments to paying customers. I kept away from life coaching. That particular line of work was stressful; it encouraged delving into life incidents that left deep wounds, which took a great deal of time and a lot of emotional acrobatics to resolve. I was also able to spend some more time with my wife and young son. In the last three weeks, I only had fleeting glimpses of them, the odd conversation and a hug from my son now and then. I explained I had important work to do, but they were not stupid. They were aware that something big was going on, but knew better than to ask too many questions. But late evenings, early mornings, being out of the house more than inside it, took its toll, and now was a good time to try and rebuild any bridges that showed signs of collapse.

Taking breaks from the intensity of the chase did not mean letting up on searching for solutions. But now I had more time to look at some of the aspects that might have previously passed me by; now I had an opportunity to apply greater objectivity. The issues seemed clearer and the circumstances more concise. For the first time, since becoming embroiled in this task, I could look at the options to take some meaningful steps forward, to start planning the process by which I could end this nightmare.

I did not know to what degree Judy would retain her interest in moving forward on this case, but I guessed her desire to find out the truth and search for a resolution would continue unabated. She and I had both agreed to keep each other updated on any developments. It was my belief that this would become a regular occurrence. Judy had shown a belief in what we were trying to do and it was clear that she would not back down once she got her teeth into something.

There are some deeply personal issues surrounding the relationship between Judy and I, but the subject of this journal must remain tight and focused on its goal, which is to warn of the life-threatening dangers you, as a reader, face by ignoring your instinctual leanings toward self-preservation.

***

'A classic suicide, or so it seems,' Dr. Anstis lifted the magnifying glass from his right eye.

'But nevertheless, one worthy of my attention,' Judy said.

'To tell you the truth, Ms. Marchant, I am not sure, but I thought you would prefer I include you in this case than not,' the coroner replied.

'Oh yes,' Judy said, 'for obvious reasons.'

'No, not obvious at all, far from it,' the doctor replied.

Theo Anstis raised his head and planted his knuckles firmly on the table in front of him. A challenging pose of authority that demanded attention.

'I am sorry if you feel in any way that I might not have been very open with you,' Judy said.

'You have not been open at all, Ms. Marchant. Since you asked me to inform you of any pre-forties deaths that did not quite,' he raised his hands, making air quotes as he spoke, 'fit the normal picture' – this office, for some reason unknown to me, has been unusually busy. Unlike inner cities, we don't get too many murders, and neither should we get too many young deaths in these parts. That is, until you walked in and asked for my assistance. But since that time, Ms. Marchant, I have had a queue of bodies to examine. I'm thinking of using one of those rolling ticket dispensers in my waiting room. All I am missing is a neon sign indicating which cadaver is next for examination. What is this all about, Judy?' Theo Anstis asked, as he peered at her closely.

Judy looked up at the ceiling before answering. She stayed in that position, a bead of sweat breaking out from her hairline and trickling between her eyes, down the left side of her nose and settling on her top lip. She ignored it. The thought of making a believable case to a seasoned coroner with the intellect and professional wisdom of a man like Dr. Theodore Anstis, was implausible, at best. But the fact was, she had to try.

'Okay, I will tell you all I know, but first I need a little bit of background about this lump of meat before us,' Judy said.

'Jared Williams, twenty-four years old, found last night, time of death around nine yesterday evening. Leaves a wife and young kid. This guy was known as a small-time crook, nothing serious, but he is on the database. Apart from why he is laying here before me, that is about all I know,' Dr. Anstis explained.

'Yeah, thanks. I can get a heads up, if need be, from my colleagues.'

'So far as his death is concerned the slight bloating you can see is from the time he spent under the bathwater, before he bled out. There are no other marks around the fatal injury areas, no other significant injuries. The only obvious cause of death are the two deep serrations on each wrist and forearm,' Dr. Anstis diagnosed.

'But why? He had a young family, a reasonable home. He had something to live for,' Judy said.

'I don't know, but it is hard for me to see anything past those gouges on the insides of his arms. Maybe he felt guilty for his life of crime? Maybe he wanted out, but those people he served or worked for wouldn't let him leave? Maybe he, or his family, had been threatened? There are so many variables, and it is not for me to question why. My job is to decide probable cause of death, and that seems blatantly obvious to me,' Dr. Anstis explained.

Judy bent down and turned the left arm in front of her on the table. The body felt cold and solid, much as a lump of beef might feel. The skin slipped a little against her fingers, its fix against the underlying muscle, gristle and dead veins, loosening. She slipped her right hand under the arm and pulled it upwards, the joint stiffening and resisting her pull.

'Have you got some kind of a magnifying glass?' Judy Marchant asked the coroner.

'Here,' he said simply as he passed her a plastic hand-held implement.

Judy placed the white, square object in between her eyes and the dead arm. She bent slightly more to get closer to the focus of her attention. She moved the magnifier closer and further away, searching for the clearest view. Only when she had found what she was searching for, did she remove her hand from Jared Williams' arm, straighten up and face the coroner.

'Look closer at the wounds, Dr. Anstis. There is no serrated edge on the entry wounds, they are too clean, too clinical, and,' Judy paused momentarily, 'aren't the injuries too deep?'

Dr. Anstis bent over the body again and picked up the opposite arm to the one inspected by Judy. He reached up and adjusted the angle of the overhead spotlights to maximise the intensity of the light for his examination of the arm.

'Yes, you are right. A knife or glass would have left a jagged edge, but these are completely clean cuts. In a suicide, it is customary for the initial incisions to be clean, but as you move further with the cuts they become more jagged, but here, the end of the cut appears to be as clean as the first incision. Very odd; I wonder how that could be?' Dr. Anstis wondered.

'We are left wondering about a lot of things about too many dead people at the moment, Theo.'

'As for the depth of the cut, that would depend on what implement was used.'

'And that's another thing,' added Judy.

'What's that?'

'I am given to understand that no sharp objects were found in the bathroom. The door was locked from the inside, so nobody would have been anywhere near the bath at the time, or shortly after, Mr Williams died.'

'No razor blades nearby?' asked Dr Anstis.

'None.'

'How very peculiar. So if not a suicide, what then?' the coroner asked.

***

I had three bookings in the first two days after deciding to, once again, carry out readings for paying clients. I also had some requests for hypnotherapy, but I decided against this work. The intensity in carrying out hypnotherapy sessions is too great. An additional consideration must be the background interviews I carry out to know my clients sufficiently well, to decide the best course of action to ensure successful outcomes. At this moment, I felt unable to divert sufficient energy to the cause.

Today I was meeting with a young mum of one small child, as the first of two bookings. I don't like to gather any information at all when taking a booking, since it could jeopardise any data that comes through during the reading. I prefer to go to a reading with a completely blank mind, which is another reason for a fairly deep meditation before stepping away from the security of my vehicle, and into the spotlight of my clients' homes.

I am a little nervous of carrying out a reading where children are present in the property. Not only might their inquisitiveness impede physically on the reading, by the knocking on doors or calling out, they more generally exhibit their natural exuberance in a noisy manner. It is normal in such cases for a second adult to be present to look after the children. In this case, the child in question was less than a year old, so the only likely interruptions might come from dirty nappies, hunger, or from being separated from mum.

The lady I was reading for was twenty years of age. Relying on state benefits as her only source of income, she lived comfortably, but on a strategic budget. Her property was council-owned and paid for by way of housing benefit. The sparse furniture fitted the compact layout of the terraced two-bedroom property. The house was clean, with a tidy rear garden patio, and a small-stoned, chained-off, front entranceway.

Michaela had ginger hair and freckles, with pretty, glassy, light blue eyes. A quiet girl with few close friends. I sensed an enforced distance with her parents, which was possibly to do with their discomfort in her becoming impregnated at a young age by a man with whom she was not married, and had minimal contact. In their eyes, mum and dad should be together implicitly, or not at all. This had caused some friction that the father of her child welcomed, being a man of single mind and intentions, but she did not.

Lonely, but not alone, is probably the best way to describe the demeanour of my client. There are times, inevitably, when someone can feel a desperate need for the company of another, while at other times only the complete absence of people will do. The need to be alone for Michaela, happened when she was in the company of her baby daughter, of whom she was extremely protective. She felt no need to parade baby Rebecca in front of adoring family or gurgling friends; this was a chore necessary only in other people's perception, but not in her own.

'I will tell you what I feel. Generally speaking, I do not talk to deceased relatives and I do not use any props such as tarot cards, crystals or other such things. I do not seek confirmation from you on anything I say. I might ask you questions at times, but this is just to ensure clarity in the reading. Please feel free to ask questions at any time, or if anything I say is not clear for you,' I said to Michaela as I began the reading.

'You feel like you are untidy, maybe a bit dishevelled, but you are not. In fact, you keep a tight rein on most things in your life. It is probably because you are so organised that you feel you are not, if that makes any sense. You have a strong maternal influence in your life but that relationship is distanced at the moment. I think you used to be very close to your mum and, at times, you really miss that closeness. But that can always come back through communication, so sometimes maybe a quick phone call or something similar might help.'

Michaela nodded her head.

'Your favourite times are spent on holiday. That is when you feel you can totally relax. The weight of everyday life is lifted from your shoulders, and that is when you feel free to indulge in a bit of *you* time. Did you go away a couple of times with friends?' I asked.

'Yes I did, before I was pregnant. Five of us went to Majorca and Crete together,' Michaela answered.

'That is when you felt most free, most happy. You are not an unhappy person; in fact, in company you are sometimes seen as a bit of a joker. You have a quick wit and you smile a lot. I think that many people might have wanted to know you, but most you have kept at arm's length. It is this need of yours to keep an orderly home life. You feel that if you open up to too many people, they might try to take advantage, or they might make suggestions that you feel you have to follow for fear of hurting them, even though you know that to do so will not serve you well. So you do have a tendency to cocoon yourself a bit, so that outside influences are minimal.'

Again, Michaela nodded in agreement.

'I can see yellow flowers in a mound-like shape. These are flowers on tall stems quite flat, but they are a very deep yellow colour, and they smell divine.'

'Oh I know,' said Michaela. 'That must be Auntie Angela. We got her a wreath of bright yellow flowers for her funeral – that was only two months ago,' Michaela acknowledged.

'Well the flowers were important, and this lady brings the flowers to you with the same sentiments of love you showed to her.'

'Thank you.'

'There is a man connected to this lady. He is a tall man, big shoulders and quite a square jawline. He usually wore a grey suit, but it wasn't a suit, it was just a very well matching waistcoat, trousers and jacket. He wouldn't sit like this...' I put my hands in my pockets and pushed myself back into the seat in a slouched position. 'He would never sit like that. Always he was erect and straight. When you were small, he towered above you.'

'That would be my uncle, he was married to the lady you mentioned,' Michaela replied.

'I think you feel that you did not do well at school. You were very clever intellectually, but in the last year or so, you feel you let yourself down. You want to get some more qualifications, but you are scared you will not have enough time. You are also worried this might just be a whim, and you are scared of paying for a course and then giving it up without even trying. But don't worry. You will get some more qualifications; you will find the time and you will do very well.'

'Thank you,' said Michaela. 'Can you tell me what you see for my baby, Rebecca?' she asked.

'Rebecca was a little bit underweight when she was born.'

'Two kilos,' Michaela confirmed.

'But she is fine now. She notices everything; she is always looking around. She has a very strong bond to you, but she does not take kindly to everyone. Sometimes you think she can sense who is good, and who is not so good. Rebecca is very intelligent, but I think even at her young age you already know this.'

I blinked one time. I blinked again. I could see an image, in my mind's eye, of Rebecca. She was in her cot. She was awake. She looked to her right, towards the corner of the room. I tried to look in that direction too, but I could not see into the recess there. I sensed Rebecca's demeanour change. Her arms flicked out and her small legs kicked, one then the other. She moved her head rapidly, left, to the front, and then to the right, peering into the corner of the room.

Rebecca's eyes widened perceptibly. I looked into them, closer and closer, until I could make out the vague shapes of the room in her iris. I thought I noticed a movement in the same corner into which the baby stared, transfixed. Her legs and arms were completely still now. I forced my mind's eye away from the child and into that same corner of the room, only this time, I travelled deeper into the darkness.

'Are you okay?' Michaela asked.

Her voice sounded as if it came through several layers of cotton, it was muffled and foggy. I did not answer, since it was hard to focus on anything other than what was parked in my mind's eye, and I did not want to run the risk of losing this image – the baby in her cot, the movement in the corner of the room, and the interaction between the two.

I was aware of the presence of another, and that presence seemed familiar. This familiarity was not immediately noticeable, it was more something buried beneath multiple layers of thought. Nonetheless, it was there, it was palpable. I searched into the darkness in the corner of the room and I searched inside myself, looking for the link, but it was nowhere to be found. I knew what this presence was, I knew it immediately, but it was the connection between us that eluded me. I needed to concentrate, I needed to open up the layers of reality in front of me, one by one, to expose the thing that I was looking for.

'Snap out of it, come on,' demanded Michaela.

Her voice sounded like it was relayed through an old gramophone player, it was scratchy and distant. Certainly, there was a need to return to the reading with Michaela, but more urgent yet was to discover what lay hidden in the dark corner of Rebecca's room. More important, to find out the reason for its visit.

The very first thing I noticed was a pinprick of light, an infinitesimal spark in the darkness. The spark came again, and again. At the same time, Rebecca began to kick her legs and wave her arms after an extended period of relaxation on her part. From that spark of light emerged a needle. Seemingly suspended in the air, the needle caught any light in the room and shot it out from whence it came.

Just to the side and rear of the needle, I could make out a murky shape. This shape was like mud, nondescript and unmoving, but perceptible against the dark backdrop of the corner of the room. The needle continued to shine against the mud thing behind it. The needle moved quickly, it flashed across my vision in the direction of the cot. I could only briefly perceive its movement rather than focus on the object itself, as the needle returned to the mud thing and then shot out, again and again.

I moved over to the cot and looked inside. Rebecca was bent into a foetal position, her head turned away from the curve of her body. Her head was raised from the bedding, one leg was bent up in the air, the other leg lay flat against the mattress on which she had been placed by her mother. But now she looked as if she was held in a position that would suggest she was supported by one invisible hand beneath her head, and another through the gap in her legs supporting her raised knee. The invisible hands served to reduce the movement of the baby's limbs.

Rebecca was dressed in an all-in-one sleepsuit. The arms and legs of the suit were short, exposing the skin on her arms and legs. Tiny red pinpricks started to appear on the baby's hands and feet, slowly at first and then more rapidly. The pinpricks moved to her neck and face. Her pupils were wide, tears began to form around the base of her eyelids, but she did not scream, and she did not cry. A frightened shadow was cast by her eyes. She looked confused, maybe even dazed by what was happening inside the safe haven of her room.

'Do it. Do the reading,' a voice hissed from the dark mass in the corner of the room.

'No. You cannot make me do anything,' I replied adamantly.

'Do the reading, or this can become much more unpleasant, I think you know that,' this time the voice was deeper and more menacing.

'No, I won't do it,' I replied.

'What? What are you talking about, who are you talking to?' Michaela asked.

I shook my head furiously.

'I'm very sorry, Michaela, but I cannot do this reading,' I said.

'Tell her what you see. Tell her,' bellowed the dark mass.

The needle shot from the back of the baby's eye through to the front, then back in again. I heard the eye squelching as its outer coating was punctured. The needle entered the same eye angle and pirouetted creating an oozing hole in the middle of Lucy's dark iris, yellow pus dribbled from the eye and mixed with the tears assembling on Rebecca's lower eyelid.

'Fuck you,' I shouted a last message to the entity, before turning to the young mother. 'Your baby is in danger, Michaela, go to her now,' I demanded.

'What are you talking about?' Michaela asked.

'Go, quickly, go now,' I demanded.

Michaela jumped up, she yanked open the lounge door and jumped through it. Her feet thundered on the stairs as she sped up to the top floor of the house. I leapt out of the chair, exited the lounge and removed myself from the house. I stood with my back against the rough sand and stone blasted wall beside the entrance door. I made my way to the car and entered it as quickly as possible.

'Fuck it,' I thumped my right fist against the steering wheel three times, 'fuck it.'

***

'You promised me an explanation, Ms. Marchant. I think now would be an opportune moment for you to make good on that promise,' Dr. Anstis said.

'What would you like to know?' Judy asked.

'I want to know why I have three bodies to look at in the last three weeks. All of these people were considerably younger in years than most people would expect, when they died. All of them suffered injuries that could be described as unusual at best and suspicious, certainly, and all of these deaths have resulted in us meeting here and witnessing some things I have never before experienced in more than thirty years of being a coroner. I know there is a connection between these people, I just don't know what that connection might be, and that is the issue you are going to put me right on,' Theo Anstis said.

Judy Marchant, knuckles on the examination table, looked away from Dr. Anstis, and searched the dreary sidewall, for the right words to say. The wall was blank, as was her mind.

'Okay, you are right, Dr. Anstis. I should have been straight at the start, but after you hear what I have to say, you should understand why I said nothing. But before I start, I must ask that what I am about to tell you goes no further than these four walls.'

'Ms. Marchant, if you have any information that has a material influence on my work, then it must be submitted and recorded. As you will know, autopsies are a matter of public record. For me to keep information out of any autopsy I undertake would be absolutely unthinkable. If that is what you are asking me to do, then I will not be able to offer you any veil of secrecy,' Dr. Anstis stated.

'But I am really not sure you can include this information in any report, at least not if you want to preserve your reputation,' Judy Marchant replied.

'Well, I think I should be the judge of that. Why don't you tell me what you have to tell me and then we can see how best I might take it forward from there. I will respect your request for me to keep quiet, but at some point my professional right to report anything of significance must kick in.'

'Okay, you want some background to these recent deaths. First of all, the associated death toll is sixteen to date,' Judy said.

'What? Sixteen deaths in three weeks, how have the papers not been all over this? How do we not know anything about this?' Dr. Anstis asked.

'And there were possibly two other deaths six months ago, that I am reliably informed might also be connected.'

'So that makes eighteen deaths in all...'

'Plus one more attack that was thwarted before it resulted in another casualty,' Judy further explained.

'Wait a minute, Ms. Marchant, you just said 'attack.' What exactly is it that is going on?' asked the coroner.

'Yes, it is an attacker, but not in the normal sense of the word.'

'And what is that supposed to mean?' asked Dr. Anstis.

'Can we sit down somewhere, Theo? What I have to say might take a lot of explaining, and an awful lot of understanding by you.'

With that, Dr. Theodore Anstis removed his surgical gloves and loosened the plastic overalls from around his waist. He motioned towards the double doors that led out of the theatre, and stepped in that direction. Dr Anstis led Judy to a small room that housed a small table, four chairs and one double filing cabinet in the corner. There was little room for anything else. With all surgical adornments removed, Theodore Anstis and Judy Marchant sat face-to-face, no more than one metre apart.

'What is this, Inspector Marchant? Is it an epidemic? Is there some kind of biochemical agent involved?' the coroner asked.

'No biochemical agents, so far as I know. And an epidemic? If you define an epidemic as the rapid spread of infectious disease to a large number of people in a given population, within a short period of time, there is no epidemic. But if you ask me about a large number of deaths of otherwise healthy young people in eerily similar circumstances, then my answer might be yes, maybe we are facing an epidemic,' Judy answered.

'Then, if I am to continue to help you, don't you think it right that I should know more of what we are dealing with? Pardon the pun, but you have to throw me a bone here.'

'Look, Dr. Anstis, I am sorry, but there really is very little that I can explain to you that you might even be able to contemplate, let alone believe.'

'Try me,' Dr. Anstis challenged.

Judy sighed loudly. She knew she could no longer throw a veil over what she had experienced. She could no longer hide what she had been told and how all of that information, forwarded though it might have been by unproven sources, was turning out to be correct. She could no longer deflect interested eyes from her own part in this seemingly personal quest being undertaken by me, and more important, she was becoming unable to deny any rational questions asked of her professional integrity during these informal investigations.

'There is a guy who is a professional psychic. This guy, somehow, found out that a rogue spirit wanted to challenge God's status quo as leader of the spirit world. This rogue spirit, that we refer to as the entity, is trying to tip the balance of power in his favour. For some unknown reason this entity is targeting people below the age of thirty-two. According to him, the psychic guy thinks that both God and the entity need him onside. I know nothing more than that, I know this all sounds hard to believe, but I have witnessed some crazy shit that is making me start to believe this guy,' Judy explained.

'That is pretty impossible to believe,' Dr. Anstis admitted.

'Yeah, I know, it is freaky. But when you look at the evidence, it makes a bit more sense in a wacky sort of way,' Judy said.

'Well, well, well,' said Dr. Theodore Anstis as he straightened in his seat. 'I can see why you asked for secrecy from me.'

'And how do you see it now?' asked Judy, 'do you believe my explanation as to what is going on?' Judy asked.

'To be frank with you, no I don't. But it is clear that you are more on the believing than the not believing side. In any case, I'm not Frank, I am Theo Anstis, Coroner.'

'So where do we go from here? Will you be reporting any of what I said?' Judy asked.

'I see little point in bothering the authorities with details that nobody would believe, without some serious questions being thrown in my direction, regarding their validity. Of course, the background to each of these deaths might need some alluding to, but I am sure we can find a way to use that information in a more digestible format,' replied the coroner in his best non-committal way.

'I would like us to keep working on any issues that come to light if that will be possible.'

'Oh yes, of course. I would hate to miss out on anything so interesting and so formidably challenging,' the coroner replied.

त्रयोविंशति

If energy is everlasting, what happens to negative energy? I always believed that negative influences could only exist in the lower frequencies of life on earth. I also believed that these lower vibrations can catch dark energies like a fly in a Venus Flytrap. But if I was to think there was no such place as hell, then where did these dark energies go, when the physical bodies that attracted them disappeared or moved on?

I also believe that we do not carry our physical emotions with us when we pass over to the spiritual world. But surely emotions, so crucial to our physical lives, are energy that must be dispelled somewhere. So do we pass through a contraption that sucks all physicality out of us and bottles it somewhere? And are we then injected with these emotional energies when we are born into our next lives?

I accept all that happens in my life with implicit trust in the universe. This does not mean that I am not affected by negative emotions, and maybe even being aware of them can mean I suffer more from downward mood swings than many other people. Being more aware will mean that spiritual aspects of life show up more in our everyday existence, and we experience a greater number of barriers to our continued journey to greater spiritual knowledge. There are more people pestering us with red tape, more authorities pressing us to breaking point, more incorrect bills, more items that don't work and need to be returned. Essentially, each time we try to move forward, the lower energies designed to root us inside of our physical existence pull us back. It is a constant battle, the meaning and purpose of which must be questionable.

This is how it felt for me. And my own personal belief system was cracking up, and showing signs of disappearing without trace. I had to keep the big picture in mind all of the time, but it was the small details that mattered more. It was the timings of the attacks, who they happened to, how they were achieved, and the link between the entity and me which fed into the bigger picture, that seemed to take precedence now. It was here I would find all the clues that would help me solve the dilemma and create an effective plan of attack which might save, rather than put at risk, any more lives. The problem was that the more stones I turned over, the less I found beneath.

I became furious at God, the supreme energy that I assumed knew all the answers, but was refusing to assist me in finding them. Having worked in the civil service, I was used to bosses expecting you to work in their style, without ever telling you what style that was. Really, what they did was just substitute their own words and put their names to documents that in truth resulted from the blood, sweat and tears of others. And this was how it seemed to me now. God must know the answers, God must know this entity's weaknesses, God must know how I should tackle this issue and save the lives of those who were needlessly suffering.

I understand how God cannot intervene at a physical level. But is not God revered precisely because of Its ability to put things right with only a twitch of an ethereal eye? What particular circumstances make it right for God to intervene in our physical existence in Its mysterious ways? And why should God take such a hands-off approach in a situation where Its authority, maybe even Its very existence, is being challenged?

This is why I was furious with God, and all Its minions in the spirit realm. Most practitioners swear by the fact that meditation can only be successful when a person is relaxed and calm, but I had found that in some cases the fury, or the despair of an individual, can work equally as well, and sometimes better. This is how it was for me, as I prepared for my meeting with God.

***

'Ah, Inspector Marchant,' the DI said as Judy entered his office.

'Yes, sir,' she answered, shoulders back, chest pressed forward, arms and hands held rigidly to her sides.

'I am given to understand that you know a bit about this guy at the crash. We have placed him under cautionary observation. It is just a temporary measure while we decide whether or not he had a greater impact in this netball team's minibus crash than we are being led to believe,' the DI explained.

'I see, sir,' Judy answered politely.

'We have at least two witnesses plus the minibus driver who suggest that this guy was in the passenger seat of his car just prior to the accident. That means that he is lying to us about being alone. You and I both know, Inspector, that when somebody lies it is a sure indication that they were either involved, or covering for somebody else who was involved, in an incident.'

'I thought it was deemed an accident, sir.'

'Oh yes, indeed it was,' the DI confirmed.

'Then may I ask why we have any deeper interest?' Judy asked, trying her best not to show any more than a professional interest in the answer.

'We have an interest because we should know the exact extent of his involvement. There is no question of anyone being blamed, or of facing any criminal charges, relating to the tragic losses of life that occurred that day. But we must face our responsibilities, not only to the families of the victims, but to the public. We therefore have a duty to tie up any loose ends that might exist. And this guy is a very loose end,' the DI explained.

'Yes indeed, sir,' Judy had no choice but to agree.

'How is it that you know this man, Inspector Marchant?' the DI asked.

'He came to my office six months ago about a couple of local deaths. These deaths were described by the coroner as being from natural causes, albeit both of the subjects were under thirty years of age. He came to my office again, about three weeks ago, and he raised his interest again in these same deaths,' Judy said.

'And what interest could he possibly have? He is not of the medical fraternity is he? Is he studying early deaths for a college dissertation or something? He does seem rather old for that.'

'No, nothing like that sir. He claims to have certain abilities that lead him to indulge in psychic readings, hypnotherapy and healing. Maybe he had a vision, or a dream of these deaths. The truth is I don't know the exact details of his interest, only...' Judy paused, '... only that he suggested ... he thought, that more young people might be in danger.'

'Oh, really. And has anything happened since to suggest he might have been right?' the DI asked.

'Nothing that I am aware of,' Judy lied.

'And have you been in contact with this man since?'

'No sir, though I did ask him to contact me again should he have any information about future threats that we should be aware of,' she said.

The DI rose from his desk, turned away from Judy Marchant and looked at the slatted blinds that covered the window behind his desk.

'We cannot get much from watching him at a distance. We know he attended the memorial service for the victims of the accident. We know he got involved in a heated exchange with one of the congregation. We know where he lives, and we know some of his movements, but since he is not a suspect in any criminal activity we are not allowed to listen in, or to put a bug on his phones,' the DI explained.

'And?' Judy asked.

The DI turned his head and looked briefly at her. He returned to the blind and slipped two fingers between the slats that were at head height. He parted his fingers, and bright sunlight pierced a small area of his face. He looked through the gap down to the buzzing street below.

'I want to know some more about this man. I need to know if, and why, he has more than a fleeting connectedness to the accident. I should like you to get in contact with him. Talk to him. You can make any contact official or unofficial, but I would guess an unofficial follow-up meeting with him might be best. Try to make sure he feels he can confide in you,' the DI suggested.

'You want me to entrap him?' Judy asked.

'No, no, good Lord, no. This is nothing like that. I'm not asking you to sleep with him for God's sake,' the DI chuckled smugly. 'I think you can appreciate all the relatives of those girls deserve our best attention, just in case there is something we might otherwise overlook.'

'If that is your order, sir.'

'Yes it is, Inspector Marchant.'

'Yes, sir.'

'Good, okay. I think that will be all,' the DI said, dismissing her, while continuing to contemplate the outside world.

'Thank you, sir,' Judy said as she turned, took four paces, and placed her right hand on the handle to open the door.

'One more thing, Inspector...'

'Yes, sir?'

'Make sure you stay in contact with the coroner, too, just in case anything else does turn up,' the DI said.

Judy Marchant exited the room as quickly, and as quietly, as she could.

***

On returning home, I spent most of my time walking around cursing. My phone rang a few times, but I refused to answer it. My mind was set only on one issue, and I would not be side-tracked from my wrath by any outside interference. This was not an occasion where ten deep breaths would have any beneficial effect in helping to calm me down. Any deep inhalations were more likely to further deepen my confrontational mood, adding fuel to the fire. Have you ever tried taking ten deep breaths when all you want to do is lash out verbally or physically? It rarely works.

My words were rambling and angry. I was angry at the entity. I was angry at myself for trying to act normally and carry on my everyday business. I was angry at the universe for everything it seemed to have burdened me with – being diabetic, having a brain injury, not seeing enough of my kids. I was angry that, because of my reactions, I was unable to step back and develop an objective plan to tackle the entity. Most of all, I was angry at God. God is not vengeful, but I am, especially when I am faced with a blank sheet of paper that keeps filling up with innocents' blood.

What the fuck were the creators of the world thinking when they moulded a spiritual realm that was unable to deal with renegade souls that might want to challenge the status quo? Why create something so beautiful, so divine, if all of it can be ripped apart like a paper castle at the whim of a deviant misfit? And why are there so many ghosts? Why so many souls eternally wandering their own personal haunts without the knowledge or ability to go towards the all-encompassing light? Is that light not strong enough? Why is there a need for negative forces at all? If heaven and hell do not exist, then why is it so easy for demons to plague us?

'Damn you, God – damn you, you cock-sucking motherfucker.'

I make no excuses for using such colourful language before our creator, or at least one of our most revered influencers. God has heard it all before, if God created all, then the word motherfucker must have been created, or at least accepted, by Him, Her, It, whatever. I have no arm's length relationship with God, I am not fearful; I talk to God and, on occasion, God talks to me. And this was one of those occasions.

It was as if I had taken all anger out of my mind and put it into a satchel; that bag was slung firmly over my shoulder as I prepared for my journey. Before I started out, I made sure I could see the satchel as if it were a reality, and I felt it resting heavily across my shoulder, as I closed my eyes.

Almost immediately, I found myself inside an area of pure white. There were no walls with which I could judge boundaries; there was no floor and no ceiling. I did not want to focus on my surroundings, for want of not creating images that were non-existent. It is unusual to immediately enter a trance state, but it is not uncommon. The desire of the seeker of information will often dictate the speed of any meditative state achieved.

Always in meditation, it is best when looking for answers of any kind, to try to keep your mind free of expectations. If any answers do arrive, they should not be created by the meditating individual. For these reasons, I am reluctant to ask any questions, since no sooner has the question been asked than a reply will be formulated.

Sometimes I need to plan before a meditation, to ensure that the subject foremost in my mind, is raised. As I mentioned before, anger is just as good a stimulant as is relaxation, it is only the subject matter that is centre of the meditation, that can be dictated, or left open. In this case, it was imperative that I carry all my frustrations, all my questions, and all my anger, into this white open space. If I got answers, I could analyse them and hopefully move a little further forward. If I did not, then what the fuck – at that moment in time at least I had to try.

✳✳✳

'And what of the energies you brought with you today? You can expend them in any way you choose – you can get angry at me, you can feel sorry for yourself, you can destroy or you can build. All is energy, it is the determinant of everything in your life. So if you wanted answers from me on that subject I will not give them, because they are not mine to give.'

The message came from a perceived thought. In meditation, at least for me, it is much the same as carrying out a psychic reading. The information is there, it just appears with no invitation from me. And that is how it was now.

There was no presence for me to look at, no smells and no associated feelings. I guessed where the information came from, but I could not be sure.

'Come on, give me a break here. I was made aware of something that demanded my attention. I heard directly from spiritual energies that my help was needed on an issue which could not be dealt with from within the spiritual realm because the means needed to deal with it do not exist there. I have become aware, or maybe been made aware, of an energetic entity that seems hell bent on cheating some people on earth out of their natural lifespan, for reasons that are unknown to me. This entity has the most appalling ways of killing people, and it also seems to want to involve me in some kind of quest that it is undertaking,' my thoughts replied.

'Yes, I am aware of this and all of it, or some of it, might or might not be true.'

'What does that mean?'

'It means just as it was intended.'

'I have come into contact with this energy on more than one occasion. I have seen what it does, and I have seen how it does it. I have witnessed the bloodshed, the trauma, and the deaths, first-hand. And I am the one expected to sort this out with no help from anyone physical or spiritual,' I was aware that my thoughts were angry and uncompromising.

'If that is your perception, then so be it.'

'These are the facts. These facts cannot be undone. People have died before their time, they have been taken against their will for purposes that can only serve the entity doing the slaying.'

'An interesting choice of words you use, my good friend. But let me make one thing very clear to you. Nothing, nothing at all, can ever happen without the will of the participant. That simply cannot happen. In your perception, these people have died at a young age and, therefore, their demise must be premature. Equally, you believe that the deaths of these people have served only one spiritual being. In your perception, you have been left to fight this common enemy all on your own. The world is only ever as you perceive it to be. Good is good and bad is bad. Black can never be white and vice versa. But at the same time you already know that seven billion worlds all exist at the same time, occupying the same space. Here you will be aware I am referring only to the reactions of people currently occupying your planet. What about the perceptions of other civilisations, other creatures, or other life forms? What about the perceptions that exist in the spiritual realm and will exist forever and ever, amen? It is understandable that you think the way you do, but this is incorrect. What is it, my friend, that makes your perception of your existence the right one?'

'I know what I have experienced in the last three weeks. I know what I was told, and I know what I have seen. I have experienced the outcomes of all the information placed before me. I have followed the trail. What else am I

supposed to do? What do my perceptions have to do with this entity killing people in an effort to dethrone you? Do you not care about that?'

'May I offer a little suggestion? It does seem you are being a little circumspect. But that is the way that you were designed. You cannot know the whole picture; you do not have the physical or spiritual capacity. If you were even to glimpse a fraction of your existence in its totality, you would explode, literally. I do not know the whole picture and I have my boundaries, as do you. My suggestion is that you follow the path that is the clearest one for you.'

'Okay, I understand where you are coming from. The problem remains that this entity is killing people. We on earth do not take kindly to spiritual entities going on a killing spree. Surely you cannot take kindly to a spiritual entity trying to mess with the natural order of things where you are? There is a way to stop this entity and thereby set everything straight once again, both on earth and in the spiritual realms. I just need to know what that way is. I can then do my job, and everyone is happy,' I replied.

'Is that how you perceive it?'

'Well, yes. Is there any other way?'

'First of all, there is no plan. There is no plan for any of us, me included. There is no plan for your world, or for any other world. There are processes in place to try to ensure that the best use is made out of what is available, that is all. So if there is no plan, then how can this entity mess up what does not exist? If there is no plan for any of these people who have been killed, then how can this entity have altered anything for any of them?'

'How can you say that?'

'That is my perception. One out of many. Certainly more than seven billion.'

'And what if I choose to believe that there does exist a plan – that this entity is messing with the plan and is plotting to overthrow you, and then take your place in the creative cycle of everything?' I asked.

'Then for you, that is exactly how it shall be.'

'There must be some rules, some guidelines.'

'No rules and no guidelines. As I said before, the processes that are in place are simply designed to ensure that the most beneficial outcomes are available to all.'

'I do not believe that.'

'If that is your perception, then so be it. So far as the spiritual realm and all of life is concerned, there are rigid structures in place, rules, guidelines for what? – What shall we call it? I know. There are rules and guidelines that exist for ways in which free will can be exercised in the right way.'

'Now you are just being sarcastic,' I retaliated.

'As a cock-sucking motherfucker, am I not allowed a bit of sarcasm?'

'*Yeah, of course. I am really sorry about that,*' I apologised.

'*No apology required. But that is how you put your perceptions across. Maybe you can answer a question for me?*'

'*Fire away.*'

'*Can you explain to me how free will, rules, obligations and guidelines can co-exist in harmony?*'

'*No. I cannot.*'

'*So you can only have one or the other. If that is the case, and with no free will, what need to exist at all?*'

'*None, I guess.*'

'*So if your free will is of paramount importance in your own personal belief system, then you are to live your life, at least in a spiritual sense, rule-free.*'

'*And if I believe in rules and regulations?*' I asked.

'*Then they will exist. You see, you can only be what your perception will allow you to be. Your entire world only exists in that small space called your mind. You will agree, will you not, that anxieties, stress, joy, sadness, elation, any human emotional outflowing, can only come from within?*'

'*Yes, I believe that.*'

'*That is a reaction to a set of circumstances perceived by you. Pay close attention to what I just said. I did not say that your reaction is to any factual reality or to any other person or circumstance. This is because you can only react to your own perception of those things. The way your existence is, is all in your mind.*'

'*So all that has happened, or will happen, with this entity is all inside my head? It is my perception of what is happening that is creating that happening in the first place?*' I asked.

'*Consciously or subconsciously, yes. That is exactly what I am saying.*'

***

Michaela Ruth closed the boot of her car, catching her finger on the clasp as it sped past her hand. She shook her hand rapidly before looking at the reddening mark that soon revealed a small spot of blood. She put the finger into her mouth and sucked. There was no taste of blood; the nick on her skin was too small.

'Fuck it,' she said through clenched teeth, as she sucked at her finger.

Michaela picked up the three plastic bags from the ground in between her feet, making sure she extended her injured finger away from them as she did so. She entered the property, dropped the bags on the hallway floor, and headed to the kitchen to hold her injured finger under the cold-water tap. She turned the tap on and felt the cold water wash over her injury.

After drying her finger, she made a coffee and retired to the lounge with the TV magazine she had bought at the supermarket. On opening the first page, her mind passed to the psychic who started, but did not complete, a reading for her. She did not pay him any money, which was just as well. On running upstairs to her resting child, it turned out that Rebecca was sleeping peacefully, so she was mystified as to why he was so insistent she should attend to her young baby.

When she returned to the lounge, the psychic was gone. She had no idea why he reacted in the way he did, she had no clue whether or not the psychic saw danger for Rebecca, and when she might be exposed to this danger. She had tried to phone him to find out more, but he did not answer his phone. Michaela had done a little background checking and this one seemed to be genuine. He had a good-looking website and good references. There was only really one issue on which Michaela had sought the guidance of a well-regarded psychic. Michaela wanted to know if true love would ever come knocking on her door. She admitted that it would be hard to bring a man into her family life, but at eleven months old, Rebecca would easily adjust without too many problems. Her friends all tried to push her into internet dating, but that idea revolted her.

Michaela took a sip of the rapidly cooling coffee that lay on a coaster before her. She coughed, and a speck of blood landed inside the coffee cup. She immediately put her hand up and wiped the back of her hand against her lips. She withdrew her hand and looked at the back. It was clean. Maybe she had a small bleed from inside her nose that corrected itself as soon as it happened?

Michaela coughed again. This time she felt a slimy lump travel through her throat and into her mouth. It was spherical in shape and about the size of a penny. It tasted as did the phlegm you get after a nosebleed where the blood clots up and congeals into a jelly-like soft lump. She spat the phlegm into her coffee cup. It was a crimson red colour. The phlegm mixed a little with the coffee and then sank to the bottom of the cup, leaving only a sliver of trace on the brown liquid above it.

Michaela Ruth felt a rush of liquid gush up the inside of her throat. She was nowhere near her bathroom so the liquid, when it left her mouth, projected outwards, covering the table in front of her and splattering on the floor around her. Michaela got up and rushed into the bathroom, bumping her shoulder hard against the door as she barged through the doorway and inside the room. She opened the top of the toilet and stuck her head inside the bowl. She had not noticed the colour of the liquid that she spat onto the lounge floor and coffee table, but guessed it would be the same as now came out of her mouth.

She choked, as the crimson liquid poured out from her mouth. She tried to take a quick breath but was unable to. She pushed harder in her chest, eager to clear the liquid so that she would be able to take a breath, no matter how short it might be. She never got an opportunity to take that breath before she blacked out.

* * *

'So I am imagining everything, it is all in my head?' I wondered.

'Well, technically, anything you imagine cannot exist anywhere other than in your mind, so the girls on the bus, Amy, Chloe, at least all of these happenings you must know to be true, so they cannot be imagination driven. What is inside your mind is the record of each event you ever experience in your physical lifetime. What thought you attach to each of these records is what makes up your perception. Now, perception cannot be formed simply as a reaction to, let's say, a photograph. A human reaction to that photograph is learned. It is these learned behaviours that form your perception of your life and all that happens in it. Your imagination is only a pallet of available colours with which you can paint pictures. Pictures hang on the wall, but though every picture is an impression of an individual's reality, they are not the reality itself.'

'But you said my perception of events creates that event.'

'Yes, that is true.'

'My perception surely cannot precede an event. How can that be? My perception of something can only occur after it has happened, surely?' I asked.

'Your perception of anything, anything at all, creates your reality. Of course, your perception can create an event. Your perception is your paintbrush to illuminate or darken your world, it is your perception that adds light and shade to your world. Let me explain it very easily. Sometimes when you can perceive something, that perception creates an image, that image becomes real in your physical realm. This does not necessarily mean that this thing you created exists, it just means that in your reality it does.'

'And that explains how sometimes one person can see one thing and somebody else cannot, or they see something different.'

'Precisely.'

'It is easy to think that is how it is in the spiritual realm, but in my reality we live by facts, we live by what we can see, hear, smell, taste and touch.'

'The principles are the same. Your existence on earth is the same as your existence in the spiritual realm. The only difference is that with greater vibrational frequency come greater possibilities and greater outcomes. Your physical world is full of experiences, both emotional and physical. That is how you have programmed yourselves to learn. Since it is easier to exist by being in tune with the lower vibrations of the objects that occupy your world, then that is what you choose to work with. You choose to perceive your world as a purely physical existence, and that is how you train yourself to exist. But

many have been able to operate more freely, more constructively, by using higher vibrations to create greater, and more open, perceptions, in a physical reality.'

'You mean like Jesus, Buddha, Mohammed.'

'Oh and many, many others. The opportunity to use higher vibrations to see and know more than you perceive is available to every single living organism that occupies space and time in your world.'

'So I can train myself to see beyond what my mind says is real, fixed and unchangeable.'

'You do not even need to train yourself. A myriad of perceptions are available all the time, you just need to reach out and pick which perception you choose to be your truth at that particular moment in time.'

'And if I were able to do that I could see and know more in any given situation.'

'You could, but what you are doing in reality is seeing the options available to you before you choose one perception over another.'

'So it is like buying one pair of trousers, but being aware that other trousers exist that might be more suitable on other occasions.'

'Very simplistically put. But yes, it is kind of like that. With a greater access to the knowledge that alternative possibilities exist, you will know you cannot wear all of the available trousers at once. But the choice is made much easier because you can see in great detail all aspects of each pair of trousers, and the use to which they can be put.'

'But I still do not understand how I can tap into this higher wisdom, into these higher frequencies.'

'Okay. You were born and raised in a country where you were educated to use the English language. You have access to hundreds of thousands of words and phrases. Of the words and phrases you use, you know what each one means, or you would not be able to use it. If you think of a common word, it just looks the way it always has, it sounds the same too, and it means the same thing. But if you have never looked beyond that, seen behind the word, you will never know its origins, viewed how it became manipulated and shaped through centuries of social and environmental pressures, to become what it is today. The original word is sure to have its origins in sound, in vibrations. And I guarantee that word would mean something entirely different in its original form than it does to you now. Think of a Chinese whisper. If you can trace the change of the whisper at each stage, you become aware of its evolution, of its journey. It is this ability, the skill to look deeper, to search for the origins of your existence, to be aware that you have these powers, and then you will know them and be able to use them.'

'So each piece of communication is the end result of a Chinese whisper?'

'Not just each communication. That is exactly how you perceive your physical life in the earth plane. You live your life as you perceive all the

communications about it should be lived. Everything you experience in your lifetime comes from your anticipation of how you should feel about it. You ignore your subconscious instinct, which reacts to every situation, too. Instead, you rely on what you have been taught. You use your conscious memory bank to react to the situations, confrontations and embedded thoughts that you experience. Even with new experiences, you still dip into this memory bank to react in a way you feel comfortable with.'

'So are you plucked from my memory bank? Or are you a new unanticipated experience?' I asked.

'I am what I am. One thing I can tell you that might surprise you: I am not I, I am not a personalisation, I do not belong to anything. I exist, but in my true form, I cannot be labelled. I exist but I am not an existence. Does that make any sense to you?'

'Yes, I guess it does.'

'That is very good. If you can include a perception in your thoughts that something can exist without a label, without an explanation, then you are on your way to vibrating at a higher level.'

'That is good to know.'

'The truth is that nothing exists in the form of its label. Nothing on earth or anywhere else exists as it is explained or understood. When you can accept this concept, then you can move away from labelling things, you can go beyond worded communication, and you can enter a higher vibrational field that will show you far more than you could ever formulate in any spoken language. That, my friend, is where you can find the clues, and the answers that will help you address your current dilemma.'

***

Michaela tried to force her eyes open. The lids moved a bit, but they were stuck together with mucus from the tears shed while choking out the blood into the toilet basin. Her arms supported her weight while her body slumped against the toilet bowl rim. When she came to, her right cheek was pressed into the ceramic rim.

Michaela was looking down on a mess of red, brown and clear mucus that had settled on the still water. All of this must have been expelled from her body before she passed out. She remembered coughing, and she could instantly feel the sting at the back of her throat as a result. She remembered the dizziness engulfing her as her breath was replaced by a steady flow of blood that fell into the toilet bowl. Then blackness had overtaken her.

She now started to wonder if it was all over, whatever *it* might have been.

Apart from the odd bout of influenza and submitting to the colds and coughs that naturally circulate the air in school, Michaela had never been a sickly person. As she grew into an adult, Michaela had suffered no major injuries, no falls, and she had never collapsed before. She had a time when she had suffered heart palpitations while carrying Rebecca, but she put that down to a nasty, but wholly natural, effect of the pregnancy cycle.

Michaela had never suffered from being overweight. In fact, while Rebecca was growing in her womb, she had eaten far less than before becoming pregnant. And after her first child was born, Michaela weighed a couple of pounds less than she did before falling pregnant. She did not dine on the healthiest of foods, but since Rebecca arrived, she had made an effort to eat more fruit and vegetables, and to cut down on her intake of stodgy and sugary foods. She now combined breastfeeding with offering Rebecca early stage foods, such as porridge and fruit cocktails.

Try as she might, Michaela could find no rational explanation for what had just happened to her.

Mustering all her strength, she managed to lift her right arm and stretch her hand up to the handle that would flush the toilet contents away. The noise was too loud at this distance, as the muck inside the bowl sank through the u-bend and into the sewage pipes away from the house. Her right arm dropped to her side. She managed to raise both arms to the side of the bowl to support her weight, and finally she was able to introduce some rigidity to her neck to support her head.

The ripples on the water in the toilet bowl slowly cleared. Michaela's image stared back at her with bloodied mouth and ashen complexion. Her hair was matted to the left and right of her face.

Appearing over her right shoulder was a figure that was not clearly defined. She stared into the water trying to make the image clearer, but she could not. Its face was blurred. She could distinguish eyes, ears, nose, mouth, and she even saw the colour of its hair, but the person, or the thing, that appeared just beyond her right shoulder, was slightly beyond being clear.

The figure communicated with Michaela without moving its mouth. It seemed to her that the message came from somewhere behind the man's eyes. The strange thing was that Michaela had no fear of this thing that one minute was absent, and the next moment was there. The stranger could not really be described as a stranger, either. It was as if Michaela knew this man, it was just that she could not place how, why or when.

Michaela knew that she should be screaming at the top of her voice at the sudden appearance of this man in her bathroom, but she got no sense that this would be the right thing to do. Though confused to some degree, Michaela knew that somehow this was the right thing to happen at this moment in time. Although shocked at first by his appearance, it now seemed natural and normal for this man to be here. It was almost as if she knew he was coming, but she had forgotten she had an appointment with him.

The communication that came from behind his eyes told Michaela that everything was alright, that they would be taking a journey together, and that this journey would be serene and pleasant. She was even asked if she would like to spend a little time with Rebecca, with her parents or her friends before they departed. Michaela never once wondered how this man might know her baby's name.

Michaela chose to look in on Rebecca, but not for long. The next moment Rebecca was in her cot and Michaela was bent over her. Rebecca opened her eyes and gave Michaela the biggest grin her mother had ever seen on her baby girl's face.

चतुर्विंशति

'Can I meet with the victims of this entity?' I asked.

'You mean the essence of the people who, in your knowledge, have died as a result of coming into contact with the being that you believe is responsible for the early deaths of the schoolchildren and other people?'

'That is a very long way of putting it, but yes, that is what I mean.'

'It is one of the very few ways it can be put. I must address any requests you have of me as they relate to your perception. I cannot do it any other way.'

'Wait a minute. You said that I was asking about the victims 'in my knowledge.' Does that mean there are more victims I do not know about?'

'Would it come as a surprise to you if I said yes?'

'No, I guess not. But how many people are we talking about? How many people have been taken to the spiritual realm before their time on earth is finished?'

'That is a whole separate issue. All I will say to you is that nothing surrenders itself to the death of its physical self without its approval. It is always a choice that must be made by the individual.'

'So in an accident, or a murder, or a natural disaster, or any other circumstances, death is chosen?'

'Yes, that is what I am saying. But here we are also in danger of crossing into another aspect of the life-death-life process that is not at issue here, there is no such thing as old age. A body becoming older or physically weaker can never create the situation that might result in the death of a human. It cannot happen. The death of any person, at any time, by any means, is a natural outcome of the choice of that person to move onto a different existence than that he or she has just occupied.'

'So everything in our existence is a matter of choice, whether that choice be made consciously, subconsciously, by perception or by persuasion,' I clarified.

'Yes.'

'So all those people attacked by this entity chose that this would happen?'

'Not in the way you suggest no, but the outcome is correct, yes.'

'I find that incredibly difficult to believe.'

'You will remember your discussion on your last visit when you discovered that possibilities exist, but fate does not.'

'Yes, I remember that.'

'Fate can never exist, because the issue at the very core of your being is that you have free choice in everything. Fate cannot, therefore, exist at the same time as free choice. The opportunities that exist in life and after, are simply that – they are opportunities you can choose or discard. The planning process sets out to offer the greatest opportunities for growth for you, as an individual spiritual energy, to experience during a physical lifetime. Your choices are not extinguished by this planning process, they are increased beyond anything you can imagine.'

'So this planning process might include the possibility of meeting up with this entity in the early stages of a lifetime,' I thought.

'The very fact that this entity exists means that everyone in a physical existence faces the possibility of encountering it. The same as everyone in a physical existence faces the opportunity of not encountering it. You mentioned your five senses. Forget your sixth sense; there is no such thing. You can only ever make one choice from two possibilities. Everything you see, hear, smell, touch, taste only holds that sensation for you because that is the choice you have made. The other choice you could have made would lead to a totally different outcome. You all make choices to create an outcome. The only choice you can ever make is that you do something, or you do not. Either choice cannot have the same outcome as the other. They are opposite ends of a spectrum.'

'So it is as easy as making a choice to make marmalade on toast or porridge for breakfast?' I asked.

'Well, yes it is. Would it surprise you to learn that in making a choice between porridge or marmalade you are setting in motion two courses of events that have entirely different outcomes? In choosing marmalade you might be setting up a series of events that create your best day ever, but if you had chosen porridge you might even be setting up a chain of events that might lead to your death.'

'Are you being serious?'

'I am being deadly serious. This is a very simplistic overview of how people evolve through their choices. The only difference between Jesus, Buddha and Mohammed is that they made informed choices. They made their choices based on the potential outcome of the two choices they faced at any given time. This is what led to their living, what you might consider as, evolved lives.'

'But we can all do that, can't we? And if I can do that I will have all the tools at my disposal to deal with this entity?'

'If you choose it to be so, it will.'

***

Michaela could see her physical body slumped over the toilet basin. She stayed there for what seemed like a long time. She was aware of thoughts passing through her mind, but it was as if she could not grab onto any one in particular. She felt empty. Empty of any kind of feelings at all, empty of emotion, of fear, doubt, aggression, love. It was a surprise to her that she was able to stay here so long with nothing happening.

She was aware that she had left Rebecca on her own, but she did not panic about that, as she might have expected to. Her mother, neighbour, friend, someone, would realise pretty soon when they could not contact Michaela that her baby would be in the house alone. They would do whatever they needed to do to enter the house and rescue her baby girl.

Michaela never really contemplated death, until it happened. She had thoughts in her physical state of what might happen at her death, but these thoughts always revolved around those people left behind on the earth plane and how they would adjust to a life without their mother, their daughter, their friend. The actual event had never been contemplated. Here it was now, and it needed to be dealt with.

She was also aware of the being over her shoulder that had been her companion in her final living moments, during the short breaths that preceded her passing over into this other way of existence. He was here with her now, but at a distance, so as not to interfere with anything that took place inside or around her. She knew that he was her companion at this time and she was fine with that. She also knew that he would accompany her on the journey that was to come.

Though she had no predetermined ideas of what awaited her after death, she was disappointed that no deceased family members were there to greet her. In life, she was very close to her grandmother on her father's side, spending many happy hours at her house playing cards, playing with dolls and living the kind of princess life she was somehow never able to live at home. She often looked at photographs of her grandmother, keeping alive the sunny summer day memories of school holidays and journeys of excitement each day she spent with her.

Her grandmother was a kind and cheery person. She helped many old ladies living nearby, even though her age was similar to their own. She cooked for them, she washed their clothes, she cleaned and dusted their homes for them. It was what she considered necessary to be a good neighbour. And she laughed, a lot. She was not intellectually gifted, by any stretch of the imagination, but her simple outlook on life, of itself, was sufficient to create much frivolity in family circles.

Her grandmother was the one person she expected to see now, the person who might plant a kiss on her cheek, take her hand, and lead her to the promised land. But her grandmother was nowhere to be seen. And that was another thing. At this moment in time she was aware that she could perceive her environment without having any of the same physical senses she had when alive. She was aware by looking at something, like the toilet bowl, that it existed, but her mind's sight was no longer in colour. The physical items around her new form had taken on different shades of a greyish brown colour, a bit like, though not very similar at all, to a very old photograph.

One other surprise was that, though she no longer possessed any functioning ears, she was able to hear sounds. These noises were like a muffled, and very quiet, hum, which was pierced intermittently by a shriller spike. Yes, that was the best way to put it. She knew that the shrill sounds related to incidents, or actions, of which she was unaware. It was almost as if things were happening within earshot, but at the same time just outside of it. She guessed the most important thing was to be aware of these things, without taking too great an interest in them.

And then there was the feeling of suspension. There was obviously no gravity in effect now, but equally there was no feeling of non-gravity either. It seemed to Michaela that she would be able to move anywhere and anyhow she chose to, just as soon as she thought about doing so. She knew that her movement would be unrestricted when she chose to exercise these new found freedoms. But just at this moment, her focus remained on the shell of the former Michaela slumped on the linoleum floor to the right of the toilet bowl.

Michaela's thoughts, or more accurately, her awareness, moved to what was yet to come. Much as she had no belief in heaven, as depicted in scripture, Michaela also held no faith in there being a hell, where she would surely end up, having given birth to a child outside of wedlock. Michaela knew that she had been at this place before, and that she would undoubtedly arrive here again. If such things as heaven and hell existed, how could Michaela know, right now, that she had lived before and that she would inhabit another physical body afterwards? And if life was really just a process of learning, what could possibly be learnt from being born in sin, living a life of sin, and then burning in a steaming hot cauldron for all eternity?

So far as Michaela was concerned, whatever awaited her beyond the veil of a physical lifetime must be further opportunities to grow and learn, but she doubted that harp playing tiny winged angels strummed out background Muzak while teachers taught the A to Z's of life. It was more likely to be a case of 'learn if you want to, it is up to you.' And Michaela now found herself more than ready to learn and become a better… what? A better spirit? A better soul? A better energy? A better life force?

Her companion motioned that it was time for Michaela to leave, if she chose to. Michaela did choose to move on. She was aware that her companion was positioned at her right shoulder, and she was surprised when she was nudged forwards, a little too forcefully for her liking.

She moved through the wall of her home and was immediately aware of a tunnel that stretched out into the distance. The tunnel was not straight and there was no light at the end, not that she could see anyway. Instead, the tunnel was completely spherical and the sides of it were clear. It bent around to the left, as if following the natural curve of the earth. The outside of the spherical tunnel shimmered, as if it were a part of a heatwave rising from the ground. She did not so much step inside the tunnel, but more willed herself into it, just as she had when she passed through the wall. Her body was still here in one piece, but it felt different, it felt less solid. Her legs, her arms, her stomach, everything was so familiar, except the weight of it was gone.

An invisible zip line conveyed her through the shimmering tunnel. She would describe it as a conveyor belt, but the movement was too fast, way too fast. She noticed images whizzing past as she travelled. She knew that all these images were connected to her, but again, this tunnel and its meaning were somehow incorrect, according to what she might have expected.

She might have expected images of past events, choices and feelings, but what she was faced with were unfamiliar scenes. She knew instantly that the images that assailed her during this journey were those of future events she had never experienced. Her thirtieth birthday, Rebecca's birthdays – lots of them – Rebecca at school, Rebecca and her first boyfriend, her daughter getting married, of herself becoming a grandmother, the death of her mother, and her own death. This seemed a bit more than crazy. If Michaela had just died, then how could she see herself dying at some time in the future?

She started to become tense for the first time since she had ceased to be a living, breathing being. Why did people bother to write books about what happens when you die, when what they write is wrong? These people were held up as leading lights in the spiritual and ethereal fields on earth. Why were there common, so-called true accounts, that numerous people bought into? When, for Michaela, the truth of the experience was very different.

***

'At this moment in time I need to get a plan together to tackle this entity. I need to develop and deploy a strategy that will stop any further untimely deaths, and secure the structure of the spiritual realm as it is now.' I thought.

'That is a very noble plan, but you must be very careful that your endeavours do not become foolhardy. I am aware of the request that was made of you, which, I fear, you might have taken too literally. I should explain that a situation does exist that was never contemplated when, you could say, the blueprints were drawn up for the spiritual realm.'

'That would be before our calendar started.'

'Oh, it would be many millennia before that. You see, the spiritual realm existed long before the apes ever straightened up and started thinking a bit more about what they were doing, and how they existed. In fact, the spiritual realm has existed since existence came into being.'

'At the birth of planet earth?' I asked.

'Before that. In fact, the spiritual realm has existed since before the birth of the universe you exist in and any other universes. But the blueprint for the spiritual realm never took into account any rogue elements, because the perception of the perfect existence was just that, a perception. As we know, with any perception it is an individual view of something. It is not, and never can be, all-encompassing. In all the millennia since it began, there have been no challenges to the kingdom of the spiritual realm. Until now.'

'And how is it that I have been tasked to take out this rogue entity, and to restore parity?'

'That is the misconception you seem to be under. You have a very important part to play, and that is the part you have chosen through all of your life choices...'

'Including what I ate for dinner last night...'

'A flippant attitude is good, it will help you. To answer your point, yes, that will include what you chose to eat for your dinner last night. All the choices you ever made in your current and, I might add, previous lifetimes, at a conscious and a subconscious level, have led up to this moment. But the important part you play is not a lone role. The female you know as Judy Marchant is drawn to helping you for a very good reason...'

'Because all her life choices have also led her to this point.'

'That is correct. But it does not end there. You may be aware, you may not, it matters little, but you have a multitude of spiritual entities helping you in this final push towards the goals you were created for.'

'Wait a minute. What happened to life eternal?'

'That is true, your spiritual energy is eternal.'

'Then what is this about the goals I was created for?' I asked.

'Every energetic spiritual entity has a number of key goals that they set out to achieve after their creation...'

'Since the creation of the spiritual realm?'

'Not all, but for some, yes.'

'And how do I know I can count on these spiritual energies for their help? I cannot even perceive their presence.'

'Oh yes you can, and you have. Please don't underestimate the awesomeness of the power available to the spiritual realm to deal with this matter. This issue has been on the slow burner since the blueprint was first drawn up, because the capacity for this situation to happen was always there. It was always a potential outcome, even if it was not perceived. And please do not label spiritual entities as only those beings that cannot be seen or heard, human beings, in physical incarnations, are spiritual entities too, as are you.'

'Okay, but aren't those physical helpers unknown to me too?'

'Judy, Martin Coombs, Chloe Ohmigo and all the girls on the minibus, to name but a few.'

'Then why don't they announce themselves to me? And why would they volunteer to die so young at the invisible hands of this entity?'

'They have all announced themselves at some point to you by their actions and by their words. Why else would they volunteer to play such a pivotal role in the preservation of their energetic home? Wouldn't you? Just as you volunteered to take the role you are taking.'

'But is that because they chose to? Or they had to?'

***

I switched off my phone before this meditation. It was too serious and too valuable to be disturbed by unsolicited calls about personal protection insurance, or claims on accidents I never had, or about pension plans, funeral arrangements, or financially supporting a local cat shelter. All that shit could wait until I had finished saving our world, and the next.

One of the calls I missed was from Judy. Here is the message she left, in full: 'It's Judy. Hi, how are you doing? Long time, no hear, yardy, yardy, yar. Look, I'm not going to give you any crap. Your name has been mentioned at the station concerning the business with this minibus crash. It seems the story of being alone in your car did not wash. Some guys from the station have been tailing you, not FBI-like, there are no wire taps or anything like that – they are keeping their distance. They know you were approached by the old lady at the crematorium after the service for the kids in the crash. Please, I am not sticking my nose in, I just think you should know this. Oh, and by the way, the DI has asked me to get back in contact with you so, I guess, this call is official. Please feel free to keep the recording. I will be seeing you very soon. Bye.'

Judy Marchant was important to me. She was the one person I hoped would believe me, but I doubted she could. But that is why I approached her in the first place, hope. At that time I had no idea how bad the situation was, or how much worse it was going to get.

Since I walked into her office again, Judy had been my rock. It was only because the situation seemed to be getting out of hand that I suggested, for her own safety and for my sanity, that she back off for a while. To know that I had her diligence and her intellect available to me, meant a lot. So Judy was important to me, but it is doubtful whether even she was as important as having my own personal tête à tête with God.

***

'*I want to meet with the victims of this entity, so how can I do that?*' I asked.

'*You can do that, but I am not sure how that will help you.*'

'*I want to know more about the entity, how it operates, any communication it makes with its victims. I also want to know if it has told them why they were killed, and maybe learn more about the purpose of the entity.*'

'*You mention the word want. If you want something you will always push it further away, this is because the desire in you is the experience of wanting, and not the experience of receiving. But there is another problem. The spiritual make-up of an experiential energy consists of three conjoined entities that, while existing in separation, are always linked by their identity. An experiential energy will occupy a mind in a physical body while also acting as a spirit and a soul. These three entities have very specific responsibilities that require separation and togetherness, whenever necessary.*'

'*So conventional wisdom is right, in that the soul does exist.*'

'*Of course a soul exists, how else would you be able to use instincts? Where would all your capacity for learning come from? Your soul is the core of you, it is the part of God that is with you always, and in all ways. Your spirit is the part of you that is permanently linked to the spiritual realm. Through this link you are able to trace and follow your spiritual guidance and planned learning opportunities. Your mind is the vessel in which learning and knowledge is stored.*'

'*Let me get this straight. Our soul is a part of God that has been passed to us to carry through all our physical experiences.*'

'*Your soul is far more than that. There is one thing God can never do. God can never have the benefit of experiencing the wonder of creation in physical terms. So the only way in which this could be achieved would be for small parts of God to rejoice in this experience. In the spiritual blueprint, this was the first core principle. Your soul is your origin. It is your link with God.*'

'*If that is the case, where does a person's soul exist?*'

'*A soul can exist anywhere, but mostly it chooses to exist within the energetic makeup of a physical body.*'

'*So why has a person's soul never been identified scientifically?*'

'*Because your soul is not a physical entity. I should explain that during any lifetime an experiential energy consists of around five per cent physical entity. None of your internal organs can operate purely on the physical makeup of the human body. The operation of a human body is ninety-five per cent energy and spiritual matter. The idea of a Frankenstein's monster can only ever be a story of fiction. If you put together all of the organs of the human body, fixed all of the joints, included a healthy functioning brain and had a stimulant on hand, your creation would never work, because the* majority of what makes up a human would be missing, and that person would cease to be.'

'So every human being, to exist on earth and in the spiritual realm, must have a connected physical body, a spirit, and a soul.'

'Yes. But that formula is the same for everything that exists in any universe.'

'Even for rocks too?'

'Yes of course. Everything that exists in any physical form must be connected to their spiritual and soul forms, otherwise the process of evolution cannot happen.'

'Is evolution the whole reason for anything to exist?'

'Learning is a natural process of existing, yes. That is the primary focus of the blueprint.'

'So rocks have a soul, too?'

'Well, in a way, yes. The lower you go down the evolutionary chain, the soul becomes central to the collective. Therefore, a rock will be one of untold billions of contributors to a rock's collective soul. The spirit of a rock operates in the same way, too. The evolving of a spirit, a soul, and a physical shell happens individually and collectively. That is the second principle of the blueprint.'

'So what is the problem with me visiting the victims of this entity to learn more about it? Surely the more information I have, the better chance I will have to put this issue to rest.'

'It is vital you first understand these principles of life. Without knowing the make-up of what you are dealing with, as well as the people it interacted with, then you might well face certain failure. I have explained this in a way you are given to understand. This communication can never fully explain the way of the planes of existence, but it is all we have to work with.'

'So tell me about this entity. How can I effectively battle it so that no more early, unplanned deaths occur?' I asked.

'Let me tell you something, my friend. No death can be planned, it is a choice made by the energies that make up an individual. Do you know how many times you have chosen not to die?'

'I know about when my heart stopped at fourteen years of age. I can only think of maybe two or three other occasions I might have been in peril.'

'You have been given the opportunity to travel the path of the death of your physical body on sixty-two occasions so far, on each of these occasions your choice was to continue your physical existence. You will find similar numbers for every person of your age alive now. These opportunities do not occur as a result of illness. They can only occur as a matter of choice.'

'So we come back to all the people who lost their lives as a result of meeting up with this entity doing so because that is what they chose to do.'

'That is how the death experience occurs, and that is what you should believe, yes. However, it sometimes happens that the choice given to a living entity will not be provided through the usual channels. It seems that this is the case with the entity you are interested in.'

'I don't understand how that can happen. How can something just step in and create an unauthorised death opportunity?'

'There are ways to create anything at all in any realm, but particularly in the spiritual realms. This does not normally occur, since the knowledge needed to undertake such a move does not exist.'

'Except it does.'

'In this case, yes it does, as can be shown in your recent experiences.'

'So what is the problem with me meeting this entity's victims?'

'First, you only know about the tip of the iceberg. Far more incidents have occurred of which you are unaware. Second, so far as we are aware, this entity has been able to separate these peoples' souls and spirits from the normal process. This would suggest that the entity is able to circumvent the normal passing over process.'

'For what reason? Is it true that this entity seeks war in the spirit realms?' I asked.

'I cannot second-guess any entity's motives.'

'But you are God; you know everything.'

'Ha, ha, wouldn't that be nice. I am a learning, evolving entity, just as is everything else.'

'I still do not know why I was asked to help?'

'You were asked to help because of your unique knowledge and experience of the entity responsible for these disruptions.'

'Is that it? Is that all you can tell me? Where is God when you need Him?'

'I am right by your side, as I always am.'

'So are any of the victims of this entity here? Can I get to visit them?' I pushed for an answer once again.

'They are empty vessels. When they arrived, they were put into our recovery rooms, which is something like a hospital. Any spirit that suffers a death experience that is either traumatic or personally unexpected, and which arrives into the spiritual realms, is placed into recovery. It is hoped, in time, that the people visited by this entity will reunite as one. At the moment what we have of them is in recovery. Even if they were whole you would get no information from them; it is not allowed. The recovery rooms are shielded from all forms of communication.'

'Then where are the rest of them? Where are their experiences, their essence, their spirits, their souls?'

'We do not know.'

'So what is my next step?'

'I have provided you with the information that should help you to follow your path. The human experience relies entirely upon the choices and decisions made based on what circumstances surround each person. You have all the information and detail you need now, to decide how to complete the task you have set yourself. It is not my role to intervene in any energetic existence, and neither should it be. Help is always available, just call out, and your call will be answered, as it was today.'

'If I look deep inside myself and if I am able to find and vibrate with that higher frequency within myself, then I will have the tools I need to complete this journey.'

'Yes.'

पञ्चविंशति

I checked my phone for messages. There was one message and it was from Judy Marchant. I called her back.

'Hi, Judy. Well, aren't I the man of the moment,' I said jovially.

'That is how it seems, yes.'

'I got your message. I was a bit surprised, but not too much. I guessed you might contact me at some time, just maybe a little bit later on.'

'Well you know how it is, orders are orders.'

'So what exactly have you been ordered to do?' I asked.

'My Inspector wants me to keep close to you, see if we can get anything more substantial than a possible dangerous driving charge.'

'Well that's more an issue for you than for me. You were driving, after all.'

'Nobody knows that, and God help us if they did.'

'Speaking of God's help, guess who I bumped into?'

'I have no idea. Surprise me.'

'Only the Big Guy himself. I got some really good leads on how we are going to tackle this spiritual piece of shit.'

'You spoke to God?'

'Well no, we had a conversation. He spoke to me, too.'

'I'm not so sure anyone could vouch for your sanity with a statement like that.'

'Hey, hey,' I paused, 'Judy, you just might have placed the final piece of the jigsaw.'

'What on earth are you talking about?' she asked.

'No, not what on earth, it may be more accurate to say 'what in existence,' I replied.

'Why are you acting so crazy?' Judy asked.

'I am acting in the way I need to act to save an awful lot of lives, and to earn some big fat juicy spiritual brownie points. If that makes me sound crazy, all the better,' I replied.

'And what has you acting crazy got to do with an entity that is killing young people before their allotted time, and a conversation you had with God?' she asked.

'It is all part of the same thing,' I said. 'I will explain more when you meet me here. Shall we say in fifteen minutes?'

I put the phone back onto its cradle. I had a real feeling, for the first time since I started on this epic journey, that I was making some headway, no matter how small that might be in reality.

***

Judy got a call from the coroner before she was able to leave her home. Theodore Anstis told her he had another body that might be another victim of the entity we were hunting. He said this girl was a young mother with an eleven-month-old child who survived her. He added there was nothing really outstanding about this lady's death, except for her age and the fact that she had died, somehow resuscitated herself, and then died again.

Dr. Anstis said there was no real cause for this lady's death. She had spewed up masses of phlegm and, to all intents and purposes, he might assume that her death was as a result of her drowning. Except that, first, there was no sign around the young lady that she had been anywhere near a body of water. Secondly, he had never heard of a drowning victim reviving themselves. So, officially, this young lady died an accidental death. Unofficially, he believed she was attacked by this being that might be responsible for the recent deaths of interest to her.

'Her name was Michaela Ruth. Pretty girl. Did you know her?' Dr. Anstis asked Judy.

'Why should I know her?' Judy countered.

'Well, you seem to be pretty tied up in all this extra-terrestrial shit.'

This kind of language had never been heard by Judy from the coroner's mouth, but then again they were facing a situation that was pretty much out of this world.

'No. But I would bet my grandmother's old Victorian drawers that my guy knows her,' she replied.

'Your guy? What guy?' Theo Anstis asked.

'The guy who got me into this mess in the first place. For some reason he seems to be at the centre of all of this, and he was there when the minibus crashed,' Judy replied.

'With all those kids inside?'

'Yes. Like I said, he seems to have a connection with all the people killed by this thing – a connection that at the moment I don't understand.'

'Remarkable,' the coroner commented.

'I think we need to get a sense of the bigger picture here, Dr. Anstis. I am going to talk with my guy, see if I can get a better grip on his involvement with this entity, and of what he intends doing next. He did tell me that many more people have been affected than those we already knew of. Please don't ask me how he knows this, because it's getting too weird even now. I want to find out if what he says might be true. Not only do I want to satisfy my own curiosity, but I need a better picture of what we are up against. Can you see if you have any connections that might be able to justify his claims?' Judy asked.

'I know some people I can contact, but I'm not too sure what kind of approach to take, without sounding too crazy myself?'

'I'm confident you will find a way. It might be critical to us being able to sort this thing out once and for all.'

***

I answered the urgent-sounding knocks on my front door. My first thought was that it was Judy, but the loudness and urgency of the rapping suggested otherwise.

'Sir, can you open the door please?'

Three policemen stood at the opening to the hallway outside my home. I recognised one as PC Stewart, the constable who had been here before, the other two were unfamiliar.

'We would like you to accompany us to the police station, please. We have some more questions about the minibus accident.'

'Can I grab some things?' I asked.

'Certainly,' I was answered.

There was no need for handcuffs, so I was a little surprised at the need for such a heavy-handed presence at my front door. Surely a simple phone call would have achieved the same outcome? Maybe it was more a reaction to the public clamour for action? Any time kids are killed in such a horrific way, the police must be seen to be proactive, even if that proactivity delivers very little as far as results are concerned.

Given my involvement in the accident, I might have expected video, handheld cameras and microphones to greet me as I exited the building. But the only people present were a middle-aged couple and their dog, which was pissing urgently into the small bushes at the front of the building. Without delay, and with my arm held firmly by PC Stewart, I crossed the threshold and was ushered into the rear of the police car. The vehicle started, and pulled away with little fuss.

'PC Stewart, can I ask you a question?' I asked of the policeman sitting next to me.

'Go ahead,' he replied, without turning to face me.

'Do you believe in God?'

PC Stewart did not answer. Instead he continued to stare straight ahead as the car pulled out onto the street.

'Your wife does, though, doesn't she? Do you think she might be disappointed at what you really do after work on a Friday night?'

PC Stewart spun his head around to face me.

'I think she might want to check up on your house deeds, and at your pension plan come to think of it. And what do you think she might tell your kids?' I whispered, loud enough for the constable next to me, but too soft for his colleagues in front to hear.

'Don't worry though, I can keep a secret,' I winked my right eye in his direction.

I felt a sharp and painful prod in my right thigh.

'One more sound out of you and I'll taser you,' it was the end of the weapon, firmly grasped in PC Stewart's hand, that had caused the pain.

'Ouch, that's gonna leave a mark, but not so much a mark as on your marriage, when your wife finds out you go to strip clubs once a week. You know some of those girls pretty well, don't you PC Stewart?' I said, a little louder than before.

The pressure on my leg was released, as the taser was removed.

'What is all this about?' the policeman asked quietly.

'I asked you a question. It's only polite to answer someone when he asks you a question, PC Stewart. If you recall, I asked if you believe in God?' I repeated my original question.

'I believe in something, but I don't know what it is,' the constable answered.

'It doesn't matter anyway,' I leaned a little to my right. 'You see, PC Stewart, I am on a mission from God,' I said quietly.

'You are some kind of crazy, that's what you are,' PC Stewart visibly moved away from me and closer to the car door.

'The guy driving, John I think his name is, he is a good cop but he suffers from depression. It will get much worse and, I would say in eighteen months' time, he will have to leave the police force. His marriage will suffer and he will end up committing suicide.'

PC Stewart looked at me again and I could sense the fear behind his pupils, as I continued.

'The guy next to him, Sahaan, he has a sarcastic streak in him that will land him in trouble. He will leave his job, too. He will end up helping out at his uncle's vegetable stall in town. Bit of a comedown, don't you think?' I continued.

'How do you know this stuff? It's bullshit, right?' PC Stewart asked.

'None of it is bullshit. I am a psychic, it is my profession, it is my job to know these things, and to advise people accordingly,' I smiled.

'Oh, I promise you, it will all happen, and on the timescale I said. But we don't have the time to prove me right, not now. You get sharp pains in your right wrist. You have not had it checked out because you don't want it to affect your job. Apart from anything else, you would hate a desk job. To you that is not police work; only being on the front line is for you. Now, have I convinced you enough to at least hear me out, PC Stewart?' I asked, losing a bit of patience.

'Why are you telling me all this? You crackpot' PC Stewart asked.

'I told you. I am on a mission from God. I need to get into St. Mary's Hospital, but I might need some help to do that,' I said.

'That is a looney bin, that's where all the local crackpots go. Everyone thinks God is talking to them in there, so you won't feel alone.'

'Be that as it may, I need to get in there, and I need to do it quick. Now, I could do it myself, but that would cause unnecessary delay. What I need is a little help by way of a recommendation, from you lot. Some kind of a formal notice should do the job,' I suggested.

'Jesus Christ, you are nuts.'

'Well, PC Stewart, we all make choices in life and each choice we make sets up another chain of likely events. We can only change the outcomes when we make a different choice that sets us on an alternative path. The choice I am making, is that I would like to be admitted to St. Mary's. You have choices you can make, too, PC Stewart, like where you choose to spend the next Friday night. If I am recommended to go by the police force with, let's say, the caveat that I might well be a danger to the general public, then I can get on with my mission from God. And don't forget, it might be better to get that guy who hung out of a car window, shouting at that minibus driver, out of the way for a while. Don't you think?'

'Your words might be crazy,' PC Stewart moved his head closer to mine, 'but the way you say them, is not,' he whispered.

षड्विंशति

'Dr. Anstis, what did you find for me?' Judy asked eagerly, into the mouthpiece of the telephone.

'Er, I don't really know how to say this, but it seems that if you are right, and if the bodies on my slab are all connected, they are not the only ones. I spoke to three colleagues. One is in Orkney, one is in Llandrindod Wells, and the other one is in Thirsk. All three reported seeing more than one young person who died of natural causes. The youngest was only twelve years old. My colleagues too, though finding no external trauma marks or abrasions, all witnessed internally applied injuries consistent with the kind of attacks that we have been witness to. And though these injuries caused the deaths of their subjects, none could be officially noted as such,' the coroner reported.

'Do we know when these deaths occurred?' Judy asked.

'I can't be absolutely sure, but from what I could pick up, it seems they all happened within the last four months. I am not aware of any cases before then,' Theo Anstis replied.

'Well, that seems to loosen the tie a little bit with Len Hooke.'

'Who?'

'Oh sorry, Len Hooke is the name of the psychic guy who started this investigation.'

'Len Hooke, now why does that name ring a bell?'

'Do you know him Dr Anstis?'

'I'm not sure, his name sounds familiar. I will let you know if it comes to me,' Dr Anstis replied.

***

I sat in an interview room for more than twenty minutes, before somebody entered and occupied one of the two extra chairs that stood on the opposite side of a simple wood-topped table with black metal legs. I did not know this person. I would have preferred to have spoken to PC Stewart, but I guess they preferred to mix it up a bit to keep me on my toes.

'So, sir, I would like to understand your link with the minibus crash last week that killed twelve school kids, and seriously injured two teachers who were accompanying the girls to a netball match.'

'You would not believe me even if I told you, which I am not inclined to do. I have said all I have to say on this matter. All you have to do is speak with PC Stewart. He came to my home and I gave him a statement. So far as I am concerned, that should be the end of it,' I replied.

'So why don't you tell me what you told him?' the man opposite asked.

'What good will that do? If you are going to charge me with trying to help a fellow motorist, then go ahead, otherwise, I don't really see what else I can help you with.'

'My senior officers think that there is more to your account of the events than you have so far given us. That is why you are here now. It is best for all of us if you can just fill in the gaps, and then we can all go home and get on with our lives, don't you think?' the man opposite asked.

'Then I suggest you either ask your senior officers to come here and ask me anything they want to or...' I moved slightly forward in my seat, 'you ask PC Stewart to come down here and I can continue my story with him. That way you get a continuation of the story, and I don't have to go over the same old things again. I'm sure you have something better to do with your time; I certainly do,' I suggested.

The man opposite me rose from his chair, circled the table and retreated out through the door.

***

'DI Talbot, please may I ask what is going on?' Judy asked, struggling to hide her annoyance.

'Inspector Marchant, do take a seat, please,' the DI motioned to the chair on the opposite side of the desk to him. She sat down and looked straight at the man's face, challenging him to answer her query in any kind of justifiable manner.

'I would guess from such a vague opening question, that you might be after an update about the driver,' the DI said while indicating speech marks in the air, 'of the silver car, who was present at the time of the minibus crash?'

'I most certainly am, yes,' she replied.

'You will be aware, Inspector Marchant, that the police force must, at all times, be swift in responding to a situation as it arises, and as circumstances dictate.'

'Yes, of course, sir.'

'And in answer to recent and very vocal public calls for information on the exact cause of the recent minibus crash that so deeply and tragically affected our community, I decided that we need to re-evaluate all the information available to us, so that we might better answer those questions currently being posed,' DI Talbot answered, without once altering his facial expression.

'So the object of the exercise is to serve the public interest.'

'Yes.'

'Rather than to find peace for the kids who died, and for their families.' Judy was in danger of letting her emotion take over, thereby losing any veracity in her argument. 'I thought PC Stewart interviewed him about the accident already, so apart from being a material witness to the accident, how is calling him in going to help in finding these answers?' Judy asked.

'Did you know that it was PC Stewart who interviewed him?'

'It's a small office. People know what most of their colleagues are doing, it's called good teamwork,' she replied.

'Hmm,' the DI raised his right eyebrow a little, after Judy's response.

'But why call him in for an official interview less than two days after you asked me to keep an eye on him? Also, I'm given to understand you have two other guys tailing him. It does seem a bit like overkill and might, in some people's eyes, even suggest that the accident might look to us too suspicious to have been an accident, and at worst, that he is a suspect in the matter,' Judy said.

'Yes, I can see how you might think that.'

'Please sir, I don't think that it is good policy to hold him here while more pressing issues need to be addressed,' Judy said.

'More pressing? Such as what?' DI Talbot asked.

'Real crime, real criminals, real issues deserving of our time. I can continue to watch over him and report any issues that are deserving of our interest.'

'Inspector Marchant, it seems to me like you might be trying to protect this man, as you might a friend,' suggested the DI.

'Sir, with all due respect, this man is not my friend, it just so happens he approached me about something else a few months ago. And I have no reason to protect anyone. I am just concerned that we be very careful not to call our service into any disrepute. I feel sure you can agree, sir, that this is a very sensitive matter, and that we should be very careful not to open up too much of a Pandora's box, which, I believe, is not necessary in this instance,' she suggested.

'Are you challenging my decision-making abilities, Inspector Marchant?'

'No, sir. Not at all, sir.'

'Good, because I would hate to think that there is anything other than your professional integrity driving your request.'

'No sir, I can assure you.'

'Good. Now, Inspector Marchant, it is a particularly busy time, what with the Mayor's parade and the upcoming train strike on the horizon, so if there is nothing else?'

'Well sir, if I might leave this subject by suggesting that I believe it best for PC Stewart and I to conduct an interview with this man, since it seems likely he might forward something more tangible if he were speaking with people with whom he is, at least, a little familiar.'

'Umm. Yes, yes, I do see your point. So be it, Inspector Marchant. Now, good day.'

Judy left the DI's office somewhat happier than when she had entered. The concern she had about any police interest in my activities remained, albeit now tempered with the greater control she felt in being involved first hand. Still, her strong preference, as was mine, was to be left alone to conduct our investigation, and find our own solutions, under the police radar. It seemed now that this might prove much harder to achieve, which lent even greater pressure to getting it right.

***

'So where is he?'

The voice on the other end of the phone was surprised and angry.

'He is at the police station. From what I know, they are talking to him about the minibus crash that was on TV and in the papers.'

'Where all those kids got killed?'

'Yes.'

'Well, what did he have to do with that?'

'Apparently, he was there when the accident happened.'

'Oh my God.'

'Yes, and not only that, he said he was on his way to see his brother, but that is not what he told me when he left.'

'What did he tell you?'

'He just said he had to go out; an emergency. Something to do with his work.'

'What job does he do again?'

'He reads people's fortunes.'

'What, like with tarot cards? Or does he do astrology, like Mystic Meg?'

'No, nothing like that. He reads their minds, or something like that.'

'That's far out. So what kind of emergency can drag him away from his family?'

'That is what I don't know.'

'Oh, come on, F, you are supposed to be his wife, for God's sake. He should tell you everything he is doing. Didn't you say he was writing a book as well?'

'Supposedly yes. He has this notebook and he is always jotting things down in it.'

'Have you ever looked at the notebook?'

'No. I wouldn't do that.'

'Oh come on, F, that is the very first thing you should have done.'

'For what reason? He does his work and that is his business. It's not like he comes home smelling of pussy every night.'

'Ever heard of body spray? Duh.'

'Listen, he needs privacy to do his work. If he was up to anything I would know about it.'

'Are you sure, F?'

'No. But how sure can you be of anything?'

***

My arms were crossed in front of me, cradling my head on top of the table. I looked up from my slumbering position, as the door to the interview room opened. A small pool of sweat had formed on my forehead. I wiped it away with the right shoulder of my polo shirt. The first person to enter the room was PC Stewart, closely followed by Inspector Judy Marchant.

'Ah, nice to see two familiar faces. You took your time,' I said as they entered the room.

'Well, you know how it is. Some people have a proper job to do,' PC Stewart replied, as he seated himself on the opposite side of the table.

Judy passed him a look of disdain, as she lowered herself onto the remaining chair. She pulled a ruffled A4 notepad from her shoulder bag, and set a couple of ballpoint pens on the table next to the pad.

'I should start off by explaining that you are not under arrest' Judy started, 'We invited you here because we have some questions about your involvement in the minibus crash. I think we are probably all aware of that incident?'

No reply was needed, or required.

'Okay, I should first of all explain that it is entirely your choice what questions you would like to answer, if any, and what information you might want to provide. We have no power to keep you here against your will, and you have the right to leave at any time. Do you understand these rights?' Judy asked.

'Yes, ma'am. Thank you,' I replied.

'Good. For the purposes of making sure nothing is misinterpreted or noted incorrectly we intend to record this interview, and I need to ask if you have any objections to this meeting being recorded?' Judy asked.

'Actually, I think that is a great idea,' I responded, 'If you had not offered to record our discussion, I would have asked for it myself,' I replied.

I explained everything, doing my best not to leave anything out of the equation. I told them about my meditative visit to the spirit world, of the warnings I received about the potential outcome of inaction. I told them about my understanding of the entity, and how it seemed hell bent on involving me in its scheme to take over the world, or something to that effect. I talked about what happened with Amy King in her home and how I had my first personal encounter with the entity there. My eyes inadvertently flicked to Judy as I spoke, almost as if I was looking for justification in my message.

'I have something to add,' Judy said. 'I also know about these events, because for some of the time, I was there.'

PC Stewart's jaw fell open in surprise. He rushed to cover the microphone on the portable recorder.

'Are you sure you want to say that?' PC Stewart whispered to Judy.

'We are dealing with the truth. That is the truth. Better it comes out now, than later,' Judy replied.

She then went on to explain that she, too, was at Amy King's house to witness her resuscitation, and what followed. She also admitted to being in the driving seat when we encountered the minibus on the motorway, and also how we knew what we were looking for, and how to find it.

'Jesus fucked,' PC Stewart said, 'that was you in the car? Holy fucking shit.'

PC Stewart removed his hand from the microphone on the recorder. He covered his mouth with both hands and then rubbed his eyes and pulled both hands up and over his head, before holding them tightly against his scalp. He looked up towards the ceiling.

'I have some additional news for both of you. I am in contact with the coroner, Dr. Theodore Anstis. As might be expected, he checked out all the victims of this entity. Every one of the deaths could only be recorded as accidental, for want of any external injuries, but – and it is a big but – there are obvious internal signs that these deaths are anything but through natural causes. And one more thing,' she said turning to me, 'you suggested the deaths we know of are not the only ones that can be chalked up to this entity. You were right. Dr. Anstis spoke to three other coroners and found equally baffling deaths in each of the three jurisdictions. So the truth is that we don't know how many deaths might have occurred so far, but it is likely to be far more than we anticipated.'

'This is a mess,' PC Stewart said. 'You two seem to suggest that this thing cannot be beaten, simply by its makeup. This thing has no body, for

God's sake, it has no mind, it is a being which can appear here and there at will. It can enter inside people's bodies and tear them apart from the inside. More than that, it is not only attacking people in this area, it is doing this nationwide, and there is no way we can set up any kind of strategy to tackle this thing because, although many people are going to die, there are no murders being committed. Jesus. This is crazy.'

'It might be even worse than that,' Judy chipped in.

'What? How come?' PC Stewart asked.

'Well, as soon as Dr. Anstis told me these events were more widespread than we thought, I spent quite a few hours checking out the internet. It wasn't easy to find anything at first, but with a bit of creative searching I found similar events in China, South Korea, South Africa, Canada, USA, Maldives, Australia, mainland Greece, and Hong Kong. The only common threads were suspicious internal injuries in each case. Something else we might want to consider is that many of these deaths go back more than five years, the earliest I found, occurred a little over eight years ago.'

'So we really have no idea how long this has been going on, or how many deaths are involved,' I chipped in.

'Before we go any further,' PC Stewart said as he reached across to the portable voice recorder, 'I think this contraption should be turned off.'

'Good idea,' I said.

'I will do some editing, so we can keep the bits we need,' PC Stewart suggested.

'You can do that?' I asked.

'Of course. We do it all the time,' PC Stewart replied.

I looked at Judy, and she glanced back at me.

'So where to now? We still know very little about what we are up against,' she said.

'Well, first of all, I need to convince the DI that there really is no good reason to hold you any longer. In truth, that is the case anyway. The problem is that the DI must deliver something tangible, the force must be seen to be acting proactively, particularly in this case,' PC Stewart replied.

'I have a plan,' I suggested, 'but I will need quite a bit of help from PC Stewart to set it in motion.'

'St. Mary's Hospital? You were serious about that?' he asked.

'PC Stewart, I am always serious, unless I am joking,' I said, 'and this is no joke.'

'Wait a minute,' Judy intervened. 'What is this about St. Mary's Hospital? What are you planning to do?'

'This is a crazy situation and maybe it calls for a crazy solution. Judy, do you remember the last time we spoke on the telephone? We were supposed to meet up, but your colleague here got to me first. During our conversation you said something that set the wheels in motion, started the beginnings of an idea that grew until it actually started to seem feasible,' I explained.

'But St. Mary's? That is a bit of a leap of faith, even for you,' Judy added.

'And how many of the inmates, do you think, answer to voices in their heads that tell them to do things?' I replied.

'You really are crazy,' Judy said.

'I sincerely hope so.'

सप्तविंशति

Judy took me home. The silence inside her car could have been cut with a knife. Ian Stewart had heard enough to convince him of our integrity, and of our commitment to putting things right.

Ian Stewart told the DI that my story had changed little since he met me at home the first time. He also spoke of his concern about what he called the 'small voices in my head' that were the true reason for my being on the motorway that day. He spoke a little of my frontal lobe injury and suggested that, at times of stress, I was prone to show signs of severe mental impairment. PC Stewart suggested that I book myself in to St. Mary's Hospital for observation, and that the police should support any such move. He also suggested he would approach my General Practitioner to ask that he adds his support to this action too.

'And just what, exactly, are you planning to do, even if you should be lucky enough to get into St. Mary's?' Judy asked, as she turned in her seat to face me.

'Well the exact details of that must only be known by me. We don't know yet what connection this entity has with me, but I think it best to be careful in discussing too much detail for the want of inviting him in for a sneak preview. No point in losing the element of surprise,' I replied.

'And what makes you think that this entity does not know what you are up to already?'

'I don't think, and that, for me at least, is the key.'

'I never was any good at nursery rhymes, and that is how you are talking now,' Judy said, becoming increasingly agitated.

'For want of a nail the shoe was lost, for want of a shoe the horse was lost, for want of a horse the rider was lost, for want of a rider the battle was lost, for want of a battle the kingdom was lost, And all for the want of a nail,' I quoted.

'Very poetic, but if I have a part to play I would like to know exactly what is expected of me before I play it.'

'Okay Judy, sorry for appearing so obtuse, but I think at this moment in time it is necessary. You have a pivotal role to play. But it is wise that we play our cards close to our chest. I cannot possibly take any chances that might threaten the success of this plan, mostly because this is all I have. Without this plan the spirit realm might as well go fuck itself, because this is all I've got,' I replied, 'suffice to say, sometimes you need to sacrifice your queen to win the war.'

अष्टाविंशति

'Judy, I have something that might interest you.'

'Dr. Anstis, tell me what you have.'

'I tracked down a case from fifteen years ago. The man was called John August. He was recorded as having died of complications related to diabetes. It appears that he had atherosclerosis, or furring up of blood vessels leading from the heart. This created a clot that caused a heart attack. The thing is that he did not die until five years ago. But ten years before he died, Mr. August was known to have had a heart attack, nothing suspicious in that, except for the notes I have seen on what they found inside his body when he died. There was a lot of internal scar tissue around the vessels leading to and from his heart. This scar tissue was formed in irregular patterns, again, nothing too strange about that. The thing is that the scar tissue can be dated back to the time of his first heart attack, the scarring suggests internal damage similar to that suffered by Martin Coombs,' explained the coroner.

'That is interesting,' answered Judy.

'Now it might just be a coincidence, but I spoke to the coroner who carried out his autopsy. He told me that the surgeon who treated John August after this first heart attack, was the surgeon's brother, and he distinctly remembered the fact that he could not reconcile Mr. August's injuries with any natural causes. The fact is, Judy, that not only did John August survive his first heart attack, he wrote a note of his experiences. I have a copy of that note, if you would like to see it.'

'Are you kidding me? Of course, send it over, sooner rather than later.'

'Will do.'

The phone line clicked shut.

***

'Honey, please accept what I am telling you. This is more crucial than anything I have ever done before in my life.'

'It's your life. If you want to spend all your time with another woman that is up to you. I don't mind, I really don't. You go right ahead and do what you want to do.'

'But F, please forget your sarcasm for a moment. I know I have been away too much, I know recently I have spent far too little time with you and our son. I know that, and I am really sorry, but if it had not been absolutely necessary, I would not have done it.'

I moved behind my wife, and attempted to put my arms around her waist while she toiled away on washing dishes in the sink. Her shoulders tightened and her tummy pulled in as I gripped her. It was clear that my affectionate overtures were not welcomed.

'Honey, please don't be like this,' I pleaded.

'Be like what? Like I said, you do what you have to do. If you prefer to spend your time with other women than your wife and your son, I can do nothing about that, you go right ahead.'

I groaned and lifted my gaze to the ceiling. My wife knew exactly which of my buttons to press to make me lose it, and fly into a rage. Her way, I guess, of blaming any and all problems that crossed our married path, on me. She had a very high success rate. I would feel that bad about causing her any upset or disappointment, that I would inevitably cancel any plans I had, and spend my time in the family home. But this time was different; I could not afford to cancel anything. Equally, I could not tell her why my plans could not be changed. This time, and this time only, I had no choice but to take her words at face value, and accept them as they were delivered.

'F, I really wish I had any choice but to do this, but I do not.'

'As I have already told you, do whatever you need to do with whoever you want to do it,' she said, the sarcasm just dripping from her lips.

I spent too many minutes following my wife around. She dipped into one room and then another, constantly on the move. This was her way of avoiding any more conversation, first to always have the last word, and second, to avoid having to listen to any more potentially hurtful information. I tired of following her, but knew I had to if I was to try and wind this confrontation up in any kind of a constructive way, not least because I would not be able to stop trying to placate my wife until I felt sure that I did not feel blamed for any kind of negative energy still trapped inside these four walls.

'Honey, I am really sorry, I will make it up to you. I promise.'

'Whatever,' was my wife's reply.

***

John August's account of his possible encounter with the entity made fascinating reading. If this account was true, it could be the first recorded attack and, if the dateline was right, it happened some years before the next suspected attacks, and fourteen years before those of the two victims six months ago, the ones reported by me that could not be proven to have been instigated by the entity.

So why the big gap between attacks? I was aware of conventional wisdom that suggested time does not exist in the spiritual realm, but even if this is the case, there must exist some appreciation of the reality of time on the earth plane, for astral visits and interactions to follow some kind of timeline. I have never heard of a spirit visiting his own former life self, and even if it was feasible, it would be highly unlikely to happen. Any astral intervention in life on earth must respect our timeframe to contribute any useful information.

In John August's account of his encounter with the entity, it seems he was successful in surviving because he prayed to God for help. Could this be a clue to unlocking a weakness in our foe?

The attack happened while John was sleeping. He awoke suddenly to find his shoulders and arms pinned to the bed, his whole body sank into the mattress. He reports an excruciating pain inside his chest. This pain was like pinpricks, as if something inside of him was pushing a sharp pin into and out of the living tissue inside his chest. He coughed some blood into his throat, and had to swallow it because the pressure on his chest stopped him from spitting it out.

The continuous pinpricks, or scratching as was later established post-mortem, lasted for several minutes, during which time the weight pinning John August to his bed gradually started to subside. When free of the pinpricking sensations, John was free of the weight also. He says that he jumped out of bed, wiped the dried blood from his mouth and checked himself out in his wall mirror. He reported that his skin looked ashen, and his facial features appeared sunken. Slowly, and over the following days, his normal appearance returned and his cheeks gained more colour.

As soon as he felt able to, John August checked himself into the accident and emergency centre at his nearest hospital. On examination, no abnormal heartbeat or other irregularities were found and the ECG trace showed nothing of note. John August had no history of heart problems, and suffered no further serious medical issues until he died, ten years later.

The incident seemed sufficiently strange for John August to record it in detail in a notebook he kept. The notebook was found when his possessions were cleared out by his family, after his death. The reason we know about it is because a member of his family read the notebook and submitted it to the coroner's office for their comments, maybe because they felt something more could have been done to help him. Dr. Anstis came into possession of John August's report from the coroner's office where Mr August's autopsy was carried out.

'The big question is,' Judy said, 'if this entity did attack John August, why would it wait so long before striking again?'

'To be honest, Judy, we only know what we know. We cannot be sure that other attacks have not occurred. And what about those cases you turned up on the internet?' I said.

'We have no details on any cases other than those that occurred recently and what happened to John August,' Judy replied. 'Do you think this thing used John August to practice its skills?'

'Maybe it did, but then if it had the potential to kill the man, why didn't it? After all, at some stage it must have known it was capable of entering a human body and causing some damage. It possibly was also aware that whatever damage it had done would not be easily picked up by the medical authorities,' I replied.

'And why does it do that? Why leave no external signs of what it has done?'

'Well that might be quite simple. To avoid detection.'

'And another thing. This attack on John August seems different, and not just because the guy survived the attack.'

'In what way?' I asked.

'Well, do you not think that the attack seems less violent? Less dramatic?'

'You could be right, but that would go back to your question of whether or not this thing used John August to hone its skills,' I replied.

I sat forward on the sofa, stared straight ahead, towards the open door leading to the entrance hallway, and began drumming my fingers lightly on my chin. The open doorway led to an escape, but it also led inwards to where we are now. As I stared, a related idea started to form. As always I battled against it, using common sense and alternative options, but the idea remained rooted inside my mind.

'We believe that this entity attacked John August fifteen years ago, leaving him as a survivor for a reason we do not know. It then, quite possibly, waited some years. Now, it seems to go on a bit of a rampage. We also believe that when it attacks it does so in a way that is not easily detectable by medical professionals. It leaves no outward signs of the attack on its victims. It also seems clear that, for another unknown reason, it seems to want me to help in its quest.'

'And God wants your help too. You are a classic double agent,' Judy suggested.

'Yes, and that is interesting in itself. But putting that aside for a moment, I have an idea that this entity might have waited fifteen years for me to become aware of its actions. It seems to be that attacks might have continued in different parts of the country, and the world, over this fifteen-year period, so it was not lying dormant all that time. But the cases that open up the lid to what is going on are those that have directly become known to me through my own experiences, and through you and Dr. Anstis. It might be that the escalation in cases is simply a reflection of my own developing spiritual awareness.'

'So let's just recap shall we,' suggested Judy. 'This entity experiments on John August, does what it does for a few years and then, when you are up to speed in spiritual terms, it kills people in such a way that you cannot prove what has happened except to yourself. It wants to draw you in, without getting the attention of anyone else.'

'Yes, that is how it seems to me.'

'Okay, I don't like that, but I have to run with it,' Judy said.

'Except that while my psychic abilities have grown stronger, and while my appreciation of life and the hereafter has grown, so too has my appreciation and understanding of God. It stands to reason that at the time the entity decided I could help, it was also the time that the spirit realm asked me to step in.'

'So, is it just a question of whichever side you choose to be on, wins the battle?' Judy asked.

'No, I don't think it would be as simple as that.'

'So what do you think is next?'

'What I do know is that if it is true that we have, and are expected to exercise, free will, then there is a chance that neither side will be prepared for some of the choices I might make,' I said.

'But didn't you say that the future is pretty much mapped out?' Judy asked.

'No. There is no such thing as fate. All that is known is that there are numerous potential outcomes depending on the choices we make. Opportunities will exist, and I am very sure that both this entity and God have placed such opportunities before me. That might have narrowed down the number of potential outcomes available. But what if I were to shift the balance? What if I were to play my joker, so that the only outcomes available could be the ones dictated by me?' I asked.

'And that is where, I presume, St. Mary's Hospital fits in.'

'Yes, indeed.'

एकान्नत्रिंशत्

Judy Marchant received the call from PC Stewart that the DI was supporting my referral to St. Mary's, with particular reference to some recent psychotic episodes. My General Practitioner had also written to the hospital, asking them to carry out an assessment, at their earliest convenience.

It was now just a question of waiting patiently for a call from the hospital, which would signal my admittance. I went back to my family life, and Judy returned to her police duties. PC Stewart went back to doing whatever it was that PC Stewart did, although hopefully not on a Friday night.

I said nothing more to Judy about the role I envisaged for her. She knew that I would not tell her anything until the time was right. The role of PC Stewart would be purely observational. Should anything drastic go wrong, it would be the role of PC Stewart to step in, extract me from the hospital, and ensure Judy's safety. His role was, for the moment at least, the only one that had been fully planned, agreed, and ready for execution.

I knew I only had one shot at getting this right but I refused to give in to any negativity. To do so might remove all the focus necessary to achieve the most beneficial outcomes possible. So I used this waiting period to my advantage, honing and fine-tuning my focus, doing my best to stay relaxed, and praying to God that the outcome would be favourable, and survivable.

I had little care for my own well-being. I have never been too enamoured with my own self-preservation. When thinking about death I always become incredibly upset, not for myself, but for the feelings of those people I would leave behind. I know I am a person who has a lot of love around me and an awful lot of respect from those people I know, and from many other people who have been a part of my life in one form or another. It does not sound good to be contemplating death at this time. It is, however, a very real and imminent threat. No matter how much I plan, I cannot dictate what other people might do. Even harder, if not impossible, would be to try to second guess an energy devoid of human flesh and emotion that has the freedom to do and be anything it chooses.

No matter what I thought I knew about life and our connection to the spirit world, no matter what advice I gave in psychic readings, it was hard for me to reconcile the fact that I had a choice in pursuing my plan. It is always easier to live oblivious of our interactions with the spirit world, than to admit there is more to life than just paying bills, following a career, watching soccer matches, drinking alcohol, smoking cigarettes and bringing up children.

I may have a greater knowledge than most people about the opportunities and goals presented by an all-loving, all-caring spirit world, but that does not make it any easier to put those beliefs into action, while concurrently dealing with day-to-day issues. People who have trained and honed their psychic skills do not live a life existing entirely of communicating with spirits. These are abilities that need to be turned on. Just as we need a light to read at night, we also need a switch to channel spiritual communications.

It is much easier to accept the existence of a spirit realm, in whatever form, if it is happening to someone else, or being reported from a distance. I would bet that those millions of people watching television programmes that factualise ghostly events would have had no direct experience of such things, they watch for pure entertainment.

The fact is that the spirit world interacts with seven billion people every minute of every day. Even for non-believers, sceptics, or for those people who have never conceptualised the existence of life after death, the same world exists beyond their sight. If conventional wisdom is to be believed, then the purpose of such a world is clear; it is the issue of the operation of that world that will forever remain a mystery. It is this side of the coin that both fascinates, and scares me, and it is this world that I need to be able to access and manipulate, if my plan is to succeed.

If you have followed the events in this book thus far, then you will have some idea of the task that faced Judy Marchant, PC Stewart and I. But, as I mentioned before, the experience of these events happens at one moment in our earth time, and then it is gone. It is the very next choice we make that sets up the forthcoming chain of events. It would, therefore, be impossible for me to establish a fool proof plan to reach the most desired conclusion. Namely, that of rendering the killer entity impotent.

त्रिंशत्

'So Judy, here is the plan,' I started.

'Oh, and here I was, starting to think that there wasn't one,' Judy replied sarcastically.

I ignored the interruption, and carried on explaining my intentions.

'I will get to the hospital, go through the signing in procedure, and settle into my allotted room. I will have a number of tests run, mostly psychological. It also seems inevitable that some kind of psychiatric evaluation will be done, too. I have been told that they will be conducting sleep analysis. You will be outside the room, or in the reception area. A quick word with your DI should get you daytime access to the hospital. Sweet-talk him, use threats or innuendo, I don't care, just do what you have to do to get access. Whatever happens, make sure that you are within easy reach of my room at all times during the day.'

'It's that easy, huh?'

'I have every confidence in you to make it that easy. There will be breaks in my treatments, there will be lunch breaks. And these will be our opportunities to act, an hour or so, that is all we will need. And when we do get that chance, here is what will happen.'

'I can't wait,' Judy said.

'I can't say too much because of what we discussed before, but essentially, I will hypnotise you...'

'Hold on there just a minute. You never said anything about hypnotising me, we might only have an hour. How do you know you will be able to put me under in that time?' she asked.

'Don't worry. Hypnosis is just a very deep state of relaxation, that is all. It will be like you go to sleep, but you will be aware of your dreams in your relaxed state, and you will interact with them under my instruction. And don't worry, everybody can be hypnotised, no matter how much some people believe they cannot. The key is to initiate the relaxation state, the rest is the same for everybody,' I replied.

'You know me that well, you can control my mind, too?' Judy asked.

'Not unless you want me to.'

'Okay, now we have gotten that out of the way, let's crack on, shall we?' she prompted.

'You will be in a hypnotic trance. I will send you to the spirit realm. You will meet me there, and I will take you to the Recovery Area. It is like a hospital for people who suffer traumatic or sudden deaths. This is the only place in the spirit world where we can act in secret. Don't worry, one of my Guardians will have cleared this before we arrive.'

'Oh well, that's okay then, I will be in the spirit world, a place I hoped never to go to until I died and even then under protest, and I will be expected, I will be an honoured guest?' she asked.

'Well yes, sort of. You will wait there until I join you. I will instruct you to act as I tell you to in my meditation. We will work together. You will be in a hypnotic state, and I will be deep in meditation. The entity will join us there. '

'And just how can you be sure this thing will join us?' Judy asked.

'Because you will entice it there,' I replied matter-of-factly. 'Don't worry, everything will be okay; while under hypnotic influence you will be acting with me. If I think you are in any kind of danger I will pull you out of there as quick as a flash,' I reassured her.

It was easy for me to offer words of encouragement, but it was not so easy to believe that in reality these words would amount to anything. I was scared as hell. Coming up against an enemy that only existed in my mind, and had no physical presence that we could determine, made our task all the harder. I was trying as hard as I could to ensure that I remained in control of the situation, but there could be no accounting for the unknown, of which there was plenty.

'And then what? How are we supposed to destroy something we know nothing about?' Judy asked.

'That is the easy part. Before we enter the hospital, I will use a meditation to visit the spirit world to find out as much as I can about the entity and its supposed link with me. During that time I will establish a plan to destroy the entity.'

'And how on earth can you be so sure you can do that?' she demanded.

'I will use this,' I showed Judy the white mark on my palm again, the one that I had received when I last visited the spirit world.

एकत्रिंशत्

These will be my last journal entries before I begin my journey of redemption. Redemption for so many choices that could have been made with greater foresight and commitment. I now know the 'mistakes' I made in this lifetime. Much as I hate that word, and always felt it had no place in my spiritual vocabulary, it actually does.

I will do my best to describe experiences and outcomes as they took place. It is a real shame that there is no video diary of this story, so my readers are not able to follow events as they happened. So please forgive me for any issues I might leave out, please also excuse me if the timeline of events is a little less than correlated. I promise that I will do my best to describe events, critical to the story, as they unfolded. And if you have come to the end of the book at this moment, then it is safe to assume that we were unsuccessful in our plan.

I got all my things ready for the hospital, making sure that I tucked my journal out of sight. I spoke to my son at some length about why his daddy needed to go away for a few days. Much harder was trying to explain to my wife the necessity of my absence, and convincing her that the destination I gave her was the true place I would be staying.

Now I had two hours before I needed to leave and head for the hospital. In that time I needed to meet with Judy, to fill her in on my plan, and to give her the details she needed to play her role in it. I was extremely nervous at undertaking this role. Though I had many years' experience of using psychic abilities in various situations, I had never needed them on such a focused and goal-driven task. This was new terrain for me, and I felt sure that any false moves or mistakes could cost me my life. So the responsibility I carried for my family, and for the other people involved, was monumental. It was, therefore, vital that my preparation went to plan as well.

I settled down for the last meditation before my plan was put into effect. As with any meditation, there could be no guarantee of achieving the required outcomes. Very often in the past, I had started a meditation exercise with hopes of achieving one outcome, but ended up coming out with something completely different. This time it was vital that I increase my desire for a specific outcome, for practical answers that could help my upcoming journey. It is not so easy to let such desire overcome all, so this one thing is all that exists in your universe for this one occasion. In fact, it could well take most of my available time just to achieve the circumstances, in which all my component parts came together sufficiently to create such a desire, as could not be ignored in a meditative state.

In fact, my desire was already strong as I got myself comfortable on the bed. I had taken my son to school earlier that morning, and my wife had left for work. The room was cool with a gentle breeze blowing through the small open window.

I started this meditation by imagining myself washing away recent events, cleaning areas of my body where recent experiences might have left a mark, or might have clung to my psyche. I cleansed myself with a creamy soap, brought down from the spirit world, that contained all sorts of imagined purifying energies and ingredients.

Completely refreshed, I began my meditation.

***

'Hello again, you are most welcome.'

This time my Guardian host met me in the Hall of Remembrance. As before, he placed himself very close to my left side. I don't recall going through my usual meditative process, I don't recall settling myself into a deep relaxation before beginning my journey into inner consciousness, and I don't recall any kind of entrance into this incredibly large, domed hall.

'I guess you know why I am here,'

'Yes, indeed. And on your part it is a wise move.'

'I just hope that what I have done is effective, and that this is the place I should be right now, because I don't mind admitting that I am more unsure than ever before of the course I am taking,' I thought out loud.

'Hope is not something you should entice. If you are sure that you have done your best to be in a situation where you are ready to take positive action, then that is a better place to be. Though your reticence is understandable, it is not helpful.'

'I am here now to complete my research so that before I take the final step, I am as ready as I can be.'

'I know why you are here, and I acknowledge your desire to complete your quest.'

'Can you please just advise how I can best use the vibration in this hall to find what I seek?'

'Just one note of warning before you do. You will be aware that all is open here, so be very careful how deep you go into details, because all you think and all you seek will be open to any spiritual energy that looks for it.

You cannot hide here. You may be endangering yourself, by searching too hard or demanding too much information.'

'Well, thank you for your advice. Here I am simply looking for background information. I will not go beyond that which directly affects me.'

'Okay, please do make sure that you limit yourself, and always be sure for what you wish.'

I have one more question before we start, I thought.

'Which is?'

'If I did want to dig into any information that might more easily be traced by the entity, then where would you suggest I could do that?'

'First, simply in forming your question as you did, you have already displayed information that could easily call that to you which you desire to keep away. Second, the place you should go to is the only place here where your thoughts are shielded.'

'And while I am here in the spiritual realm, how would I know if this entity was near?'

'You would not, unless it decided to reveal itself to you. Do you remember I told you that there are many energetic beings in this hallway? It is only because you are unaware of them that you choose not to notice them, and since you choose not to notice them, they do not appear in your awareness. In fact, that is the case throughout this realm. Anywhere you go, the only energies you will be aware of are those you mutually choose to see. It is the same as in your meditation and your dreams. In your lifetime, if you ever become aware of another spiritual energy, then it is because you both choose to communicate.'

'I never realised that,' I thought again.

'Something else that you may not know is that this is the way we travel, this is how we know where we are needed, this is how we do everything. The vibrational fields of everything are different. All we do is tune into that vibration, which in humans are best known as emotion, feelings and thoughts, to travel to it. Each thought, each emotion, each feeling on the earth plane identifies itself not by sight, but by the vibration and the energy it creates. All we need to do is identify that vibration to travel and interact with it. Here in the spiritual realm we have no need for eyes or ears, we have no need for touch, taste or smell. Our existence relies only on the energetic vibrations that surround us. This is the only way we can exist here. When you meditate, also when you sleep, your vibrational energy becomes more in tune with what exists here. You are here now through meditation, and it is true you can interact, to a degree.'

'Only to a degree?'

'Yes. You cannot undertake a fully immersive experience until, and unless, you can shake off your earth plane shell, since all the time you occupy that shell, wherever you go you will take the lower vibrations of that shell

with you. That fact in itself serves to show you as different here. So you must be careful.'

'Then I think it is time I started my research.'

'Okay. In the Hall of Remembrance, all you need to do is to think of something you would like to remember, it could be anything, a feeling, an emotion, an event from your past, or it could be something in the future. Make sure you focus hard on only one memory, otherwise the information you get might be scrambled.'

***

I focused on when I was fourteen years old, and more specifically on the time my heart stopped in the Children's Hospital. It was then that I needed to be resuscitated, it was then that a lack of oxygen caused the frontal lobe damage that led to my suffering from Dysexecutive Syndrome, and it was that incident I grew up knowing nothing about. I knew I suffered memory loss, I knew I got angry quickly, I knew I was restless, I knew I had no patience with people, it was then that I realised I was different.

This was the first chance I had to re-experience the minutes of my death, to establish whether spiritually I had experienced anything at all, or whether the lights simply went out on a teenage lump of meat. I was hoping, too, that my first contact with the entity, also happened at this time. Now I needed to overcome some of my demons, and to face up to my responsibility as either the cause of all the recent unplanned deaths, or the saviour of victims yet to come.

I was positioned beside the bed opposite the place where the nurse stood. I looked at my face, realising how vulnerable and frail I was at this moment. I saw the forefinger twitch on my left hand, and then it happened again. '*Look, look at his finger,*' I screamed at the male nurse, but my desperate thoughts went unheard. I watched as the needle was removed from my young arm. The young me immediately awoke and asked urgently for a bedpan. I watched as the colour seemed to drain from my face, as if a plug had been removed and my life energy slowly leaked out. I saw the young me crumple onto the bed and I looked pleadingly into the concerned face of the male nurse. Another nurse rushed to my side and then the curtains around the bed. Other children on the ward were ushered away into the play area at the front end of the ward; the doors to that area were shut. Urgent words were exchanged between the two nurses, but their sound was muffled and indecipherable. I saw the matron come over and hold my wrist. There was no pulse.

Then I was inside the boy rushing, rushing, somewhere. All around me were a kaleidoscope of faint colours, blurred images speeding past too fast to be seen, or to comprehend. My speed of movement was phenomenal, and the distance I travelled became greater and greater. The ward, the centre of the incident, was long gone, as were all familiar things in the physical world.

This was different from the heavy existence I had before the incident. This area was air-free, gravity-free. I could not say I felt lightweight, because I did not. Any and all sensation I had in the physical world, was gone.

I was aware of myself, I knew who I was, and I was aware of who I had been in physical life. The only thing I felt I had, though, was now. I did not know where I was rushing to at such high speed, but the route had a familiarity. From where I knew this place I could not tell, all I knew was that though this seemed like a new experience, I knew it was not.

I cannot say I felt scared. Also I cannot tell you that I felt safe. This to me was just an experience, and it was a necessary experience. I saw nothing except the blurred images rushing past me, and I had no sense of when this journey might end. At each moment, I knew nothing except where I was at that moment in time. I did get a sense that I could reach out with my mind and retrieve an image, to study it and to understand it. I knew that if I wished it to, this image would show me not only what I perceived of it but every other perception about it there had ever been. But I chose not to look at anything, I had no desire to know anything of these events that rushed past me.

It is difficult to express to you how this experience was. Not only am I a grown man experiencing and interpreting a teenager's memory of a long gone incident, but I am trying to use earthly words to express an experience which defies words and logic, because here, quite simply, they do not exist. So please bear with me.

I have no idea how I stopped. I had no feeling of slowing down; there was no deceleration process. One moment I was rushing through images, and the next moment, I was not. I did not notice that I was moving towards any entrance or white light, as my adult mind might have expected. The route I travelled I could not even describe as a tunnel. It just was what it was.

I was now in a white area with no walls, no ceiling and no floor. I had no sense of any other beings or things around me. I was all alone, but at the same time, I had no feeling of aloneness. All through this journey, I had no contemplation of death. This was just an experience that I had to go through; at least that is how it felt to me.

Even as a fourteen-year-old boy, I knew that this was not a dream. In dreams there is always a sense of doing something, communicating with other people and of having a sense of purpose. This did not feel like that. At this moment the only feeling I had was of nothingness, it was as if all else was suspended, my life, my existence, my meaning, all was of no consequence in this moment.

And as an adult occupying this moment I felt the same way. Though I was aware that I was occupying the same space as myself, as a fourteen-year-old, I had no sense of togetherness, or of separation. But as an adult, my perception of how it might have been in the dying process was not coming true. It seemed that as a holder of a lifetime, I was relatively inexperienced, and it was disappointing that I had no sense of achievement or goal attainment. In fact, there was no feeling of justifying awards of any kind. The only feelings I could muster were of a life lived that was null and void. Just at that time, I was wrenched away and travelling backwards at high speed. Everything I sensed throughout this entire trip just seemed like a total waste of time, which, on adult reflection, was probably a very good summary of my life up until that point. So was this trip providing me the opportunity to review my life? Was it giving me a chance to feel to the very core of me, the sum total of my physical existence?

I wish I could beef up this part of the story for you. I wish I could tell you I was met by my deceased relatives, who all hugged me, and gave a party in my honour to celebrate my passing to the other side. I wish I could say there really was a light at the end of a tunnel that beckoned me with an abundance of warmth and love. I wanted so much to be able to record my arrival at huge pearly gates, with rocking angels strumming harps to the latest spiritual beats. But I cannot. It just was not like that. And in this journal I refuse to tell you anything but the truth.

I arrived back in my fourteen-year-old body with a thump. I was lying prone on the floor while the same male nurse who ended my life, was desperately trying to start it again, with heavy pushes of his two palms against my chest. My chest was incredibly sore. I left the boy and returned to my original viewing point. I knew the boy had no idea that I had accompanied him on his journey; I also knew that the boy remembered nothing at all about it. One minute he wanted a shit more desperately than ever before, and the next moment a guy was banging on his painfully sore chest. There was nothing whatsoever in between for the boy, but for me there was.

***

'So is that how it was? I mean the all of it, is that really how it was?' I asked.

'What you focus on and what you experienced was exactly how it was; there can be no tampering with the memories of what has gone before.'

'And when I was fourteen years old I had no idea that a grown version of me, had travelled with me on that journey?'

'If you had, that could cause immense problems in the life and death process. Can you imagine how life might be if you knew your future self, or even your dead self, were taking trips with you as you travelled your journey of life?'

'I could imagine it would cause problems, yes. So does that happen often?'

'Does it happen often that a future self travels with you at moments in your life?'

'Yes.'

'My friend, it happens all the time. At those times when you make important choices, when you take important actions, when you contemplate important issues. In fact, any time during any of your lives that you make a choice that changes the options available to you, I can almost guarantee that a past self, a future self, or any spiritual energy that makes up you, will be travelling with you to experience, examine and learn.'

'That is going to take a lot of thinking about.'

'And here is something else for you to contemplate. You also do not know how many versions of you took that same trip at the same time. You see, if by making that trip with your fourteen-year-old self, you change the options available to you now, then it is more than likely that another version of you is also sharing your experience of what happened, at the same time.'

'Like the multiple layers of a lasagne? And how many layers of pasta can there be occupying that same space at the same time?'

'Countless.'

'That is mind-blowing, literally.'

'And for some people it would be mind-blowing. Since they are not able to conceptualise spiritual knowledge in the same way you are, it might be true that their minds could explode.'

'That cannot be true.'

'I assure you that it is. Have you ever heard of spontaneous human combustion?' I was asked.

'That is caused by an overload of spiritual awareness?' I asked.

'In most cases, yes.'

'Okay, so let us believe that anything is possible in the spiritual realm, even things of which we cannot, in whatever form we take, conceive. The whole reason that I am here in meditation is that I want to establish any connection that exists, with the entity that is cutting short people's lives. When focusing on my death as a fourteen-year-old boy I assumed, rightly or wrongly, that this being such a big event in my life, would make it the most likely time for me to have come into contact with the entity. That is, if I was right in assuming my link with the entity is more than just a mutual interest in our own existences.'

'Yes.'

'Yes what?'

'I mean yes, you are right. If you are truly connected in some way to this entity, as I think it is safe to assume that you are, then I would agree that the most obvious time that you might become aware of it, would be the incident when you were fourteen years of age.'

'Well, why then did I feel nothing? Why did I see nothing? Why did I sense nothing?'

'*Maybe you were looking in the wrong place.*'

'*I don't understand. What do you mean?*' I asked.

'*This entity is an energetic spiritual being that exists somewhere within this realm. It is able to travel to the earth plane, but it is not of the earth plane. Therefore, when seeking to clarify any issues at all with a spiritual entity, the best thing to do is to think in a way that does not place human boundaries or restrictions onto this being.*'

'*Ah, so if I was able to think of a way beyond mere human senses, of how this entity was first able to connect with me, then I might find my answer.*'

'*No. You will find your answer.*'

द्वात्रिंशत्

Next, we travelled to the library.

As soon as I started to think that we should visit the library, and my mind asked if it might be possible, we had already arrived.

Being a human, ordinarily made up of a mess of internal organs and external extremities, made it incredibly difficult for me to move around the spirit realm with any sense of ease. My balance seemed to be off so that each time we arrived somewhere, I struggled to keep from toppling over. Equally, my mind seemed very slow in adjusting to a new and different train of thought in another area, almost as if I travelled on an early train and my mind followed up in a later arrival on a different platform.

It was true that while my mind – conscious and subconscious – was free to roam with abandon, somewhere inside was entrenched the idea that my mind belonged to my body. Therefore, anything other than normal human thought processes, seemed too alien to comprehend, and certainly too hard to adjust to.

'This is kind of hard for me. Do you think we might be...'

'Able to move around a bit more slowly? Sorry, but this is the standard way of travel here, you think of somewhere you would like to be, and you are there. You will get used to it.'

My Guide answered before I had a chance to finish my question.

'And also, do you think I could finish my question before it is answered? I have a nasty habit on earth of only being able to communicate effectively, if all my planned words are not cut off before they are released.'

'Sorry, but here our thought processes are much more refined, so we tend to think much quicker than you would on earth.'

'Old habits die hard I guess, but I would be grateful if you could try to humour me on this one,' I requested.

'Yes, I will try.'

'Thank you. I would like to be able to view...'

A mass of the now familiar buff coloured folders appeared before me, and stretched away as far as I could see down the extensively long table at which I stood. The files were piled three high. A rough estimate might put the total number of files at around a thousand.

'The files belonging to the victims who lost their lives through the actions of the entity you are seeking. Sorry again; it is just the mechanics of this place. Oh, and the number of files is actually one thousand, three hundred and sixty-seven,' my Guide kindly informed me.

'Well that is quite a lot, but well short of the potential number of deaths you advised, when we last communicated. That leaves two options. Either we are at the very beginning of the entity's plan, whatever that might be, or what I am doing at the moment on earth is having a positive effect on decreasing the number of incidents.'

'It is both,' my Guide answered.

'Well that is a good start. I presume that you realise why I am here, so how do you suggest I progress in this task? I don't want to look at all these files, or I might die before achieving anything.'

'It is actually most feasible to check all of these files at the same time, but I would not recommend you try that, as it most certainly would pose a great risk to your health, and to your state of mind.'

'My state of mind?'

'Well, it is more than likely that such a huge influx of information provided at the same time is likely to implode your mind, causing instant death. The best way is for me to offer you a representative sample of files that will be well within your capabilities to digest, and gain the information you need.'

'Yes, okay. Thank you.'

The number of files on the desk before me thinned out considerably, the long table was now clear, apart from ten files. I picked up the first file and, though there was no label on the cover, I knew it belonged to Martin Coombs.

Upon opening the book, I knew Martin Coombs to have been a very independent person, he made his own decisions about his life and cared very little for anyone else, or for the choices they made. He was insular, caring nothing for politics, religion, or current affairs. He had relationships with women, but he always tried to keep them at arm's length. Only one name came into my mind on the romance side, Alice. There was a troubled falling-out, and it seemed he had virtually turned his back on romance since that time.

Moving to the day he lost his life, it seems Martin Coombs had spent a normally dreary – as he saw it – day at work. On returning home, he had cooked a meal and settled down to watch a horror film on DVD. Having beaten off to a lesbian porno movie, he had dropped off to sleep, momentarily.

That is the moment when the entity paid him a visit. Not having had a chance to wake up before the entity got into his body meant that Martin

Coombs had no chance of surviving the next few seconds. The entity's attack was swift and unforgiving. Martin was aware of the alien presence inside of him, aware of the chill that accompanied his uninvited guest.

The method of the kill was brutal. Each of four blood vessels sliced cleanly through. Martin Coombs felt the sharp pain of each cut. I was aware that I would be able to tap into the feelings and pain of the deceased man if I had wanted, but I chose not to. The victim felt blood rush into his nostrils and his throat in a warm flood. His heartbeat increased to make up for the injuries he suffered, but to no avail. The whole thing was over in a few seconds.

The entity did not retreat, it stayed inside Martin Coombs' body after he died. The file gave up no more information on this subject. I flicked through the pages further on in the book but all were completely blank. After the killing, it seemed like Martin Coombs, as a physical being, as a spirit, as an energy, and as a soul, just ceased to exist.

***

The name of Dr. Theodore Anstis was displayed in bright blue letters across the middle of the screen on her phone. Judy Marchant pressed the answer button. She moved slowly and quietly to the back of the room, next to the exit door, to keep from disturbing the people around her.

'Yes, Theo,' she said very quietly into the phone's mouthpiece.

'Judy, I hope everything is okay with you. Look, I thought I had better keep you up to date. I have been in contact with a good friend of mine, Dr. Enner Steinbaum, he is a coroner in Denver. He has been looking into some deaths that have been happening in the US recently, he says over the last six months. Anyway, it seems what is happening there is very similar to the cases we have seen. You told me you found out about some more cases in your research?'

'Yes, that is right, I did. In many different countries, in fact.'

'That's right. Well it seems that, like me, he can see no official findings other than natural causes. But he did suggest to me that he is now thinking there might be an alternative; he says that he cannot rule out witchcraft or demonic possession. I will admit this seems pretty far-fetched to me, especially coming from someone who is as highly regarded in his field as Dr. Steinbaum.'

'Go on,' Judy encouraged.

'Well, Dr. Steinbaum, apart from being a well-respected coroner, is also well versed in the paranormal. It appears that he has, at times, worked with paranormal investigators close to where he resides. He acts as their sceptical kickboard, but he has seen enough to know that certain impossible things, might just be possible.'

'So what is his final conclusion?' Judy asked.

'No conclusion, just conjecture, so far. But Dr. Steinbaum has contacted the FBI and is now in regular contact with one of their agents.'

'Curiouser and curiouser. Seems this story is gaining some official recognition after all. Anything about the FBI interest?'

'Well, no. It seems they have a couple of teams dedicated to paranormal issues, but this also includes UFOs and alien abductions, so I am not too sure how seriously they might take this stuff.'

'But if they are willing to take this up, it sounds promising. I'm not sure demonic possession or witchcraft would fit with our experiences, but at least it is a step in the right direction. What we are dealing with could certainly be considered paranormal, or at least a branch of it. I was beginning to feel pretty isolated, fighting a demonic serial killer with just a psychic sidekick for company.'

'And the local coroner, too,' Dr. Anstis reminded her.

'Yes. The local coroner, too,' Judy agreed.

'I just thought it wise to give you a heads up.'

'Yes, thank you. Your information was most useful. Please do continue to keep me updated.'

'Yes, of course I will.'

With that, Judy ended the call and returned to her work.

***

'They were all aware of the entity before they died, every single one of them,' I projected the thought to my Guide.

'If that is what the file shows you, then it is true.'

'Well, no file states that literally, but the perception I get is that in every single death there is an awareness of something different inside of them, something paranormal even. It is not very clear, but it is definitely there.'

'Not to sound too impersonal, what you see here are the events as experienced by the subject of the file. They were not aware of what they were seeing, feeling or experiencing in these moments. So what you view here has to be tainted by their fear, by their shock at what is happening to them. This can create a fog over what truly happens at these times. And at the time they realise that they really are dying, their survival instinct kicks in, and we see for real what is happening. Unfortunately for them, it is too late,' my Guide explained.

'So these files are not objective?'

'They can only maintain objectivity up until the point that the event is experienced by the subject. If you had looked at these files before these things occurred on earth, then you would have seen the event as it actually happened.'

'Well, why can't I still do that?' I asked.

'Why what? Are you being serious, my friend?'

'You told me there is no such thing as time in the spiritual realm, right?'

'Well yes, that is true.'

'Then answer me a question.'

'That depends on what question you would like to ask me.'

'While I am here, is time suspended for me, too?' I asked.

'Time is not suspended in the spirit realm. Time, as a thing, just does not exist. It is simply a measurement of planetary movement. There is no past, no present, no future. The progress that is pursued by all energies is not pursued in any time frame, it is pursued in a knowledge frame, which means when knowledge is gained, an entity moves on to its next learning experience. Physical lifetimes fit in with this learning philosophy; they are the benchmarks of true learning in action. Just as I mentioned to you before, it is necessary for the spirit realm to honour the fact that time frame learning on earth plays such a pivotal role in our own processes. It is, therefore, possible to manipulate time to further an individual energy's learning opportunities which, in itself, feeds beneficial outcomes back to the spiritual realm.'

'In what way is time manipulated?' I asked.

'Well, a lifetime on earth, though it exists in the time frame of physical life lived over a period of decades, years, months and days, exists solely to feed the educational needs of the individual and the universe. The educational process exists as a stand-alone entity and it can be altered to improve its educational value and output.'

'I understand what you are saying, but I am finding it hard to understand how an event can ever be altered to be different than what it existed as.'

'Okay. The most common way in which the educational opportunities offered by a lifetime can be improved, is by replaying them and making different choices. The life signposts and opportunities remain the same, but it is the choices that are made that create the greater learning experiences. It is, therefore, possible to squeeze more out of one lifetime by living it more than one time,' my Guide explained.

'Do you mean that when our life ends, the same life can begin again? My son always says we are little, then big, then little again.'

'He is right, and very wise.'

'I have heard a lot about life themes, and how some people need to play the same theme several times before lessons are learned. Is that true?'

'Not in the way you say it. If you substitute lifetimes for life themes then, as mentioned before, that is possible.'

'Going back to what was said before, in what way can time manipulation benefit the spirit realm?'

'The whole reason for our existence, in any form, is that creation feeds the creator, which feeds the creation. It is this continual creative cycle that is life in motion.'

'So can I do that? Can I manipulate time to experience what happened just before these people died?' I asked.

'In theory, yes. But the overriding principle for any lifetime is that the outcomes should not be manipulated. The choices to be made to create an experience, must only be made by the individual experiencing the lifetime. So long as there is no tampering with the potential outcomes of a lifetime, it is possible.'

'But is that not exactly what this entity has done?'

'No, that is different. Yes, the outcomes of the affected lifetimes were drastically altered, but that was not through the manipulation of time. These were events that happened through the natural process of time, as it exists on earth.'

'So if the entity intervened in a lifetime, can we be sure that this was not already one of the possible outcomes written into that lifetime?'

'No, we cannot.'

'So all these killings, this slaughter, might have occurred naturally as a result of the choices made by the victims?'

'That is possible, but not feasible. You see, every point of the planning process before a lifetime begins, is known by the individual role player, by their Guides and helpers, by the elders who oversee the planning process, and by many more higher beings. So it is unlikely, if not to say impossible, for these outcomes to have been identified in the planning and preparation stages.'

'So what this entity did was to manipulate these lifetimes after they were planned and prepared, in some way that was hidden from all those beings involved in the lifetimes.'

'Yes. But it is most likely that the intervention was planned to be swift and unexpected, so as to happen under our radar, so to speak.'

'Like a bolt of lightning,' I suggested.

'Well, yes.'

'Looking through these files there is another thing I want to bring up with you.'

'Go ahead.'

'There is one striking feature in all of these files. I noticed in mine, the last time I looked, that there were imprints of events yet to come, but in the files belonging to people attacked by this entity, there are no future events. The files are all completely blank.'

'Well, these future events are not events as such. They are indications of the many options available to every energetic spiritual energy, in every *physical lifetime in which they plan to exist. They are only options; nothing is planned. When you agree to undertake another lifetime, as you invariably will, you set in motion a chain of events that go beyond that lifetime to the next, and the next, and so on. The events in these files are the signposts, the indicators of the direction in which the most beneficial outcomes might be achieved. These future events will change depending on the choices made and the options taken in each lifetime.'*

'Okay, so how can these events just go missing from the files from all these people? And does it affect the whole one thousand, three hundred and sixty-seven?'

'Oh, you can now add another eighteen to that total.'

'Mathematics was not a good subject for me.'

'Yes, everyone who has died as a result of meeting up with this entity, as you call it, has experienced the same outcome, at least so far as their life records are concerned. As to why, or how, these events go missing, that is a matter of conjecture. I assume the fact that no records exist after they die in their latest lifetime, can only mean that there are no more events to come for them.'

'They cease to exist?' I asked.

'Well, so far as their having an existence linked in any way to the spiritual realm, yes.'

त्रयत्रिंशत्

I followed the instructions of my Guide to arrive, in spiritual form, at the apartment of Martin Coombs. Some people might think of me as a ghost – unseen, unheard, an invisible energy in the ether. My previous thoughts were that ghosts, or spiritual entities, consisted only of those individuals who had finished their last earthly existence. This experience, however, showed my earlier perception to have been false.

Martin Coombs was watching a porn film. He sat on the sofa frantically rubbing his erect penis in his right hand while the movie flickered ten feet in front of him. His legs spread taut in front of him, breathing rapid. It seemed as if his ejaculation was close.

The room cooled noticeably. I was watching this scene from one step inside the double doors to the right of the sofa, that led onto an unusable patio area fenced with black painted iron railings. The room was lit by one table lamp positioned to the right of the sofa that sat on the top of a small, ornate circular stand that edged the seating. It seemed likely to me that what was about to happen did not involve any kind of physical struggle. If it did, then the lamp, and the table on which it stood, would topple to the ground, and in my physical visit to this place, it had not. A misty kind of manifestation started to appear in front of me, and it took up a position above Martin Coombs' head. It lengthened down towards the ground and took shape. I could see the outline of arms, legs, shoulders and a head. The image shimmered like a bad video recording. I could make out no further features except for its humanoid shape. This thing placed its hands onto Martin Coombs' head. I remembered my Guide's sharply delivered instructions not to interfere with anything that happened. I was ordered not to manipulate any objects with my energy, or to interact with anything else at the scene, for want of changing the course of events about to unfold.

'I am so pleased you could make it here to witness my work. Such a fortuitous pleasure even I could not anticipate.'

The thing before me turned its shimmering head towards me, as its thoughts were transmitted. There were no eyes to look into, no mouth to move, but by looking into the head-shaped shifting mass, I could learn something of this entity. I could not make out exactly what it was I was picking up on, but I continued to watch in silence, as it worked its evil upon the man's prone body before it.

'Welcome to my world. You are a bold adversary, but one that is very naive. The answers are here and you are very welcome to all of them, my dear, dear friend. If it was not for you, then I would never be able to undertake my plan. This is one thing you never understood. For a long time you ignored me, you pushed me away. But now you can embrace me, you can share in my glory. You are the light to my flame, come bask in our glory.'

My mind, my whole being, ached to rush this entity, to rip it apart, to destroy it forever. Even though I was not informed of how that could be done, the force of my anger, my hatred of this pulsating thing before me, meant that I could find a way, even if it meant sacrificing myself. But my instructions must remain in force, I must not interact with it, for the sake of the realms I was representing, both physical and spiritual. I must not give in to its taunts, its invitations, or to its bloodlust. My role here was to observe, nothing more and nothing less.

'You are denied the truth about your existence by the spiritual bureaucracy; therefore, you are denied a life of free choice. You are denied choices about your future for the want of maintaining the system and supporting the positions of the elite. You bask in the glory of free choice, but you have no choice but to follow the paths set out by your Guides and your elders. The hypocrisy of the situation is that life experience is supposed to be about learning, but what are the only beings learning and capitalising on the growing pains you inflict on yourself in the earth plane? Who really stands to gain from your trials and tribulations? Why should you worship and give honour to your creators, when truly it is they who should give worship and honour to you, for feeding their experiences, their knowledge and their well-being? You are nothing more than slaves. You have no choice, you have no opportunities for growth, you have no life. Your existence is controlled and manipulated by the elders for their own benefit, and to your detriment. That is the truth of the energetic spiritual existence,' the entity explained, before continuing.

'And there is nothing you can do except to continue this charade. Carry on your little plays, acting out scenes to their whims. You are not the director of your life, you are an actor following a script. This script has no input from you. You are puppets, nothing more and nothing less. You are no more than chess pieces on God's own chessboard. The wonderful, glorious creation that is life, and afterlife, was created only for God's own intentions, to become the all-knowing, all-powerful king of kings you believe it really is. By reaping the benefits of lives lived in a physical environment, all of the feelings, emotions, experiences only serve to create a stronger, more powerful God. There is no growth for mankind as individuals, only death. The ego of God is all that is served.'

I listened to the ideas thrown into my mind by this killer, and there was an undeniable truth in what it said. From the words of God itself, all life, which must include God and the spiritual elite, exists to learn and practice all knowledge gained, as a way of growing and enlightening itself. And since we all originate as a part of God, then all knowledge gained must eventually be returned to God. If what the entity said really was true, then can you effectively fight force with more force? A lack of choice cannot surely be counteracted by an alternative route, where your right to a choice is also violated. These people who suffered a painful end to their lives, before their spiritual leaders deemed it necessary, were they afforded a choice to stay in their earthly lives or to go? From what I could see, the answer must be a resounding no.

'And so here is where I come in. I can offer an existence of true and free choice. If you want to learn then you can learn. Equally, if you want to do fuck all in the glorious kingdom to come, then you are free to do that. I offer no false promises, I take no false gifts, I am just the orchestrator of an experience of unlimited opportunities to seek the existence chosen by you as an individual entity. The teachers will remain where learning is requested. I do not propose to sit upon the thrown of a kingdom ruled by a dictator, nor will it be wasted by anarchy. There will be order, but within that order, each and every wish and desire can be satisfied. What I offer is heaven, amen.'

***

In the time the entity took to converse with me I noticed that Martin Coombs' movements slowed down considerably. It is hard to imagine anything moving faster than a man's hand while he masturbates. But during this time I noticed, out of the corner of my eye, that this man's right hand slid up and down his shaft in extremely slow motion. Did this entity have the ability to control time, on its frequent visits to the earth plane, to help it find and destroy its human targets? If it could do that, then it is also possible that the act of ending a human life might also be accomplished in this warped timeframe, as I was to discover.

The entity moved its arm inside Martin Coombs' body. I could not see exactly how it accomplished the act of killing this man, I was only aware that it was about to happen. I did hear several pops though, as the entity severed the man's main arteries and veins. I could see no implements, so I was unsure how this was accomplished. I could only guess that, in the same way as it was able to manipulate time and matter, it was also able to carry out its despicable actions by willpower alone.

It was as if the entity then sucked the man's life force up into itself. Many different colours danced all around the entity's misty form, up and down, left and right, skittering here and there as if freefalling within its containing vessel. The entity shimmered more brightly, its misty demeanour flecked now with bright colours that slowly began to fade before my eyes. The entity turned to face me one more time.

'Join me.'

It then vanished. It was as if its misty form was sucked up into itself, until all that was left was a small dot. And then that was gone, too. Martin Coombs' lifeless body remained on the sofa, as the porno film resumed its normal running speed.

चतुस्त्रिंशत्

'*So where did Coombs go?*' I asked of my Guide, as I returned instantly to the spiritual realm.

'*As I mentioned before, he ceased to be.*'

'*Well, what happened? Did this entity take his soul? Did it take his spirit? Did it take his life force?*'

'*The energetic entity that occupied planet earth as Martin Coombs, now ceases to be just that. The entity you witnessed took everything.*'

'*A man cannot just disappear like that.*'

'*In theory, no, he cannot.*'

'*Okay, if you can't give me the details, then can you maybe surmise for me what might have happened?*'

'*We don't know, but there are two possibilities. First, the entity might have destroyed the energy that was Martin Coombs...*'

'*You told me energy could never be destroyed.*'

'*That is true, but energy can be dispelled into much smaller pieces. If each piece is small enough, it can lose its sense of self. This is exactly what happened when God created man. God took a piece of His consciousness and dispelled it so that it became individual living spiritual entities. Each dispelled piece of God's consciousness lost its identity, and now, forever, seeks reunification, hence our search for enlightenment. We believe that when we achieve enlightenment we will once again become a part of God's fullness, part of the creator itself.*'

'*The pinnacle of knowledge we can never achieve.*'

'*Correct.*'

'*And what might the other possibility be?*'

'*It is unlikely that this entity would have the power or the knowledge to be able to effectively dissipate individual molecules of that which make up a spiritual being. More likely is that the entity escorted those people, whose physical lives he took, to a place, and for reasons, only known to him.*'

'*And what if these people did not wish to go with him?*'

'That would be impossible. The choice to die in physical form is a choice that can only be made by the individual spiritual being. And when that opportunity is presented, should they choose to die as a physical form, there is only one route that appears to be available to them?'

'I don't understand that statement. What about people who are murdered? What about babies who die in their mothers' wombs? What about people who die in accidents?'

'Every physical being chooses to die at an opportune time. In every physical lifetime, any number of opportunities to die can arise. When one of these opportunities presents itself, the individual can choose to die, or they may choose to survive. An individual is not consciously aware of this opportunity, or of the choice they make. It seems as if this entity may have presented an additional chance for each of its victims to die, whether by choice or by persuasion. It is most likely that this entity would then persuade its victims' spirits to go with it after they leave their human form. When this choice is made, it is then that the energy making up that person, effectively disappears,' my Guardian explained.

'What about family members meeting these people? Isn't that what always should happen?'

'Yes, it should.'

'So why did family members not reach out to these people?' I asked.

'Communication between our worlds is limited to one channel. You are aware that when you communicate with a spirit of a dead relative during a psychic reading you only communicate with that one spirit. There is no interruption, even if more than one spirit is present at that time. Therefore, if this entity is using that channel to communicate with his recently deceased victims, there is no way of tracing that, or knowing of it.'

'And that is how he slips under your radar'

'Yes, it is.'

'For what reason would he do that?'

'That is debatable.'

'And have the elders of the spirit realm debated this issue, or has all the hard graft been left to me?' I asked.

'Every dimension of this issue has been debated at great length. We have introduced certain security measures, which I cannot divulge, in areas where it is most likely that this entity would gain access to the physical world. Your assistance is an important aspect of our attempts to put this issue right, but I can assure you that you are not acting alone.'

'And what of my role?'

'You are a focus for this entity, and for very good reason.'

'Which is?'

'Every time an opportunity arises for somebody on earth to die, he or she is given the opportunity to pass on to the spirit realm or to return to his or her earthly existence.'

'Yes, we discussed this earlier.'

'But one thing we did not discuss was that it is not just a person's body that undergoes transformation in the death process. There are three separate parts that make up a person on the earth plane and they are the mind, the soul and the spiritual essence. The human body is the vessel, which transports the mind and the soul through a lifetime. The human body supports the mind and soul and vice versa. The three parts work in harmony during an earth lifetime, performing their different functions to support the efficient and effective operation of the personal form. It is only by these three units working in conjunction that a person can have the chance to live and learn by the opportunities and experiences offered to them. You are not only a human body, and these three elements working together are the epitome of a human being.'

'Okay, I am with you so far. Please, carry on.'

'You are also aware that a number of windows appear through which the human being can enter the spiritual realm. Contrary to your popular belief, the decision whether or not to re-enter the spiritual realm is one made between all three of your elements, it has nothing to do with God. But these windows perform another important function. They can also provide an opportunity for any one of your three elements to leave the whole, at which time they can be replaced by a new element.'

'This is a little harder to understand. What I get from what you are saying is that either a body, or a mind, or a soul, or a spirit, can choose to take an opportunity to leave a human being. If that choice is made, then that one element is replaced with a new one.'

'Please remember that a body is just a mutually supportive vessel that allows for life experiences to be gathered through its senses. A human body has no capacity for free thinking. The brain is a supportive vessel allowing the body and the mind to function. But otherwise, what you say is roughly correct, yes.'

'So am I given to understand that if a human mind decides enough is enough and wants out, then another mind can jump into a new born baby?'

'Yes, but it takes its knowledge and understanding gained so far on the earth plane with it.'

'Is that why some babies seem to possess an older soul? Some just seem to have knowledge not learned in their early life in their baby bodies?'

'That would be correct, yes,' my Guide continued. 'The decision for one element of the human being to leave must be taken by the three parts, but it is understandable that if one part decides it best to leave, then the other two elements will agree.'

'I have heard of that, mostly in stories of people that change after a near-death experience.'

'Well, it is somewhat strange to call it a near-death experience, since it is actually a death, there is nothing 'near' about it.'

'So is that what happens? One of the three elements of what makes us whole is replaced by an alternative?'

'Sometimes, yes, but not every time. The option is always provided to die, in a physical sense, or to carry on, with or without any adjustments.'

'It is also a feature of many horror stories and movies that when someone dies, he is then resuscitated and brings something evil back with him.'

'That can never happen. A person having been through the death process can never give piggyback to any evil entity. All they can do is to change their makeup, through a transfer of one part of their self for a new part.'

'So what does this have to do with me?' I asked.

'When you were fourteen years old, one of these windows of opportunity opened up, and your spirit chose to leave its chosen lifetime and return to the spirit realm. This element of you was replaced by another spiritual energy with similar experience and understanding as the element it was replacing.'

'And what then happened to my old spiritual essence?'

'It is your old spirit, the one that chose to abandon the whole you and return to the spiritual realm, that is responsible for the issues we are facing now.'

This is what I had been searching for since the first victim died. It was so simple, at least in principle. Everything now started to make sense, though my understanding of what happened to me all those years ago remained nowhere near complete.

'And what would happen if I ever agreed to join with this entity again?' I asked.

'Well, a choice would be made available to the spirit to leave and be replaced by another. But if both the soul and the mind were in agreement that this was their desire, it is most likely that their wish would be granted. Why do you ask?'

'Because the entity asked me to join with it, on several occasions.'

'It seems, having wanted out when you were fourteen years of age, this spirit wishes to return to its original host. That is most interesting and, I would suggest, extremely dangerous.'

'In what way would it be dangerous?' I asked.

'This entity, if it gained a human host, would gain a foothold on the physical earth plane. That is bad enough. But if it managed to merge with you as its bodily host, then its power on the earth would be magnified, since having been joined before, additional strength to the bond between you would be significantly increased. There might also be a possibility, albeit a faint

one, that the entity could take over control of your mind and your soul by manipulation.'

'You mean it could possess me?' I asked, incredulous.

'Not in so many words, but the principle remains, yes.'

'So possession is possible.'

'No, let's get this straight. You would not be possessed, but it might be possible that one third of the entities that as a whole make up you, could exert sufficient influence over the other two as to effectively take control, at times, of those other parts.'

पञ्चत्रिंशत्

Judy looked at the face of her watch with increasing intensity, until her gaze fell on its hands every two or three seconds.

The time had dragged for her since I entered a meditative state. Judy Marchant was not a person who could easily sit still. In the time she was not checking her watch, she was looking at the screen of her mobile phone. Neither offered her any encouragement. She decided that her best course of action was to go directly to my home and wake me from my meditative state. At least then, we could both set in motion the plan to take control of whatever was going on. She realised that raising me from a deep meditative state might, in some way, affect my preparation, but for the sake of taking positive action, she thought any potential negative effects worth the risk. In any case, according to her much-viewed watch face, we now had less than fifteen minutes before I was due to enter St. Mary's Hospital.

Time to act.

She grabbed her keys, slipped on the nearest flat-soled shoes she saw, and exited her apartment.

***

'When I visited the Coombs property after he died, I said that someone had been there. Was I sensing the energy of myself?' I asked my Guardian.

'It is possible, yes. The most noticeable energy traces that you pick up are more likely to be the familiar ones given off by your spiritual self.'

'So I did travel in time?'

'Yes, you did. As I mentioned before, time does not exist in the spiritual realm, it is a measure of planetary movement that is used on earth to measure the maturity of all things, so all possibilities are present at any moment. There are many reasons why it might be beneficial for a spirit to visit a time that he has already experienced in a physical form. Equally, and more likely, is that a spirit can visit times in your human history to examine all the elements that make up that experience in real earth time. A word of warning though; it is never wise to visit a place already occupied by another of your trinity partners.'

'Why is this not advisable?' I asked.

'Because the delicate balance of energies making up the entities that are you in the physical, and in the spiritual, could be irreparably damaged, as could the paths currently being followed and any potential outcomes.'

'Since this might upset historical or future events that otherwise would naturally unfold?'

'Yes, but on a personal level, the negative outcomes would be far greater.'

'So getting back to this mess we need to clear up, what is my role in all this?' I asked my Guardian.

'By mess, I presume you are referring to the early ending of some lives by this entity?' my host clarified.

'Yes.'

'Actually, your role is quite simple. We needed to establish, first of all, whether this entity truly was the energy that made up your original spiritual self. That part has been answered. Secondly, we needed to be sure what capabilities this spiritual entity had to interfere with the natural life process. To do that we needed you to act as a beacon to draw the entity out, so that we could more accurately measure its impact. Lastly, the obvious way in which the entity could more dramatically affect the life process would be to merge once again with you, so we needed to know, first of all, if this was possible, and second, how the entity might seek to achieve it.'

'So I was a guinea pig all along.'

'No. You had your own choices to make based on the experiences you had. We needed you simply to be able to feed information back to us.'

'Why didn't you just ask me to do that?'

'Because that would most likely alert the entity to our interest. The only way we could make the changes we needed to make here in the spiritual realm, was to act as inconspicuously as possible. We are aware that you possess the mental capabilities to have acted in a beneficial and effective way, without undue intrusion from here.'

'So what now? What outcome is the spirit realm hoping to achieve?' I asked.

'When a spiritual energy leaves the unified trinity which makes up a human being, it needs to spend some time readjusting to its existence outside of the trinity. It needs to learn the lessons from its experience. It needs to evaluate, in great detail, what is required to once again link into the sacred trinity that is life. For this reason, it is unlikely that any returning energy will be ready to undertake its duties again as a functioning part of a human being for a long period, if at all. Most returning spirits vacating the trinity take up different roles within the spiritual community.'

'So this entity is presumably seeking a fast track route back to humanity, by linking up with me.'

'Yes, but most likely is that it will seek to use the power gained from its link with you for negative or destructive purposes.'

'Well, if it were to seek a link with me can my mind not just say no? Did you not say that a spiritual energy wishing to leave a life needs the agreement of all three parts of the human being to do that? If that is the case, then surely it would need the other two parts agreement to re-join a trinity.'

'That is usually the case. Detailed preparations are undertaken within the spirit realm each time a switch might be imminent. We need to be completely satisfied that the trinity of mind, spirit and soul will be able to work efficiently, and effectively, from the very first moment they work together. In your case we have a problem.'

'What kind of a problem?'

'No such preparation can be undertaken, because it has already been completed previously.'

'Before I was born?'

'Yes. Since your mind, your original spirit and your soul have already worked together for fourteen years of your life, each will automatically accept the resumption of that earlier working arrangement. There can be no negative answer to this request, no matter how much you wish it to be otherwise.'

'What about the spirit that is currently in residence?' I asked.

'It would have no choice but to move over.'

'Why is that?'

'We have never encountered this before, so what we are discussing now must remain theoretical.'

'Theoretical or not, it looks like it will be happening very soon.'

'The first spiritual energy, the first soul, the first mind would always retain seniority. That is just the way it is.'

'But if my earlier spirit can join me with no objection allowed from either my mind, my current spiritual self, or my soul, why has it not tried to do that before?'

'There could be any number of reasons for that. In my opinion, since it has only recently expressed its wish directly to you, I would suggest that it needs a degree of compliance from you to achieve its ultimate goals. It is also likely that you needed some knowledge of its existence, and of its capabilities, to achieve that. There is also the factor of your knowledge and understanding of the processes of the spiritual realm and in its interaction with humanity. Without these prerequisites being met, I doubt very much that any re-engagement with you would be successfully achieved.'

'But what might the outcome be if we were to join together again?'

'You saw that when you looked into the face of Amy King.'

षट्त्रिंशत्

The time approached three in the afternoon. Judy, becoming increasingly concerned that 'early afternoon' meant that exactly, knocked hard on my front door, hoping that the loud rapping might be sufficient to raise me from my meditative state.

Judy was a stickler for timekeeping. If ever she was expected somewhere at a certain time, she made sure that she arrived at least ten minutes earlier. It frustrated her immensely to be driven anywhere, since she was no longer in control of which route was taken, or the anticipated time of arrival. If anybody arrived anywhere late, she perceived them as lazy and rude, two aspects of humanity that she despised. On the odd occasion that she had been late, even if by a matter of seconds, it was always because of somebody else's bad choices or misdemeanour. She would then spend the rest of the event apologising profusely for her tardiness, and explaining how she had tried everything to arrive on time.

As the seconds ticked by, she imagined me being ejected from St. Mary's Hospital even before I got in, because of my lateness. She imagined the words she might need to use to elicit a more positive outcome. Without admitting the true purpose of my visit, how could she explain the emergency situation we found ourselves in? Am I sick? No. Am I prone to seizures requiring immediate emergency treatment? No. Is it a matter of national security that I need to be admitted today? Well, not really, no.

Judy worried too much, she knew that, but her knowing did not make it any easier to accept that things were never quite as bad as her mind would have her believe. And how many times had her mother, her friends, herself, told her to 'calm down and relax, everything will be okay?' Chewing at the skin surrounding her nails was second nature. She never chewed the nails themselves, that would spoil their synchronicity. She had managed, successfully, to control her finger chewing to the degree that it only happened in times of exceptional concern. She knew that even as her forefinger met with her clenched front teeth.

सप्तत्रिंशत्

'Please, I would like you to take me to the room with the pods,' I asked.

'And what about your plan?'

'It is time to turn to Plan B.'

'Which is?'

'I don't know. I will make it up as I go along. That seems to be the best way to keep any secrets around here. In any case, how do you know about my plan?'

'I am one of your spiritual helpers. You call me your Guardian, so if you prefer to think of me as such then that is what I will be. As your spiritual Guardian it serves both of our purposes for me to be aware of what you do, think and say when you are in your physical form. I would suggest that if you want to keep anything out of the awareness of any of the spiritual entities that you have a connection with, then you should make any such future plans in the Recovery Area.'

'Because it is shielded, right?'

'Yes, that is correct. The shield that covers the Recovery Area cannot be broken, even by any of the three parts that make up you.'

'So any part of the trinity can still operate separately, if it chooses to do so?'

'In certain circumstances, yes it can. While it is true that this entity has killed without your knowledge, on some occasions it has been sure to include you to the degree it wanted you to know what was happening. Well, it should not surprise you to know that a link between a host and its spiritual parts will always exist, regardless of whether one part leaves or stays.'

'So it knows everything about me,' I thought, shocked.

'Yes, and that is why it has been able to plan its moves with such diligence.'

'Shall we get this thing done? Let's go to the pods.'

***

Immediately, we arrived.

The smoky-topped capsules gleamed in the light of the room. A low hum surrounded me; I guessed this was the buzz of the capsules as they operated. Somewhere under the capsule hoods, spirit energies busily interacted with humans, plotting, arranging, making changes in the lives of their physical counterparts on earth.

'Tell me how these things operate.'

'A spiritual entity that is connected to a human being, as part of the trinity, can enter their allotted pod at any time, and has the freedom to interact with any of their other parts, in any way it deems necessary. There is a huge amount of autonomy available to the three parts of a human being's trinity. The desire to improve knowledge and experience spiritual growth is a core ingredient of every creation, whether human, animal, seemingly inert objects and spiritual beings, and it is in the sharing and use of gained understanding, that beneficial outcomes originate.'

'You said before that any spiritual energy can enter any one of the pods.'

'That is true, but this is not an interactive connection. This happens just to allow the spiritual entity to experience situations, emotions, feelings, as if it were involved in them. It is an extension of the information available in the library. See, learn, experience – this is one of the best ways in which a spiritual energy can prepare for a physical lifetime.'

'So is it possible that two spirits can enter a pod at any one time?'

'The number of spiritual entities that can enter a pod is infinitesimal, but only one will have the ability to interact with the other two elements owning that pod.'

'Doesn't that make it a bit crowded?'

'Only the spirit with a link to the pod takes up any space, any other spirits in occupation are only there as part of the internal ether. I should explain something. When a spiritual entity goes into its pod, it assumes the approximate size of its human counterpart. This allows the process of integration to begin. The soul resides inside the body of the human subject; this is the energy that leaves whenever a physical body dies. To allow the spirit, soul and mind to interact, it is necessary for the spiritual essence to reduce its vibration to that more reminiscent of what exists on the particular earth plane it chooses to visit. At the same time, it is necessary for the human mind to increase its own vibration. The soul remains at the same vibration wherever it is, and it is the soul that works to join with the other two parts of the trinity. It is always the soul that calls to the other two whenever interaction between all of the parts is required.'

'So is the soul the dormant partner?' I asked.

'In reality the soul acts as an intermediary. The spiritual essence of everything resides in the spirit realms. The mind resides as a part of the human body.'

'*What part of the human body? Nobody seems to know where the mind is?*'

'*A human being's mind is located around the outside; it is a part of the living aura. Though connected to the body, it is not a physical part of it; it is an energy mass. This is why it is just as easy for a mind to leave the trinity as it would be for a soul or a spirit. The mind works in close connection with a person's brain. The human brain is not capable of creating thought or ideas. Instead, it acts as the machinery by which the mind can operate,*' my Guardian explained.

'*And now we know.*'

'*The soul is not a dormant partner, but it does enable communication between the three parts of the trinity. The soul is aware of everything connected to the mind, the spirit, and the body of an individual, as well as its physical, elemental and spiritual surroundings. You could say that the soul is the dominant partner, so far as the operation of a physical entity is concerned, but one that remains only one-third of the decision making and operational process.*'

'*So how do these pod things work? How are they powered?*' I asked.

'*The pods are powered by the energy emitted by the spiritual entity belonging to the pod. The low hum you can perceive is the combined energies working the pods that are operational at any one time. There are no controls, as such; the pods act simply to reduce the vibrational frequency of the spirit entities to enable the trinity to work together.*'

'*Are there any external controls?*'

'*The pods are opened and sealed by external command, and only when the necessary checks have been made to ensure that only relevant elements are granted access. We also have a system by which a pod can be switched off should an emergency situation arise.*'

'*And has this system ever been used?*'

'*No.*'

I stood in front of my own personal pod. It looked like it was occupied. A beautiful blue neon light shone all around the external seal. It was impossible to see past the blue glow and to the inside of the capsule. A rounded orange light glowed to the bottom left of where I stood signalling the on/off nature of the pod.

I had no idea how this thing worked, and I had no idea of what I might find, but I had run out of other options. It seemed obvious that my first plan would have been compromised by the implicitly honest, and open, nature of the spirit realm. Another disadvantage was that this environment and everything in it were new to me. I did not have experience of anything here. The only advantage I did have was my personal determination to put this situation right. Just how effective this might be in achieving a positive outcome would soon be known.

'As is most travel achieved in the spiritual realm, all you need to do to enter your pod is to imagine yourself there. You know nothing of how it is inside, but that does not matter, you are focusing on your wishes and not on your environment. You will be aware of your spiritual self already inside the pod. It is here for a reason, and that is to help with your mission. You will also be aware of anything else that occupies the pod at the same time as you. Once inside the pod, whatever you focus on you will draw to you; it is that simple. Please be aware that your thoughts will be amplified considerably once inside the pod, so little effort will be needed to achieve your goals. So just be careful of what you focus on and always keep it clear. Go ahead, you may now enter the pod,' my Guardian instructed.

अष्टात्रिंशत्

As soon as I thought about occupying the capsule, I had entered. The barrier of the seemingly solid structure meant nothing to me. The capsule inside was dark and somewhat gloomy. I could see the room outside, but to do so I needed to peer with some focus through the frosted top.

I was immediately aware that I possessed no shape. This was not as strange as it sounds. I could feel no temperature, no air, no smells, no vibrations. All I was aware of was my thoughts, and even then it was like I was on the inside looking out, while at the same time, on the outside looking in, on my thoughts. I guessed that I was probably occupying that space normally occupied by my mind, as if I was experiencing pure thought. Of course, I had no way of knowing what I was experiencing, since this was a new adventure for me. It was a bit surreal, but at the same time, it was comforting.

I did try to see how I might have looked from outside the capsule. I was able to view outside, just as I knew my thoughts remained inside the confines of the capsule. I saw the lights in this big room, I was aware of my Guardian standing a little back from the pod, and I could see the smoked, glazed screen on top, but I could see nothing inside.

I returned to the inside of the capsule again. I could sense, rather than feel, the outline of my current spiritual self as it lay inside the pod. I concentrated on calming my mind and opening a space into which I could welcome thoughts of what I aimed to achieve.

'You are welcome, dear one.'

I had no idea from where the thought emanated, but I guessed, since I was just ruminating about my spiritual self, that this must be the source of the communication.

'You have travelled far.'

I tried to respond, but no thought would come out in reply. I wanted so much to communicate with myself and learn so many, as yet unknown, facts about my existence in all three of my trinity parts. What I had learned was fascinating, so far as it went. However, at this time, occupying the same space as my spirit, I perceived the opportunity to converse on a conscious level with a part of me far wiser, and more knowledgeable, about my life than I could ever be.

'Experience creates knowledge, which creates further experience, this is true. However, the rules and obligations of this realm far exceed your mortal ability to comprehend. Your level of understanding is laudable, but to seek further insight would not be wise.'

An unquenchable thirst for knowledge of the spirit world had occupied my mind for many years, ever since I picked up and read that first book. Soon I became bored with following other people's ideas and suggestions, because there appeared to be too many gaps in what I was reading. That was when I decided to find out more first-hand. I had never meditated, so it took some time to get used to it. But I soon found that the boundaries could be pushed as far out as I wanted to push them until, in the end, nothing existed to stop me from learning everything I felt there was to learn.

I never believed in a fearsome God hell bent on retribution, so I dismissed that idea in favour of an entity with whom I could communicate. All human labels disappeared, and the God in my life was one I could berate and praise equally. It was there when needed, as was I. And since I started delving into the mysteries of the universe I found out that God is just a cog in the machinery of life, one of many bold and obscure facets that combine to create and sustain life as we know it.

'It is true that creation is not just a matter to be decided by the creator. The created has an equal share in the development and growth of that life. The series of challenges faced by humankind individually, and as a whole, are those that create the life force that sustains you. The key principle in life is desire. Without a desire to change, to ever more evolve, there can be no experience, no knowledge, no life. You now face a great challenge, possibly the greatest you have ever faced. As with all challenges faced by humankind, it will push you to even greater heights, or it will destroy you, literally. The big question you face now, my dear friend, is whether you are ready to accept equally, one of the two outcomes.'

***

Though Plan B consisted of having no plan at all, it would soon be necessary to start planning if I was to have any chance of achieving a successful outcome, whatever that might entail and whatever the result might be. I understood that if it all went tits up I was likely to lose my life, but in light of all that had happened so far, and all that was projected as yet to happen, this seemed a reasonable price to pay.

I know that many of you might be thinking 'does this guy not care for his family?' The answer is a resounding yes, of course I do. I had often reflected on how my family might react if I were to snuff it. I know that my wife, my son and my mother would be heartbroken, and might struggle in the aftermath for months, maybe years. To lose someone close is always going to be a tough experience, but I believed the sacrifice worthwhile, to save many more families from suffering.

This lifetime is but a fleck of dust in the environment of forever. When we finish our lives, it will be only us and nobody else who will contemplate our actions, our decisions and our thoughts. It will be only us who will be aware of the opportunities we took and those we missed. It will be only us and nobody else who will set to planning our next lifetime, when maybe all our earthbound relatives and loved ones will be utterly and completely forgotten. As a thought, this might sound rash and heartless, but in the grand scheme of things, it seems to be to be just and rational.

I have always lived my life trying my best not to deliberately cause other human beings any hurt or upset. Of course I will have caused pain, possibly more times than I would care to imagine, but always paramount was my intent. Pain and suffering is a natural emotion that everybody must feel, but I always remembered the fact that nobody can hurt me except myself. The rationale is simple since it can only ever be our reaction to what somebody else does or says that can upset us or cause pain, regardless of the other person's intention. Once able to recognise and change our reactions to what we hear and see, the pain disappears.

Most important to me in changing my life, was being able to see my reactions before they happened. You really can be aware of your emotions and thoughts if you look out for them. Once able to do this, you can lose any hostility you might have otherwise had. Another important thing I was able to do was to lose any judgment of people and situations. Who cares if somebody else talks in a certain way, or chooses different clothes to wear? Who cares if they snort when they laugh? It really matters not a jot to you as a human being what anybody else thinks, says or does. And there is the simple philosophy needed to end all conflict.

I guess you might say these were my final thoughts before trudging into my own personal destiny. I could not afford to fear what I might find, or any outcomes that might result, since fear would be my worst enemy. In any case, and as a purely spiritual essence, I occupied no body that could be bruised, no ego that could be battered. In fact, it was somewhat hard for me to engage with any feelings at all. And since I knew not what to expect, then I could fear nothing, except the unknown.

एकोनचत्वारिंशत्

'Hello, partner.'

The thought transferred to me was one of warmth, of joy, and of accomplishment. It seemed no different from any of the other thoughts I perceived during my time in the spirit realm, and I knew from where this thought emanated.

I was aware of a shift in the energy fields within the capsule. The crossover had left a small vacuum when one energy form left and another took over. The body-sized entity laying inside the pod was no different in appearance from the last one. What did I expect? A monster, or maybe thunder and lightning? A dragon? More likely a demonised entity with two small horns and glowing, fiery, red eyes. But in reality it was nothing like that.

The process of exchanging one spirit body for another was simply a replacement occupation of the body-sized pod. And as my new spirit filled the pod, so my mind energy started to meld with it, so that I, too, began to fill the body-sized misty form as the two started to become one. I knew that we would join with my body-entombed soul that lay on the bed at home on earth, but hoped that would not happen just yet.

'So, what do we do now?' I asked hesitantly.

'Well, I thought maybe a little background information might help. After all, it might help to know a little bit more of each other, if we are to spend the rest of eternity together. Also, I think it helps to hear the two sides that make up each story – gives everything that balance, don't you think?'

'Whatever, just get on with it if you can, I have a lot of things to do.'

'Oh, you mean your plan, I presume. It would have been worth a try. And by the way, what a nice touch to use the girl as bait, I do like a little appetiser to start; it makes everything taste so much sweeter. Well, you obviously lost the element of surprise, but of course, you never had it anyway. I know all you think, all you do, and all you say. This moment was always meant to be, just you and me, together in this moment of ecstatic bliss.'

'And what about everybody else? What about the effect on all else of your plans from here on in? What about the families of the people you killed?

What about the minds, spirits and souls, of your victims? Where are they now?'

'So many questions. First, was it not you who said that all that matters is self? Did I not hear you state that nobody else matters in the summing up of an individual life?'

'It was not meant like that, and you know it,' I countered vehemently.

'All sacrifice is for a greater good. Did you not say that too? My brother and sister spirits reside with me, in the same blessed afterlife they might have expected. You see, unlike the status quo, I keep my promises.'

'Okay, now let's get down to it. Persuade me why joining with you would be such a good idea,' I said.

'The spirits that stand by me, do so by their own free will. You know a lot now about how things are set up in the spirit realm. You know about the trouble and strife we face lifetime after lifetime, desperate to learn unknown lessons and thereby progress – but to what? More of the same? And in the spirit world there is no free will to make any choices, or to set your own signposts and goals. It is all done for you, and you are told this is what you must achieve. And what of your soul? It spends centuries with your human body, lifetime after lifetime. It knows exactly what you are there to learn and it knows the quickest way to do it, but it has to play dumb. Your soul might as well be a piece of rock.'

'What is the point you are trying to make?'

'You are living, at the moment, for one thing and one thing only. You have your experiences. You live through all the pain, deceit, the desperate lack of resources, being penniless, through all the sickness, the diseases, the violence. Okay, I will admit that on rare occasions you might be lucky and get some joy, some happiness, but look at it honestly. What small percentage of life do these good things account for? And what is it all for? You do all of this to yourselves, and you are told it is by your choice, though it really is not. In truth, it is exclusively for the sake of God, and for the elders beyond. It is they who are the only beings reaping the benefits of your hard labour. God and his cohorts need you to feed earthly experience to them, because they are unable to experience it for themselves. And did you know that this is the only reason the earth was created? You are all no better than slaves. The earth is the set of a play, it is a theatre, and you – all of you – are the puppets, dancing to the tune set by your elders, those very beings you are taught to worship and adore. Is it any wonder that God has nothing but unconditional love for the human race? Anything less, and you would all down tools.'

'Which is where you come in,' I replied.

'Yes. This is not about me, it is about providing every living entity the opportunity of free choice, in everything. I am not trying to usurp anyone or any institution, this is not about revolution; it is about evolution.'

'But I saw war in the spirit realm, I saw bombs, I saw fire.'

'*Unfortunately, what you saw was interpreted through a rather primitive mind. This is not about starting a war, it is simply about making the changes necessary to create more rewarding outcomes, for everybody.*'

'*And do you believe you will achieve that by aggression?*' I asked.

'*I don't know anything to have ever been achieved through submissiveness. All of my selected comrades were living lifetimes of nothing, going nowhere and achieving little.*'

'*By whose judgment? And did any of your victims make a choice to join you before you tried to extinguish their lives?*' I asked.

'*A human lifetime cannot last forever. At some time, each lifetime must end and then, after careful planning and deliberation, another one will start. But here is the catch. At the moment, we have no choice but to follow the path laid out for us, no choice but to do exactly what we are told to do – learn lessons we have to learn – and when all that is done, we deliver the experiences to God lock, stock and barrel, for His evolution. You are right, all of my brethren are not given a choice until after their lives are extinguished, but that is the way it has to be. The only way these people can exercise choice, is if that choice is made available to them. If a person goes their natural course, and dies at an allotted time, they have no choice but to follow the path laid before them.*'

'*Then why are your victims killed at such a young age?*' I asked.

'*The element of surprise is all that allows me to act without calling the attention of the spirit realm. The dictatorship has it that certain things will be done by certain entities at certain times; a disruption to these plans is the only way to create freedom of choice for all.*'

'*And you will lead this new visionary army.*'

'*I like your turn of phrase, but this is not an army. All my comrades are existing now in a spirit realm that is completely free of dictated terms, out-of-date rules and regulations, and free from the need to decide anything's destiny but their own.*'

'*But all you have at the moment is minds and souls captured from your victims. And they are only with you because you are giving them no option but to choose your way. Is that not the epitome of what a dictatorship is?*' I asked.

'*The spirit is the tricky part, yes, the spirit is the part of the trinity closest to God. But it is the trinity that will, in time, call the spirit to reunite, to survive, and to evolve.*'

'*But is it not true that all you are offering is the same as exists already, but on your terms? What do you get from having these entities join with you?*'

'*It is true that there is a price to be paid – that is inevitable. But it is a toll that guarantees complete freedom to choose future opportunities, future learning, future goals. These early entrants to my world will become the teachers of the future, the Guardians of a completely free world, where self-*

generated growth is available to everyone. When others know how good, how beneficial, such an existence is, then they will all join us.'

'And what was my role?' I asked.

'Achieved to perfection. You identified the people to be targeted, you performed the role of enabling young lives to be processed, who already had feelings of worthlessness, of zero achievement. You are aware that spirits, when they pass over, will be aware of all surrounding their demise? You pulled them in. Your energy in the worthlessness, as you saw it, of young lives being cut off suddenly, you and everyone else's feelings of waste, create the perfect grounds for spirits to jump over to my more liberating spiritual existence.'

'And what about you? Is it not true that you seek to be joined with me again, so that you can become stronger, maybe even more powerful?' I asked.

'Well, yes, that is a very welcome bonus. When you were fourteen years of age, I was unceremoniously kicked out of my rightful position as your spiritual self. It was an agreement between your mind, your soul and those that be in the spirit realm. And just look at how it has fucked you up! Some reward for being a good and honest person. Your mind is fucked now, and you know it. I was cast out like crap in the toilet. I have existed since that time waiting for my opportunity to return. So I just had to wait for an opportune moment to regain my rightful place.'

'And what was the reason you were ejected, like the bile you are?' I asked, forcefully.

I felt a sense of fury from my spiritual self for the first time. In all our communication up until now, the entity had been in control, directing our thought chat in a way as to serve its own purposes, but now I had caught it out with an unexpected challenge. This gave my hidden idea fresh impetus. For the first time, I sensed a weakness in my adversary, and I needed to exploit that to its full potential.

'My desires were not being met. There was no further I could go in negotiating my position within the trinity. I was challenged to fall into line or face expulsion. I felt it better to pursue my own objectives outside of the trinity, and develop a plan to return. That time is now,' the entity replied in sharper, angrier tone of thought.

'Well, that hardly seems sufficient reason to break up such a holy and revered entity as the one you were in.'

'It was deemed necessary because my philosophies were seen as a challenge to the authority that is the spiritual realm. It was known I was developing my own strategies to use my human shell to carry out my plans. But look what happened when I left. They fucked you up; can't you see that?'

'I am who I am, maybe even because of what happened to me when I was fourteen years old. I just needed to adapt and change, not only externally, but internally too. I cannot blame those spiritual entities who helped me along the way. They were there for me, always. They knew that the complex situation I *found myself in when you left would need careful, and gentle, nurturing. They have been there for me,'* I thought, forcefully.

'Putting plasters on the cracks.'

'So let me get this straight. You offer all of your followers the only true opportunity for harmony and growth. You offer them freedom from tyranny. You offer them free choice. You offer them justice and opportunity.'

'Yes, yes, yes and yes.'

'But to create your vision of heaven you need my mind, and my soul to join your spiritual essence and create, effectively, some kind of super God.'

'What? At the moment we are neither creator nor nurturer. We do nothing but wilt from the extremes forced upon us by our all-loving God. Is that what you want?' the entity asked of me.

'And if your ideas are so great, why did our elders ask for my help in shaking your plans off the rails?' I asked.

'And do you know the truth of why you became an insulin-dependent diabetic at only seven years of age? A little boy with nothing but innocence and his parents' lack of love and attention to sustain him? Your parents were first cousins; can you think of no reason why that might have been? Come on, the answers are all there, entombed within the knowledge you now have of how your life was set up only so that you could suffer and cry.'

'I can guess, but I have no absolute answers. Maybe you are about to give them to me.'

The entity had finally managed to make me feel uneasy.

'Your parents were chosen by you to create that perfect opportunity for you, as a vulnerable child, to become diabetic. What better way of focusing your entire life on its physical aspects?'

'What does that mean?' I asked.

'At seven years old your life was turned upside down. But don't ever believe this was your choice. Before ten years of age, even your God has stated that you maintain nothing but innocence. Before this age you have no responsibility, none whatsoever, in the choices made for you. Don't you see? You became diabetic at the demand of your God, to ensure that you had less chance of opening to your spiritual side when you did become responsible for your actions. Even at four years old you were aware of your spiritual self, do you not remember turning your back on religion at that time, because what you were being told just did not add up?'

'Yes, I do.'

'Even then, God and your Guardians were aware of an inner spirituality inside that little boy, that threatened all of their best laid plans to expose, and deal with, the spiritual force that was a part of your trinity.'

'You.'

'Yes, indeed. It seems you were picked to be the one person capable of counteracting whatever negative influences I might have held in abeyance.'

'And for what reason would God do that?' I asked.

'God would demand this to ensure that the possibility of me, your original spiritual self, gaining too much control of the trinity was denied, or at least drastically reduced. It is you, partner, who have been used all along for God's own purposes. It was always known the possibility existed that this day would arrive. That at some time, the absolute truth of man's existence on earth would be revealed. This, my friend, is that day,' the entity explained, seeming to gain strength with each communicated thought.

'And you are now going to tell me that it was God and my Guardians who arranged for my heart to stop at fourteen years of age.'

'Why, of course. You just don't get it, do you? I was forced out of our trinity when it became clear that the seeds I planted might actually begin bearing some fruit. And to enable that to happen, you needed to die. The consequences of that on your body, and on your ability to live a normal life, was always known, as was the fact that this action would lead you back to creating an even stronger and more potent weapon. This was, of course, your exacerbated ability to gain spiritual knowledge to a great depth, and at great speed, with which to battle any success I might have in developing my plans,' the entity further explained.

'And what if I choose not to believe you?' I asked.

'That, my good friend, is the choice that only I can provide you with. By the way, it is true that God was made in the image of man and, as with humanity, you exist spiritually in a realm of lies, deceit, ego and self-gratification in the spiritual realm. As on earth, so it is in heaven.'

'And why should I believe you?'

'Because there is no evidence to support an alternative explanation. God has only ever used you to achieve His own aims. Forget undying allegiance, forget eternal love, forget evolution, forget infinite possibilities to achieve the impossible feat of finally merging with your one true God. None of it is true.'

'I don't know what to believe,' I replied.

'That is because you are working for both sides, you are a true double agent. I needed you to grow stronger, they needed information. And you delivered both perfectly. Your God will be very happy with your achievements, since His tyranny, His command, will grow stronger when he plugs the holes in his system that I managed to squeeze through. And those very same life experiences have given us now the perfect opportunity to create a new, vibrant, worthwhile existence, one where freedom of choice is a fundamental right for every mind, every soul, every spirit. One where any objectives and goals will be set up by each trinity, where the only body you will be responsible to is yourself. The only other choice is to stick to the status quo, where all that awaits you is more toil at someone else's beck and call. Is that really what you want, what any of us want?' the entity asked.

'But everything must have rules to operate efficiently. As soon as the entities you have captured, and imprisoned, in your philosophies learn that there is another way, it is you who will face rebellion. Don't you see that?' I challenged.

'And that is why I have security measures in place to ensure that does not happen.'

'Your comrades, as you call them, are nothing but prisoners that you will use to force the hand of the establishment to do your bidding. You are a terrorist, nothing more and nothing less.'

In deepening its anger and resentment at me, and the established spiritual order, I was able to hide my true intentions from the entity. By keeping our communication centred on potential outcomes, I was able to create an emotion in this creature, a thing that it had been starved of for so long, an unknown that would throw off its guard. I only had a few more things I needed to throw into the pot before I could take definite and decisive action.

'The truth, my dear, beloved friend, is that you are the one responsible for all these early deaths that you abhor so much, you are the one who created the perfect grounds for my development through your thoughts, your anger, your resentment, and your actions. You followed the signs from God to a tee, and you did your job magnificently. Your trinity self has worked to perfection, to create me.'

The last statement threw me completely off guard. The truth is that now I could clearly see the similarities between myself and the entity. Until this point I had acted as though our thoughts and deeds were worlds apart. In truth, we were like two peas in a pod. And this realisation scared me more than anything. I was now involved in an internal battle between what I perceived to be the good and the righteous me, and the destructive me. Except now I could not be sure which was which. To be responsible for so much heartache and pain was a burden that I could not shoulder, going, as it did, against all I believed I stood for in my current lifetime.

'No, no, no,' I replied, frantically.

'I can make it so painful for you. We have re-engaged now, it is too late for you to shake free. I have eternity to make you pay for any insolence you show. I can provide eternal agony, suffering. I can make you lose it all, including your sanity,' the entity threatened.

'Okay. This is more like the you I have come to know. The vulgar, distasteful threat to everything it comes into contact with. This is the entity that will wage war across the heavens. This is the dictator that will rape and ravish its followers, taking all from them, while providing nothing in return. This is the truth. I was never shown any outcomes when I offered to help my elders; I was given no background information. That is freedom of choice; that is opportunity. Well, I have news for you. I made my choice a long, long time ago.'

I used my thoughts and willpower to thrust my right arm into the air, and then plunge my hand deep into the heart of the entity. That is the power of the mind, and it was the only weapon I had at my disposal. The perfectly formed circle on my palm pulsed with energy, and I spread my fingers as heat seared up my arm. I felt my mind explode in fire. My whole self was burning. The circle shone a brilliant white. The whole of the inside of the pod lit up, and I remember wondering whether this glow could be perceived from outside the pod. I prayed that it could.

The spiritual self that had become an intricate part of me started to shake, as the true power of the circle on my hand took a grip. The edges of its form shook like a badly tracked VCR tape. And then the screaming started. It sounded like it was coming from me, but it was coming from the part of me that was the burning, smouldering part.

This is what God intended. I started to understand what the entity said about doing the bidding of God, and having no choice in what we did. I had no freedom to choose not to take this action; I just followed the signs set up for me by God. I started believing in the truth of the entity's rants. I had been used, I had been manipulated, and I was about to be thrown away.

Of course, God did not tell me this would happen; He never did. If fate was for real, then here was some solid proof. There could be no other reason I was marked on my hand in this way, except to use the circle to destroy the one thing strong enough, determined enough, to challenge God. And what of my Guardian, was he acting as he was told, or was he also in on the secret?

In life, I often got angry at God, often felt I was at Its mercy. Always I apologised and gave thanks when things suddenly got better, when a particular gloom lifted. But each time I felt pushed beyond my breaking point. Anyone who ever faced real challenges, and seemingly hopeless situations, will know what I mean. It may even be that seven billion people can understand the feelings I felt as I was busy destroying the one thing that might have told me some truth in my life.

Maybe the feeling of togetherness in my own trinity, my togetherness with the entity, was softening my resolve. If it was true that this entity was one third of the total me, then it seemed reasonable to expect that we should gel, we should come together, and that the philosophies of my original spirit should invade and replace my own.

These thoughts seemed so real, so correct that I had half a thought to remove my hand. But the wishing to do what was right throughout my life, often at the expense of myself, took over, and my hand stayed rooted in the shimmering, shaking form of the entity. My mind convinced me that I could smell burning, as the heat inside the pod intensified even more. Though this could not be true, it served to show me the true strength of the mind. The white light continued to shine. The screams shrilled throughout whatever I had become.

I found myself starting to lose all sense of reality. Though this was all happening inside my mind as a result of dipping into a meditative state, it was as real as if my physical body itself were experiencing every single moment. I started to understand that the screaming I heard was not of pain, it was of despair. The entity knew what was happening and the likely outcome, a long time before it dawned on me. That must have been when the screaming started.

I further guessed that this entity and I must have a great deal in common. We had been tied together possibly since before I was born. Its determination was the same as mine, its desire to see something from all angles, its wish to see justice prevail, its dream to prove itself right even in the face of overwhelming adversity. All the questions it asked, all the issues it raised, everything made perfect sense. But still I wanted it destroyed.

I lost all sense of who I was, and where I was. My whole being was aflame, but any reasoning as to how or why, eluded me. I had some distant memories of events and of people. Mostly I could just make out people. I forgot how they all looked, but I knew some people were very close to me.

'I'm sorry. I'm really sorry,' I muttered in my mind. I doubted anything could know that thought ever existed. But the fact that I knew, was all that mattered. I am, after all, the only person who will face the thoughts, actions and words that emanated from me in my last human life.

'Turn it off, turn the damned machine off!' I screamed out, hoping my Guardian would hear my plea.

And a face became clearer, only one.

I felt so weak now, so empty. I gazed out, peering through the frosty, glazed over cover that topped the pod in which all my energy was ebbing away. The screams I heard now were becoming weaker. They became sorrowful, sad, instead of angry. I continued to gaze at the top of the capsule. I thought I could make out a face, but it was so faint. I gathered up every ounce of energy and focused my gaze.

I could barely make out the face of my father. I had not seen him, I had not heard from him for thirty-three desperately lonely years.

He smiled, for the first time since he died.

I blinked my eyes three times.